## EXPERIENCE THE MAGIC OF LOVE
## WITH FOUR SPELLBINDING TALES

There's no time of year more magical than autumn. Summer has come to an end, and winter will soon be arriving. The holiday season is still a bit away, but for now there are full moons, gold and crimson leaves, crackling fires and brisk walks in the woods. Days have become shorter, but nights—meant to be shared by lovers—have become longer. And Halloween will soon be arriving, bringing along witches, ghosts and goblins—who are not always easily recognizable. Although appearances can sometimes be deceiving, there's no denying the magic of love once it's touched your heart. No matter what season of the year it is, love is always in the air, captivating hearts in wonderful and mysterious ways. Magical ways. All it takes is just one kiss.

So treat yourself to a special collection and sit down with Caroline Bourne, Colleen Faulkner, Ashland Price and Becky Lee Weyrich as they take you back to the past with four pairs of lovers you won't soon forget.

# Spellbound Kisses

Caroline Bourne · Colleen Faulkner
Becky Lee Weyrich · Ashland Price

**ZEBRA BOOKS**
**KENSINGTON PUBLISHING CORP.**

ZEBRA BOOKS are published by

Kensington Publishing Corp.
475 Park Avenue South
New York, NY 10016

First Printing: October, 1993

Printed in the United States of America

# TABLE OF CONTENTS

# Phantom's Caress

## by

## Caroline Bourne

# One

As the shadows of evening twilight slowly descended upon the ancestral home of Zelpha Prudhomme, Kristina Hartman was fairly certain a pallid form had suddenly snapped the draperies shut in an upstairs window. She took a moment to study the house, approached through corrugated iron gates a quarter of a mile behind her, magnificent, and yet neglected over the years, serene in its seclusion, mysterious in its history. A green shutter had lost a hinge and was hanging against the peeling white paint like a broken limb. A railed balcony surrounded the second floor from which private doors opened. Stately white columns graced a wide gallery littered with fallen leaves and pecans tossed by a recent storm from one of the many trees that speckled the lawns.

Kristina imagined that the house had once been beautiful, before the war that had devastated the South. But in the eleven years since that conflict had ended, the house had fallen into such neglect that its beauty might never be recaptured. What a pity, she thought, that brother fighting against brother had taken away the beauty and allure of such a culture. She could not know that the decay of Oak Shadows Plantation had begun fifty years before, when her own father had left his childhood home. Still she imagined that many memories were keeping this old house alive.

Her first trek to Oak Shadows Plantation in the heart of Louisiana, the home of her only living relation, had thus far proved quite an adventure. She'd quickly learned that superstitions abounded in this strange place; she'd seen a dock-worker in the nearby town of Alexandria spit upon his finger because his foot had gone to sleep, another sneeze in order to expel the evil spirit attempting to enter his body through his nose. Or so Cleveland, now offering his hand to assist her down from the carriage, had explained with carefully chosen words.

"Is Aunt Zelpha expecting me this early in the evening?" Kristina asked, easing her gloved hand into the gnarled, twisted one of the old, black gentleman. She had caught an earlier train in departing St. Louis three days before; otherwise, she would not have arrived in Alexandria until well past midnight.

"Expectin' you, sho' 'nuf, Miz Hartman," Cleveland replied after a moment. " 'Spect she's pert near excited 'bout meetin' you's, as you's be 'bout meetin' her. Lawd"—Cleveland's fingers rummaged through the scant gray hairs at his temples—"she be's a character, that Miz Zelpha, fo' sho', an' you's proper fo'warned."

As Kristina now stood before the house, twisting a small handkerchief nervously between her fingers, a thought came to her. "How is it you were in Alexandria so early in the evening, Mr. Cleveland?"

"That be's jes' Cleveland. Ain't got no first name what's 'Mistah.' " He chuckled. "An' ta answer yo' question, Miz Hartman, yo' ol' aunt, she *knows* you's be earlier 'n 'spected. Jes' knows them things, jes' like ol' voodoo woman can tells you yo' future, sho' 'nuf."

A cool breeze washed across the lawns, catching in her hair and threatening to tear it loose from the matching gold filigree combs. Why she thought of her father just then, she was not sure, but she could imagine his footfalls on the wide gallery, a careless shoulder relaxing against one of those thick columns from which the paint was now flaking . . . could hear his laughter drifting with the wind over the bayou they had just crossed. But why would she think of his laughter, as rare in the years they had spent together as pure, unblemished memories? She thought of the many times she had watched him in silence, always wondering what caused the pain glazing his dark and tortured eyes . . . It had pained her almost as much as his unspoken thoughts surely must have tormented him.

He had been almost fifty when he had married Kristina's mother. The great difference in their ages, considerably more than twenty years, had put a terrible strain on their relationship. Her mother had died before the age of thirty and one of her parents' house servants, angry that she'd been dismissed from service, had accused her father of being responsible, of stifling his wife's youth and driving her to an early grave. Kristina had been only seven at the time, but she remembered the tense encounter and the sullen silence that had followed as her father, shamed by the accusation, had avoided her for several days. Then he had drawn her aside, explaining that the servant had simply been "a vicious gossip-monger."

And now, here she stood, outside the house in which her father had been born, where his aging sister still lived. Zelpha, described by Cleveland just moments ago as a delightful lady. But why hadn't her aunt rushed out to greet her? Cleveland had mentioned that Zelpha was the picture of health, though her mind tended to wander at times, and at the age of seventy-eight was still able to break into a run like the child she had once been . . . many, many years ago.

The lawns of Zelpha Prudhomme's house, swathed in moonlight this early September evening, gave him a perfect view of the woman alighting from the carriage. The macabre and twisted shadow stirred against the great

11

marble crypt, then hauntingly withdrew, becoming one with the towering tombstones as neglected as the house on whose land the cemetery stood. Here rested the remains of those who had passed into eternity . . . and the soul of one who waited . . .

A chill traveled the length of Kristina's spine, causing a visible shudder to rock her slender shoulders. She turned, her gaze narrowing, the vague outlines of the cemetery suddenly rising against the gray-black shades of evening.

"A cemetery?" questioned Kristina, hugging her cloak to her slender frame.

"Yas'sum," spoke Cleveland. In the moonlight, Cleveland was thinking how very much Kristina favored her aunt as the older woman had been when young. Cleveland had just been a lad—a slave at Oak Shadows—when he'd first been taken into service as a house servant by Master Tiberius Prudhomme, Zelpha's father . . . but he remembered the way Zelpha had looked. Tall, slim, youthfully graceful, with hair the color of a pale moon and eyes as green as the clearest emeralds. Cleveland knew that if the master had been aware that he'd been looking at his daughter, he'd have taken a whip to him. Those days were long past . . . He was no longer a slave, though he still had no business looking at the women of Oak Shadows and assessing their beauty. Thus, he looked away, mumbling, "Yas'sum, a cemetery."

"So near Aunt Zelpha's house?"

"That's where she wanted it," said Cleveland, Kristina's few canvas bags now clutched in his hands. Then he mumbled something the young woman could not have heard, something he did not repeat when she raised quizzical eyebrows. He was not being disrespectful, merely remembering something from past years.

Kristina's attentions returned to the darkness, and for

a moment she could not take her eyes from the haunting shadows of the cemetery. Had she heard a twig break underfoot? Had she seen a dark figure merge into the darkness? Had she seen a mist rise slowly to envelop the ground?

Or had her imagination gone awry?

Turning, attempting to take one of her bags, which Cleveland protested with a good-natured chuckle, she now watched the massive front door of Aunt Zelpha's house slowly creep open.

In the next few moments she was silently approached by a woman who had to be her aunt, a woman whose looks still echoed the beauty she had been in her youth. Her skin, the color of alabaster, glowed beneath heavily applied rouge, bright red lipstick hid the pale color of her mouth, and blue shading clung somewhat precariously to the sagging skin beneath her eyebrows. So bright were her eyes, the same color as her niece's, that Kristina was sure they could see into her soul, and she found it a shade disconcerting that the woman might know all her innermost secrets. Somehow, that made her feel almost as uncomfortable as the fact that her aunt hadn't spoken a word to her. Kristina remembered saying, "How are you, Aunt Zelpha. I am Kristina." But she could not remember getting a reply.

Now she was surrounded by aging servants interrogating her on life "up Nawth," passing through a foyer as cluttered as a well-stocked food cupboard and being half-dragged into a large sitting room. The servant named Sophronia was a diminutive woman whose skin was pale and heavily freckled, and she spoke with a happy lilt in her voice. The man Joseph was quiet, merely nodding when they were introduced, and he kept his eyes downcast. Kristina imagined that all three of the house servants had been at Oak Shadows as long as Aunt Zelpha had, if not a few years longer. Cleveland had told her in the carriage that Sophronia was the youngest and that

13

she was Zelpha's age. But Cleveland and Sophronia were spry and friendly, and they had welcomed her with arms a great deal more open than her aunt's.

Just as Kristina felt she might be smothered by the adoring attention, Cleveland came to her rescue, his gnarled fingers waving through the air. "Sophronia, bring Miz Hartman some o' that cinnamon tea you makes so good, an' Joseph, how's 'bout he'pin' me take the bags up to the gues' room."

The drafty silence, the result of their departure, brought Kristina under the narrow scrutiny of her aunt. She could see herself in a large mirror perched over the mantel, the color rising in her cheeks, the untidiness of her hair . . . the profile of her aunt, watching her, she thought, much as a waiting cat might watch at a mouse hole.

"You are very lovely."

Startled by her aunt's first words, Kristina turned her attentions to her. "Thank you," she replied, making a discreet scrutiny of her aunt and the room beyond her. "Father always said I look a lot like you did at my age."

"Did he, indeed?"

The short response was a little intimidating; Kristina wasn't sure if mention of her father might have caused the coolness reflecting in her aunt's gaze or whether it was simply Zelpha's "way," as Cleveland had warned her on the trip to Oak Shadows. She managed a small smile, her gaze drifting away to study the room in light of her aunt's continued silence. Well, this wasn't going at all the way she'd planned. She'd thought Zelpha Prudhomme would be a little warmer; after all, they hadn't met until this night and they were each other's only living relation.

Like the exterior of the house, this large room whispered its antiquity . . . the harsh lines of scuffed furniture, the fingers of frayed darkness hinting at the sagging sofa's age . . . the floor by the mantel littered with gilt that had peeled from the mirror's frame. There again was

14

the reflection of her aunt, watching her . . . thinking what? That she had intruded upon her solitude? Kristina shuddered; her aunt's only letter to her had been warm and inviting . . . why the chilly reception now that she was here?

She was almost glad of Cleveland's return, and when he stood in the doorway, politely waiting, Kristina turned to smile at him. But the smile would not linger, and her fingers began to fidget among themselves in the folds of her gown. She wasn't sure what she should say to her aunt. The mention of her father had received a curt response. Perhaps she should simply allow her aunt to bring up the subject for conversation between them. Then, as the silence continued, she found herself wishing that Cleveland would find a gentle way to extricate her from her aunt's company.

But he did not. So, Aunt Zelpha did it for him. "You'll be tired after your journey. Cleveland will see you to your room." When she arose, Kristina did also, and without further amenities, Zelpha, carrying a cane that she did not seem to truly need, moved toward a doorway at the back of the parlor.

Kristina felt a pang of hurt. Her aunt was none too pleased with her, if the woman's actions were being properly read, and she really wasn't sure why. Her aunt had invited her to Oak Shadows, even sending the money to pay her fare, with a little left over for incidentals, and now she was acting as if she wished Kristina were a thousand miles away. Then Cleveland, as though he had been able to see into her thoughts, smiled apologetically, explaining, "She'll warm up to you, Miz Hartman."

"She hates me," mumbled Kristina, biting her lip, a familiar habit she resorted to when she thought she might cry.

To which a now-laughing Cleveland replied, "Naw'm, she don't hate you, a'tall. You'll see." Cleveland turned toward a wide, spiral staircase. "Come along, Miz Hartman. You'll have the brightes' an' happies' room in this whole house. Come along . . . I'll have Sophronia bring you up a supper tray, along with that cinnamon tea she's been slow to bring you."

"Thank you." Except for the parlor, the house was ominously dark. Cleveland took a pewter candelabra from a side table and led the way up the carpeted staircase. Like the rest of the house, the carpet had seen better days, and occasionally her heel snagged in the rotting remnants. Perhaps if her attention had not been so completely upon the family portraits, she might have managed to maintain a steady footing. There were vague likenesses of Zelpha, and very vague ones of her father . . . portraits that may have been of grandfathers and great-grandmothers, of relations dating back to the seventeenth century, glared somberly back at her. So dark and foreboding was the stairwell and the corridor into which Cleveland escorted her, she could hardly believe a room in this dreary old house could be bright and happy, an unblemished cloud floating in the fiercest of storms. Immediately, guilt flooded her. She thought her aunt had been quick to condemn her. Now she had given Oak Shadows the same harsh treatment. But the house made her skin crawl, as though something dark and sinister would momentarily drop a bony hand to her shoulder.

Then Cleveland opened the door to a room no less than thirty feet long and wide, and Kristina was instantly delighted. A velvet-covered Chippendale love seat rested at the end of a canopied bed, all draped in filmy white; plump rose and blue embroidered pillows tucked gracefully among the ones against which her head would rest. A wicker rocker sat beside a gauze-covered window, and the hazy gray of evening beyond the clean pane of glass was almost inviting. Moving from the planked floor onto a brilliant Oriental rug, newer by decades than anything else in the house, she declared, "Cleveland, this is, indeed, a beautiful room. Are you sure Aunt Zelpha meant for me to occupy it?"

Cleveland chuckled, "Ordered ever'thing brand spankin' new from Baton Rouge when you write that you was comin', Miz Hartman. An' had workmen a scrapin' an' paintin' the woodwork an' puttin' that purty pink on them walls. Sho' it was meant fo' you." When Kristina turned to face him, he said, "Well, I'll be leavin' you ta yo'self, Miz Hartman. Sophronia'll be along presently." As Cleveland turned to leave, he paused to ask, "You'll be wantin' ol' Sophronia to he'p you unpack?"

"No, I can do that myself. Thank you."

The door closed with a dull thud. As she listened to the retreat of Cleveland's footfalls on the tattered carpet of the corridor, she found herself becoming aware of other sounds . . . a distant rumble of thunder . . . the call of a night bird . . . a long, wailing cry from the bayou . . . the gentle whistle of the wind through the pecans and oaks. At her window a bare pecan branch began tapping against the pane . . . *tap . . . tap, tap . . . tap . . . tap, tap, tap . . .* and she moved toward it, hoping the offender might be brittle enough to be broken off and, thus, cease its irritating rattle.

Stepping to the window, she found that the branch was hitting against the top of the glass. Though the bottom half of the window was open, she could not reach the offending branch, even when she leaned across the sill. If only her arm were two inches longer . . .

Then she saw him. Standing amid the tombstones, the hazy masculine form seemed to rise from the ground mist.

He was tall, slim, dark-clothed; she could not see his features, though she was sure that his eyes shone like diamonds. His booted feet were apart in a careless stance . . . his arms crossed . . . a brimmed hat flipped back from his forehead. Then the mist slowly enveloped him, and her gaze now held only the swirling darkness grabbing at the tombstones of Oak Shadows cemetery.

# Two

Kristina came out of her sleep so quickly that she might have been physically thrown from it. Her slim hand immediately attempted to block out the light invading her eyes. For a moment she forgot where she was; the warm sun hardly seemed to be the same as that shining down on her home in Lexington.

No, of course it wasn't. This was a Louisiana sun . . . and she was in a strange bed on the upper floor of Aunt Zelpha Prudhomme's plantation house.

Then she recalled the sorry impression she had made upon her aunt last evening when she'd arrived, and silently vowed to make a better one this morning. Thus, she bounded to full wakefulness, protesting the coldness of the floor as she approached the armoire where her dresses were hanging. Thinking that she would have to search the house for an iron, she was surprised to find that all her dresses had been carefully pressed. She touched the one she would wear this morning—a modest dress of sky-blue cotton—and found that the fabric was still warm. She would have to remember to thank the thoughtful soul who'd seen to her gowns, dear, old Sophronia she was sure.

Downstairs, a hearty breakfast was awaiting her and Cleveland informed her that the lady of the house would not leave her rooms today. So why the extra plate at the dining-room table? thought Kristina, cutting questioning eyes toward the old gentleman.

How perceptive he was, for with a little laugh, he replied, "You'll be takin' breakfus', Miz Hartman, with the school marm, Miz Leanna Gilbert. She rents that ol' overseer's cottage in the orchard."

"Will I like her?" asked Kristina.

To which Cleveland replied, "Ya can't he'p but like Miz Gilbert. She be's a delightful lady."

And delightful she was. Leanna Gilbert was certainly destined to be the redeemer in Kristina's visit to Oak Shadows Plantation. During the day, the two women chatted about their separate lives, Kristina visited the one-room schoolhouse and was introduced to each of the seventeen children attending that day, and she enthusiastically agreed to assist Leanna with the autumn festivities throughout the month of October that would culminate in the costume ball to be held on Halloween night. Things were definitely looking up.

Or so she thought. When they sat down to supper that evening, Cleveland informed them that "Miz Zelpha be joinin' ya for sup."

The two young women sat patiently to wait. So eerily silent was the atmosphere of the large house, Kristina was momentarily startled when Leanna asked, "What do you think of your aunt?"

Kristina could hardly tell her that she thought Zelpha curt, rude and unfriendly. So she replied, with carefully chosen words, "She's, ummm, staid, rather reserved, I suppose—"

Leanna drew her table napkin against her mouth and snickered. "Reserved? Miss Zelpha? Surely, we're not thinking about the same Zelpha Prudhomme."

Just then, a brash, aging, feminine voice began to croon, "My love for you is all I knew, my love for you

19

is all I knew, My love for you is all I knew. Hope I will see you again. Farewell, my darling, farewell! Farewell, my darling, farewell! Farewell, my darling, farewell! Hope I will see you again."

From their position at the table, Kristina and Leanna watched as Zelpha seemed to float down the wide, circular stairs, then entered the dining room, the most godawful spectacle either of the young women had ever seen. Dark green lace cascaded across the front of Zelpha Prudhomme's shimmering gold satin gown; the décolletage was edged with gathered lace adorned by ravishing red roses in full and glorious bloom. To complete Aunt Zelpha's outfit, a wide gold satin bow sat atop her carrot-colored wig of shoulder-length ringlets and bell-shaped earrings hung from the stretched holes in her earlobes. Her rouge was like red apples against her pallid features, and her bright red lipstick was grotesquely smeared beyond the lines of her shrunken lips.

"Greetings, my young lovelies," she said, dropping to her chair at the table with a grand flourish and a crinkling of crisp satin. Only then did the rubies of the large ring on her left hand gleam in the light of the chandelier. Drawing that same pale, withered hand to her gaunt cheek, she smiled again for the younger women in attendance.

"Good evening, Aunt Zelpha," said a still-startled Kristina. This was not the quiet, melancholy woman she had met last evening upon her arrival at Oak Shadows Plantation, and she was quite at a loss for words beyond her initial greeting.

Though Leanna, in her six months in residence at Oak Shadows, had been exposed time and time again to Zelpha's eccentricities, she had never seen them to this extent. She bowed her head and mumbled, "Good evening, ma'am," then drew slightly back from the table as Joseph and Sophronia approached to set covered plates before them.

In the moments that followed, an eerie silence settled over the room. Kristina was sure that some invisible source had dragged long fingers of shadow across the muted walls, that she could hear the gilt from the mirror frame falling to the planked floors . . . Darkness veiled the windows so quickly, she could scarcely recall the fading of the sun . . .

Aunt Zelpha had fallen silent, her attention upon the soft foods that had been placed upon her plate. Her lipstick was smearing even more, in a macabre pattern, as she ate, and Kristina self-consciously began dabbing at her own rosy lips. But the only color upon them was that which nature had given her.

There were so many things she wanted to ask her aunt, but at the moment she was not sure Zelpha could carry on a sensible conversation. Surely, a rational person would not be dressed so, nor would her features be so garishly painted. She wanted to ask Zelpha, her father's sister, why her name was Prudhomme, why her father's name had been Hartman. She wanted to ask her about other family members that might still be living. She wanted to ask—

"What will you wear to the costume ball?"

Kristina's eyes cut across the short expanse and settled upon Leanna's. "The ball? I don't know. I really hadn't thought about it, and, well, needless to say, I haven't a costume. Perhaps I'll be able to sew one by then."

The night called from beyond the window, an eerie, long, whispering sound such as no wind had ever made. Kristina's attentions strayed toward the mesmerizing darkness. Without conscious effort, she arose, placing her napkin gently to the right of her plate. "It's a little stuffy inside. Do you mind if I walk outdoors?"

"Shall I accompany you?" asked Leanna.

To this, Aunt Zelpha immediately interjected, "The girl needs time to herself." As Kristina turned to leave the stifling warmth of the house, her aunt's voice halted her retreat. "It is because he was my half brother, Kristina, and . . . no, there are no other living relatives."

She turned, confused for the moment, unsure of what the woman was saying. In a hushed voice, she said, "What?"

"You wanted to know why our last names were different . . . Well, it was because we had different fathers."

Kristina instantly recalled the questions that had been in her thoughts just moments ago. "But how . . . I never asked . . . how could you possibly . . ."

Aunt Zelpha waved a weak wrist. "Doesn't matter how, girl. Go on to your walk. You're looking a little pale."

What a strange woman she is! thought Kristina, dismissing at once the coincidence between her aunt's answers and the questions she had had in mind. Giving the other women a cursory nod, Kristina moved into the chill of the outdoors, caring not that her shawl was upon the hall tree a scant half-dozen feet behind her in the foyer. She stood on the planked boards of the wide gallery and peered into the encroaching darkness.

Something strange and hypnotic compelled her to merge with the shadows of night. She moved with confidence along a narrow footpath, as though she had always lived at Oak Shadows and knew its every fault and character. Skirting a slight dip filled with muddy water, although she did not see it, she stepped over a protruding stone that could as easily have been the shadow of a Live Oak root. She ducked the cool dampness of Spanish moss, though it could have been the ever-changing hues of the evening sky, and before she quite realized where her feet were taking her, she stood in the great shadows of the cemetery, dwarfed by the monuments of those lost to the world as she knew it.

Though she wasn't sure why, tears sprang to her eyes. She did not notice the haunting mist floating eerily along the ground, skirting the bases of the tombstones and set-

22

tling, like deathly cold fingers, around her slim ankles. She dropped to the edge of a chair-high sepulchre, hoping the occupant wouldn't mind, then covered her tearful eyes with her hands.

Her sobs might have been an integral part of the night, as natural as the hoot of the owl across the timberline . . . her sorrow might have been one with the gentle wind stirring the bayou currents gleaming through the stand of cypress just down the slope of the hill . . .

And the sounds of the night slowly drifted away, leaving behind a void in which her thoughts magnified and tortured her . . . the only too recent death of her father . . . the loss of her New England home to the mortgage company, because her meager wages as a seamstress had not been adequate to pay for its upkeep . . . and now, this journey she should not have taken . . .

A twig snapped. Sucking in a short breath, Kristina drew herself erect, her ear sensitizing to pick up the sound. Again . . . Boot steps . . . heavy, like a man's . . . and yet her gaze could discern nothing more threatening than the massive tombstones and sepulchres . . . the rich, marble crypt at the core of the cemetery . . . The ground again trembled under the weight of a man's boot . . . there, again . . .

Kristina shot to her feet, dragging up her voluminous skirts as she prepared to break into a run. But the tears she had wept had disoriented her, and shadows and hanging tentacles of Spanish moss were all around her, feathering her pale features, while twigs snagged her tender flesh. Though she tried with all her might, she could not call out.

Dear Lord . . . Kristina, do not panic, she warned herself. Stop! Get your bearings. You're not that far away from Aunt Zelpha's house!

Relaxing her fingers so that the folds of her skirts fell from them, she drew in a breath to steady her nerves. Did she catch the gentle aroma of magnolias? But that was not possible! Magnolias bloomed in the spring. Were strong, masculine fingers closing gently over her shoulders? No, she couldn't believe that, though she was much too fearful to open her eyes and assure herself that she was still very much alone. Shadows skipped across her closed eyelids, and in that moment she was sure her heart had ceased to beat.

"Ma'am, are you all right?"

Had it not been for the gentleness of his voice, Kristina might have released a blood-curdling scream. But his tone had a calming effect, and her eyes slowly came open. He had now drawn her closer, so that the rangy smell of him filled her nostrils. He was tall, slim, dark-haired, and dressed completely in black. She could not clearly see his features, but she could tell he was young, somewhere within ten years of her own age of nineteen. "I-I . . ." she stammered, her feeble attempt to extricate herself from his grip causing it to tighten. "I'm all right," she finally managed to say, "you gave me somewhat of a fright." Then on a bolder, more accusing note, "Were you prowling the cemetery last night, also?"

"I never *prowl*," he responded. "Only cats prowl."

Now, she found the strength to break his hold upon her. "Didn't I see you last evening from my window?"

"You probably did."

"What are you doing here?"

"Well . . ." A boyish charm came into his tone. "I'm not prowling."

"This is a private cemetery, located on private property. You hardly have a right to be here."

"I beg to differ, ma'am," he said. "My understanding is that it's a community cemetery."

"Oh?" Kristina was a little embarrassed. If the gentleman was right, then that proved how very little she knew about her only living relation's affairs. To save grace, she continued, "Since you won't tell me what you're doing here, perhaps you'll tell me who you are?"

"Ummm, won't do any harm, ma'am. The name's—" He stopped in mid-sentence, the dark, hooded eyes Kristina still had not been able to distinguish suddenly looking across her shoulder. Then he gazed back into her features and said, "Name's Relin Trosclair de la Cerda."

"That's quite a burden to carry," said Kristina, offering her hand, which her night visitor immediately took. Warmth washed from his hand up her slender arm and pierced through to her heart. In a small, shaky voice, she said, "I am Zelpha Prudhomme's niece, Kristina Hartman." Then with more inflection, and the slightest touch of humor, "I suppose you're a ghost haunting the place?"

"Haunting you, Miss Kristina Hartman. The place be damned." Then, "Sorry, I'm not usually in the company of a lady." He did not release her hand; rather, his long, sinewy fingers were gently massaging the smooth skin of her palms. She attempted to take a step back, so that her hand might ease from the warmth of his own, but her foot caught on a length of trailing grass, knocking her off balance. Suddenly, she was in his arms, not even the smallest space separating them, the iron-hardness of his chest crushed to her soft one.

His mouth was ever so close to her own, his warm breath rushed upon her cool cheek and his eyes—heavens!—his eyes were black as onyx, the tiny silver flakes circling them caught, and magnified, by a sudden moonbeam . . . His angular good looks were rangy . . . Western . . . and Kristina suddenly became aware of the long hardness of his muscular thighs and of calves disappearing into Western boots. He was as completely out of his environment here at Oak Shadows Plantation as she was . . . and certainly, just as mortal. If he was a ghost, then, by George, she was Ulysses Grant!

For some strange, wonderful reason, she did not want to be away from his arms. Her gaze held his ample mouth, her own lips parting, trembling ever so slightly. She wanted him to kiss her. He was warm, virile, strongly

25

masculine, and . . . what was he waiting for? Her eyes gently closed. Imperceptively tilting her head, she waited for the caress of his mouth upon hers.

"Kristina!"

The sharp, feminine voice echoed from the darkness behind her. And before she could prepare for it, he had withdrawn from her, stepping back into the heavy mist floating upon the ground like storm clouds. She tried to follow the vision of him with her eyes, but it was almost as though he had never existed. All that remained of him was the warmth flooding her body . . . and the pressure she was sure she could still feel where his arms had held her.

Leanna Gilbert approached. "I was worried about you. What a spooky place for you to be all alone. Aren't you afraid?"

"I'm not . . . and I wasn't alone." She was a little angry that an interruption had made Relin Trosclair de la Cerda withdraw so suddenly. She didn't want to think that her mind might have been playing tricks on her and that he had been a figment of her imagination. She knew that couldn't be so . . . She could still detect the manly aroma of him . . . and she knew he had been as flesh and blood as she. She just wasn't sure how he had disappeared so quickly, or why he had felt the need to do so.

Well, she would see him again; she'd make sure of it. Turning, smiling at the shorter woman, she said, "We'd best get back to Aunt Zelpha's drafty old manor. Has she retired to bed?"

"She's in the parlor, sipping a hot toddy and wanting to get to know you better. Just promise me, whatever she says to discourage you, you won't back out on your promise to help me entertain the children this month. They're such a handful, I'm not sure I could manage alone."

"I promise." Kristina laughed, moving to Leanna's side

26

for the short walk back to the house. "I enjoy children. One day I'll have a brood of my own."

At the gallery, Leanna said, "I must retire to the cottage to grade papers. I'll see you tomorrow."

"Yes . . . tomorrow." Kristina lifted a hand in farewell, then stood quietly, watching Leanna disappear into the darkness.

Only now could she feel the deepening chill of the night. The large house loomed before her against the violet sky, and behind her the wind rustled through the trees.

She looked back for a moment, sure that she could almost see the blurred figure of him through the mist, leaning lazily against the marble crypt so hauntingly visible beneath the overhang of Spanish moss.

# *Three*

When Sophronia entered the parlor with the tray, she found Kristina leaning across Zelpha, briskly patting her cheek. With a small cry, she set down the tray, tipping one of the delicate china cups and spilling the tea. Taking Zelpha's hand, she showed alarm as she asked, "Good heavens, Miz Kristina, what happened?"

"I don't know." Sheer terror softened Kristina's answer. "I was telling her about the man in the cemetery, and all of a sudden, she just—"

Zelpha began flailing her wrists and making a feeble attempt to sit up. "I'm all right now," she fussed, her lipstick smeared grotesquely across her right cheek. "How silly of me. Why"—a small smile briefly touched her features—"you'd think I was a sick old lady, wouldn't you, *ma chères?*"

"We should fetch the doctor," said Sophronia.

"We should do no such thing!" argued Zelpha. "I'll take that tea now, Sophronia, if you'd be so kind." Cleveland, drawn by their arguments, now entered the room. At which time, Zelpha continued, "Better yet, I'll take my tea in my room."

As she arose, Sophronia offered, "I'll bring it, Miz Zelpha."

Kristina was stunned beyond words. She sat back against the plush fabric of the divan, her velvet-clothed

28

elbows pressed into its softness, watching her great-aunt shuffle from the room with Sophronia, the teacup clinking against the saucer as she moved. As Cleveland, too, departed, shaking his head, Kristina had the good sense to silently question her reckless decision to come to Oak Shadows; she was certainly not good for her aunt's health.

She gradually became aware of the silent scrutiny of the woman who had become her friend. She looked up, her gaze tracing a path along the rich, ornate walls, then halting at Leanna's stare. "I thought you went to your cottage, Leanna?"

"I heard you scream. I thought something terrible had happened."

Kristina gave an apologetic smile, but it was as weak as winter-killed weeds and didn't have the decency to remain upon her mouth. So, she pushed herself forward, then stood up, one slim foot shuffling from beneath the hem of her gown. "I suppose you're wondering what happened?"

Leanna lightly shrugged her shoulders. "Well, I was actually."

Kristina looked to her once again, the apology like a renewed beacon in her eyes. "I really don't know. One moment my aunt and I were talking; she seemed so interested in my mysterious visitor, and a little worried that I had been accosted by a stranger, and then all of a sudden, she fainted away on the divan." Kristina's narration immediately ceased. Running a long, slim finger across her slightly parted mouth, she thought a moment, then continued, "It was when I mentioned his name . . . yes, that was it." She smiled now, proud of herself for being able to explain what had upset her aunt, though it really wasn't a rational explanation at all.

"And what was his name?"

Kristina did not hesitate to respond, "Relin Trosclair de la Cerda."

"Oh, of course," snapped Leanna, without truly meaning to appear rude. "Why not the Oak Shadows ghost

29

in residence? If I were so fortunate as to be accosted in the cemetery by a stranger, I would certainly want it to be none other than Relin Trosclair de la Cerda."

Tears popped into Kristina's eyes, though she was not sure whether they were tears of anger or of hurt. The sarcasm in Leanna's voice had left a nasty odor in the air, and Kristina wasn't sure what had provoked it. Drawing in a steady breath, she responded, her own sarcasm clearly evident, "Well, perhaps you'll tell me just what exactly it is you're talking about?"

Leanna approached and settled on the divan, then took Kristina's hand to coax her down beside her. "The man whose name you mentioned to Miss Prudhomme died years ago. His is the great marble crypt at the center of the cemetery. That is where Relin Trosclair de la Cerda has lain for the past fifty years, and he certainly could not have talked to you in the cemetery tonight. You must have given Miss Prudhomme an awful shock."

"It wasn't my intention," assured Kristina, her fingers now plying the curves of the cameo at her neckline. "And I assure you the man I met tonight has not been dead for fifty years. Why, I . . . I . . ." She stumbled over her words now, a pretty crimson flooding her cheeks. Leanna's smile instantly relieved the tension. When Kristina felt a gentle squeeze upon the fingers of her left hand, she continued with haste, "Don't jump to the wrong conclusions. We—he and I—it's just that . . . Oh, for heaven's sake!" She breathed deeply, collecting her thoughts. "He was a man. I felt his flesh—warm, hard, masculine flesh—and he breathed warmly against my cheek. Ghosts don't breathe! Besides, he was a stranger . . . and he meant nothing to me!"

"I would love it if a man who meant nothing to me made my face as red as yours is now."

Kristina's mouth stirred into a cockeyed smile. Then she laughed and was instantly joined by Leanna. By the time Sophronia returned to remove the tray, the young women had collapsed into uncontrollable laughter. Sophronia, shrugging her shoulders in her usual way, simply picked up the tray and moved toward the kitchen. *Lawd, Miz Zelpha be strange as pink molasses. Don' be 'spectin' her niece to have a loaded attic either!*

In the moment of silence to follow, though she sat in the overly warm parlor, Kristina found herself mentally being swept away into the brisk outdoors, surrounded by the darkness of the cemetery . . . a darkness that should have been cold and damp . . . but her memories were, rather, of warmth and virile strength. She could feel the tickle of the rake's breathing against her hot, flushed cheek; his iron-hard arm at her back, pulling her ever so close; the broad expanse of his chest against her soft breasts . . . And his eyes . . . Their rich, black shade, their silver specks . . . like beacons penetrating the darkness below the rim of his hat.

He was no apparition! He may have teased her, recklessly giving her the identity of some fellow who lay buried in the cemetery, but she certainly wasn't going to allow his little joke to make a fool of her.

She might have completely become lost in thought if Leanna hadn't unexpectedly shot to her feet. "I'm retiring to the cottage, again, to grade those papers before bedtime. Can you properly entertain yourself for the balance of the evening?" Winking, she asked, "Or will you take a saunter and be swept into a blue-eyed stranger's arms?"

"Not blue eyes," Kristina pouted. "They're black as pitch."

Leanna favored her new friend with a wicked giggle. "Of course, stormy eyes . . . how romantic." She sauntered a few feet across the parlor, then turned, loosely linking her fingers before her. "Don't forget, we'll take the children out at eight o'clock. It's Skull Night . . ."

Kristina shuddered. When she and Leanna had spoken earlier, she'd learned of the macabre practice of taking the children out to find the "haunted" skull of the murderous slave, Pierre, who had killed his master's family eighty years before and had sunk their bodies in the bayou. The local folks believed that the knobby roots of the bald cypress at the bend in the bayou were their restless souls and that the water hyacinths blooming in profusion there were the spirits of the children, reaching to the sky in a vain attempt to recapture life. Though Leanna had assured her the Halloween rituals were for the children's enjoyment, Kristina couldn't help being repelled by the tragedies from which they had sprung. Murdered families and dead school teachers . . . all in the name of enjoyment.

"I'll come along," offered Kristina after a pause. "But I'll not be wanting to find Pierre's skull."


*The Following Evening*

Fingers of darkness stretched grotesquely along the edge of the bayou. The water's surface, at once beautiful and ugly, gleamed with algae and the knobby roots of the cypress breaking the currents. The giggling children had failed to locate Pierre's skull by plunging short, stocky fingers into the murky shallows and now had scattered through the encroaching darkness of the nearby woods, following the leader, a brave boy named Willard. Leanna and Kristina walked slowly along, supervising the children, keeping a wary eye on each, especially the little "snail heathens," as Leanna called the precocious boys, and watching the attic window of Oak Shadows for the "lighting of the lamp" that would end the search for another year.

Momentarily, Kristina pointed a graceful finger. "There—look. There is the light in the attic window."

Instantly, Leanna began calling the children to her. When all had appeared and their heads had been counted, Leanna reminded them of the hot cocoa and cookies Sophronia and Cleveland would have waiting for them.

"Are you coming, Kristina?" she asked, at once aware of the dreamy look in her friend's emerald eyes.

"I think I'll walk for a while," Kristina said, absently flicking her wrist. "I'll catch up to you."

"Going in search of your ghostly rake?" Leanna laughed and, before an answer could be offered, was coaxing the children toward Zelpha Prudhomme's old house vaguely outlined against the lavender sky.

When the children's chattering had become muffled by the distance, Kristina turned her gaze toward the bayou. A surreptitious movement here and there failed to capture her attention beyond a perfunctory glance, and she found herself looking toward the cemetery. She knew he was there, among the tombstones, perhaps watching her through the thin stand of pines and the oak saplings. With the absence of the children's laughter, the night became strangely soundless; even the frogs were quiet.

A small skiff sat at the edge of the bayou. Kristina wished she had the courage to get in and push herself out into the middle of the water. But the bayou was haunting and frightening. She knew that creatures lingered there, creatures only the dense darkness of a Louisiana bayou could harbor. Where she stood, enclosed by the dim, vaulted chamber of the moss-enshrouded cypress, she could smell the sweetness of the tea-colored water, its surface like a delicate mosaic of tiny leaves. Her father had told her how hauntingly lovely the bayou was, but she had never been able to imagine its true allure. She knew that she could stay here forever. It seemed the land itself had grasped her tender flesh, holding her prisoner, and willingly so.

Then she heard a twig snap. Leanna and the children were long gone; could it be a night creature, perhaps a raccoon venturing into the night in search of food? Or could it be a human intrusion? And if so . . . was it him?

Then she turned, her gaze narrowing to discern a human shape among the stand of cypress. Yes . . . There he was, that slim, masculine figure standing tall and straight.

"Do you always sneak up on girls in the dark of night?"

"Aren't you frightened?" came his low, masculine response.

"Should I be?"

He began to move, his arms, crossed just moments ago, falling to his sides. When he raised a hand to touch her hair, she stepped back, her eyes suddenly dark with rebellion.

"I don't know who you are, sir. You could be stalking the woods killing and eating little children, for all I know. You're a liar, a sneak and a fraud, and I have no reason in the world not to flee from you in fear for my life."

His hand fanned out. "Then flee, Miss Kristina Hartman. If you think I intend you harm, flee to the security of Zelpha Prudhomme's stuffy parlor."

"How do you know it's stuffy?"

An endearing chuckle followed. "All little old ladies keep their parlors stuffy." A suddenly raised arm startled her; again, she stepped out of his perimeter. "Do pardon me, ma am," he drawled. "But I believe there's a child over there, and I haven't had my supper yet."

Try as she might, she could not prevent the smile from curling her mouth. How charming was this black-hearted rogue who had come out of the night, claiming to be a long-dead gentleman buried in Oak Shadows cemetery and dropping his little jokes as casually as he might compliments. She had no earthly idea who he was, and yet she felt as comfortable—and as safe—with him as she had ever felt with anyone. For now, she would not fret over his identity, or his reasons for prowling the night. She knew only that she enjoyed his company, and he obviously enjoyed hers. Why else would he have sought her out two nights in a row?

Now she found herself noticing little things about him . . . the fullness of his mouth, the way he tucked his thumb into the pocket of his trousers, the scuff marks on his boots. Instinctively, her gaze attempted to pry away the darkness from beneath the rim of his hat, so that she could see the haunting shade of his eyes.

"Are we just going to stand here staring at each other?" he asked. "Or shall we walk along the bayou?"

"A walk sounds good to me."

The man who had identified himself to her as Relin Trosclair de la Cerda now fell in beside her as she began to move onto a path skirting the bayou. When he saw her struggling with her shawl, he picked the garment up and settled it comfortably upon her shoulders. "Is that better?" Her sigh whispered into the night. "Tell me," he continued, "what were you and the school marm and all those children doing in the woods tonight?"

"Looking for the haunted skull," she casually remarked. Amused by the bewildered expression immediately touching his features, she told him the story, ending with, "And there'll be some activity or other until the night of the costume ball at Zelpha's house on Halloween night."

"Will you be there?"

"I imagine that I will." Suddenly, Kristina halted, remembering something Cleveland had told her. "Oh, that's right. You're supposed to make an appearance on Halloween night. That is"—she grinned—"if you are, indeed, Relin Trosclair de la Cerda."

He was surprised when her hand came to rest on his forearm. She said nothing, merely smiled, but he knew what she was thinking. To save face, he offered in a husky voice, "All right, Miss Kristina Hartman. I lied. I am *not* the ghost of Relin Trosclair de la Cerda."

With a soft laugh, she asked, "Then whose ghost are you?"

Without warning, he pulled her into his arms, the musky, manly scent of him assailing her senses. "I am *your* ghost."

"I beg your pardon," she responded, her attempts to extricate herself from his arms as vain as they had been the night before. "If you are not flesh and blood, then . . ."

In the instant she paused, he asked, "Then what?"

She was a lady and, as such, would not betray that she was very aware of the hardness of his loins against her abdomen, a betrayal, without spoken words, that he was a mortal man affected by the nearness of mortal woman.

Kristina knew, of course, that she should not be in his arms; he was, after all, a stranger, certainly not from these parts, nefariously prowling cemeteries and bayou trails. She wondered how many other women he had accosted in the darkness. And she wondered where he lived, what business had brought him here and why he felt he had the right to hold her like this, ever so close and oh, so gently . . .

But there was not time for her thoughts to instill any sense of rationality within her. For suddenly his mouth was upon her own, and though she had not intended to allow such an assault, she found herself responding wantonly, hungering for the way his lips claimed hers. Her fingers moved over the strong, sinewy muscles of his arms, encircling his shoulders, and her right leg rose slightly, to feel the hardness of his thigh.

Luke Chandler had not left the vast, open plains of Texas behind him to come to the Louisiana bayous in search of a woman. But now that he felt Kristina Hartman in his arms, her body melting into his own in the haunting darkness of night, he could not imagine being apart from her. He didn't give his heart easily, but if she were to ask for it, this very minute, he would toss it to the ground at her feet.

And because he didn't want to feel that accessible to the alluring, pale-haired beauty who had suddenly appeared at the plantation, he pulled away from her so quickly that she nearly lost her balance. He was polite enough, however, to offer his hand for support.

He could see surprise on her features, and for the moment he felt a little guilty. But rather than betray the vulnerability he had felt, he said huskily, "It's going to rain. You'd better get back to Zelpha's house."

"Rain?" Briefly, her gaze cut skyward, at once noticing the hazy darkness of rain clouds hanging on the horizon. The gentle rumble of thunder seemed far, far away. "Yes . . . yes, I suppose it might."

Still, she couldn't imagine this place being blasted by the gusts of wind a storm might bring. She felt warm and secure inside, like on a balmy spring day. She wanted to be back in his arms, but his gaze was dark and foreboding . . . She didn't imagine that he would again open his arms to her, though she couldn't for the life of her understand why.

His head moved slightly. "Go on . . . Don't get caught in a downpour."

"Will I see you again?"

"Perhaps . . ." He turned, his long strides taking him toward the trail dipping into the woods.

But before he could merge into the darkness, she called out to him, "Please . . . tell me your name."

He halted abruptly. Turning his head only slightly, he called back to her, "Luke," then merged into the stand of oaks, willows and cypresses. She heard a splash in a shallow stream where his booted foot had stepped, and then he was gone.

Something stirred in the reeds, a rabbit perhaps. Gathering her shawl to her, she broke into a run toward Zelpha's house.

As she ascended the steps to the wide gallery, a lightning flash of dim white brightened the sky for a moment. Before the warm house could envelop her, drops of rain began to rattle the leaves strewing the lawn of Oak Shadows Plantation.

# *Four*

*A Week Later*

Kristina couldn't sleep. It was hours before dawn, and she rested against the pillows, her arms crossed as her gaze swept the niches and crannies of the large, comfortable chamber. The case clock at the foot of the stairs chimed the hour of three as, somewhere beyond the window, a night bird called out in the darkness. She could almost hear the haunting melody of the bayou's waters in their never-ending southerly travels . . . she could almost see the night sky beyond the sheets of rain draping the long windows of her room.

Her hand absently began to massage the rich harmony of the jacquard coverlet, feeling its bold texture. Overhead, the delicate lacing of the canopy floated gently, like spider webs caught on the slightest of breezes. Listening to the chorus of rumbling thunder, the creakings of the old house, the songs of the bayou frogs, Kristina became instantly aware of the sudden silence, as if all sounds of the night had been frightened into submission. She sat forward, listening for any small sound, even the scurrying of a mouse between the ancient walls of Oak Shadows.

But there was nothing . . . not the growling of thunder, not the chorus of frogs, not the creakings of the old house that had magnified in the stillness of the night. Then she heard it, long, low, haunting. . . .

*Kris-tiiiiii-naaaa . . . Kris-tiiiiii-naaa . . .*

Slowly, hypnotically, she slipped from the bed and moved cautiously across the planked floor toward the window. The exterior darkness seemed deeper than that in the room. For a moment, she could not see who had called her name.

Yes . . . There he was . . . his tall, slim frame in darker silhouette against the timberline. "Luke?" She spoke his name quietly, watching for a movement. Then she saw his left arm move skyward and begin to wave back and forth. Was he calling her to him? And for what reason?

But did the reason really matter? It had been a very long week since she had seen him, though not because she hadn't taken the walks she enjoyed through the cemetery. Stepping back from the window, she retrieved her robe from across the chair and began to pull it on. Somewhere beyond, a peal of thunder brought the noises of the night back to her. She was still pulling on her slippers as she quietly opened the door to the wide corridor.

Not aware of her stealthy footfalls and her deliberate effort to create no noise in the household, she wanted only to be out of doors, with Luke, and she did not want an audience from the house. He had called to her, and the summons must be important. It was scarcely past three in the predawn. He must have known, somehow, that she had not been asleep. Would he have risked calling her name if he had thought she would not hear him?

Soon, she stood beneath the swirling, bloated sky and felt large droplets of rain pounding her slender frame. She cared not about the cold or the rain or the occasional streaks of lightning; she cared only that Luke had called to her and was waiting in the darkness of the timberline. She moved in that direction, her feet slipping upon the muddy roadway.

She breathed a sigh of relief when she saw him, almost

as one with the stand of hardy pines. But when she began once again to close the distance between them, his hand went up and a harsh, masculine voice said, "You are not Kristina! Who are you?"

It did not sound like Luke's voice. Cautiously, she said his name, "Luke? It is Kristina. I . . . I saw you from my window."

Again, he said, "You are not *my* Kristina." Then slowly he began to withdraw into the darkness of the timberline.

The rain was cascading down Kristina's head, plastering her hair to her face and neck and blinding her against the night. Her robe and gown clung to her body, and she felt bound by the shimmering fabric. Still, that did not stop her from fleeing after him to demand an explanation.

Which was, immediately, a decision she wished she had reconsidered. The prickly limbs of brambles tore at her tender skin and snagged the fabric of her robe. She found herself mired in ankle-deep mud, fighting to gain her equilibrium and her bearing. In which direction had he fled? In which direction was the house?

Panic began to grab at her heart. An ache in her shoulders traveled through her arms and down the length of her back. She was not sure how she maintained her footing. Suddenly her legs felt flaccid and weak, so Kristina closed her eyes tightly, began to count slowly . . . one . . . two . . . three . . . And when she stopped at ten, she opened her eyes, breathing a little easier. The sky had lightened to a silvery gray through the thick stand of pines, and she saw at once the bold outlines of the tombstones at Oak Shadows cemetery. At least, this was a place from which to begin to find her way back to the house, for in her few ventures there she had learned every trail and path leading among the monuments.

As she sloshed through the mud, she watched the crypt at the center of the cemetery. Occasionally, her gaze would wander and she would catch the glint of dark water beyond the trees or the pale, eerie glow of a lighted window somewhere far, far away. The sky pulsated through the great ceiling of clouds and seemed to dip dangerously at their center.

Before she quite realized the distance she had traveled, Kristina stood a hundred feet in front of the great marble crypt bearing the name of Relin Trosclair de la Cerda. A gentle light flickered from within; she knew it was not natural, and yet she did not feel afraid. Rather, her feet began to move toward it, stepping onto the brick path half a dozen feet from the iron gate, and when her fingers closed over the iron filigree, the light within pulsated to blinding dimensions, forcing her to drop her gaze.

She called tentatively, "Luke?" But no one answered. Again, she spoke his name, and again she was met by silence. She pulled on the gate, hearing its lock click open, its ancient hinges protesting the movement as she held it wide enough to allow for her slender form to pass through. A dozen steep, carefully laid brick steps led downward, and still the light grew . . . pulsating like heartbeats against the smooth marble walls and the reds and muted browns of the mosaic floor.

Why would Luke come down here? she wondered, pausing on the last step, aware now of the icy chill grabbing at her tender flesh and the painful cold of her water-soaked feet. What had compelled him to flee from her? And why—dear Lord, why?—had she followed him here, into the crypt of a man long dead? She should be safely tucked into her bed on the second floor of Zelpha's house, anxiously awaiting the breaking of another dawn over the haunting bayou of her father's childhood home.

Soon, Kristina became deeply immersed in determining the source of the muted light, of the pale shadows floating around the crypt like the scattering colors of a kaleidoscope. Fixing her gaze upon the grates at the top of the crypt, near the ceiling, she watched as occasional flashes of lightning permeated the chamber, and yet she knew they were not the source of the strange light. It was as if the marble itself was creating the soft illumination, striking every feature of the crypt . . . even, frighteningly, the dust-shrouded coffin resting sedately on its iron bier. Constructed entirely of teakwood, its brass finishings had long ago tarnished to a dark green color like that of the algae floating on the bayou's surface. She was not sure what compelled her feet to move, but now she was near enough to touch the cool wood with a trembling palm.

A creak somewhere nearby caused her to jerk her hand away. Then she saw a mouse scurrying across the floor of the crypt. With a small sigh, she whispered, "There are no ghosts . . . there are no ghosts . . ."

Then she heard it again, oh, so very close, *Kris-tiiii-naaaa* . . . And she whirled about, the sight before her immediately causing her to go rigid with fear, the scream she wanted to release frozen in her throat so that she thought she would choke on it. He stood upon the stair, his heavy black cape pulled across his torso by one hidden arm, his features pale and luminescent, and beyond him, every feature of the stairwell and the marble walls distinguishable through the hazy darkness of his transparent form.

Then he said, "You're not Kristina. Who are you?"

She somehow managed to say, "But I am Kristina," then on a soft, panic-stricken note, "There *are* ghosts . . . there *are* ghosts."

Though frozen tendrils of fear grabbed her from within, she refused to be intimidated, even by a ghost. Just as she would have taken a step toward the strange creature who had spoken her name, she heard a crumbling at the top of the crypt. She had just turned to look up toward the source of the noise when something very hard struck the right side of her head. As if a fog were wrapping her in its embrace, she felt herself gently folding to the dusty floor at the foot of the coffin.

If she remembered anything at all after that, confused

and disoriented though she was, it was that her visitor certainly was not of this world.

The case clock chimed half past five. Kristina rubbed her eyes with an index finger and thumb, hoping that she might catch the first glimmer of dawn this early Tuesday morning. But the first glimmer she saw was the blazing fire in the hearth, and she sat forward, stretching her arms and then drawing them back to hug her slender frame.

What a nightmare she'd had! She recalled every vivid detail of it, and could almost feel the ominous presence of the ghost she had encountered in the darkest recesses of sleep. Drawing herself up on her pillows, she cast a wary glance around the room, hoping she would not see him again or hear the eerie whisper of her name on his ghostly lips. She drew up the coverlet, feeling its raised, geometrical pattern press into her skin, then tucked it beneath her chin. All at once, she became aware of her bed gown, the rose-colored one with muted pink and mauve flowers intertwined in the fabric. Her brows pinched in perplexion; this was not the gown she had pulled on last evening.

She had worn the silky one, the one her father had said a single woman should be ashamed to wear. But, she had liked the filmy femininity of it. So . . . where was it now?

Quietly, she withdrew from the bed, immediately feeling a pounding ache in her head. She bent over, clutching the site of the pain and felt a lump the size of her fist behind her right ear. Well, that was the first tangible proof that her evening had not been a dream, or a nightmare, whichever term was most appropriate. Finally able to straighten, and waiting for the pain to subside somewhat, Kristina attempted to locate her slippers. She was positive that she had placed them just beneath the edge

43

of the footboard. But they were not there now. Giving up the search almost as quickly as it had begun, she traversed the short expanse of Oriental carpet and protested the first touch of her bare foot upon the planked floorboard. In the armoire she found her satin gown and its matching robe, hanging together on a brass hook. They were clean, though slightly damp.

All right, now! What kind of trickery is going on? Kristina spun about, much too quickly since her head began to pound again, her gaze moving around the wide, warm chamber. It had been a dream . . . hadn't it? And if it hadn't, then how had she gotten back in her chamber, and who had changed her into a clean gown? "Damn!" She muttered the expletive as she drew her hands to her hips.

Hearing a shuffling of feet in the corridor outside, she quickly traversed the floor and flung the door wide. Sophronia, carrying a lantern, paused, then turned to look at her rather curiously. "Sophronia . . ." Kristina wasn't sure what she intended to ask her. She imagined that she must look a little peculiar to the elderly servant, standing in the doorway in her bed gown and failing to speak beyond the initial greeting. Gathering her thoughs, she mumbled, "Do I . . . did I . . . ? Good heavens, did anything out of the ordinary happen last night?"

"How'd you know?" asked Sophronia, her thick, gray eyebrows meeting in a diminutive frown.

"Ah-hah! Something did happen!"

"Sho', Miz Hartman . . . lightnin' struck de silo las' night, burnt it plumb to de groun' befo' anybody even noticed. Mistah Lamont's boy, he come ovah ta tell Miz Zelpha jes' few minutes ago." Again, the servant asked, "But . . . how'd you know 'bout dat?"

Kristina sheepishly shrugged her shoulders, a quizzical, apologetic smile easing up the corners of her mouth. "I must have heard the announcement from my window," she explained. Before Sophronia could argue further, she said, "I'd better get dressed for the morning," then pulled the door to.

I must be going completely and utterly mad! she thought, leaning heavily against the closed door. She knew that the pale glow she had seen last night—if, indeed, her experience had not been a dream—had not been a fire in a silo across a meadow or field. It had been close . . . too close . . . and she had encountered a ghost.

At least, she thought she had. Kristina made up her mind to find out before the day was over just how much of her experience had been real and how much an illusion experienced in sleep. One thing was certain; she had received a painful blow to her head, though she couldn't remember where.

As she sauntered over the lawn, Kristina could hear the school bell ringing across the bayou and, occasionally, the laughter of a child responding to duty and education. Kristina hugged her shawl to her as she cut a deliberate path along the bayou, soon entering the footpath to Oak Shadows cemetery. Last night's rain had chilled the air and made the ground an unpleasant mixture of mud and slime. By the time she stepped onto the brick path leading to the marble crypt, her feet were weighted down in muck and mire.

She stood for a moment, staring at the elaborate marble crypt. Leanna had said it had been built for the first Oak Shadows schoolteacher who had died in a tragic accident. Kristina couldn't help but wonder why a schoolteacher had been laid to rest in so elaborate a crypt. Surely, the pittance he had received in wages at that time could not have paid for the expensive tomb. One day, she hoped Leanna might tell her the whole story . . .

A rustling in the leaves nearby chilled her through. For a moment, Kristina rested her chin upon her left shoulder and watched the source of the disturbance, a

45

scraggly black cat that looked as though it had fought every battle of the Civil War and been soundly defeated. Its ears were tattered, its fur missing in patches and it walked with a noticeable limp. But its hearing was intact, for within moments, it had snagged its prey, a large black field rat coming up out of the earth at the base of a tomb.

Morning was a soft gray above the timberline. Gathering her resolve, Kristina pulled the crypt's iron gate open and began to descend the steep brick steps. So familiar did they seem, she had no doubt she had been here last night. The silence within the marble walls was solid and almost deafening, shutting out the noises of the dreary morning. Now she stood on the last step, staring at crumbling marble large enough to have made the lump on her head, and the high corner from which it had broken. Then she looked at the teakwood coffin with its tarnished brass fittings. There, crumpled and scarcely recognizable, was one of her satin slippers. Quietly, she approached, then picked it up, dropping it immediately as sticky red mud grabbed at her fingers. Her nose twitched in revulsion as she attempted to pry the mud loose against the edge of her white shawl.

Then a gleam caught her attentions. Moving across the darkened interior toward the right corner, she bent and picked up a gold coin. The twenty-dollar gold piece bore the date 1875, only last year, and she wondered how it had gotten in the crypt. One of the school children wouldn't have possessed that much money. So . . . who?

Luke, perhaps? Or, should she say the man who had given her the name "Luke." It might not be any more genuine than the first name he had given her, Relin Trosclair de la Cerda, the name of the man in whose crypt she now stood, clutching a twenty-dollar gold piece that had not been here in the predawn hours.

Did the coin belong to the person who had taken her

back to Aunt Zelpha's house and changed her into a clean gown and tucked her into her bed?

And was that person the nocturnal rake whose arms she had enjoyed just last night?

She stood there, wistfully dreaming of him, closing her eyes in an effort to recapture the angular lines of his lean, hard face.

And to remember the kiss he had taken . . . and that she had willingly returned.

Luke Chandler had allowed his investigation of the crypt to intrude into the morning. He, too, had heard the voice calling Kristina's name, and he was determined to find its source. He did not usually allow himself to be caught in the cemetery by daylight, and had been pondering ways to return to the cabin undetected. Secrecy was important if his mission was to be successful.

He remained very still in the niche of the crypt, watching the beautiful Kristina Hartman and noting the dreamy expression upon her soft, oval face. He had been about to retrieve the coin from the mosaic floor when he'd heard her descending footsteps, and had barely managed to tuck himself away before she was staring into the crypt.

She had not noticed his distorted shadow in one corner of it, or she had and simply hadn't recognized it as human. He was wondering what she was doing here . . . after the experience she'd had last night.

He had been so careful to take her back to her chamber on the second floor of Oak Shadows Plantation, undetected by the other residents of the house. He thought he had taken care of everything, even his shameful, though enjoyable, duty of cleaning and dressing her in a fresh gown and tucking her into the folds of her bed. How could he have left the blasted slipper on the mosaic floor at the foot of de la Cerda's coffin, a dead giveaway that her experience had been real and not the dream she might otherwise have believed it. She was too smart to be fooled . . .

Even as he chastised himself for not being thorough, he recalled the beautiful ivory body that had lain unconscious beneath his tender ministrations last evening . . . the small, firm breasts . . . the tiny waist and womanly hips . . . the long, lithe legs that seemed to go on forever. He had wanted to be a gentleman, to turn his head away while he had washed away the mud and had dressed her in the only bed gown he had found available at the time, but—damn it to hell—he was a normal, red-blooded American male, and she was the most beautiful, alluring female he had ever encountered. He had thought Texas gals were the top of the line, but Kristina's pale hair, emerald eyes and flawless ivory flesh made them look plain in comparison. And he admired her spunk; how many girls would venture into a crypt in the dead of night, as she had done? And here she was again, the little detective trying to figure out what had happened and how she had gotten back to her aunt's rambling old house.

If he had wanted to, he could have reached out from the niche in which he'd wedged himself and touched her arm; she was that close. He held his breath, fearing that the smallest movement might be detected by the astute New England beauty, and when she finally began to saunter toward the steps, looking back only once, he breathed a sigh of relief.

Turning, pressing himself to the cool marble, he watched her voluminous mauve and brown plaid skirts disappear as she ascended into the morning light.

Wrapped in the warmth of her hand was the first piece of evidence that what he searched for was close by. He was sure the coin she'd retrieved from the mosaic floor was part of the rich bounty he had tracked across the border into Louisiana.

## Five

Kristina moved down the lawn, away from the big house where her father had been born. Dusk was in evidence, with a full moon shining weakly in the darkening sky. Although the grounds were said to be haunted by Relin Trosclair de la Cerda, there was nothing to upset her. A heady fall aroma was in the air, the musty odor of rotting leaves not really so unpleasant; and pampas grass swayed along the drive. She could hear a small animal, perhaps a rabbit, moving in the timberline, and a night bird trilled across the bayou. Kristina smiled at the beauty of it all, and swinging her hands vigorously, began to hum a silly little tune her father had taught her.

Suddenly, a slight chill fanned her, so very different from that of the still October air. What was it that so lightly touched her face, like the kiss of a butterfly, and yet hauntingly familiar? She began to move faster, though away from the house rather than toward it, where she might logically have sought the safety and comfort of its interior.

She had left Leanna in the parlor, playing a very slow game of chess with Aunt Zelpha. Now she wished she had stayed with them. But as usual, the parlor had been too hot and stuffy, and several hours of Aunt Zelpha's fussing had grated on her nerves.

It had been three days since she had ventured from

the house at night, though she had watched for Luke from her second-floor window. Several times she was sure she had caught the soft glow of a lantern in the cemetery, but too many watching eyes in the house had kept her from going in pursuit. She didn't want to think that she was foolhardy; rather, she considered herself adventurous and unafraid, to a degree, of the unexplainable.

Now, as she moved into the darkness of the timberline separating the lawns from the Oak Shadows cemetery, she reassessed her decision to venture into the night. But she was determined to find the man who had identified himself to her as Luke, and to find out what he was doing in the cemetery, what he was looking for and where he lived. After some questioning of the house servants and Leanna, she had learned of a small cabin at the edge of the woods where a crotchety old slave had dwelled years ago. There she would begin her search for Luke's living quarters. She knew he could not be commuting between Lecompte and the plantation, because no one, as far as she knew, had seen him on the road . . . it was simply a matter of patience before she located the man who kept her awake at night.

Now there was a concession she did not wish to make. He would be pleased if he knew that she thought about him so obsessively she could not sleep. He would swell like a banty rooster ruling the barnyard, he would swagger like an arrogant drunk looking for a fight . . .

The darkness closed in on her. All of a sudden, she felt she was no longer alone. Heavy thunder clouds rested on the far horizon, and the trees amongst which she stood seemed to be reaching toward her with dark, treacherous tentacles. She pulled her shawl up and hugged her slender frame, trying to gain her bearings.

Why hadn't she gotten better directions? She knew only the general vicinity of the cabin, between this meadow and that, just beyond the apple orchard, to the right of the road leading to Lecompte . . .

She tucked her hands into the pockets of her skirts. In the left pocket, her hand closed over the gold coin she had found in the crypt several nights before. She must remember to give it to Aunt Zelpha; perhaps her aunt would have an explanation as to how it had gotten in the crypt. But . . . might Aunt Zelpha be angry that she had *been* in the crypt? Perhips she should hold on to the coin and try to find out for herself who had dropped it in the crypt.

Pale moonlight swathed the clearing into which she stepped, allowing her a wider view of the meadow and its vague shadows. She took a step forward, finding the ground solid despite the week of rain, and again tucked her shawl more securely about her. She would find that cabin, even if it took all night!

Lucas Chandler uttered a curse. "Where the hell is she going?" he grumbled, making his tall, straight frame a part of the pine behind which he hid. His fingers absently dug into the bark as he watched her move confidently into the meadow beyond the timberline.

Hell! Hadn't she heard of the treacheries of the night? Didn't she know that Old Man Jenkins from across the bayou poached on Oak Shadows property and frequently laid traps? He'd sprung all the ones he'd found, but suppose Kristina's slender foot should land in another one? Blast it all! Why wasn't she in the safe haven of Zelpha Prudhomme's home, away from traps and treacheries . . . and men like him? Why couldn't she be like the other women he had encountered hereabout . . . afraid to look at their own shadows without their men's permission?

He should dislike her immensely, he supposed. Since she'd come to Oak Shadows, she had made his quest for the gold much less appealing. For months he had thought of nothing else, but now she was all he thought about. She filled his dreams when he was sleeping and his thoughts when he was awake. She had crawled into his soul and made herself a vital part of it.

To hell with the gold! He wanted far more of a treasure. He wanted to touch ivory skin as smooth and flawless as porcelain, to gaze into eyes that were as green and vibrant as an ocean current, to caress a full, sensuous mouth that trembled against his touch, to lock his fingers in golden tresses and feel their cascading softness—to love her as he was sure no man had loved her before . . .

Yes, she was the treasure he wanted.

But—blast it all!—he had to see her safely through this latest adventure, if he ever wanted to claim that treasure. The night veiled her from his view, and he had only the soft echo of her footfalls to guide his way. For a moment, he caught the heady fragrance of lavender, her familiar scent, and when her footfalls ceased, he could still have found her.

Then, too, his own steps ceased. She might detect him on her trail, and that he did not want. This strange, mysterious young woman who had left her lifelong home to visit an eccentric aunt was something of an enigma to him. She was rather like a water hyacinth, pale and beautiful, surrounded by vibrant colors, her roots dangling invisibly below her. He had seen her flawless beauty shift faintly with the light; he had seen her shimmer in the passing of a cloud. How would she feel if she had known that he had spied on her during her daily morning walks?

She thought he was a creature only of the night.

But he was a creature falling deeply in love . . .


Terror caught in the slim column of Kristina's throat. She heard nothing, saw nothing, but she could not shake the fear that something—or someone—was following her. Could it be a raccoon—curious as to her presence, merely wishing to see where she was going—or could it simply be the darkness following her in her nocturnal walk?

No . . . She knew in her heart that the stalker was of the two-legged variety.

And her heart also told her that it was Luke.

She halted, hearing the echo of boots halting just as suddenly. What game was he playing? Why didn't he simply step forward and make his presence known? Kristina could almost hear his breathing catch, as though he were afraid that one natural human function might betray his position in the dark timberline. Was he trying to frighten her, and dare she let him know that he was succeeding?

No, she was much too stubborn for that. Thus, she slightly lifted her skirts and took one precarious step forward. Finding the edge of the footpath beneath her shoe, she cautiously stepped onto it and began to head to the southeast, toward the meadow and the road and the cabin where she thought Luke might be staying. If he was hiding anything, she was sure he would want to reach the cabin first, so that he could dispose of any small giveaways. She kept alert, waiting for the sound of breaking twigs and masculine footfalls as he passed her in the darkness.

She was quickly rewarded. The smile she felt inside did not appear on her lips, because her fear was too strong to allow her features to relax. And that made her angry, as did the thought that Luke would try to make it to the cabin before her in order to hide any evidence as to his true identity. Perhaps if she peeled her ears to the heavy fringe of darkness, she would be able to hear his footfalls and keep up with him in the unfamiliar terrain.

But as he quickly outdistanced her, she paused on the trail, listening for the sounds of his retreat. The woods were strangely silent; not even a cricket chirped.

Then the wind began to swirl eerily through the tops of the trees, descending upon her in fragile silence. She now stood on the path amid wildly twisted live oaks whose branches stretched out into vast moss-draped shrouds. And still, the wind descended, until she was wrapped in its icy embrace.

"Kristina? Kristina, is that you?"

She spun about so quickly that she nearly lost her footing, her fingers wrapping around the bare limb of a diminutive fig tree which was the only tangible thing nearby to steady her. She saw no one, but into the darkness from which her name was spoken, she said, "Yes, it is me . . . is that you, Luke?"

The shadowy, dark-clothed figure stepped from the timberline, his face hidden beneath the rim of his hat. "Who are you? You are not Kristina."

She reeled, instantly recovering from her rigid fear. This wasn't the voice she had heard before; this one was strained, almost forced.

She fought the urge to turn and flee. She wanted to, of course, but she would not give this nocturnal menace the pleasure. "By George!" she whispered harshly, her slender fingers immediately closing over the folds of her gown so as not to hinder her movement. Giving herself no chance to think rationally and perhaps reassess so rash a decision, she charged toward the dark-clothed figure and grabbed it by the lapels of its coat before it could get its bearings and flee. All of a sudden, she was falling with the weight of the creature, and was sure she felt the crack of bones as her backside hit the hard trail. Then feminine snickering rolled gently toward her, and she looked around just as the moonlight touched upon Leanna's thin, amused face.

She, too, was sitting on the ground, now dragging the heavy cloak from around her and retrieving the hat she'd taken from the house. "I thought you'd run like a buckshot poacher." Leanna laughed, dragging up her knees as she prepared to arise. "I didn't think you'd attack me."

Kristina was sure all the blood had drained from her

features. The paleness left behind was as chilly as a grave. "Leanna, what on earth are you doing. My goodness, are you six or twenty-six? I can scarcely tell sometimes." Indignation edged her voice as she added, "I should never have told you about my strange visitor the other night!" She hoped her venomous look might properly chastise Leanna, but a second glance into her friend's face told Kristina otherwise. She wanted to remain angry, she truly did, but her heart simply wasn't in it. Slowly, her mouth eased into a slight smile; then her soft laugh joined Leanna's renewed one. As Kristina found her footing, then offered her hand to assist Leanna up, she said, "You did give me a fright, Leanna Gilbert. And since you did, you owe me a favor."

On her feet now, Leanna dragged off the black cloak and laid it across her arm. "I won't take you to that cabin. There are snakes prowling the night."

"Snakes . . ." Kristina fluffed off the probability. "Better snakes than goblins and ghosts."

"Those, too," responded Leanna. "And this is the month of things that go bump in the night."

Kristina laughed. "Then bump along this trail and show me where the cabin is."

Placing the black cloak and hat over a fallen log, Leanna heaved a weary sigh. "Remind me to pick these up when we return," she said, turning on the trail. "Are you coming?" she called to Kristina, and waited for her to fall in beside her.


Luke took a last look around the cabin, lit only by the moonlight invading it by the single window. He had spirited his personal belongings out to the edge of the woods and hidden them, his horse was tied in a small clearing through a stand of pines, the hearth was cool and the linens were stripped from the small bed in the corner of the room. Confident that he had removed all traces of human occupation, he picked up the bedroll he'd untied from his saddle and the oil lamp, soon leaving the cabin. He would have to wait until Kristina ceased her nocturnal prowling before resuming his search of the cemetery. Blast the girl! If she defied the conventions for single women and remained at the cabin—unchaperoned—he would have to sleep out in the clearing with his horse.

He had just reached the overhanging shadows of the woods when the two women appeared. Ducking low, he watched them cross the clearing to where the cabin stood, cursing the fact that Kristina had picked up an accomplice. The two women paused for a moment; he could hear them assessing the dangers. But they quickly dismissed them and entered the cabin. Instinctively, Luke's gaze turned skyward, as he watched the slow travels of a dark cloud. Just moments ago, he had been thankful for the moonlight that had allowed him to clear his belongings without lighting a lamp; now he cursed it, wishing the thundercloud would erase the pale light from the sky.

He waited a few minutes, listening to the gentle movements of the women from within the cabin. Occasionally, a feminine form would stand in silhouette at the window, and he could tell that long, tapered fingers were easing over dusty sills and sparse furnishings, trying to find out if the place had been occupied.

Suddenly, absolute darkness fell and Lucas relaxed, confident that the arch of shadows would hide him from view. He knew the cabin's interior would also be dark and thought perhaps the women would leave. Then something happened that surprised him. A pale halo of light suddenly lit the windows. In that same moment he remembered another oil lamp and matches he had left in the niche beside the hearth.

Rain began to pelt the earth, the wind rattling the tree branches as if they were dangling skeletons.

Luke was furious. As he crossed his arms, feeling the raindrops soak his clothing, he looked toward the lighted windows of the cabin he had inhabited and heard the laughter of the women within. At least, they were warm and dry!

Gnashing his teeth, the brim of his hat failing to keep the steady flood of rain from pelting his features, he began to shiver in the chilly October night.

*Blasted women! Blasted! Blasted! Blasted!*


"What is he like?"

Kristina tucked her shawl into the crooks of her arms and allowed herself to settle onto the dusty rug before the hearth. She wished a healthy fire blazed there, to take away the chill of the night. Her thoughts ricocheted for a moment, then came back to settle on Leanna's innocent question. "What is he like?" she repeated. "It's really hard to tell since I've met him only in the dark. But . . ."—she sighed wistfully, her eyes closing for a moment to allow the image of him to form in her mind— "he's tall, slim, rather like the Texas cowboys I've read about. His hair is the color of chocolate—a little darker, perhaps—and his eyes are as black as the night."

"And his kisses?"

Warmth and color flooded Kristina's pale cheeks. Instinctively, her hands rose to cover them, immediately falling as she asked, "And what makes you think I would know about his kisses?"

A comical grin came to Leanna's thin features. "I'll just bet you do, Kristina Hartman."

"Well . . . I don't," she lied, unwilling to give away all her secrets. Nor would she admit that the rake had seen her naked! "The rain is letting up. Shall we return to Aunt Zelpha's?"

A laughing Leanna drew up her knees and wrapped her arms around them. "Wishful thinking, since it's raining harder than ever. You just don't want to talk about your beau."

"He is not my beau!" The argument, a little too sharply given, was quickly amended. "I mean, I hardly know him. Luke is the only name he's given me, and that one might not be a true one. After all, he did first tell me he was Relin Trosclair de la Cerda, didn't he?"

"Some of the children have told me they've seen a man digging around the cemetery at night and poking into every nook and cranny. Do you suppose it is your"— she had been about to say beau, but amended it—"gentleman?"

"I wouldn't be at all surprised at what that . . . that snake is doing! He might be a robber hiding out from the law." Oh, she had read too many of those dime Western novels, always in secrecy, of course, since her father had forbidden them in his house. Rising, stretching back her shoulders as she moved toward the window, Kristina continued quietly, "He might even be a figment of my imagination. My father always said I had a very active one."

"I'm curious . . . why did your father leave Oak Shadows? Surely, as the son, he would have inherited it from his parents, and he might have been able to make a profitable venture of the place."

Absently, Kristina asked, "I asked him several times, but he always evaded the subject. He didn't like to talk about Oak Shadows . . . or Zelpha . . . or his past. My father was a very sad man, and I never knew why. I probably never will."

"Ask your aunt," suggested Leanna.

"I've tried several times, but never could come up with the proper words to introduce the subject. Sometimes when I mention Father's name, I see tears in her tired old eyes. I didn't come to Oak Shadows to cause her pain; I simply wanted to know her. She is my only living relative since Father died, you know." Hearing the dull plodding of horses' hooves, Kristina's gaze returned to the darkness beyond the window. "Someone's coming."

Leanna jumped to her feet, approaching the window

to look out with Kristina. Very soon, the vague outlines of two horses could be seen, and a man, small in stature, dismounted the lead horse.

"It's Cleveland," said Kristina, moving to the door just as it opened. Gazing into his dark, reproachful eyes, she quickly apologized, "We got caught in the rain. I hope you weren't worried."

Cleveland politely removed his soaking hat. "Miz Zelpha, she's a mite worried. Sent me to fetch you two ladies. I seen the light from the trail. Otherwise, I might'a rode clear to Lecompte." Cleveland fought a grin as he added, "It ain't safe out here in the woods, ladies. Why, some bold young rooster done walked right inta the kitchen at Oak Shadows an' stole my long coat 'n' my fav'rit hat. What you think o' that?"

Leanna grinned sheepishly. "And do you know Cleveland, I think I saw them hanging over a log beside the trail."

"Yas'sum," replied Cleveland, turning in the doorway. "I found 'em. Now, let's git that lamp snuffed real good, an' ol' Pruny'll take you two back to the house. She rides double real good-like."

As they left the cabin, the leaves fluttered with the strength of the driving rain. Within moments, the two old saddle horses were plodding along the muddy trail, the sucking noises of their hooves scarcely detectable in the howling storm. The forest bent beneath the force of the wind, and the dark, ominous clouds against the copper glow of the horizon hinted that nature's wrath had only just begun.

Guilt flooded Kristina as she watched the fragile old gentleman who'd come looking for them struggling to keep in the saddle when the wind worked so hard to drag him out of it.

# Six

By the time the three riders arrived at Oak Shadows, the rain fell in fierce streaks and curls, thrashing through the trees like a viciously wielded whip. Had it not been for the sad state of the two young women, Aunt Zelpha would have taken sufficient time for the tongue-lashing they deserved. But with a few carefully chosen words of criticism—they should, after all, be old enough to know better—both were dismissed, Leanna to the cottage across the lawn, and Kristina to her room on the second floor. Sophronia had prepared a hot bath there, and as a soaked and freezing Kristina finally slipped into the water, the protective heat chased away her chill.

The storm was fierce beyond the long window, and it was, perhaps, her security and safety that caused Kristina's eyes to close. She felt that she'd been wrapped in a warm blanket, and the stillness within the room was like the peace of springtime. Behind closed eyelids, she could see soft blue skies and rolling clouds . . . she could almost detect the heady fragrance of gardenias and roses blooming in profusion . . . she could hear the angry chattering of a mockingbird protesting an intruder too near its nest . . . How secure her dream was. She wanted it never to end.

But the water was already beginning to cool, so she forced herself to full alertness, then climbed from the tub and began briskly rubbing her skin and hair. Wrapping a thick robe around her, she sat on the edge of the bed to continue drying her waist-length tresses. Exhausted as she was, this did not take long. Falling back to the bed, she wondered if she had strength enough to pull on her bed gown, which was lying half beneath her body. She made a feeble attempt to free it, gave up and tucked her feet into the warmth of her robe. Her eyes closed once again, and sleep rolled across her like a storm without sound.

She quickly lost herself in the depths and dimensions of her dream, experiencing emotions she had not allowed herself to feel in many weeks . . . visiting friends she hadn't seen in a long while . . . enjoying a casual saunter in the park with her father. Dreams often gave life to that which had passed, allowing it to be part of life once more, though for only a brief while. Kristina knew she was dreaming, and in her dream she warned herself not to wake up and lose contact with her father. Her mind obeyed, willing her into the dimensions of the past where dreams were made.

But then the past was gone, the comfort of her father's arm resting casually across her shoulder could no longer be felt, and a rangy, dark-clothed Texas rogue slowly approached her from the foggy darkness at the edge of her dream. She watched him saunter toward her, watched the darkness of his eyes deepen as he neared; and when he took her in his arms, roughly, firmly, commandingly, the musky aroma of him filled her nostrils—

Kristina lurched from sleep, her hand instantly covering the wildly beating heart beneath the thick fabric of her robe. She looked around her bedchamber, sure that the nearness of him lingered, sure that he lurked in one of the dark corners beyond the perimeters of the lamp's glow, sure that he was waiting to pounce upon her like a lion attacking its prey.

Wild panic filled her, and just as she was about to

laugh off her unreasonable fear, *he* stepped from the darkness of the alcove where her writing desk sat.

"The emerald of your eyes is as dark as a midnight forest," he said huskily. "I hope this fear is not of me."

Kristina was furious that he had invaded her privacy. Suppose she had thrown herself upon her bed in her altogethers and fallen asleep? Would this cocky, self-assured man have rudely spied upon her even then? But she fought the instinct to scold him for this intrusion, replying instead, "I wouldn't waste my time fearing you. Why you're just a big old pussycat!"

For a moment, he said nothing, his dark, somber gaze raking in her ivory features and the tantalizing softness exposed between the lapels of her robe. A rare moonbeam touched upon her pale tresses, like a glimmer of gold in a foggy sky. Then he said in a low, husky voice, "Don't you wonder how I got in here?"

"Through the door, I'd imagine," she shot back.

"There are other ways into rooms."

"Such as?" she instantly retorted.

"Dreams," he murmured, his movements bringing him close enough to her that the tips of his fingers caressed her tangled tresses. She drew back, anger darkening her eyes. Then his knee was upon the bed beside her, and his mouth was ever so close to her own. "Let us make the night complete, Kristina . . . the lady and the rogue . . . as one."

"You are such a bore!" she hissed, scooting out from beneath him, then nearly losing her balance on the edge of the bed. She gave him a narrow, dark scrutiny, before asking, "Why aren't you wet? It's pouring outside."

His jaw became taut. What was the point of a ridiculous question that mattered not a whit? Couldn't she see that he wanted her, wanted to feel the rebellious heat of her mouth against his own, to take from her that rebellious passion that mortal man had never enjoyed? Why was she being such a child, when the woman inside her ached for release? He was tired of being the gentleman—if, indeed, she considered him one—but a healthy male could exercise just so much control before his basic instincts took over. Then he smiled, and before he could alter his expression, he knew she had perceived it as evil and dangerous. Her eyes were wide with horror, her parted mouth now trembling against the snowy white of her teeth.

"Why . . . why are you looking at me like that?" she uttered. "I think I would like you to go away."

He eased toward her, his hand edging across her shoulder with strange gentleness. "Like what?" he responded. "The wolf devouring the lamb?"

"Something along those lines," she said, "but you'll find this lamb has fangs, too."

Lightning struck one of the oaks on the lawn, and Kristina started. A line of fire and sparks instantly felled a great limb, and in that moment, the distance closed between Kristina and her intruder. She did not protest the strong grip on her arm, drawing her closer; rather, her gaze boldly met his dark one, and her fingers rose to sweep the strands of dark hair from his forehead. Then his mouth touched hers, taking her breath away so completely that she thought she would smother.

He became a blur of strong, masculine features unable to gain depth and clarity. His hard body pressed upon her soft one, enflaming the very core of her being. At that moment, Kristina lost herself in the essence of him. As her senses soared, desire commanding her every response to his caresses, she knew that this strange, mysterious, oh, so wonderful man possessed her very soul . . . She belonged to him . . . and he to her.

There was no turning back.

Not now, not ever . . .


"Luke?" she purred sleepily, turning beneath the mound of covers to gaze into his eyes. Then, finding herself very much alone in the cool room, she quickly sat up, snatching the covers up to hide her nakedness. Well, love them and leave them, dear heart? she thought, pressing her mouth into a thin, angry line. Then she fell back to her pillow, her hand touching the smooth fabric above her tousled hair. What else could he have done? Stayed and been caught in an uncompromising position by Sophronia, or—God forbid—her dear, garish old aunt?

Well, at least she knew one thing for sure, he was no apparition. She had felt gentle, masculine arms around her last night, not the cold aura of a ghostly presence. The whisper of his kiss had become passionate, commanding, as his hands had caressed her and awakened her most secret desires. Her life no longer seemed cold and sterile and empty . . . now she knew love and passion and hope for the future, a future she hoped to share with Luke.

Merciful heavens! she thought, jolting forward once again. She had made sweet, wonderful, wicked love to a man whose last name she did not know, a man whose first name might not even be Luke.

A knock echoed gently at the door. Scooting forward to retrieve her robe and pull it on, she called out, "Yes, who is it?"

Leanna was now looking toward her. "Good morning, Kristina," she said vibrantly, entering the room. "Don't forget the field trip this morning."

"Field trip?" As she echoed the words, Kristina remembered Leanna mentioning it yesterday. As she thought of that conversation, she recalled the purpose, to collect names from the tombstones beginning with each letter of the alphabet. The child who collected the most different letters, and no two children could collect the same name from any given tombstone, would be awarded a prize after lunch.

"Don't you remember?" continued Leanna, now dropping casually to the edge of the bed. "The rubbings . . ."

"I remember," responded Kristina. Then she wondered

if she looked different this morning, after being with Luke, wondered if Leanna would notice. But if her friend did, she said nothing. Kristina smiled.

"What is so amusing?"

"Nothing," said Kristina, her hands moving smoothly beneath her hair to drag it from her neck. "Isn't it a grand and beautiful morning? I do think we shall see sunshine today . . . don't you?"

Leanna shared a puzzled look between Kristina and the long window across the room. Upon the timberline she could see those same dark storm clouds they'd been seeing for the past week or more. If there was even the smallest speck of blue in the sky, then Kristina's eyesight was much better than her own. Rising from her seated position, she sauntered toward the door. "Get dressed, lazybones, and I'll see you downstairs."

The door closed; Kristina dropped back to her pillow for a moment, her hands gathering her hair into a tight ball. Then she swung her feet to the floor, stepped across the carpet and protested the chill of the planked floor. As she readied herself for the morning, she hummed a happy tune, thinking of Luke and the wonderful night she had spent with him.


Kristina looked up at the bare limbs of the trees dotting the lawns of Oak Shadows. Then she began to move among them, slowly at first, and with a mindless fixation she could not clearly explain. It had to be here . . . She had seen lightning strike one of these trees and yet . . . now she could find no evidence of it . . . no charring, no fallen branches . . . nothing.

Mercy! She must have dreamed that part of it; surely, lying in Luke's arms had been real. Her heart told her it had been, and yet some part of her deep innermost soul was quick to contradict that.

She chose to believe that Luke had been real, and

lightning striking the tree had not. She wondered how she might broach the subject to him when they again met, so that he would not think her totally daft.

Well . . . she would think about that later.

Kristina moved along the path, watching the children dart among the tombstones while making their rubbings. Leanna had returned to the schoolhouse to tend a cut finger one of her students had suffered, leaving Kristina in charge of the other children. Every few steps she would pause to count heads, taking into account the missing child. She thought of her father just then, and the way he had frequently scolded her for "worrying about everything, even that which cannot be altered."

Perhaps she did worry too much, and perhaps this was one of those days. But she felt so wonderful, vibrant and alive and eager to meet the future, something she had actually given very little thought to. She watched the darkening sky, thinking of Luke, wondering where he was at this very moment, and remembering that she had never seen him in the daylight hours. He was, indeed, a creature of the night . . .

But that didn't matter. She could adapt to his environment, even if it meant perpetual darkness. The cool October wind touched her skin, but warm memories of Luke surrounded Kristina like a blanket. She moved along the path, occasionally kicking out at an imaginary stone, and when she reached a small stand of pines, she turned, leaning heavily against the larger one. Tucking her hands into the small of her back, she took a visual count of the children busily making rubbings of the tombstones and, finding them all there, relaxed for a moment.

The storm was rolling in, though, perhaps an hour or so away now, and Kristina thought that the darkness of the forest was rather like the night, vague and foggy, with a ground mist creeping eerily toward her, wrapping itself around her ankles.

Then, suddenly, a hand touched her shoulder, and with a small, startled cry, she pivoted about. Fear instantly became relief, as she met the amused gaze of the man who had become such a wonderful part of her life. "My goodness, aren't you afraid you'll melt in the daylight?"

Gently, he gathered her to him. "What do you mean? I'm not even here . . . only in your dreams . . . in your desires—"

"Yes, of course . . . in my dreams . . . like last night—"

He drew back slightly, favoring her with a slightly cockeyed smile. "You dreamed about me last night?"

"Dreamed about you? Why, you scoundrel, you know it was more than that."

"Ah . . . one of *those* dreams. Well then, it is all right for me to tell you I had one, too, and you were in my arms."

She *knew* she had been with him. She just knew it! But she would play his little game. "While you're holding me, count the children and make sure they're all there . . . so that I will not have to turn from this warm hug." Silence. Kristina pressed her cheek into the cool fabric of his shirt, her eyes closing dreamily. "Well?"

"There's sixteen of the little buggers scooting around out there." He had made a rare daylight appearance because of the activity in the cemetery. And he simply had to know, "What are they doing?"

"Part of the Halloween rituals," she replied absently. "I'll explain it later."

Suddenly, a horse's hooves echoed on the road. And before Kristina could prepare for the parting, Luke had stepped away and disappeared into the deepening shades of the woodline. She tried to follow him with her eyes, but he had become one with the darkness. Feeling betrayed and angered by his unexplained departure, she rushed onto the trail directly in the path of a mounted

67

horse. She cried out as the beast reared back on its haunches, and a deep, masculine curse rent the air.

Sheriff Roy Saunders immediately regained his composure. Dismounting his spooked horse, he managed to sooth it with a few carefully chosen words, then turned to Kristina. "Miss Kristina Hartman," he said, his voice patronizing, "up there in the North, I suppose stepping into the path of horses is something everyone does?"

"Sorry. I was talking to a gentleman and wasn't paying attention."

He gave her a skeptical look. "I saw you from a good ways down the trail, young lady, and I didn't see anyone else."

Kristina's eyes narrowed as they studied the burly sheriff who had visited her aunt for a few minutes the other day. He was a most unprepossessing man, tall and bulky, the large gun strapped beneath his overhanging paunch the kind of weapon she imagined an outlaw would wear. Indeed this tall, middle-aged man was hardly someone she would have pictured on the respectable side of the law. She thought that he might be able to read her thoughts, and to redeem the moment, she smiled her most sincere smile. "Really, Sheriff Saunders, up North we don't normally walk into the paths of horses," she offered. "Even there, some people have good sense.

"Glad to know that, miss. I'm on my way out to see your aunt. I see"—his eyes scanned the cemetery—"that you've got your hands full here."

"Yes." Mentally, she counted heads, then saw that Leanna Gilbert was returning to the cemetery. "What you said just now, Sheriff Saunders," Kristina continued, her gaze lifting to the burly mans face, "I don't see how you didn't see the man I was speaking to a few minutes ago."

Saunders turned and mounted his horse, returning his hat to his head. "Just saw you, miss." Nodding imperceptibly, he eased by her on the trail. "Nice to talk to you."

"Yes . . . you too." But he could not have heard her

reply, because he had coaxed the horse into a slow trot down the trail to Oak Shadows.

Leanna approached with the child whose index finger was wrapped in much more gauze that the small cut actually required. "Was that Sheriff Saunders?" she asked, her hand at the little girl's back, urging the child to rejoin the other children.

"It was," said Kristina, pressing her mouth into a thin line. "I was talking to Luke when he was on the trail, but the sheriff said he didn't see him."

A musical "Ooo-ooo-oooh" followed as Leanna lifted her fingers, curling them into an unnatural position. "Your ghost made a daytime appearance . . . and Sheriff Saunders didn't see him. Doesn't that tell you something, Kristina?"

Beneath Kristina's glaring scrutiny, Leanna dropped her theatrical pose. "It tells me there's a conspiracy in the works. Why is everyone so determined that Luke doesn't exist?"

Leanna's mood became serious as she fell in beside Kristina on the path. "Think about it. Who else has seen him?"

Kristina thought for a moment before answering, "No one."

"Then I would suggest that he exists only in your mind. Tell me"—Leanna's voice grew serious—"were you troubled in your heart when you left New England?"

"Not enough to invent a friend," Kristine retorted, a little angry now. "Only children need imaginary friends. Luke is real. He—" She'd been about to confess last night's encounter, but thought twice about it. Taking a moment to compose her thoughts, she amended, "He's flesh and blood—a man just as surely as I am a woman." The sudden, high pitch of Leanna's voice calling the children startled Kristina, and she felt a jab of pain along with the burning of tears held at bay. "If you have the children under control now," she continued, "I'll spend a few hours with Aunt Zelpha."

The chattering children were falling into a straight line on the path, holding their pencil rubbings tightly against the breeze that might work to rob them of their work. Absently, Leanna said, "Yes, I'll see you later," and she clapped her hands to signal the start of the children's tidy march toward the schoolhouse. They were easy to control when a prize was waiting for one of them and no one yet knew which one. Leanna had, however, purchased hard candies for all the children. These were now neatly bundled in orange papers.

Kristina waited until Leanna and the children had disappeared in their descent of the hill. She stood on the path, biting her lower lip in an effort to keep from crying and linking her fingers tightly against the pain that rippled through her.

She was furious, with Luke for the little games he enjoyed playing and with every human being in the vicinity who would not confess that they had seen him. Surely, one of the children had seen a man fitting Luke's description in the cemetery . . . surely, Roy Saunders had fibbed when he'd said he hadn't seen him.

What was going on here? Was this some macabre plan to drive her insane . . . and for what reason?

She vowed, as she began to move on a somewhat shaky course toward Oak Shadows, that she would not see Luke again, not tonight . . . not tomorrow . . . not ever.

She would have a lock installed on her bedchamber door, so that he could not invade her privacy.

But her heart fell a little. Could she bear the future without him? If she knew he stood outside her door, would she be able to bar his entrance?

Did she really want to cut herself off completely from him?

Or would she take him into her arms again . . . and again . . . and again . . .

She knew the answer.

But it was an answer she tried mightily to deny.

# Seven

*Halloween night*

Kristina could scarcely believe her eyes. She floated down the stairs, her feet barely touching each step, the sight before her making her breath catch. She had never imagined that Aunt Zelpha's run-down old house could be so magnificent, brightly colored streamers hanging from the chandeliers, tables laden with fruit and meat, and side dishes, silver plates laid out as if this were a king's banquet. The parlor had been cleared for dancing; yet the costumed dancers spilled into every room, even onto the stairs, forcing Kristina to the bannister to stare in awe and wonder. She felt almost insignificant in her emerald ball gown and her gaily decorated mask of ostrich plumes and scarlet ribbons.

Though the gala had gotten under way at ten o'clock, Kristina had deliberately waited until well after eleven to make her appearance. Sophronia had been pleased to assist her in dressing and doing her hair, which was piled high and held in place by matching silver combs. She wanted to be charming and alluring, for if her scoundrel made his promised appearance, she wanted to be swept into his arms for the dances they would share.

Then she recalled her talk with Sheriff Roy Saunders a few days ago. She was still angry with him, still an-

71

noyed that he had felt the need to lie to her. Of course, he had seen Luke! Why had he told her that he hadn't? If he, too, was trying to convince her that her trysts in Oak Shadows cemetery were with a long-dead spirit, then . . .

Then what?

She knew that in her arms she had felt gentle masculine strength. She knew that upon her mouth had been pressed the sweetest of kisses, and she knew—dear Lord, she knew—that the musky, manly breath whispering across her cheek had not been the stirrings of a ghost defying mortal boundaries to be with her. Warm, living, male strength had made her feel like a woman, and neither the servants nor Aunt Zelpha, Leanna or . . . or that deceitful Roy Saunders would convince her otherwise. She didn't know whether or not his name was really Luke, but she did know he was a living, breathing human being!

Searching across the sea of brightly plumed and costumed heads, Kristina spotted Aunt Zelpha sitting in an overstuffed chair she had referred to earlier in the day as "the queen's throne." Befitting her self-appointed role, her regal ivory and gold costume portrayed her as Marie Antoinette, and the way she was tipping her brandy goblet to her mouth, Kristina hoped she would not lose her head this night.

So, with polite amenities, Kristina made her way through the guests and soon bent to place a kiss on her aunt's strangely pale cheek. She had forgotten the ritualistic application of her daily ration of rouge. "What a splendid party!" exclaimed Kristina. "I didn't realize so many people lived in this area."

"Come from as far away as Naw'Leans," came Aunt Zelpha's throaty response. "This is one of the most popular affairs of the year here in Louisiana. There's no telling at all who will show up . . . even the governor himself! If he does"—Zelpha leaned close and wickedly whispered—"just look for a fellow dressed as the court jester. His politics are to be taken just as seriously!"

Kristina smiled, though she saw no true humor in her aunt's declaration. To say that a politician was like a court jester was to say that a rooster was poultry; it stood to reason.

Something excitingly familiar caught Kristina's eye . . . A black eye patch, red satin shirt with billowing sleeves, skin-tight pants tucked into knee-high boots, a tricornered hat, a saber strapped to a slim waist . . . could it be him? Aware that she was staring, she discreetly lifted her mask to her face and peered through the eye holes. He appeared to be searching among the revelers himself.

Their gazes met . . . feminine green eyes, wickedly wild ones the color of onyx. His mouth pursed, then turned up in a cockeyed smile.

The man she knew simply as Luke, the man all in the region had been trying to convince her was a ghost, slowly began to ply the ocean of dancers toward her. She could not tear herself from her aunt's side to meet him halfway, perhaps because she knew she should be terribly angry with him.

Kristina had thought nothing could sway her attention from the dark-eyed rogue she had learned to love and to hate. But, suddenly, though she couldn't recall having seen him approach, a tall, slim young man was bending politely over her Aunt Zelpha, proffering his hand. Kristina turned, mesmerized, listening to the deep, resonant voice with its noticeable French accent ask, "Mademoiselle Prudhomme, this dance, *oui?*"

Kristina was charmed by the crimson hue rising in her aunt's sagging cheek and the coyish dropping of her eyes, as she replied, "Why, *monsieur,* I am sure you could find a younger, prettier lady to dance with."

"Ah, younger, *oui* . . . but not as pretty as you, *mademoiselle*. I have waited a long time for this dance, *ma chère.*"

Then Luke was beside Kristina, his fingers gently closing over her elbow, and she turned from her retreating aunt and the young man who had asked her to dance. As her gaze lifted to Luke's she tried very hard not to betray that she was happy to see him. Rather, she jerked her arm from him and said, "All right, you've made your appearance. Now I demand to know what you are doing here."

"Why, joining in the festivities," he drawled pleasantly, tipping the tricornered hat so that it rested crookedly on his head. "I told you I'd be coming to this shindig. How do you like my costume?"

"A pirate," she mused, refusing to smile. "I can't think of anything more befitting a scoundrel." Now her tone grew even more serious. "You said you would have a full explanation," she reminded him.

Actually, he had never said anything like that. He thought that her eyes flashed green fire through the delicate feathers of her mask. He smiled, even as he felt the inclination to duck the swinging palm he anticipated. Taking her hand, he pulled her out to the veranda and, before she could launch a protest, pulled her into his arms and kissed her deeply and passionately.

As soon as she was physically able, she drew away, breathless. "And what was that for?" Even as her tone chastised him, she thought how boyishly charming he was, his pirate's costume bold and flattering, his scarlet shirt gaping so that the wide, hard expanse of his chest was mere inches away from her trembling mouth. So that he would not look into her mind and know where her thoughts were directed, she quickly added, "You are going to explain?"

"I never said that I would."

"But don't you think I deserve an explanation?"

His hands closed gently over her shoulders, then moved in a slow, seductive path down her arms and back again, settling over her shoulders and lingering there. "You look absolutely stunning, Miss Kristina Hartman."

"And you—you rake and you rogue—you are using unconscionable flattery in an attempt to change the subject."

"Very well, I'll give you an explanation." Taking her hand, he moved toward a small table beside which two wrought-iron chairs sat. Settling her into one of them, he pushed the French doors closed to shut out the noise of the ballroom. Still, the melodies settled around them, as did occasional laughter. Sitting across from her, Luke took Kristina's hands and held them against the table top. "Where do I start?" he mused.

To which she immediately responded, "The beginning would be nice."

"How about a name?"

"That, too, would be nice."

Actually, he had decided several days ago to confide in her when he'd admitted to himself that he was wasting his time looking for the gold, so he really wasn't being coerced into doing so, though he imagined that she thought he was. "Lucas Chandler." Releasing one of her hands, he tipped his hat politely, his smile so brief as to be nonexistent. "And up until two months ago, I was one of the elite, one of the Texas Rangers stationed just west of the Brazos."

"And now?" She raised a pale eyebrow, awaiting his response.

"Now I'm just an obsessed, unemployed ex-Ranger trying to find a chest of twenty-dollar gold pieces buried in Oak Shadows cemetery. But if it's out there, I can't find it . . . and if I can't find it, nobody will."

She thought of the coin she had found in the crypt, wondering if it was part of the booty he sought. "And just what makes you think it's on Oak Shadows?"

"Of the three outlaws that robbed the train that morning near Beaumont, only one rode away alive, with the money and with a bullet in his lower back. I trailed him into Louisiana, and caught up to him about six miles east of here. Before he died, he told me he'd hidden the money here. I've been looking ever since."

"In secrecy, so your quest would not attract treasure seekers, I'd imagine. I suppose Sheriff Saunders knew, though?"

"He knew," Luke admitted. "I'm real sorry about what happened the other day. Roy felt bad about it, too."

"And why did you lose your job as a lawman?"

"Louisiana is out of my jurisdiction. I was told that if I trailed the man across the border, I wouldn't have a job when I got back." Silence. Luke looked up, unable to read the expression in Kristina's eyes. He watched her slowly remove the mask and settle it into the massive folds of her gown. When she began to flex her fingers, he said, "I suppose you're bristling to slap my face?"

"Don't you think you deserve it?" she quipped, sliding her fingers beneath the mask and out of his view. "You lied to me—over and over and over. What did you think? That if you pretended to care about me I might aid you in your search for the gold? That my walks through the cemetery might have brought me close to your precious gold and I might accidentally have discovered it? Is that why—"

Before she could get out another angry question, Luke was on one knee before her, taking her hands to hold them close. "No . . . no, Kristina. I don't give a hoot about the money now. I just care about you." Was it the proper time to admit his love? Would she be receptive to it? She had every reason in the world not to trust him, not to believe anything he said.

"I simply must know, Luke. The other night . . . you did come to my room, didn't you?"

Ah, the dream! he thought, grinning boyishly. "I'll never tell."

"You do know that I hate you, don't you?" Kristina

76

retorted, her mouth pursing as she feebly attempted to free her hands from his stronger ones.

"That's all right, Kristina," he whispered huskily. "But I promise you . . . you *will* love me. Because I will relentlessly pursue you until you do."

"Is that so, Mr. Ex-Texas Ranger Lucas Chandler?"

The boy, Willard, approached, standing just out of touching distance of Luke and Kristina. Meeting Kristina's gaze, he said, "Me 'n' Paulie . . . we was wonderin' "—his gaze now connected to Luke's—"can we be touchin' ya, Mr. Ghost?"

Luke laughed, extending his right hand. "How about a handshake, young man. Will that convince you I'm not a ghost?"

Cautiously, Willard took Luke's hand, then yelled across his shoulder. "Come on, Paulie, he ain't no ghost." When the younger boy, peering from the safety of a corner, did not come forward, Willard withdrew his hand, explaining, "Paulie, he's skeered of ever'thing. He wouldn't come out, even if ya paid 'im."

If that had been a hint, Luke did not take the bait. Rather, he lifted his fingers to his forehead and gave a careless salute to the fearful child. Then both boys scurried off, soon becoming lost in the swell of merrymakers.

When Luke's attention returned to Kristina, she said, "I don't know what to make of you, Lucas Chandler. One moment I want to slap your face, and the next . . ."

He grinned boyishly. "And the next accept a kiss, eh, little princess?"

"I'm not a princess," she immediately responded, "I'm the Mardi Gras queen." Lifting her peacock mask to her features, she added, "Do you see the resemblance now?" Kristina wasn't sure why she could not remain angry with him. She saw in him a man as tortured by the secrets he had kept as she was by his secrecy and his need for it, a man who really was not sure what the future held for him.

But Kristina knew what *she* wanted it to hold. She wanted to be part of his future, even if she had to pick up her roots again and go to Texas with him. She looked toward her aunt dancing in the arms of the young man. The other day they'd had a nice chat while sitting in the coolness of the gallery. Her aunt had been openly affectionate, and Kristina had felt that she truly was fond of her. She hadn't known how true the feeling was until her aunt had asked her to remain at Oak Shadows. Now she felt guilty at even considering fleeing to Texas with Luke when she had promised Zelpha that she would keep her company in her final years.

But as suddenly as it came upon her, the guilt was gone. Something strange and wonderful had happened to her aunt. Her back did not appear as humped, her eyes were bright and alive . . . youthfully coy in the way they looked into the eyes of her dancing partner, visible despite his satin mask.

Zelpha Prudhomme whispered again, "Do tell me who you are, young man. I don't believe I've seen you before. Who is your family?"

*"You* are my family . . . *ma chère* . . . *ma* Kristina . . ."

Zelpha's movements instantly ceased. "No one has called me Kristina . . . no one. Not since—"

Suddenly, the case clock at the foot of the stairs chimed the midnight hour . . . the witching hour . . . the hour when *he* had promised to appear.

That was the moment he chose to remove his mask . . .

Zelpha's small, dark eyes opened wide . . . in horror . . . in wonder . . . in surprise. She opened her mouth to speak, but no sound materialized. Her legs felt flaccid and weak. She knew she would not be able to stand for any length of time, and the noises of the ballroom suddenly drifted away . . . leaving her alone, the brilliant colors of a kaleidoscope surrounding her.

She knew she had collapsed and readily offered her hand into his proffered one . . .

Though she felt the surrounding warmth of his grip, it was not her hand she saw but a slim, white, youthful one . . . She came to her feet with the agility of a girl, to feel the gentleness of an embrace . . . a kiss . . . that she had not enjoyed in half a century.

He held her close as he turned; then they took their first step together into eternity . . .

Kristina was not sure how she made it through the crowd so quickly. She dropped to her knees and touched her aunt's cheek with a hand trembling so violently she could scarcely maintain control of it. Then Lucas was beside her, pulling Zelpha's head onto his lap.

Sophronia approached in silence, then handed Kristina a damp cloth. But Kristina knew there was no need.

Her charming, eccentric old aunt was dead.

A tearful Kristina, wanting explanations, looked about for the young man in whose arms her aunt had danced her final dance.

But he was nowhere to be seen. All that was left of him was the black satin mask he had worn, gently clasped in Zelpha's right hand.

Three mornings later, Zelpha Prudhomme was laid to rest in the marble crypt beside Relin Trosclair de la Cerda, the man she had loved and would have married had not fate intervened. The skies were heady and overcast, the distant rumble of thunder upon the far horizon painting the morning in bold shades of gray and black. Kristina was glad of the weather; her aunt had said not too long ago that she felt safest when rain pelted the earth.

"What are you thinking?"

A black-clothed Kristina tucked her hand into the crook of Luke's arm as they exited the cemetery. "About rain," she said truthfully, "and how much Aunt Zelpha loved it."

"Do you think she's happy now?"

Kristina sighed deeply. "I always wondered how a preacher could say that the recently deceased was safe and happy in the bosom of the Lord, when I was always sure that the person would rather have been alive, but yes, I do believe Aunt Zelpha's happy, because she is now with her one true love."

As they entered the lawn of Oak Shadows, the rain began to fall in large drops, coaxing the young people into a run toward the gallery. There, protected by the overhang of the porch, Kristina scooted her bonnet from her wheat-colored tresses, then dropped into the porch swing to watch the rain. When Luke joined her, she wrapped her arms around him and dropped her head to his shoulder.

Though she wanted only to enjoy being with Luke, and the comfort and security of his arms around her, Kristina couldn't help reflecting on things that had happened in the last few weeks . . . strange, unexplainable things . . . things that, properly interpreted, might even be wonderful. One experience, in particular, popped into her mind, and she quietly said to Luke, "It must have been him that night I thought you were calling me."

"Who?" he answered, a little absently, his cheek moving gently against her pale hairline.

"Relin de la Cerda . . . It was about three weeks ago, and beginning to rain. I thought I saw you from my bedchamber window, and I went down to meet you. But when I started to approach, you—or rather, him—he put up a hand and asked me who I was. I told him I was Kristina, and he said, 'But you are not *my* Kristina. If it was Relin de la Cerda, and he was Aunt Zelpha's love, then who was Kristina?"

"I can 'splain that." Kristina started, her eyes noting movement at the end of the dark gallery. Slowly, old Cleveland came forward. "Din't mean ta startle you, Miz Kristina . . . an' I wasn't eavesdroppin' on you . . . jes' happen't ta be goin' into the house."

"That's all right," Kristina responded. "You said you could explain?"

"You see, Miz Kristina, when Mistah de la Cerda, he was courtin' Miz Zelpha, he tells her Zelpha be an ol' lady name . . . he tells her she looks mo' like a Kristina, because he say Kristina a romantic name, an' she be's real fine lookin', like you 'spect a lady named Kristina would be . . . so he calls her that name what is yo' name now."

Kristina drew slightly away from Luke, a little embarrassed that the old gentleman was witnessing her intimacy. "But that doesn't explain why my father named me Kristina, Cleveland. If he had wanted to honor his sister, he would have named me Zelpha."

Silence. Cleveland looked deeply into Kristina's emerald eyes. Should he tell her that her father had been on the roof of the school that Halloween night with the schoolteacher, that they had both been drinking, and that her father's friendly slap on Relin de la Cerda's back had sent the teacher down the steep slope of the roof to die on the ground below? The two young men had been the best of friends, and her father had never forgiven himself for causing the death of the man who had died in his sister's arms, promising that he would return to her— *"ma chère,* in fifty years, on this very night." Relin had exhibited his humor right up to the end, for with a final kiss upon Zelpha's mouth, he had winked, and then died. His death was the reason Kristina's father had left Oak Shadows Plantation and settled in New England, eventually marrying Kristina's mother . . . and it was the reason Zelpha's niece had been named Kristina, in honor of her father's grieving sister and the man who had given her the affectionate nickname.

"Cleveland?"

He straightened quickly, a little taken aback by hearing his name falling from the young woman's lips. Shaking his head, he replied, "Naw'm . . . don't know why yo' father named you Kristina. A coincidence, I s'pose." A thought came to him. Lifting his hat and crushing it between his gnarled fingers, he said, "Miz Kristina, me an' Joseph an' Sophronia, we's worried 'bout maybe you won't be intendin' fo' us to live out our lives at Oak Shadows . . . we's been here fo'ever . . . an' we's just wonderin'—"

Kristina arose, her hand slipping from the warmth and comfort of Luke's. "I imagine that when Aunt Zelpha's will is read on Friday provision will have been made for the three of you. Aunt Zelpha would never have expected you to leave Oak Shadows. I am sure the new owner—"

"But you be's the new owner, Miz Kristina."

"That can't be." The protest rose in her throat, choking her. She had only known her aunt for a month; before that time, they had been strangers, not even corresponding with each other over the years. Surely, there were others closer to Aunt Zelpha and more worthy to inherit Oak Shadows Plantation. Then Kristina looked around at the neglect and decay that had virtually left the house in shambles; even from her perch on the gallery of Oak Shadows, she could see the fields grown high and pitted by young pines that had taken root over the years. Only then did she wonder how Oak Shadows had sustained itself and paid its bills without the fields being planted in the rich crops of cotton, corn and sugar cane her father had told her about. Dropping into the slatted swing, she said once again, "That can't be."

"I took her into Alexandria to her lawyer, Mr. Huntington, early las' week," Cleveland continued dourly. "I saw her sign the new will. An' she says, when we was

82

comin' back in the buggy, that she done made you the new owner."

Kristina looked to Lucas. "I don't know anything about running a plantation."

Cleveland said, "Excuse me, Miz Kristina . . . Mistah Chandler . . . got chores inside." When he had disappeared into the house, Lucas drew Kristina into the circle of his arms. "What am I going to do with this old run-down plantation?" she whispered.

"We could fix it up, maybe even plant those fields that haven't seen seed in a good number of years."

"What are you saying, Luke? That you will stay here and run the place for me?"

"That's a thought. But, I was really thinking about getting married. Would you mind if I stay here with a new wife?"

She drew back, horrified, the floor suddenly a hundred miles from her feet as she tried to find it. How could he have held her and kissed her so deeply and passionately—how could he have made love to her?—if he was planning to marry another? The floor came back somehow, and her feet touched it. Just as she stood and prepared to flee from him, fingers wrapped firmly around her wrist.

"Where are you going, Kristina?"

"Away—away from you—as far away as I can get."

Luke knew exactly what had happened, that she had misinterpreted his declaration and thought he would take her up on the job offer and bring another woman onto the plantation. Though he enjoyed the color that had suffused her cheeks and thought it quite charming, he could not bear the thoughts running through her mind. As his fingers relaxed into a gentle caress, he whispered, "But if you leave, you will spoil my proposal." He rose to his feet, pulling her close. "Miss Kristina Hartman, will you do a humble ex-Texas Ranger the honor of becoming his wife . . . and the mother of his dozen or so children."

83

Tears moistened her eyes. "You want *me* to marry you, Lucas?"

"I sure do. And if you're worried that I can't pull my weight around here, then you haven't seen me working my fingers to the bone. I have a little money that my father left me when he died—sitting in a bank in Beaumont—a tidy enough sum to get those fields cleared and planted in the spring. So, what do you say, Miss Kristina Hartman, will you marry an ex-Texas Ranger and make a planter out of him?"

Her hands flew to the back of his neck as she pressed herself to him. "Oh, yes . . . yes. I will marry you."

"Hot damn!" In his enthusiasm, Luke lifted her off the planked floor and swung her around. As her feet once again touched the ground, their mouths met in the sweetest of kisses, sealing their hopes for the future, their love for each other—and their determination to make a working plantation of Oak Shadows.

Kristina laughed. "Will you be content to be my husband, or will you keep looking for the money in the cemetery?"

"That money? I don't believe it'll ever be found."

# Eight

*Six months later*

Kristina had really planned to keep the ceremony simple. But now she stood before a full-length mirror, studying her appearance and thinking that perhaps the gown was too elaborate for a "simple" wedding. The white satin dress had been hand-tailored by Leanna Gilbert's aunt, touted as the best seamstress in all of New Orleans. It was lavishly trimmed from neckline to hem with lace and richly embroidered with diamond-patterned tulle. The two-layered shirred tulle veil was gathered in a tight circle at the crown, under a floral headdress of peach and white satin roses; and her bridal bouquet matched the headdress. She was wearing Aunt Zelpha's pearl brooch and earrings Leanna had given her.

"You is lovely, Miz Kristina." Sophronia approached and looked across her shoulder at her vision in the mirror. "Why, just look at them cheeks, them's faintly blushin', jes' like a bride."

"I'm so nervous," whispered Kristina, feeling that she might faint from the excitement of her wedding to Luke Chandler. She wished her father and Aunt Zelpha could have been with her on this special day.

Sophronia snickered. "Ya thinks yo' nervous, Miz Kristina, why, ya should see Mistah Chandler. Why, they be's sweat a-pourin' down his fo'head an' into his eyes. An' he's a jerkin' on that tight collar like a preacher caught in the bushes with his britches down."

"Sophronia!" Both turned as Leanna Gilbert, Kristina's maid of honor, entered the chamber, resplendent in her gown of lavender brocade. She brushed a light kiss against Kristina's cheek, then turned a look of feigned disapproval toward Sophronia. "Talking about the preacher like that?" She smiled then, easing her arm across the elderly servant's shoulder. "And on Miss Kristina's wedding day! Why I'll bet our blushing bride won't even be able to look the old scoundrel in the eyes as she says her wedding vows."

The organ downstairs, that had until now been droning in off-key notes, now began to play some semblance of the wedding march. Sophronia said, "I'll be goin' out ta find Cleveland and Joseph, so's I can watch ya meet yo man befo' the preacher."

Kristina lifted a hand in farewell, instantly jerking it down when she felt its violent trembling. Now, alone with Leanna, she whispered in somewhat of a panic, "Am I doing the right thing by marrying Luke?"

Leanna laughed. "He's been running the plantation since Aunt Zelpha's death. Those fields are cleared and planted—and this house! My goodness, it hasn't been so beautiful in fifty years! I suspect if I told you to run him off, you'd run me off first. Yes, my friend, you are doing the right thing. He will make you a wonderful husband—for a ghost!" She hugged Kristina carefully so as not to crush her careful appearance. "Now, let's go downstairs before he thinks you've changed your mind and faints with relief."

"Oh, you!" Kristina laughed, gladdened by her friend's good humor, which helped to alleviate her nervousness. But moments later, as her descent of the stairs brought her face to face with a hundred happily smiling guests, she felt her knees become as flaccid as weeds.

Then Kristina saw her bridegroom, standing at the end of the aisle between the chairs placed in the parlor. She had met him and fallen in love with him in the veil of darkness, and she had seen him sweating in the fields that had been cleared and planted, but she had never seen him looking so grand . . . calm and self-assured, the only hint of nervousness the tight clenching of his hand where, she imagined, the gold ring he would place upon her finger was hidden. Her beloved was so handsome in his formal suit of finely woven wool gabardine with satin lapels. His crisp white shirt was magnificently pleated and closed with diamond studs in golden bezels. Mother-of-pearl buttons gleamed on his white jacquard vest, and—she smiled—Cleveland had perfectly tied the silk bow at his neckline. She'd been told he'd fretted over it himself for half an hour.

The organ played the wedding march; Kristina did not notice the wrong keys being occasionally struck by the matronly player. She knew only that the man she loved was about to make her his wife and spend the rest of his life with her.

Now, she stood beside him, scarcely aware of the steps that had brought her to him. Though she had passed by many guests, she could not recall a single face; if any comments had been made on her appearance, she could not remember one. She felt that she and Luke had stepped into a glass bubble and were the only two people who existed.

Afterward, she would not recall the words spoken by the preacher or the congratulations of their guests. She would not recall the precise moment when the simple gold band was slipped on her finger and she said, "I do." The ceremony had been a wondrous vortex of silken shadows imprisoning them in the confines of each other's loving gazes, and the only words she could recall were the preacher's: "I present to you Mr. and Mrs. Lucas Chandler."

The reception would be held out-of-doors, where banquet tables had been set up for the many guests. In the typical tradition of weddings attended by many of Cajun descent, the merriment lasted well into the late hours. Then, an exhausted Luke and Kristina gave the festivities over to the guests, with an invitation to stay as long as they wished, and they entered the house they would share together. There, in the confines of their bedchamber, their exhaustion was quickly forgotten. Tenderly embracing, they held each other for a long, long while, without spoken words. This night was the beginning of their new roles as husband and wife, and they wanted only for their togetherness to go on forever.

"I love you, Mrs. Lucas Chandler," he whispered tenderly against her hairline. She had removed her veil hours before, and her hair had fallen loose during the day's merriment and festivities. Now, his fingers grazed the disheveled silken tresses. "Beautiful," he murmured, drawing them against his cheek to feel their softness. Then he chuckled, putting her gently away from him for a moment. "Those blasted curls are out of your hair . . . how about climbing out of your wedding dress? You must be uncomfortable."

Her long, tapered fingers gently struck his chest. "You're not thinking of my discomfort, Mr. Chandler . . . you are thinking of the pleasures of the bed."

Drawing her to him, he held her firmly, a low growl echoing against her ear. "You're right, wife." Then he began unfastening the stays of her tight-fitting gown. Soon, its weight dropping from her slim form, she stepped out of it and her voluminous petticoats as though they were all one garment.

"Luke . . . Luke," she murmured. "I simply must know . . . before the Halloween ball . . . that night . . . in this very bedchamber . . . were you here, or did I dream it? Oh, I simply must know!"

He grinned rakishly, his mouth teasing the crease at

the corner of her own with gentle kisses. Then he whispered his usual response, "I'll never tell." Before she could offer further protests, Luke bent and touched a kiss to one of her white shoulders, his fingers soon easing the straps of her camisole down her arms. When, moments later, she was completely free of her clothing, he thought how beautiful she was in her tantalizing state of nudity. Quickly freeing himself of his own clothing, he took her in his arms and moved toward the bed, which had been turned down sometime in the afternoon in anticipation of their night of wedded bliss. Gently laying her among the pillows, he covered her soft, warm body with his hard one. The urgency he felt, he could tell she, too, felt. Both seemed anxious to forgo the preludes to their lovemaking. Her body moved erotically beneath his caresses, and her womanly curves rose to meet his hands. When, at last, he was part of her, they rocked together in gentle unison, so completely enflamed by desire that nothing existed as their ecstasy reached into the farthest expanses of the universe, refusing to return to reality.

But after the culmination of their love, as they slowly were dragged from the clouds and back to the satin sheets, they clung to each other, refusing to allow their bodies to become separate and distinct. In their passion, they fanned the flames of their unfulfilled hunger again and again . . . until in the predawn semi-darkness exhaustion drew them to the clinging tentacles of sleep.

With her tousled hair lying against his shoulder, Luke asked, "Will that blasted money ever be found?"

"Only in your dreams," she murmured, snuggling against him.

"No . . . not there." His arm tightened, then relaxed into a gentle caress against her shoulder. "My dreams are only for you, Kristina . . . Chandler."

"And the night, too," she whispered, sleep quickly claiming her.

As her long, pale lashes flickered against his cheek,

Lucas held her close, protecting her, loving her, knowing that forever, she would be in his arms.

Like this.

He didn't give a damn about the lost money. She was all the treasure he wanted of life.

Still, when he closed his eyes, he instinctively envisioned where the cache might be in the vast, deathly silence of the cemetery . . . hidden from the eyes of man forever.


The base of the sepulcher bearing the mortal remains of the beloved slave who had been Cleveland's father had cracked many years ago. The gap disappearing into tall grass was just wide enough to accommodate the ragged shape of the cat who had survived nearly two decades, a good number of years longer than any other feline in the neighborhood. He slithered through the gap in the stone, thinking that he'd spook up another rat for his dinner. But there were none, so he curled against the oblong chest that had been placed there by a fleeing outlaw some months ago. Yawning and stretching out, he prepared for a few hours of sleep after his night of prowling. When something round and hard fell against his haunch, only vaguely disturbing his sleep, he gave it a perfunctory glance as it rolled down and settled onto the packed earth. The bit of sunlight invading the crack caught upon the coin, sending a bright array of lights onto the age-darkened walls of the sepulchre.

Catching his much-needed bit of sleep, the old cat paid no attention to the rattling inside the broken chest . . . a pack rat preparing to carry away another of the coins to its nest in the marble crypt . . . a rat that had evaded capture as long as the old cat could remember . . .

*Lovespell*
by
Colleen Faulkner

# One

*Virginia Colony*
*The Peninsula*
*All Hallows Eve, 1701*

"Ach, Sarah! Come along!" Robert Cameron halted in the center of the road leading into the small town of Koshatak. The mule he was leading stopped behind him and the small basket tied to the animal swayed slightly, bringing a wail from the baby inside.

Rob groaned and leaned over the basket to retuck the tattered quilt around the little boy. "Now look what you've done, child. You willna listen to your uncle, will you?"

Sarah Commegys crouched on the hard-packed dirt road arranging a pile of sticks. "I'm coming!" she called. "I just have to lay down these traps to keep the witches off our backs when we come back from town. You told me it might be dark before we make it home."

The baby's wailing nearly drowned out his sister's words.

In frustration, Rob ran his fingers through the blond hair that fell over his face as he tried to soothe the babe in the basket by awkwardly patting a little flailing hand. "Ach! How many times must I tell you, child? There's no such thing as witches! Now come along or I leave you behind. I told you, I have to get to the auction before it begins!"

The red-haired child dropped the last broken twig onto the carefully arranged pile of sticks and then ran to catch up. "My grandmama said there was witches."

"And I tell you there's no such thing. 'Tis naught but tales to scare wee children into bed."

Sarah stared up at the trees that hung low over the road cut through the forest. They were so dense that even at mid-day much of the sunlight was blocked out by the branches. The skeletal limbs cast long fingers of eerie shadows across her path. "Grandmama said witches hang from the trees at night, by their toes like bats." The little girl glanced over her shoulder suspiciously. "Them and ghosties."

"Well, your grandmama was a liar." He caught her by the shoulder and gave her a gentle push toward the mule. "Now try to soothe your little brother. He's not been asleep ten minutes and he's howling like a Highland banshee again. The boy is dry, his stomach's full, and I've wrapped him in enough blankets to keep him warm 'til Candlemas Eve." He dropped his hands to his hips. "I tell you Sarah, I'm at my wit's end."

Sarah peered over the side of the basket, but walked on. "Can't shut him up. You said so yourself last night, Uncle Robbie. Pity for you grandmama brought him back. I'd have thrown him into the bay was I you and he screamed the way he does, keepin' me up all hours of the night."

"Hold your tongue," Rob chided softly. "The boy's my sister's child, as you are. The both of you belong with me. I should never have let your grandmother take you home to Annapolis in the first place."

"She was nice enough, but she just didn't understand children. Not like you, Uncle Robbie." The little girl slipped her hand into his.

Rob squeezed her hand and then let go. He clicked his tongue, and the mule lifted its head to stare at its master sullenly.

Rob clicked his tongue again and gave a hard tug on the leadline. After a moment of indecision, the mule moseyed on along. Sarah fell into step behind.

Rob cursed, a Scottish oath, beneath his breath. What more bad luck could possibly befall one man in a single lifetime, he wondered miserably. The incidents seemed more than bad luck. His sister was right; he had to be cursed. As long as he could remember he'd been a boy and then a man of misfortune.

His parents had brought him from Scotland as a wee lad. Here on the eastern coast of the Chesapeake they had cut fields from dense forest with their bare hands. They had forged a wilderness plot into a tobacco plantation, small but prosperous. But since Rob had inherited it upon the passing of his mother and father, he had brought nothing but trouble to Sarah's Stand.

Three years in a row, Rob's crops had been poor. He'd been plagued by hailstorms in the fields, fires in the tobacco drying houses, and sinking transport ships. Of course there were also the pirates to worry over. Though so far Sarah's Stand had been spared, there'd been a string of raids along the Virginia and Maryland shores of the Chesapeake. The pirates came to steal, but raped and killed in the process.

Six months ago, when the boy was only a few weeks old, Rob's sister and brother-in-law had drowned in a storm crossing a river on a ferry. The children's grandmother had taken them to Annapolis, but that just hadn't worked out and they had soon been returned home to Sarah's Stand where he now knew they rightfully belonged.

Of course he found himself the guardian of a precocious six-year-old female and a six-month-old boy child who screamed most of his waking hours.

With the children to care for, he was unable to properly tend to his chores about the plantation, and with winter setting in, he knew there was much to do if the family was to survive that season. That was why Rob had decided to purchase, with the last of his coin, a bondwoman to tend to the children, and cook and clean. With his sister and brother-in-law dead, it was simply too much work for one man, especially a man who sat awake all night rocking a wailing babe.

With all this to worry over, to add insult to injury, this year Rob had finally managed to get a decent tobacco cutting, only to have the ship he'd shipped his tobacco on be reported sunk half a day's sail into the Atlantic. How one man could lose his tobacco crop two years in a row, he couldn't fathom.

Rob turned right off the road and walked past the first house in Koshatak. He knew he would have to hurry if he was to see the bondwomen before other buyers arrived and the auctioning began. Joe Maddon had been emphatic: if Rob wanted the older woman with child-rearing experience, he would have to make the sale on time. Rob was hoping Joe would just take pity on him and sell him the woman rather than auction her off. Then he could be on his way.

"Sarah!" Rob waved his hand. "Come."

The child had fallen behind again and was now spinning in a circle, her hands over her ears as she attempted to touch her tongue to her nose.

"Ach! What are you doing now, girl?"

"Warding off the evil spirits. It's All Hallows Eve, Uncle Robbie. Don't you know this is the night all spooks come to claim our souls?"

Rob rolled his eyes heavenward. The girl's grandmother had seemed a sensible enough woman to Rob the two times he'd met her, but she'd been extremely superstitious and had apparently passed the trait on to her young granddaughter in the few months she'd cared for her.

Spotting the auction platform in the town's center, Rob picked up his pace. A small crowd had already gathered around.

Rob halted near the platform and pressed the mule's

lead line into Sarah's small hands. "Stay put with your brother whilst I buy us a nursemaid."

"Don't need a nursemaid," Sarah said, thrusting out her lower lip.

"No? Well, you may not, but the lad does." He pointed to the boy in the basket who was finally beginning to drift off to sleep again. "Now just stay where you are, Sarah, and no more spook nonsense."

"What if Sugar tries to run away?"

"Have no fear of that, child," Rob called to her over his shoulder. "I can barely get the beastie to move at all. He'll not take off on you."

Sarah waved to her uncle and Rob took the plank steps two at a time, bound straight for Joe Maddon. The sooner he bought this woman, the sooner he could get some semblance of order back into his life.


Katie stood stock-still on the raised platform, watching the Scot whose long blond hair brushed his shoulders in the autumn breeze as he approached and then spoke to the auctioneer. She couldn't hear exactly what he was saying, but she could make out the slight burr of his Highland speech. She twisted her hands in the rough hemp ropes until they didn't rub at her wrists quite so badly.

The Scot was discussing the purchase of the buxom, matronly woman three bondservants down the line. You don't want her, Katie thought. She looks the motherly type, but she'll not spare the rod on your children, Scot.

The Scot spoke to the matron, paused to hear her response, then frowned and moved on to the next adult woman to be auctioned off. The wail of a baby echoed behind him. He turned to glance in the direction of the mule he'd walked into town with. A small red-haired girl peeked into a basket on the animal's back. She shrugged her shoulders at her father—no, not her father, Katie decided. She's not comfortable enough with him.

The little girl and the baby crying were orphans. The Scot, a single man, no doubt, had for some reason taken it upon himself to care for the children. How admirable. That's why he had come into town, Katie surmised, to buy a bondwoman to care for the children.

*To buy* . . . The words echoed in Katie's head. Here she was, being sold once again. How human beings could sell other human beings, she didn't know. After her mother's death she'd been sold at the age of four into bondage for twenty-one years. Four more years of this, she thought, of being passed from house to house, kitchen to kitchen. Good heavens, by the time she was free, she'd be too old and worn out for the life she dreamed of! She'd have been a slave to others too long to ever be able to have a life of her own.

Katie looked up. The Scot was only one woman down from her now. He still hadn't made up his mind who he would purchase. She liked him. Though his broadcloth breeches were patched and his hands were rough from walking behind a plow, he had a handsome face and a strong jaw. Her mother had always said you could trust a man with a strong jaw. Katie's father had had one.

Now she could hear the Scot speaking. She watched him out of the corner of her eye.

"Ach, Joe. Dinna I tell you, I can't afford that kind of price! I speak truth when I say I'm down to my last shillings, man. You know every hogshead of tobacco I owned was on the *Mary Jane* when she went down."

The man called Joe, who'd transported Katie and the others here to the tiny town on the Chesapeake, pushed back his wool hat. "I'm not in this business to give a bondwoman away, Rob. Sad story or no, I got to make a living somehow. I can't sell her for a copper less."

Rob . . . What a pleasant name. A pleasant name for a pleasant face. A pity he was scowling again. A man down on his luck, no doubt. Katie smiled. A man who needed a good woman.

The baby in the basket wailed louder. The little red-haired girl was ignoring her little sister or brother and playing in the dirt beneath the mule's feet.

Katie could see the Scot was growing impatient. He had a cow at home to milk, no doubt, and the screech of the poor babe in the basket would be enough to wear on any man's nerves.

The Scot moved on to Katie. She lifted her lashes hesitantly. He smelled good, like the forest, like her father had.

Rob Cameron dropped his hands to his hips, narrowing his blue eyes speculatively as he studied the black-haired girl before him. She was a damned sight too comely for him, with her coal black eyes and rosy lips, that was for certain. He needed a nursemaid and a cook, not a whore. But he was fast running out of options. He had little cash, and if that nephew of his didn't stop that infernal wailing, Rob was certain he'd go mad.

"What of this one?" Rob asked.

Joe shook his head. "No. You don't want her, Robbie." He dropped a hand onto his shoulder. "The woman's a witch. A few years back, they'd have burned her at the stake up in the northern colonies."

The Scot lifted his gaze to study Katie's face. She was nearly as tall as he was. He looked at her eye to eye as if he considered her his equal. "The man says you're a witch."

Katie's mouth turned up in the barest smile. "And do you believe in such superstitions, sir?"

"Nay. Like I tell my niece, tales to scare wee ones."

*So the girl was his niece, not his daughter.* Katie nodded in the direction of the children, wishing she wasn't hog-tied. It was hard for a woman to make a good impression with her hands and feet tied like a criminal's. "Your babe cries a lot?"

"My nephew. His mama and papa died last winter and he's done nothing but scream like the banshee since." He considered her carefully. "You ken you could soothe him?"

"I tell you, you don't want her, Robbie," Joe interrupted. "She's been nothing but trouble at the last two homes I put her in." He settled his blood-shot gaze on the Scot. *"She's the one that cursed old man Thompson Matthews last spring past,"* he said meaningfully.

Rob looked back to Katie. "Did you curse Matthews like they say?"

She lowered her voice so that only the Scot could hear her. "Now does that make sense to you? A kitchen maid giving the master a limp rod?" She lowered her head toward his. "Not that the man needed it, with as many bastard children as he's spawned."

A smile tugged at Rob's mouth. The woman was sassy, but she had a level head. And she was right about old man Matthews too; he was a womanizer. Everyone in the county knew he slept with his servants and their daughters as well. If he had been cursed with impotence, it couldn't have happened to a better man.

Rob still studied Katie's face carefully. "You cook and clean?"

"A neater house can't be kept on the shore."

"And the babe?" He pointed in the direction of the shrieking child in the basket. "Please tell me you've got the touch with children. It might well take sorcery to shut his wee mouth."

"A salve on his gums and a woman's bosom and he'll be right as rain."

Rob crossed his arms over his chest as he turned to Joe. "How much?"

"I'm tellin' you, Robbie. As cursed as you are, she's liable to turn you into a horned toad, you cross her."

The Scot twisted his worn boot on the rough-hewn plank beneath his foot. "I've livestock to feed up at home, Joey. No time to prattle. How much?"

Joe named a price.

Rob swore. "I told you what I could afford. I wanted the older woman but you named a price so high, Midas

100

couldn't buy her. How about the witch, Joe? Who the hell you going to sell a blessed witch to?"

Katie watched the Scot as he dickered for her. It wasn't that she particularly wanted to go with any man or woman, but if she had to be sold, he seemed as good an owner as some, better than most.

Joe hawked and spit. "I got to make a profit. I got little'uns to feed same as you, Rob."

"So sell her to me at a fair price."

Joe scrunched up his face, staring up at the taller Scot. "All Hallows Eve and you're going to buy yourself a witch for a nursemaid? She'll have your soul and your bloody heart as well in her pocket afore you reach your property line."

Rob rolled his eyes impatiently. "I told you, I don't believe in witches or fairies either. Now name a fair price and let's be done with it. I tell you"—he poked a finger into the auctioneers hollow chest—"you make me sit up another night with that boy and he'll be on your doorstep screaming come morning."

Joe sighed and named a lower price.

Rob swore again.

"Take it or leave it."

"Pirates are better than you," Rob complained, pulling out a money pouch from inside the waistband of his breeches. He counted out his coins.

Katie noticed that when he tucked the bag back into his waistband, it was empty.

"She's yours," Joe said, "but don't blame me if she curses your cock, too."

Rob frowned. "Untie her."

Joe took a step back. "What if she sprouts wings and flies? Better to keep her tied to something at all times. The man that had her after Matthews did."

Rob thrust his hand into his wool stocking and drew out a hunting knife. Katie watched him as he cut first the ties at her ankles, then her hands.

101

"Thank you," she said softly, rubbing at the raw flesh at her wrists.

He pointed toward the children. "Now will you please shut the boy up? Show me you're worth my last shilling, woman."

Making a quick curtsy, Katie grabbed up her skirts and ran across the platform, down the steps and toward the screaming baby. The crowd gathered for the auction parted to let her by. Katie heard whispers as she passed them.

"Witch," someone hissed.

"Devil's spawn."

A woman made a sign to ward off the devil, another turned her back to Katie as she passed.

". . . gave Nancy Moore the evil eye last summer and cursed her with the pocks . . ."

But Katie ignored them. Reaching the mule, she bent over the reed baby basket and lifted the screaming little boy up and out. His face was red and wrinkled, but he had the clearest blue eyes Sarah thought she'd ever seen. She brought him to her chest and thrust her forefinger into his mouth to rub his gums.

He immediately ceased his wailing.

"I'll be damned," Rob muttered, appearing at her side. He stared at the little boy's face and then at Katie. "How did you do that?"

"'Twas naught but—"

"Rob, Robert Cameron!" A man's voice interrupted.

A short, stout man with a balding head came pushing his way through the crowd. "Just what do you think you're doing?" asked the man.

Rob turned to the sheriff. "What does it look like I'm doing? I bought the girl's indenture. I'm taking her home to care for my sister's children. You know full well their parents drowned months ago."

"You got no other woman on that place of yours?"

102

"No. I had to let them all go. You know that. Everyone in the county knows it."

The sheriff made a clucking sound between his teeth. "Can't let you do that, then, Rob."

"Can't let me do what?"

"Corrupt this woman thusly. We ain't Maryland, Rob. You know we got laws here. Laws that keeps decent people decent. It would be immoral to take that young woman back to your place way out on the bay. God only knows what would become of her virtue come a cold snap. Hell, even the bonded got rights, Rob."

Rob wiped his mouth with the back of his hand. He was trying to remain calm, but there was an edge to his voice. "I just bought her, Jesse. I haven't got another copper to my name. I can't buy another woman to bring wi' her and you know what my credit's like."

Katie held the little boy in her arms, rocking him and murmuring in his ear. The little girl with the red hair stared up at her curiously.

Rob looked at the sheriff, then at Katie and the quiet babe, and then back at the sheriff again. "Just what did you want me to do, Jesse, tell me that?"

The sheriff shrugged. "Go on home peacefully without her."

"I can't. That boy's not been silent in two weeks time. I got to have her, Jesse." He raised a fist. "Got to, curse you."

"Sound like a desperate man," the sheriff muttered thoughtfully. He chewed on his plump lower lip for a moment. "You could marry her, I guess. Then I could let her go along with you."

Rob leaned forward as if he'd misheard the man. "Marry her?"

Katie stopped rocking the baby in midswing. "Marry me?"

The little boy began to wail again.

# Two

Rob took a step toward the sheriff, his face growing red with anger. "Marry my bondwoman? Have you taken leave o' your senses, Jesse?"

The sheriff shrugged. "It's my job to be certain the citizens of this colony obey the laws. I don't care if you marry her or don't. I don't care if the boy screams till he's grown. All I'm telling you, Rob, is I can't let the maid go with you unwed, with no chaperone."

Katie listened to the conversation between the two men. She resented the way they spoke about her as if she were an inanimate object. Marry a man she'd never laid eyes on before five minutes ago? Not a chance in everlasting hell!

But Katie was a woman of logic, and once she allowed her mind instead of her emotions to take control, she began to consider the possibilities.

What did the Scot, Rob Cameron, want? A woman to cook, clean, and care for the children.

What did she want? Her freedom. A chance to have a life.

She glanced at the Scot in heated conversation with the High Sheriff. Perhaps a bargain could be struck.

She cleared her throat. When no one paid her any mind she reached out to touch the Scot's arm to get his attention. It was a nice forearm, banded with muscle.

"Rob, might I speak with you a minute." Katie knew she was taking liberties to address her new master in such a familiar way, but heavens, if they were discussing marriage, first names were certainly appropriate.

Rob glanced at the black-haired woman. "What is it?"

While still cradling the little boy in one arm, she crooked her finger. "In private, might I speak with you?"

He gave an impatient huff. "Hold on there a second, will you, Jesse? Can you wait a minute before you haul me off to the stocks for immorality?" The sheriff nodded and Rob followed Katie around to the other side of the mule. "What is it, woman?"

"Katie."

"What?" He leaned into her.

"My name is Katie," she said patiently.

He pushed a lock of golden blond hair off his shoulder. "Katie, then."

She watched his face carefully for a reaction as she spoke. "I'd be willing to marry you," she said softly.

He lifted an eyebrow. "I guess you would, me owning a thousand acres of prime tobacco land and you owning the clothes on your pretty back."

She bit down on her lower lip, keeping a flare of anger in check. "I'd be willing to marry you on conditions. You would get what you want, I'd get what I want."

Her words tapped his attention. "Just say what you want to say, woman. I'm not a patient man."

She rocked the little boy in her arm. "I'm saying I'll marry you"—she lifted a finger—"in name only, for one year. I'll cook, clean, and care for the little ones."

"And at the end of the year?"

"Come All Hallows Eve again, I'm free to go on my way with two crowns in my pocket"—she glanced at the mule he'd brought the baby in on—"and the animal to ride out on."

He threw back his head and laughed. "Do I look a fool to you, woman?"

Without a moment's consideration, she pushed the baby back into his arms and started for the auction platform.

The baby began to scream.

Rob ran after her, jolting the boy. "Wait!"

Katie walked along quickly. "Best tend to your nephew, Rob Cameron. He cries."

"Two crowns! And I thought Joey was the highwayman. I just bought your indenture for four years! I just spent the last shilling I owned and you're willing to give me one year and for that you want two crowns and my mule?"

Katie was on the platform steps now. The baby was screaming even louder. Though she wanted to reach out and soothe the little boy, she kept her hands to herself and her face impassive. "Upset him too much and he may well give you back his supper."

Rob stood on the bottom step jostling the infant awkwardly in one arm. With the other hand, he reached out and grabbed her homespun sleeve to stop her. "All right."

She stopped on the step, but she didn't turn to look at him.

"All right," he repeated.

She crossed her arms over her bosom, turning to face him. "On my terms. I'll not lay with you, I'm warning you now, Rob Cameron. You touch me and—"

"You'll curse me with a limp rod, right?"

"I'll kill you."

He almost smiled at the look of determination on her face, but the baby was screaming so loudly that he could barely hear himself think. He jiggled the baby harder. "Right now, taking my pleasure is the last thing I've got on my mind, woman. Just, please, take him." He offered her the wailing baby.

After a moment's hesitation, she reached out and took him.

The boy stopped crying.

"Witch . . . witch . . ." colonists in the crowd hissed.

106

"You'll regret this day," a man in a red wool cocked hat warned.

"Think you got bad luck now, Cameron, wait a day."

"A witch in the home, a death come early, that's what I always say . . ."

Rob turned away from Katie, ignoring the townsfolk and walked back to the sheriff. "I'll marry her," he conceded, "but now. Today. This instant. I can't waste another day walking into town, and I can't go another night without sleep, Jesse."

The sheriff grinned. "You're in luck. The parson just rode in last night from down south way. He's in Sally Gooden's house right now eating sweet potato pie."

Little Sarah, who'd been surprisingly quiet through the entire incident was now bouncing up and down at her uncle's side. "Is it true? Did you buy a wife 'stead of a nursemaid, Uncle Robbie?"

Rob turned to Katie, who had followed him back to the mule. "The girl is Sarah. Like I said, my niece. She's mouthy, but she's a good little girl."

Katie smiled down at the child. "Nice to meet you, Sarah."

The little girl curtsied. "You too." She peered up at Katie. "Is it true what they say? Are you a witch, Katie?"

"Ach. Hush your mouth, child, and come along." Rob glanced over his shoulder at Katie, but avoided eye contact. "It's to the Goodens and then home." He grabbed the mule's lead line and started down the dusty road. Katie, with the little boy still in her arms, took Sarah's hand and followed.


An hour later Katie walked down a dirt road behind her new husband.

Husband. She almost laughed aloud. She'd never thought she'd marry. Marriage was too one-sided—all for the man and naught for the woman but babies tugging at her breasts and an early grave. Now here she was, married to a man she'd known an hour.

She wondered if she would have any trouble with him trying to demand some sort of husband's rights now that he had the official document tucked in his tattered coat. She thought of old man Matthews and smiled. Rob Cameron had best not be any trouble.

Katie looked up at her new family. Sarah was skipping along ahead of Rob, who led the mule. After another half a mile Rob dropped back a little.

"I understand the coin, but why the mule?" he asked, glancing at her curiously.

Katie took an extra step to catch up with him and walked at his side. She shrugged. "I don't know. I walked into this agreement. I thought I would ride out."

Sarah's bell-like laughter rose in the cool late afternoon air. It was already growing dark, the shadows of the forest lengthening. "He'd probably give you Sugar now. He hates her." She beamed at her uncle.

Katie tucked the baby tighter in her arms. "Oh?"

"Sarah, hush," Rob warned.

"Oh, yea," Sarah went on. "See, Uncle Robbie, he has this old mare Penny, and he paid Mr. Noah to breed old Penny with Mr. Noah's racin' horse, only she didn't take."

Sarah tried not to laugh at the serious expression on the little girl's face as she went on with her tale.

"'Stead, old Penny, she broke out of the pasture and met up with Mr. Noah's donkey." The little girl nodded her head. "That's how old Penny had a mule instead of horse. Now Uncle Robbie's so mad, he says we're gonna eat old Penny come winter." She scrunched up her face. "But I think he's just foolin' 'cause we got hogs to eat and bacon tastes better than horsemeat any day."

"By all that's holy, Sarah, must you tell everything you know?" Rob muttered good-naturedly.

Katie covered her mouth with her hand to keep from

laughing. This was obviously a sore subject with her new master . . . her husband.

She looked to Rob. "Sounds like you've had a string of bad luck."

He tugged on Sugar's lead line, trying to make the animal walk faster. "You don't know the half of it. Six months ago I lost my sister and her husband. His mother came from Annapolis to take the children, but it didn't work out. The boy, Josh, cried, and Sarah"—he lowered his voice so that the little girl couldn't hear him—"Sarah just couldn't get used to town-life. Then her grandmama decided to remarry and the prospective bridegroom wouldn't have her with the children."

"So you took them back?"

"They're my sister's children. I should never have let them go in the first place, but everyone told me I couldn't care for them, that they needed a woman. They were wrong, and I ken that now. They belong here with me on Sarah's Stand. They came back two weeks ago."

"So the children coming back was really good fortune, wasn't it?"

"Aye, I suppose I could look at it that way. But then last week all my tobacco went down on the *Mary Jane.*" He lifted a broad palm heavenward. "I'm as sunk as she is noo. I don't even know how I'm going to feed the lad and lass through the winter snows."

"I hear she was only reported sunk. Mayhap—"

"No. I'm telling you, you don't know my luck. This is a man who started for town this morning riding his horse, only to have to turn back because she threw a shoe. You'll notice I ended up walking into town leading a mule." He sighed. "This is the second year in a row I've lost my crop and now I'm out of cash. With no coin to hire help in the fields for next year, I don't know what I'll do. Sell land, I suppose. Our nearest neighbor, Noah, has been asking me to sell for years."

"But you don't want to?" Katie inquired gently.

"My parents' land. They came from Scotland and cleared much of it themselves. Sentimental foolishness."

She smiled at him. He had the clearest blue eyes, identical to the baby's. "Not foolishness at all. I have nothing left of my mother or father. Nothing but memories."

Their gazes met and locked. For a moment their thoughts seemed to connect. He understood what she meant. He understood her loneliness. He was lonely too. She could see a smile playing at the corners of his full mouth.

A foolish thought crossed her mind. What would it be like to kiss that mouth? she wondered.

"Look Uncle Robbie," Sarah cried, stopping in the middle of the road ahead of them. "Look!" She pointed toward the ground. "Somethin' come by and broke my witch trap!" The little girl looked up wide-eyed in Katie's direction.

Rob looked to Katie. "Her grandmother went on to the child about witches and goblins and such," he explained. "Superstitious nonsense, all of it."

Katie walked to the scattered pile of sticks in the center of the road and crouched beside Sarah. "You know, my mother always said that her father back in England used to talk about the witches riding on the backs of the horses out to pasture," she said softly, her hushed voice carrying on the wind. "And at night, when her father would bring the horses in, their manes would be braided."

Sarah's mouth dropped open. "By the witches?"

Katie shrugged. "She said they braided the horses' manes so they'd have something to hold onto when they rode them."

"Did you hear that? Did you hear that Uncle Robbie?" Sarah shouted bouncing up and down. "There is witches! I told you!"

Rob cut his eyes at Katie. "Now you're filling her head with nonsense. She'll be up in the night, crying."

Katie stood and started walking again. "Just tales to amuse, nothing more." She dropped a hand over Sarah's

110

shoulder. "You'll not be afraid, will you? You know it's just a story."

She beamed at Katie and shook her head. "I won't be afraid, not if you tuck me in and tell me another story, Katie. I promise."

Suddenly, for no reason at all, the mule halted in the middle of the road. Rob cursed beneath his breath as he tugged hard on the lead line. "I knew she'd not make it to town and back."

Sarah looked to Katie. "Sugar don't mind. She stops and then she don't go another foot. Last week Uncle Robbie got so mad, he left her in the west field. She stood there all night in the same spot. We thought she was stuck like glue."

"Going to turn her into glue," Rob mumbled as he jerked harder on the line. "I've got to get home to milk."

Katie looked up into the darkening sky. The sun was disappearing below the treetops in the west, setting the sky ablaze with color and the forest in darkness.

Katie turned her attention back to Rob and the mule. "Here, let me try."

"It's no use, " Sarah offered. "Sugar won't budge. Not when she gets like this. Not for no one."

"Anyone," Rob corrected.

Katie lowered the sleeping Josh into the basket tied to the mule and took the leather lead line from Rob's hand. As her fingertips brushed his, a strange warmth spread from his hand to hers.

When she looked up, he was looking at her. She felt a little silly. "Let's go, Sugar" she said softly under her breath. Then she leaned and whispered in the mule's ear. She didn't pull at the line at all, but instead, scratched it beneath its chin.

The animal raised its head as she drew away her hand. Katie took a step back, and Sugar followed. Then she scratched it beneath its chin again. The mule took another step. A moment later, she had Sugar walking behind her down the road.

Sarah clapped her hands together, jumping up and down. "Look at that, Uncle Robbie! Never seen anyone get Sugar to move before! She is a witch, isn't she?" Sarah whispered loudly.

"Hush," Rob chided. "There's no such thing as witches. I told you that, noo run ahead and show Miss Katie the way to Sarah's Stand. We're almost home."

As they came over around the bend in the road the land opened up into wide fields, fields Rob's parents had cleared, fields he had cleared. But to the left he saw a yet-to-be-plowed plot. To the right was the pasture fencing that he'd been meaning to mend. Even from here he could hear the cow bellowing. He was late to milking again.

Walking up the road, they passed the original log cabin Rob had lived in as a child. Beyond it, overlooking the bay, was the home he and his father had built of brick from their own kiln . . . the home he had meant for the bride he'd never wed.

The solicitor had made all the arrangements. Rob had paid the fees. But when he had gone to meet his bride on the docks, she had walked off the gangplank on the arm of the ship's captain. She'd wed him crossing the Atlantic.

More bad luck.

He glanced at the woman, Katie, who was leading the mule while being pulled along by Sarah.

Katie. The name was fitting. She was an intelligent woman who apparently had a touch to make things right.

Well, God knew he could use a little good luck.

"Oh," Katie breathed. "What a beautiful house!"

When Rob looked up at the family home all he saw was the shutter that needed repairing and the front step that creaked. When he thought of the house, he thought of the bride who had never seen it and all the money he'd wasted bringing her here for another man. Of course now he was bringing his bride home, but she wouldn't last either, would she?

"Don't expect furniture," Rob said, his tone short. "I sold most of it the winter past."

She looked at him. "Who needs furniture? You could make some this winter when the weather turns cold. Oh, Rob, I've never seen a house so fine."

"It's small. Two rooms and a hallway down, two up."

"It's a perfect house. The land is beautiful. A plot in paradise."

"So I once thought," he said more to himself than to his new bride.

She followed him up the drive toward the house breathing the fresh tangy air that blew in off the bay. The plantation was beautiful with its stretches of turned black soil and lines of pin oaks and pines dividing the fields. In the distance she could see the flat sheet of the glassy bay that stretched into the horizon. "Do you always look at things this way?"

"What way?"

"With your cup half empty instead of half full."

He stopped at the front steps leading up onto the small porch. Sarah ran ahead and through the door. "With the ill luck I've had, it's hard for a man to see things otherwise."

Leaving the mule to stand behind, she walked up to him, dropping her hands to her hips as she happily surveyed her new home. "Well, Rob Cameron, your luck is about to change."

He turned to her, lifting an eyebrow. He watched her as she scooped the baby out of the basket and started back for the house. What a beauty she was with her rich, black hair and dark haunting eyes. They were Indian eyes. "Oh, is it?" he murmured, a hint of amusement in his voice. "Are you tellin' me you're a witch like they say, Katie-girl?"

She started up the steps, but turned back to wink at him. "No such thing as witches, is there, Rob?"

# *Three*

With baby Joshua and little Sarah tucked snugly in their beds, Katie closed her own bedchamber door and lifted her single candlestand to survey her surroundings.

The yellow candlelight cast long shadows across the large, airy room. This was obviously Rob's bedchamber. Though it was plain, it had his touch. There was a large, handsome bedstead with a blue and green quilt thrown over it. A cold brick fireplace dominated one wall. To her left was a chest of drawers, with his clothes folded neatly inside, she guessed. An oval mirror hung over a washbasin stand in the corner of the room. A pair of old boots rested on the floor under one of the windows. The walls were whitewashed, with blue painted chair railing and molding, but lacy curtains hung over the inside window shutters. On top of the chest of drawers was an old painted Indian pot with a sheath of wheat standing in it.

Katie smiled to herself. Rob liked things plain and in place, but he had an eye for beauty, nature's beauty.

She was glad he had given her this room.

Of course, he'd had a mind to send her into the attic when they'd first come this evening. Then, over the supper of cold beaten biscuits and fried bacon he'd insisted upon making her, he'd changed his mind. He said he thought it would be better if she slept near the children who were across the hallway. He said he'd sleep better on the tick on the third floor where it was quiet, but it was obvious to Katie that what he said was not always what he meant. He wanted her to have the comfortable room, maybe he even liked the idea of her sleeping in his bed.

Katie was no fool. She had seen the way he looked at her tonight when he thought she wasn't watching. She had seen him reach out to touch her hand casually, only to withdraw before he made contact. She knew enough about men and their ways to realize that Rob Cameron found her attractive, even if he didn't know it himself yet.

Suddenly realizing how tired she was, Katie carried the candlestand to the bed and set it down on the cherry table. She unlaced her stomacher, folded it neatly, and laid it atop the chest of drawers. Then came her sage homespun gown, and then her shoes and woolen stockings.

Just as she was about to climb into bed she got the oddest feeling. She turned to face the west windows, feeling the hair rise on the back of her neck. Fear . . . She listened but could hear nothing but the wind. Then the feeling was gone as quickly as it had come.

Must be my imagination, she thought. A new house, so many changes . . . Wearing nothing but her shift, she climbed into Rob's bed, beneath the quilt, and blew out the candle.

The goosefeather ticking was firm but comfortable. She could smell the faintest scent of Rob on the sheets. Chilled by the cold night air, she snuggled deeper into the feather tick, the quilt pulled up to her nose, and drifted off to sleep.


*Running . . . Mama was running. Mama slammed the cabin door shut and threw the bolt. Why?*

*"Katie, stay," Mama said, leaning over her and brush-*

ing her lips against her cheek. "Your papa will come for you." She was crying.

"Mama, don't leave me."

Then came the sounds . . . angry voices . . . "Witch! Witch!" they accused. Light from torches shone through the cracks in the cabin wall.

She huddled on the floor wrapped in Mama's cloak. It smelled like Mama, like her herbal poultices and the pine forest. "Mama don't leave me . . ."

"Witch! Witch!" the voices were louder.

They were beating on the door and shuttered windows now. Mama blew out the only tallow candle they owned, leaving them in complete darkness.

"Hush, Katie," she soothed. "Be a brave girl."

"Witch! Sorceress!"

"Whore of a redman!"

Suddenly the cabin was filled with the ominous sound of splintering wood and the door burst open . . .

"Mama!" Katie screamed.

"I've done nothing! Leave me and my child in peace!" Mama cried, holding a staff, her only weapon against the angry crowd that now filled the room.

Katie drew up into a ball on the floor, trying to remain invisible beneath Mama's tattered cloak. She was so frightened that her tiny body shook. The men and women were shouting. They were saying Mama was evil. They were saying she was devil-spawned.

A man reached out to grab Mama by the arm, and Mama swung the staff and hit him hard across the face, knocking his old battered hat off his head.

The man howled in pain.

Two more men reached for Mama.

"Witch! Witch!" the woman carrying a baby shouted. "Kill the witch!"

It all happened so fast . . . a blur of confusion in her mind. Mama took a step back. A man with a crooked *nose lunged for her and Mama tripped. Mama fell hard on the stone hearth and hit her head.*

*Then Mama didn't get up.*

*"No—No!" she cried, crawling toward Mama. "No, mama! Don't leave me alone with them. No! Noooo!"*

*"Katie! Katie!" a voice called from above, from somewhere beyond the horror of the dark cabin.*

*Katie felt someone shaking her. She thrashed about, fighting her mother's attackers.*

*"No!" she screamed. "Not a witch! God's gifts. You killed her! You killed my mama!"*

"Katie!"

But the voice wasn't the dream. It was a gentle voice. A man's voice rich with Scottish undertones. "Katie," he said softly. "Wake up. 'Tis only a dream, hinny."

Katie's eyes flew open. The room was dark. She could feel her heart pounding, her entire body shaking with fear.

Someone was holding her. The past day's events flashed through her head. Married? Had she really married the Scot?

"Rob?"

"Yes, it's all right, lass. Just a bad dream. I'll not harm you. I swear by all that's holy, I won't."

He was holding her in his arms. His strength and the scent of him enveloped her. She was so afraid, but of what? The nightmare . . .

She closed her eyes, still trembling. She lowered her head to rest her cheek in the hollow of his bare shoulder.

Why couldn't she remember the nightmare? Why couldn't she remember what happened to Mama? Why couldn't she remember anything of her father but the smell of him, the color of his suntanned skin, and the turquoise amulet that had hung around his neck on a leather cord?

Rob was running his hand over her head, smoothing her tangled hair. He was speaking beneath his breath,

117

making soft soothing sounds as if she were a small child or an injured animal.

Katie squeezed her eyes shut, clinging to him. She could still feel her heart pounding in her chest. The nightmare was always the same. The cold, suffocating terror and then no memory. When she woke, she was left with nothing but the fear.

"There, there," Rob murmured in her ear. "You're safe enough here, Katie. You're at Sarah's Stand. No one will harm you here. Not as long as I breathe, I swear it."

She took a deep breath, fighting the dizziness that always followed her nightmares. "I'm all right," she managed. Now that she was fully conscious she was all too aware of Rob's touch, of the feel of his hands around her waist, the warmth of his fingertips through the thin material of her shift.

She lifted her head from his shoulder to look into his blue eyes—eyes as blue as the waters of the Chesapeake. "I'm sorry," she whispered. "I . . . I'm here to see that the children don't wake you and—"

"Hush," he chided gently. "Dinna I say it was all right?" He touched her cheek with his work-roughened fingertips, peering into her face. "What made you so afraid? Who's hurt you so?"

She took her hands from his shoulders and dropped them into her lap. She stared at her hands, thinking how much they looked like Mama's. "They say my mother died. They said she fell in an accident when I was four. I was there, but I don't remember it. They took me away and sold me on the auction block for an indenture of twenty-one years."

"Your father?"

She shook her head. "He was supposed to come for me. I remember waiting. But he never came." A smile lifted the corners of her mouth. "I don't remember anything about him except that he was tall, and kind, and

118

he had the blackest hair . . . and he smelled good." She looked up at Rob. "Like you."

His mouth was so close to hers that she could feel his breath on her lips.

"I could kiss you so easily, lass," she heard him say.

"Then why don't you?"

"Our agreement?"

"Our agreement," she whispered, mesmerized by his mouth.

"Our agreement, remember?" he echoed. "A marriage of convenience. You get your freedom." He got up from the bed suddenly, as if realizing for the first time what he was about.

"You get your housekeeper for a year's time," Katie said, drawing the quilt around her bare shoulders.

He backed toward the door. "Purely a platonic relationship."

"An annulment come next All Hallows Eve."

He had reached the doorway now. He stood there awkwardly for a moment, the silver light of the moon across his bare chest. He was barefoot, wearing nothing but a pair of broadcloth breeches. His chest was as broad as any Katie had ever seen, and his muscles were well defined. A trail of blond hair ran from his breast bone to disappear beneath the waistband of his breeches.

"If . . . if you think you're all right now, I . . . I'll go," he said.

She tightened the quilt around her neck. "I . . . I'm fine. I'm sorry." She could feel her cheeks coloring. She'd never thought herself shy, but the sight of Rob's bare chest made her heart flutter. It wasn't that she was a stranger to a man's body. A tavern keeper who'd once owned her indenture had taken her virginity when she was thirteen. She hadn't been a bit sorry when a few weeks later he'd fallen off his horse in a drunken stupor and broken his own neck.

Many men in the last few years had tried to take Katie

by force or sweet talk, but no one had succeeded, not even old man Matthews who'd threatened to sell her to the Iroquois Indians if she didn't lift her skirts for him.

Rob still hung in the doorway looking at her. "Good night then," he finally said softy.

She watched him close the door behind himself, and then she rolled onto her side and slept again.

Katie rose early the next morning and immediately set to the task of getting the household in order. She threw open every window to let the warm autumn sunshine in and allow the soft, salty breeze coming in off the bay to blow away the stale smells of the house.

She fed baby Joshua oatmeal mush and sat him on the cleanly swept floor in the kitchen, giving him a pewter spoon and an old tin funnel to play with. She sent Sarah to the hen house for eggs and began to make up a bowl of hotcake batter. Finding an old spider pan in a cabinet, she set to work frying hotcakes on the kitchen hearth for the morning meal.

By the time Rob came into the house from milking the cow and feeding the livestock, she'd set the table in one of the two empty rooms on the first floor and was serving warm cakes to Sarah.

"Uncle Robbie! Look what Katie done!"

"Did." Rob entered the parlor a little hesitantly. Katie noticed he must have shaved outside. He wore his blond hair tied back in a queue with a leather thong, but several short tendrils of damp hair curled at his ears.

"Guess what she did?"

Katie began to slide hotcakes onto the pewter plate at the head of the sturdy table.

"What did she do?" he asked, taking his seat.

"She made hotcakes and she even found a jar of honey." The little girl swirled her finger in her plate and then licked the sweet stickiness from it.

120

"Honey?" Rob looked up. "I thought the honey was long gone. We've been eating our bread and cakes dry for weeks. My sister was always the one to gather the honey. One bee welt on my back and I'm useless for a week."

Katie shrugged as she dropped another cake onto Sarah's plate. "Found the honey in the cellar—a whole crock."

"Where's the boy?" Rob cut off a corner of an oatcake with his fork and thrust it into his mouth. The cakes were light and sweet. "I haven't heard him all morning."

"Sleeping." Katie pushed the plate of extra hotcakes to the center of the table and started for the kitchen, a frame building built onto the back of the brick structure. "I moved his cradle into the kitchen. I hope you don't mind."

"No." Rob took another mouthful of cake, thinking he hadn't had anything this good to eat in years. His sister's cooking had been adequate, but never like his mother's. "Do whatever you like to make your tasks easier. I just always put the lad to sleep in his room because that's what his mother did."

Katie brushed at a cobweb on the doorjamb. "It's scary for a boy so young to be alone in a room so big. I thought he'd sleep better down here with me and Sarah."

"The noise won't wake him?" Rob reached for a second helping of hotcakes.

"Noise doesn't bother babies as much as silence, I always thought." She offered him a hesitant smile.

They both seemed to be slightly uncomfortable with each other this morning. Katie couldn't help remembering what Rob's touch had felt like last night. She looked at him. Perhaps uncomfortable was not right—awkward maybe. Neither seemed to be sure how to behave. They were married by the law. They were going to live together in the same house for the next year. Some sort of relationship acceptable to both of them had to be found.

Katie turned to go back to the kitchen.

"Where you going?" Rob asked. He was drinking down a cup of warm buttermilk.

"Back to the kitchen to clean up."

"You've eaten, already?" He almost sounded disappointed.

"No." She twisted her hands in the apron she'd found in the pantry.

"Then sit." He tapped the wooden chair beside him. "Eat with me and Sarah. We want you to be part of the family, don't we Sarah?"

"Yea!"

He pointed to the little girl with his fork. "For the sake of the children, of course."

Katie slid onto the chair. "Of course."

Rob lifted the serving plate from the center of the table and dropped it down in front of her. Before she could get to her feet, he was up and retrieving a pewter fork from the silver box on the mantel.

As Katie sampled her breakfast she looked about the room. It was true the house was sparsely furnished, but what was here was of the finest quality. The walls were covered with floral wall papering, no doubt, shipped from England and carefully hung. Brocade curtains of hunter green hung over the huge windows. A picture of a woman with red hair rested over the fireplace mantel. She wasn't beautiful, but she had a strong jaw and a pretty smile.

"My mother, Sarah," Rob said as if reading her thoughts.

"My grandmama," Sarah said. "I was named after her 'cause of my red hair."

Katie laughed. She liked this sitting down to eat with Sarah and Rob. It was as if she belonged to a real family. In all the other homes she'd worked in she'd eaten standing up in the kitchen, or even on the back stoop. As a child she'd always dreamed about what it would be like to have a family. "I'd never have guessed she was your namesake if you hadn't told me," Katie teased Sarah.

Sarah turned to her uncle. "Uncle Robbie, mama cat Maria's kittens is runnin' all about in the hayloft."

"Are running," Rob corrected her.

"Are running. She's got a black one. I call him Puddum. Can I have him in the house to sleep with me? Can I?"

"Cats don't belong in the house. You know that."

"Grandmama said black cats were really witches and that's why you didn't let them in the house."

"That's nonsense." Rob wiped his mouth with the linen napkin Katie had left for him. She'd worked in enough fancy houses to know how a table was set. "You don't let cats in the house because they're liable to make a mess on the floor."

"Not Puddum, Puddum wouldn't do that."

"Sarah," Katie said gently. "Hush, and finish eating now. You can help me with the dishes."

Rob pushed out of his chair, the wood scraping wood. "Excellent breakfast, Katie," he said, patting him stomach. "Can't say that I've had that good a meal to start off the day in a long time."

"I found some dried meat in a barrel in the cellar, and Sarah showed me the root cellar. I thought I'd make stew for supper."

He walked to the open window. The sunlight poured through the bull's-eye glass panes to highlight his blond hair in golden warmth. Katie watched his back ripple beneath his thin muslin shirt as he leaned on the sill.

"I've the wheat in the back west field to cut today, but I think I'll wander over to Widow Hartly's and see that she's got enough wood cut to last her a while. Her property borders Sarah's Stand to the south. You can send Sarah on Sugar to bring me a bit of bread and cheese at noonday. She knows the way."

"All right." Katie rose and began to clear the plates.

She thought it was a little odd for a man who had as much to do as Rob claimed to be standing around with the women staring out the window at the bay.

As she lifted up the stack of dirty pewter dishes, he reached across her. "Let me take them in the kitchen for ye on my way out."

She pulled back, lagging. "Allow me to earn my keep while I'm here. Now out with you. Tend to your fields while Sarah and I tend to the house."

She followed him to the lean-to kitchen, where he took a three cornered leather hat off a peg. She opened the back door for him and watched him walk away from the house, disappearing into the cool morning sunshine. A half-grown black kitten curled at Katie's feet, and she shooed it inside.

"Puddum!" Sarah called, scooping the kitten up into her arms and carrying it off into the house. "I knew Katie would let you in. Katie says there's no such thing as real witches."

As Katie swung the door shut, she could have sworn she heard Rob whistling as he cut across the yard.


Katie spent the remainder of the morning cleaning up the kitchen and surveying her new surroundings. After rubbing baby Joshua's gums with a soothing paste she made from dried herbs hanging from the kitchen eaves, she took the children down into the cellar. There, she arranged the foodstuffs so that she had a better idea of what was on hand and what must be gathered before the first cold snap.

At noonday she put Sarah on Sugar's back with a tin of bread and cheese, and a crock of water sweetened with mint. She encouraged the little girl to spend the afternoon playing near her uncle, saying the sunshine made little girl's grow. Then, after putting the baby down for a nap in the kitchen, she set herself to the task of washing dirty clothing. After scrubbing and wringing out the laundry, she went out in the back yard to hang it up on the clothesline.

As she was hanging up one of Rob's shirts, facing away from the house, she felt the hair rise on the back of her neck. Someone or something was watching her. She spun around, but saw nothing save a red hen scratching in the dirt at the back step. She turned back to the clothesline and Rob's wet, lawn shirt in her hand.

Another minute passed and she moved down the clothesline with one of Sarah's smocks. She glanced uneasily over her shoulder. Then she saw it.

Through the kitchen window she saw two dark eyes staring out through the wavy glass.

Katie threw the wet smock over the line and ran for the kitchen. All she could think of was little Joshua sleeping in his cradle near the fireplace. She grabbed a shovel left by the back door and ran up the two wooden steps into the kitchen, her weapon in hand.

Seated on the stool in the corner of the room was an old Indian man. He was dressed in a quilled leather tunic and leather leggings, a knife sheath on one hip. His waist-length silver-gray hair was worn in a single long braid. Katie didn't know how old he was, but it was obvious he'd seen many years come and go. His sun-bronzed faced was as wrinkled and creased as a pair of damp breeches left in a heap on the floor too long.

He held a leftover hotcake in one hand and the honey pot in the other. He looked up at Katie and dipped the hotcake into the honey. He took a bite. "This man wondered when you would come. I have waited many years, *daanus* of my *giis.*"

She stared at him. For a split second something seemed so familiar about him, and then he was just an old man again. Intuitively knowing the Indian meant her no harm, Katie lowered the shovel. "What did you say?"

125

He lifted his lined palm. "Nothing but the rambling of an old man." He went on eating his hotcake.

"Who are you?"

He sucked the honey from the cold hotcake and dipped it again, taking his time in replying. "This man did not mean to frighten you, child."

"I . . . I wasn't afraid." She leaned the shovel against the doorframe and went to check on Joshua. He slept, oblivious to the intruder. "You just startled me."

Finished with his hotcake the old man set down the honey pot and licked his long fingers. "Good." He nodded. "Like my wife made many autumns ago."

Katie dropped her hands to her hips. "I don't mean to be unfriendly, but why are you here?"

Just then, Sarah came running through the door. "Grandpapa Two Bears!" She threw herself into the old man's arms. He caught her beneath the armpits and swung her around in a circle, his strength remarkable for such a wizened old man. "What did you bring me? What did you bring me?"

The Indian set her gently on the floor and tapped his buckskin tunic. "Nothing, nothing at all for bad *ommamundot.*"

"But I wasn't a bad child!" Sarah hopped onto one foot and then the other. "Was I, Katie? Was I?"

Katie watched Sarah and the old man. Obviously he was a familiar visitor. "No, you haven't been bad."

From inside his tunic he pulled out a tiny leather fringed bag on a long leather cord. Sarah oohed and ahed. "What is it? What is it?"

Two Bear dropped the leather pouch onto her head. "A medicine bag to keep away the evil spirits."

Sarah pulled at the top of the bag. "It's sewed shut," she said, wrinkling her face. I can't see what's inside."

Two Bears brushed her hands away with his larger ones. "You do not look inside. That is part of the magic, Sarah Tshitshikniin."

The little girl beamed at Katie. "That's what Grandpapa Two Bears calls me because I chatter. It means mockingbird in his language."

Katie stared at the old man. What was it about him that made her feel so odd in the pit of her stomach?

Just then Rob came into the kitchen from outside. He tugged off his hat and dropped it onto a peg near the door.

"Uncle Robbie, look who's here!"

"Two Bears." Rob offered a dusty hand. "We've missed you."

Two Bears squeezed Rob's hand. "I told you she would come, she who would bring the magic back to these lands."

Katie watched as Rob gave a little nod, and then laughed off the old man's words awkwardly. "Well, we'll see, won't we Two Bears. Naught but time will tell."

Sarah pulled on the old man's hand. "I have a kitten called Puddum. Want to see him?" She led the Indian through the kitchen and into the larger wing of the house.

Rob stood awkwardly in the doorway. "I guess you met Two Bears."

She wiped her hands on her homespun apron, though they were no longer damp. "Yes . . . yes. He startled me. He came inside whilst I was out hanging laundry. He was watching me through the window."

Rob walked to the drinking-water bucket and lifted the wooden lid. "I'm sorry. I dinna think to warn you. He comes and goes as he pleases on Sarah's Stand—has since I was a lad." He drank from the ladle. "Sometimes he goes months without coming. Then he stays a month. Once we dinna see him for two years. I feared he was dead."

Realizing she was staring at Rob again, standing there in the center of the kitchen like a knot on a fallen log, she went to the hearth and began to busy herself raking the coals to start supper. "He said some strange things," she remarked.

127

Rob wiped the water from his mouth with the back of his hand. "Aye, but he is old. I ken he's not always right in the mind, but he's a good man. I'll not turn him away from Sarah's Stand, not as long as I breathe."

Katie knelt on the brick hearth and reached for the heavy iron spider she'd fried the hotcakes on that morning. "I didn't mean to say he shouldn't be here." She looked up to see Rob bending on one knee to lift the iron spider from her hands.

"I ken you didn't," he said softly, his hand brushing hers.

Here they were again, too close. She could smell the scent of the sweet Virginia soil on his calloused hands and the slight hint of mint on his breath. Katie found herself staring into his clear blue eyes, drawn to him as she had never been drawn to anything or anyone before.

"I don't mean to make this awkward between us," he said. "I can't seem to help myself. I keep thinking about you, where you've spent your years, doing what—just a lonely man, I suppose, too long without companionship."

She reached out and brushed her fingertips against his cheek. It was stubbly from the day's growth of blond beard. "I thought it was me, the way I can't keep my eyes from you." She could feel her cheeks growing warm, wondered what had possessed her to say such a thing.

"Just one kiss," he said, surprising them both. "That would end the curiosity and we could go on with our duties, me in the fields and you in the house with the children."

Her mouth turned up in a hesitant smile. "One kiss," she whispered.

"Just one," he murmured as he brought his lips to hers.

It was an innocent enough kiss, lasting barely a second, but the heat of his mouth made her hands tremble and her heart beat skip a beat. When he pulled away, she touched her finger to her mouth. "Curiosity satisfied?"

"No," he whispered.

This time when he kissed her, she raised her hands and lowered them to his shoulders. She heard him drop the iron spider. She felt his broad strong hands wrap around her waist and pull her against him.

This time his kiss was not one of naive inquisitiveness. This was a man's kiss filled with strength and demand. Katie parted her lips, reveling in the feel of his arms around her, the taste of him. As his tongue delved deep into her mouth, she wondered, How long have I waited for a man to kiss me like this? How long have I waited for this man?

"Hinny," he murmured, his breath warm in her ear. "I dinna mean to take advantage of you."

She pressed a finger to his lips. "You took nothing I didn't offer. I'm a woman full grown. I know what I'm about."

He stood and pulled her up with one sweep of his arm. "That's good, because one of us should."

She laughed, brushing a stray lock of blond hair that had escaped his queue off his forehead. It was an innocent enough gesture but in the scheme of things seemed strangely intimate. "I . . . I don't know what it is that's between us, but I'm not opposed to the thought of waiting to see," she said carefully.

He caught her chin with his hand and lifted it until he was staring into her eyes. "I tell Sarah there's no such thing as witches, and yet I feel under a spell, your spell."

"There's no such thing as witches, Rob Cameron," she said softly and then she turned back to the hearth to begin the evening meal.

# Four

The sound of a thunderstorm rolling in off the Chesapeake Bay woke Katie. Far in the distance she could hear the rumble of thunder; she could smell the impending rain. Grabbing the flannel nightrobe off the end of her bed, she slipped into it.

Last night, after the children were tucked into bed and Two Bears was settled in the barn, Rob had brought her an entire chest of clothing that had belonged to his sister.

"Sturdy clothes," he had said. "Perfectly good, if you don't mind wearing a dead woman's skirts."

"As long as it won't hurt you to see them on me, I'd be honored," Katie had answered, standing in the doorway of her bedchamber, wanting to invite him in, but knowing she couldn't.

So he had left her the trunk and now she was the owner of more clothing than she had possessed in her lifetime. There were homespun everyday dresses, linen nightrails with tiny white buttons, thick wool stockings, embroidered stomachers, and even two Sunday sacque gowns fashioned of expensive French cloth. The funny thing was, when she had opened the chest after Rob had gone, she had felt a sense of comfort, a closeness to Sarah's mother. The woman seemed to be calling out to her. *Love my children as I have,* she said in Katie's mind. *Make them your own.*

Katie went to the west window in her new nightrobe. It was barely dawn. She couldn't yet see the bay below, but she could hear the tide washing in. She could feel the strength of the approaching storm. She could taste the salty, damp air on the tip of her tongue. She pulled on her wool stockings and padded down the hall to check on the children. They were still asleep.

She came down the front steps. The house was quiet and chilly. She halted on the landing. There it was again . . . that strange feeling in the house that came and went so quickly that it would be easy to ignore.

Doom. Fear.

But Katie wasn't afraid, not for herself, at least. It was someone else's fear she felt. The children's parents' perhaps? She didn't know. All she knew was that there was some terrible sense of foreboding that at this instant hung heavy in the morning air.

Then it was gone.

She came down the steps, walked through the hallway, and took the two steps down into the kitchen. Rob was there adding a log to the glowing embers on the hearth. He looked up. "Startled you?"

She offered him a hesitant smile. "A little. I didn't hear you rise. I thought everyone else was still"—she watched him walk toward her—"asleep," she finished softly. Heavens, but he was handsome this morning, all rumpled and sleepy looking. But he was freshly shaved and his farmer's hands clean. The smile on his face was for her.

He didn't stop until he was half a step in front of her. She could feel her skin tingling. She watched him with round, dark eyes. Everything was happening so quickly, so unexpectedly. Katie kept trying to tell herself this was mere physical attraction between two lonely adults, but her heart told her it was more . . . and that was what frightened her.

"You slept well?" he inquired, quietly, as if fearful to

131

shatter the morning silence and this strange, magical excitement that leaped between them.

"*Yes*," she answered. *In your bed, where I dreamed I slept in your arms.* "Thank you for the clothes." She picked at the sleeve of her soft flannel nightrobe, realizing for the first time that she was standing here in the kitchen with Rob in her nightclothes . . . as if she really was his wife. "The fit is nearly perfect."

He touched the high collar of the nightrobe with one finger. "Soft," he murmured. "Like you."

She took his hand, entwining her fingers comfortably in his. "So what are you about so early in the morning?"

"It's going to rain," he said. The smile faded from his angular face as he withdrew his hand from hers. "I've still that whole field of late wheat to cut. The rain will ruin it." He turned away, sinking his fist into his palm. "Damnation, I should have done it yesterday when the sun was shining."

Her gaze rested on his broad back. He had done a good deed, spending all of yesterday cutting the Widow Hartly's wood and now he might lose his entire crop of wheat for his kindness. Thunder echoed ominously in the distance. "You've still time."

"The entire field and me a man with only two hands? Only the All Mighty could save my wheat noo."

"So pray to the All Mighty, but row toward shore." She grabbed his hat off its hook and tossed it to him. "You get yourself to the field and start cutting. I'll be there directly."

"It's too cold out for the children, and I don't want them left here alone. I'd be lying if I said I couldn't use your help, but the boy and Sarah are more important than any field of wheat. If we lose it, I'll manage this winter somehow. We've heard nothing of the pirates for weeks but—"

"I wouldn't leave them. I'll take them to the Widow

Hartly's. No doubt she'd appreciate the company on such a dreary day."

"The Widow Hartly? I dinna ask for help before, and I'm not about to ask for it now," he said hotly.

"Then you're a fool, Rob Cameron." She looked him straight in the eye, her hands resting stubbornly on her hips. He stared at her as if she'd just sprouted wings, but she went on. "When you give a friend a hand, you must let them repay the favor, else it's not a favor any longer. You constantly do for others, the way Sarah says you do, without letting them help you, and they become beholden to you. No one wants to be beholden to anyone, save to the good Lord."

He looked down at his dusty work boots.

She softened her tone as she brushed her fingertips across his sleeve. "Just go on with you, and hurry. The storm will wait."

Rob looked up at her, a strange look on his face. Then it was gone. He took his hat and pulled it down over his neatly combed hair and walked out the door.

Katie ran out of the kitchen and up the stairs to wake and dress the children. If they were really going to beat the storm, she would have to hurry.


An hour and a half later as Rob turned on a row, swinging his scythe, he spotted Katie and Two Bears cutting across the field toward him. Katie's long dark hair whipped about her face in the wind and her blue homespun skirting clung to her legs, flashing a fair amount of shapely ankle and calf. She waved to him as she tugged her bonnet down further on her head. Two Bears struck out toward the mule and cart Rob had left standing at the edge of the wheat field.

Rob waved back and leaned to take another swipe at the golden ocean of wheat that stretched out before him. Thunder rumbled in the distance, closer than before. The storm was moving in off the bay fast. Already he could smell the rain in the air. He'd never get the wheat in. Not half of it—not before the storm hit.

"You cut, I'll go along and pick up behind you, tie up the sheaves, and load them," Katie called above the whistle of the wind.

"Harvesting is nae woman's work," Rob argued.

"This will not be the first time a woman's taken a man's load upon her shoulder. Once the cart is full, Two Bears will take the wheat to the barn where it'll stay dry."

This black-haired Katie of his was a bold, brave woman. This Katie of his . . .

Rob kept his head down as he swung rhythmically. The wind was so cold it bit through his clothing, chilling him to the bone despite the heat of his exertion. But wheat was flour, and flour would make bread for little Joshua and Sarah, for Katie, to see them through the winter. "It's too cold for you and the old man out here," he hollered to her as she began to fill her arms with sheaves of wheat. "Go back to the house. Go back to the children."

"The children are with the widow." Katie knelt, pulling cornstring from inside the canvas coat she'd found in the kitchen, and began to tie up the bundle of wheat. "She was pleased to have the company, just like I said."

Two Bears, wrapped in a hide cloak, sat hunched on the bench seat of the two-wheeled cart, the reins clutched in his hand. He nodded to Rob and went on puffing the clay pipe clenched in his teeth.

"We'll never make it," Rob called to her. "The sky's going to open up any minute. We're going to get drenched."

"Just cut! The storm will wait, I tell you." Katie walked to the cart and dropped the tied sheaf into it. She gazed up at the sky. Dark, black swirling clouds hovered over the bay to the west and they were moving quickly

134

this way. "Hold back," she whispered fervently. "Just a little longer."

Two Bears glanced up at the sky and then back at Katie. "The great *kumhaak* will wait, *giis daanus?*" he asked in his gravelly voice.

"It will wait," she answered softly, her gaze meeting his.

He nodded in understanding, and looked to Rob who was bent over again, swinging the scythe in long fluid movements. "If my *giis daanus* says the great clouds will wait, they will wait." When Rob made no response but to scowl, Two Bears went back to puffing his pipe.

Katie glanced west again. "Easy," she whispered. "Easy does it."

Rob turned around, wiping his perspiring forehead with the back of his hand. "Did you say something, Katie?"

She bent to grab another armful of wheat. "Just the wind," she answered, running for the cart. "Keep cutting!"

In two hours' time, she had picked up all the wheat Rob had left in the field and now she was following behind him, picking up what he cut and dropped. With the cart filled with stacked sheaves of wheat again, Two Bears started for the barns.

"Just a little longer," Katie whispered, looking up at the storm that now hung over them, blacking out the sun. "No rain," she murmured beneath her breath. "Not yet . . . please."

Rob turned to look at her as if he'd heard her voice again, but he didn't question her this time. He leaned on the handle of the scythe, catching his breath. "I've never seen a storm like this. It should have hit us full force an hour ago."

Katie looked up at the dark swirling clouds that seemed so close now she thought if she stood on tiptoe she could pull one down into her arms. Thunder boomed

135

and lightning zigzagged directly overhead. There was a hint of the smell of charred wood in the air. "I told you it would wait," she said. "Look, we're already half done."

Staring at her for a split second, Rob lifted the long straight-handled scythe and began to swing to and fro as he'd been swinging it since he was a boy.

Two Bears returned with the mule cart and Katie began tying and loading the sheaves of wheat. Time passed until Katie lost all concept of the hour. Lean over, pick up the wheat, tie and carry . . . Lean, pick up, tie and carry . . .

After what seemed an eternity, she stood and pressed her hands to her aching back. How long had they been out here? Five hours? Six? Her arms throbbed so badly they were weak, and her fingers had lost all feeling from the cold; but she could see the end of the last row ahead. She smiled, glancing up at the sky. "Just a few more minutes," she murmured.

When Rob felled the last standing stalks of wheat, Katie gathered them in her arms and tied up the bundle. "Let me help you," Rob said, dropping beside her on one knee.

"No." She pushed his hands aside. "The last of the wheat, the *maiden,* is woman's work." As Rob watched her, she pulled a long blue hair ribbon from inside her canvas coat. She wrapped it around the sheaf of wheat and then closed her eyes, murmuring a blessing of thanks for the harvest. Then she looked up at the angry dark clouds overhead and whispered, "Thank you."

Two Bears appeared over her shoulder. He lifted his birdlike arms heavenward, spreading his tattered hide cloak like wings, and closed his eyes, chanting in his native tongue. His words finished, he laid his hand on the ribboned sheaf of wheat and smiled.

Katie smiled at the old Indian and then picked up the wheat sheaf and pushed it into Rob's hands. "You have to save it until next year. It will bring good luck." She looked up into the sky and then back at him. "Looks like it's going to rain," she said, still smiling.

A grin tugged at the corners of his mouth. "I did'na think it was possible, lass. Ye couldn't have convinced me this morning that we would get this wheat in, not for all the tea in China." He was staring at her, his arms wrapped around the wheat. "How'd you do it?" he asked, his voice barely a whisper.

But Katie only laughed and turned away. She laid her hand on Two Bears' shoulder. "Thank you for your help, friend. Better get the last of the wheat into the barn. I think I feel rain."

The old man was grinning as he loped to the mule cart and pulled himself up onto the seat. "This old man needs no thanks. Thanks are not needed for family."

Rob dropped the ribboned *maiden* sheaf into the cart. He put his hands out to Katie. "You ride. I'll give you a boost up."

She patted the mule, and Sugar lifted her head and the cart rolled past them, bound for the barnyard. "No. Let Two Bears get the wheat in. I'll walk." She looked up at him. The first drops of cold rain were just beginning to hit her face.

For a moment Rob and Katie stood watching the last cart of wheat pull away. Then she felt him take her hand. He looked up into the sky as the rain began to fall harder. "We'll have to make a run for it if we're not going to get soaked."

She laughed as he pulled on her hand and she ran to catch up. "We'll not make it," she warned.

Sure enough, they were not halfway across the cut wheat field, when the heavens opened up and cold rain fell on them like overturned buckets of well water.

Katie and Rob ran hand in hand across the field, down into the gully and up toward the house beyond the row of trees. By the time they reached the barn and Rob flung open the door, they were soaked to the bone.

"Oh!" Katie cried, her teeth chattering. "I've never been so cold in my life!" She pulled off her bonnet and shook her head. She knew she must appear a sight with her black hair plastered to her head. Self-consciously, she tried to brush her tangled wet hair with her fingers.

Two Bears had driven the mule cart right into the barn and was now unloading the wheat sheaf by sheaf to stand in neat rows on the barn floor.

"I know the wheat should have lain in the sun a day or two, but as long as we leave space between the sheaves, I think they'll dry fine."

Rob pulled off his hat and wiped his wet face with a soggy sleeve. "Come inside, Two Bears, and have something hot to eat and drink."

The old man waved a hand. "This man did not get wet. We were too fast for the rain, the mule and I." He shooed them with a wrinkled hand. "Go inside. When the rain ceases I will walk to the widow's and share her English *manake* tea with her. I'll sleep the night in her kitchen and bring the little ones home in the morning."

"No." Rob pulled his wet hat back over his head. "I'll go get them in the cart."

Katie laid a hand on Rob's forearm. "The widow asked if they could spend the night. She and Sarah were going to make gingerbread. I said it would be all right."

"The children belong here with us at night. They—"

"They wanted to stay. I asked Sarah. Besides, it will be good for Martha. She says she needs something to occupy her. She says she's lonely in that big house now that her son's moved further north."

Rob looked as if he wanted to protest, but he didn't.

What is he thinking? Katie wondered. That it will be just the two of us alone here in the house tonight? Of course, that hadn't occurred to her when she'd agreed to let the children stay the night with Widow Hartly, but now the thought burned in her mind.

138

Katie hugged herself for warmth. "I'm going in to change and start something to eat."

"I'll check the stock and be in behind you." Rob opened the squeaky door for her, and a gust of wind cut through the barn.

Katie made a run for it.

Inside the kitchen, she peeled off the soaking wet, canvas work coat and her hat. Even with the overcoat, she was soaked through to the skin. Shivering, she went to the fireplace and stoked up the coals. She was just adding a log when she heard the kitchen door open and close behind her. She didn't turn around. She knew it was Rob.

He came up behind her slowly and lowered his hands to rest on each of her hips. She turned in his arms to face him. It was as if she had lost control of her own movements. It was he who controlled her thoughts, her emotions, her feelings now.

"Tell me how you did it," he whispered. He leaned to brush his lips against hers as if it was the most natural thing. "Are ye a witch, sweet Katie?" he asked in his deep Scottish burr.

She closed her eyes as their lips touched. She was so cold she was trembling, but there was a heat beginning to build in the pit of her stomach, a heat that ran through her veins warming her from the inside out. "Nay. Hush your talk of witches." She rose up on her toes, this time being the one to initiate the kiss. "To accuse someone of witchcraft is wrong. It can damn not just the witch but the accuser."

He threaded his finger through her wet hair. "Ach, Katie, I try to tell myself this isn't right." He kissed the tip of her nose. "I try to tell myself I'm taking advantage of the situation." He kissed her chin, her cheek. "I try to tell myself this will pass, that it's naught but an infatuation."

She ran her hands over his broad back, feeling the ridges in the cold wet cloth that clung to his skin. He was kissing her, confusing her. "I tell myself the same," she answered, a husky catch in her voice. "But . . ." She looked up into his blue-eyed gaze. "But I don't know."

He pulled her hard against him, crushing his mouth against hers. Katie dragged her nails down his back, pressing her body against his, wanting to feel his hard, muscular form against the soft curves of her woman's body.

"Rob, Rob," she whispered against his lips.

When he brought his hand up to cup her breast she heard herself moan. This was not the first time she'd ever been fondled, but it was the first time any man had awakened such heat in her, such sudden, overwhelming desire.

"Rob, Rob . . ."

"Katie . . ."

He pushed her wet gown off her shoulders and tugged at the drawstring at the bodice of her linen shift. When the material gave way, her breasts sprang from their wet confinement into the warmth of his hands . . . his mouth.

"Katie, let me love you," Rob crooned, going down on one knee, guiding one full rounded breast to his mouth until his tongue touched her puckered nipple. Katie rested her hands on his broad shoulders, her head flung back as she gasped for breath. What he was doing with his mouth . . . sucking, tugging at her nipples, filling her with the most exquisite, rippling pleasure.

"Rob, we shouldn't."

"We be husband and wife," he said in a breathy masculine voice, thick with the sound of a Highland burr. "There can be no shame in it, hinny."

She wrapped her arms around his neck, standing, he down on one knee, his wet head nestled between her breasts. "Married, yes," she managed. "But we can't use that as an excuse. Make love to me, Rob, and I'm no longer your servant. I will be your wife, forever . . ."

He pressed a kiss to one breast and then rose so that he was looking directly into her eyes again. "I'll not

140

force you, not ever, Katie. I swear by all that's holy I won't. 'Tis your choice to make."

She brushed her fingertips across his lips. "A little time, please, Rob. Just so we know it's right. Forever is a long time."

"If it's my commitment you're fearful of, lass, I dinna think it will be a problem." He laughed easily. "I'm a man with two wee children who need a mama. I'm a man in need of a woman like you to love."

Katie felt tears gather in the corner of her eyes. When had she fallen in love with Rob Cameron? Was it this instant, or the moment she saw him at the auction two days ago? "It's not you, Rob, it's me I worry over. You don't know me. You don't know——"

He touched her lips with the tip of his finger. "It doesn't matter. None of it matters. Be ye Satan herself, I'm willing to pledge my troth to have ye."

She kissed him full on the mouth. "A few days, a few weeks. Let's give ourselves that—just to be certain it's what we want."

He pulled her against him and rested his chin on the top of her head, smoothing her wet hair with his hand. "Take all the time ye need, Katie. Just know that I'm ready when ye give the word . . ."

# Five

Katie sat on a milking stool in the yard, churning butter in the wooden churn trapped between her knees. Sarah frolicked, rolling a big orange pumpkin in the grass that had turned from green to brown in the last week. The canopy of pin oak branches over their heads was now stripped of leaves and hung silent and skeletal. A cool autumn breeze blew in off the bay, warning the citizens of the tidewater that Father Winter was not far behind.

Little Joshua slept in his cradle in the cozy kitchen, with the door slightly ajar so Katie could hear him. Yesterday two pearly teeth had popped through his swollen lower gums, the source of his contrariness, she was certain. Rob swore it was a miracle that such an unhappy babe could so suddenly turn into a laughing, hand-clapping child.

Nearly a month had passed since Katie and Rob and Two Bears had brought in the wheat. Since then, Katie and Rob had fallen into a comfortable daily routine. He worked all day in the fields and in the barnyard, while she cared for the children and prepared the house for the coming winter. But come evening, the hours were Katie and Rob's alone. With the children asleep and Two Bears bedded down in the Widow Hartly's kitchen where he'd decided to spend the winter, Katie and Rob had time to talk and get to know each other.

They talked for hours on end, sometimes about trivial matters, the children's manners, Rob's plans for their schooling, the old mare who was miraculously pregnant by the neighbor's prized steed. But other times they talked about the future—their future together. Despite the desire they both felt for each other, they had abstained. They kissed and held hands, they talked and laughed. Rob played his violin and Katie sang for him. Rob swore she really had brought him good luck. The days passed so quickly, so pleasurably, that sometimes even Katie found it hard to believe her good fortune. The only thing that cast a shadow over her happiness was the strange foreboding that still haunted her in the house, and now even outside in the yard.

Katie looked up from her churning. She could feel that the butter was almost set. Where had Sarah gotten to now? "Sarah?"

The little girl came running around the corner of the house from the direction of the apple orchard. "Katie! Katie!" she called.

Katie jumped up in alarm. She could tell by Sarah's voice that something was wrong. "What is it?"

"Oh, Katie!" Sarah halted at Katie's feet, something clutched in her small hand. "Katie, it's dead." She opened her hand to reveal a small brown wren lying lifeless in her palm. A tear ran down her cheek. "I know it's silly to cry over a dumb bird, but it was one of the wrens hatched in the nest in the apple orchard. They was my mama's wrens. She left out her hair cuttings for them to make a nest." She looked up at Katie with Rob's blue eyes. I don't want the bird to be dead."

"Oh, let me see," Katie said, taking the little bird from her hand. It was still warm. "No, no," she soothed, petting the little thing with one finger. "Maybe it's not dead. Maybe it's just sleeping."

"It's dead," Sarah whimpered. "I'm not a baby that I don't know what dead is. The leaves on the ground are dead. My mama and dada are dead, and that wren is dead."

Katie covered the bird in her hand with her palm and closed her eyes. She brought her forehead to her cupped hands and whispered beneath her breath. Then she opened her hands and threw them open.

The little wren flew off her palm and soared into the blue sky.

Sarah squealed with delight. "Oh! You did it, Katie! You did it!" She jumped up and down. "You saved my bird!" The she turned back to Katie. "You saved my bird," she repeated slowly. "It was dead and you made it alive again."

"I told you it wasn't dead," Katie said, trying to laugh off the child's seriousness.

Sarah's voice dropped to a hushed whisper. "You really are a witch, aren't you, Katie? It's just like the people in town say."

Katie stared down at the little pigtailed redhead she loved as her own. She grabbed Sarah's hands and sank down onto the dry leaves, pulling Sarah close so that she could look into her eyes. "You mustn't say that, Sarah, not ever," she insisted.

"But you are a witch! You held back the storm so Uncle Robbie could get in the wheat. You make the mule walk when no one else can. You made old Penny horse get a baby. You made Joshy stop crying, you—"

Katie grabbed Sarah and pulled her against her chest in a tight hug. She smoothed her bright hair. "You mustn't say it, Sarah. My mama died because people said she was a witch."

Sarah looked up at Katie. "But—"

Katie brought a finger to her lips. "We all have talents Sarah, all of us. They are different, but they're God-

144

given. You have to remember that. Do you understand what I'm trying to tell you, sweetie?"

Sarah gnawed on her lower lips. "You're saying not to call you a witch?" she asked slowly.

"Witch is the word people use to accuse others, to hurt them when they don't understand them."

"I wouldn't want to hurt you," Sarah said, looking up at Katie earnestly.

"I know you wouldn't." Katie hugged her again. "Now go check your brother." She pushed her up out of her lap and in the direction of the kitchen.

Just as Katie sat down to finish her butter, she heard a strange hoot of glee from the barnyard. Rob? Was that Rob hollering like a madman? Was everyone vexed this afternoon?

"Katie! Katie!" Rob appeared around the corner running toward her. "My ship, Katie! My tobacco!"

"Rob?" She couldn't help smiling at the sight of him running toward her, his blond hair loose and blowing across his shoulders. "What did you say? What of a ship?"

He grabbed her around the waist and swung her in a circle, her linsey-woolsey skirts billowing out. As he put her down, he kissed her soundly on the mouth. "The ship. The *Mary Jane!* She didn't go down." He grabbed Katie and spun her off her feet again. "She was disabled in a storm, but she never sank! I just heard from Widow Hartly who heard it from the mill. Damnedest thing anyone's ever heard, a false reporting like that. It's never happened on the tidewater, not as long as any of us can remember."

"Your tobacco's safe?"

"My tobacco's safe! God willing, it's in London by now being sold at an exorbitant price!"

"Oh, Rob, that's wonderful." Katie threw her arms around his neck and hugged him. When she lifted her head from his shoulder, his gaze was locked with hers.

145

Rob's touch made her hot and cold at the same time; it made her giddy with want of him. She touched her lips to his. Did he feel the same physical ache for her that she felt for him?

"You did it, Katie. My luck really has changed, hasn't it?"

"It wasn't me." She laughed off his suggestion. "I can't bring a ship up from the bottom of the ocean! It was a mistake, just like you said. As for your luck, you changed that, Rob Cameron. You've become optimistic. You believe in yourself."

He clasped her hands in his. "If I have, it's because of you." His voice had a husky catch to it. "You changed my life, hinny."

She touched his cheek, wondering if his heart was pounding as hard as hers was right now. "Rob," she whispered.

"Katie . . ."

Say it, she thought. Tell him you love him. Tell him you want him to make love to you now, here in the brittle grass with the late afternoon sunshine beating down on our faces. She parted her lips to speak.

"Uncle Robbie!" Sarah came running out of the kitchen door. "Me and Katie made cornbread for you for supper because Katie said it was your favorite!"

"Katie and I." Reluctantly, he released Katie and swung Sarah into his arms.

"That's what I said," Sarah answered smugly, grinning first at Rob and then Katie. "Didn't I, Katie?"

Katie laughed at the two of them as she went back to the butter churn, her skin still tingling from Rob's touch. She pulled open the round wooden lid of it and peered inside. Perfect butter. She picked up the heavy churn and headed for the kitchen door. She could hear Josh just beginning to stir.

"Wash up and we'll eat and put the children into bed early tonight. I thought we'd all ride into town tomorrow for church and Cassie Malton's baptism, if it's all right with you," she called to Rob.

"What of us?" he called, the insinuation in his voice obvious. He wanted to know if tonight would be the night, if tonight they would share a bed as true man and wife. He still held Sarah in his arms, trying to appear casual.

Katie looked over her shoulder. Could they finally make love? Was the relationship solid enough? "Patience," she teased, aware that she wouldn't know if the moment was right until it arrived. "Patience, Rob Cameron," she called as she disappeared into the house.

After a supper of venison stew and cornbread with sweet butter, Rob pushed up out of his seat, following Katie to the kitchen, a stack of dirty pewter dishes in his hands. He'd been restless all through the meal, reminding Katie of a young boy anxious for a birthday gift.

As she leaned over the pine work table in the center of the kitchen, he rested his hands on her hips and leaned over to kiss the back of her neck.

He whispered into her ear, and Katie felt her cheeks grow warm. "I've the meal to clean up, the children to bathe and tuck into bed. Do something with yourself, Rob. You make me nervous skittering about. Make yourself useful," she teased, pushing his hands away and walking back toward the dining table in the other room.

He stood in the doorway running a hand through his hair. "You're telling me I'm in the way in my own home?" he huffed in feigned indignation.

Sarah passed her uncle on the way to the kitchen, a dirty mug in each hand. "You're in the way, Uncle Robbie."

He sighed. "Well, you ladies said we're out of honey. Mayhap I'll go and gather a comb or two. It'll be the last of the year, I'll wager."

"Better not get bit by any bees, Uncle Robbie. You know bee bites make you sick."

"Ach." He waved his hand as he reached for his three-cornered hat on the wall peg near the back door. "I'm too fast for bees, Sarah."

"I'll bathe them and put them to bed." Katie didn't look up, afraid he would see her desire for him plain on her face. "Don't be long."

He slipped into his canvas work coat, winking at her. "No need to fear that, hinny." He winked at her and then he was gone.

Katie stopped to watch him disappear out the door and then clapped her hands. "All right Sarah, time for all good girls to be in bed."

"But I'm not a good little girl." She giggled. "And Joshy isn't good either." She sat on the floor with her brother who was playing with an empty wooden thread spool. "We're not good children—are we Joshy?—and we don't want to go to bed." She looked up slyly at Katie. "Even if it is to let Uncle Robbie and you play kissy-face in the parlor."

"Sarah!"

The little girl squealed with laughter. "Uncle Robbie said it was all right for him to kiss you because he's married to you just like my mama was married to my dada."

Katie scooped the baby up off the floor, unsure of how to respond. "Oh, he did, did he?"

Sarah nodded, grinning. "Uncle Robbie said if he kissed you really good, you would stay at Sarah's Stand forever."

Katie took Sarah's hand and pulled her to her feet. "Would you like that, Sarah?"

"Oh, yes." She beamed. "I've loved my mama and dada, and I miss 'em; but I love Uncle Robbie and you too."

Katie brushed a kiss across the top of her head. "I love you too, sweetheart. You and your brother."

"How about Uncle Robbie?" Sarah eyed Katie sharply. "Do you love him?"

"Enough questions! Now run upstairs for your nightgown whilst I pour hot water for your bath."

"But Katie—"

"Now, Sarah."

Sarah skipped away, and Katie could hear her laughter echoing off the plastered walls as she ran up the front staircase.


An hour later when both Sarah and Joshua were asleep in their room, Katie slipped out of the house and into the barnyard. The wind off the bay was so cold that she lifted the hood of her nut-brown woolen cloak to protect her head. It had grown dark while she was preparing the children for bed, but she wasn't afraid of the inky blackness that had settled over the peninsula.

Lantern light shone through the cracks in the barn walls, and she walked toward it. But halfway across the yard, she stopped and listened. The wind howled, and the iron sailing-ship weathervane on the barn roof squeaked. There it was again, that ominous, suffocating fear. Only this time there were voices. Screams. The sounds of frightened animals. She balled her hands into fists at her sides, concentrating. Where was the fear coming from? Was this a premonition or just an imprint of sorrows past? Before she had time to think on it, the feeling was gone.

Katie hugged herself for warmth as she hurried toward the barn. For the first time since she'd come to the house and felt the fear, she was truly afraid. "Rob, are you there?"

She pushed open the barn door and the sweet smell of alfalfa overcame her. "Rob!" He sat, his back to her,

149

on a small bench near the rear wall. The lantern rested on the end of the bench beside him.

"Rob, why didn't you answer me?" She closed the door behind her, thankful for the warmth of the barn and the comforting smell of warm-blooded animals and clean straw. It drove away the fear that made her chest tight and her palms damp. "I called you, but I—" She stopped in mid-sentence. His shoulders were hunched and even from behind him she could tell his breathing was labored.

"Rob, are you all right?"

She came around the bench to face him. He had stripped off his coat and had lifted his muslin shift above his flat stomach. It was splotched with red welts.

Katie went down on one knee in front of him. "Rob, I said are you all right?"

He touched his chest. "Aye . . . or at least I will be . . . in a minute. Just give me a chance to catch my breath." He wheezed.

"You got stung." She touched the welts with her fingertips. "Anywhere else?"

He shook his head. "They . . . the blessed beasties flew in under my coat." He smiled weakly. "But I got the honey. I got Sarah's honey."

Katie touched his forehead. He had no fever, but he was trembling slightly and it was becoming harder for him to breathe. She grabbed his hand. "You have to come inside and let me tend to the stings. "I've a poultice that will take out the venom." She hoped he wouldn't hear the quiver in her voice.

He shook his head. "No, hinny, I think I'd best stay put another minute or two." He waved his head. "It will pass. It always does."

"You've had this before? The shaking, the welts, the difficulty breathing?" She brushed back the hair off his cheek, noticing the thin sheen of perspiration that was appearing over his upper lip.

"Aye. No." He shook his head and struggled to take

a deep breath. "Welts, but not the breathing, but . . . but it will pass. Don't worry your sweet head over me. I'll be fit enough in a few minutes."

She thought for a second and then got up. "You sit there and I'll be right back, all right Rob?"

He looked at her, seeming to be confused.

"Did you hear me Rob? I said I'll be back with a poultice."

He put out his hand to her. He was trembling. "Don't leave me, hinny. Married we be and married we'll stay if you'll have me."

She squeezed his hand and then pulled away. "I'll be right back, Rob."

Katie's hands trembled as she pulled open the barn door. He was having some kind of reaction to the poison of the bee sting. He acted like a man bit by a water moccasin. Water moccasins killed men. Their poison made them shake so hard they went into convulsions, then died.

"Oh, God," Katie murmured under her breath.

She ran back across the yard and into the kitchen. Not taking the time to slam the door behind her, she grabbed a crock of water and a small basket and began to clip herbs from the neat rows of bundles that ran along the low-hanging rafters. What would she use? She racked her brain, running through her head all the herbs she had learned about and the results they gave when combined.

Satisfied with what she had chosen, Katie grabbed her mortar and pestle, dropped them into the basket with the water crock, and then ran for the barn, slamming doors behind her.

She reached Rob and went down on her knees. His breathing was now very shallow. His eyes were beginning to glaze over. He was leaning forward, supporting himself on his knees. She whipped off her woolen cloak and laid it over a pile of freshly raked straw.

"Hinny, that you? Katie?"

"It's me." She grasped his arm and tugged hard. "Rob, you have to listen to me. You have to get up and lie down over here where I can tend to you." She tugged harder. "Rob, you have to help me. I can't carry you."

Slowly he rose. She guided him to her cloak. He dropped to one knee and then down on the other. She barely had to push on his shoulder for him to fall. She took a paring knife from the basket and cut open his shirt from neckline to hem.

Rob had closed his eyes. His chest rattled with each labored breath.

"Rob, listen to me." She ground herbs as she spoke, trying to calculate in her head. "You're going to be all right; just don't go to sleep.

"Cold," he muttered thickly.

She mixed water with the ground herbs, making a paste. "You're cold? Just a minute. Let me care for the stings and then I'll warm you up, I swear I will."

She knelt and scooped up some of the paste with her fingers and rubbed it on the welts on his chest.

He took a shuddering breath. "Ach, damn, that . . . that stings. You . . . you trying to kill me wife and . . . and inherit my land?"

She smiled, thinking that no matter how desperate things got, Rob Cameron still kept his sense of humor. She smoothed the rest of the paste on him, murmuring beneath her breath, concentrating on the thought that the herbs would draw the poison out of his blood.

When she was done, she folded the cut sides of the shirt back together over his bare chest. He was shivering now. She grabbed his canvas coat and shook it to be certain there were no bees left inside. Then she covered him.

"Hinny?" He opened his eyes to look up at her. "I'm cold." With great effort, he lifted one corner of the coat. "Crawl inside with me and keep me warm."

She slid under the coat beside him. His breath sounded

152

as if it was coming a little easier. She wrapped her arm around him and rested her head on his shoulder. "Better?" she asked.

He smiled, letting his eyes drift shut. "Better."

And he was breathing better, she could tell. His head seemed to be clearer too.

"I feel like an ass," he said after a few minutes.

She smiled. He was going to be all right. Rob was going to be fine. "What do you mean?"

"I had all these romantic intentions." He pulled her closer to him. His voice was stronger now. "I was going to come into the kitchen, my whiskers freshly shaved, and I was going to bring you a wildflower." He pointed to the bench and sure enough there was an orange-yellow flower lying beside the lantern. "I was going to take you in my arms and kiss you the way I know you like to be kissed." He nuzzled her ear. "I was going to touch your breasts with my hand, tease your nipples with the tip of my tongue."

Katie could feel herself growing warm. "And then what?" she whispered.

"And then," he said. "Then I was going to lift you in my arms and carry you upstairs to your bed, to mine." He kissed her cheek. ". . . To ours."

Katie could feel her own breath coming shorter now as she thought of being in Rob's arms, as she thought of his hands touching her, as she thought of the way she knew he could make her feel. "And then?"

He lifted himself up on his elbow, his breath practically normal again. "And then I would make love to you as I've wanted to since the day I laid eyes on you on that auction block."

"Rob." She looked away. "Rob, I'm not a virgin."

"It doesn't matter, not to me, hinny."

She looked at him, forcing herself to meet his gaze. "It matters to me. I was raped."

153

He leaned to kiss her tenderly. "You didn't have a choice, then."

She traced the outline of his lips. "But now I do," she whispered.

Their lips met again, but this time Rob rose up and gently pushed her back into her cloak and the soft straw that cushioned them. "Let me make love to you, Katie girl. Let me wash away the bad memories." He brushed back her hair with his fingertips. "I don't really understand you or some of the things you do. I don't know where you came from, but listen to me, hinny. I don't care."

"There will be those who will say you married a witch," she murmured.

"I don't believe in such nonsense."

She looked into his eyes. "But if you did?"

He pressed her deeper into the straw, bringing his mouth down to the soft valley of her breasts that rose and fell above her bodice. "'Twould make no difference, hinny, because I love you. I do."

Katie closed her eyes, hugging his head to her breasts. "And I love you, Rob Cameron."

He lifted his head, his eyes sparkling with mischief. "So what shall we do about it, Katie love?"

She giggled. "I don't know, you tell me. You were the one with all the plans a short time ago."

He laughed deep in his throat. "Shall we do this?" He brushed his lips against hers.

"Um hmm. . ."

He cupped her breast beneath the fabric of her gown with his hand. "And this?"

"Yes," she breathed.

Slowly he brought his hand across her embroidered stomacher and down to her inner thigh. His caress was light and deliciously tantalizing. "And what of this?" he whispered, his breath hot in her ear.

"Oh, yes. Yes, Rob . . . please." She drew her hands

over her head, relaxing in the cushiony straw. "Love me," she said, her gaze locking with his. "Love me, husband."

He kissed her mouth, his tongue darting out to tease her. Then he kissed the tip of her nose, her cheek, the dimple at her chin. He kissed his way down the curve of her neck to the low-cut bodice of her gown, and all the while he was touching her.

Even through the material of her gown and underthings, Rob's touch burned her flesh, making it white-hot with desire. When he pushed her gown off her shoulders and unlaced her stays, she could do nothing but sigh. His tongue drew a wet line from the cleft of her breasts to one peaked nipple and then the other. As he tongued the tip of her breast she moaned softly, weaving her fingers through his honey-wheat-colored hair. She murmured his name, and he whispered words that fanned the heat of her excitement.

"Rob . . ."

"Katie, my sweet Katie . . . Wife . . ."

"Husband . . ."

He removed her clothing so gently, so naturally that Katie felt no shame when she lay beside him on her cloak in the straw, naked for him to see her. Instead, she laughed as she pulled off his shirt and wiped the remainder of the poultice from his skin with it. Then she began to kiss the bee welts that were disappearing already. She kissed the hard taut muscles of his chest, even dared to catch the nub of one male nipple between her teeth and tug gently.

Rob groaned. "Ach, for an innocent, you have a touch, Katie girl."

Made bold by the power of knowing she could give as well as take pleasure, Katie traced the line of his flat stomach above the waistband of his breeches with her fingertip. Then, curiosity outweighing her hesitation, she pulled at the string of his breeches. He nuzzled her neck, whispering words of encouragement.

Katie couldn't resist a smile as she released his burgeoning member from the confines of the broadcloth. Her husband was well endowed. He would bring her not just pleasure but many children.

Katie brushed her fingertips across his warm flesh, fascinated by the softness of his skin and his reaction to her caress.

"Ach," Rob groaned, laying his hand over hers. "Enough, or I'll not make it to the coupling." He rolled over onto her, shifting his weight to make her comfortable. As he lowered his mouth to hers, he pressed his hips against her rhythmically.

Katie remembered little of the time she had been forced, except that it was quick and uncomfortable, but this, this was the most wonderful thing she had ever experienced. Her mind soared until all conscious thought was gone. All that mattered was this man and the feel of him, the pressure of his loins against hers.

When he entered her, he went slowly. A tiny gasp escaped her, but she was smiling, her eyes half closed. After giving her a moment to adjust to the new sensation he began to move over her, and Katie quickly picked up his rhythm. Suddenly they were not two, but one, rising and falling to that ancient rhythm only true lovers know. Everything was spinning in Katie's head. She could taste the saltiness of Rob's shoulder on her tongue. She could smell the heady scent of his masculinity.

Then suddenly she felt as if her entire being were hurled far into the air. She couldn't catch her breath, she couldn't speak, couldn't move. All she could do was hold onto Rob as her world burst into a thousand shards of white sparkling light. Katie was vaguely aware of Rob's last thrust and his sigh of contentment. The next thing she knew he had withdrawn from her and was cradling her in his arms.

"I love ye, hinny." He kissed her. "I love ye, and I'll care for ye always. Know that."

She opened her eyes, her lids so heavy that it took great effort. She smiled up at him. "Life's good, isn't it?" she whispered.

"That it is."

Then suddenly that feeling of fear came over Katie. This time it was so strong and so sudden that she bolted upright.

"What is it?" Rob asked sitting up with her. "Are you hurt, Katie?"

She trembled violently. Then it was gone.

"Hinny?"

"No, no, I'm fine," she lied. "I just thought I heard one of the children, but it was only the wind." She lay back on the soft straw and reached up to stroke Rob's cheek, praying desperately that this sinking feeling in the pit of her stomach was not a premonition of events to come.

# Six

Katie hummed to herself as she carried a second armful of wood into the kitchen; the wind caught the door and flung it open behind her. The flames of the hearth fire wavered in the draft. It was twilight, that strange time between sunset and darkness when the entire sky is cast in eerie light.

Rob was in the barn feeding the stock, but he would be in soon.

A tremor of excitement rippled down Katie's spine. They had been man and wife in the true sense of the word barely a week, but these last few days had been as perfect as any Katie had known. Rob was a passionate lover and a thoughtful man, the man she knew she would spend the rest of her days on this earth loving.

Katie dropped the armful of wood into the woodbox and went back to close the door. Out of the corner of her eye she spotted Sarah and Joshua playing with their black cat on the floor in the hallway. Katie had just grasped the doorknob when she heard Two Bears cry out. Across the barnyard she saw him come sprinting toward her; at the same time the second-story doors of the barn swung open and Rob hurled himself out the door to the ground below, a musket in his hand.

*"Uishameheela!"* Two Bears shouted at Katie, flailing his arms as he ran toward her faster than it seemed pos-

sible for such an old man. "Run, Kat-ie. *Ommamundot!* The children!"

Without hesitation, Katie spun around, that same sense of doom she had been feeling all these weeks falling suddenly over her like a death veil. This was it. Whatever she had feared had come.

The children! her mind screamed. Save the children . . . though from what, she still didn't know.

Katie raced though the kitchen, scooping little Joshua into her arms and jerking Sarah off the floor by the wrist.

"Ouch! Katie, that hurt!"

"No time, Sarah. The root cellar!"

Little Sarah stumbled to keep up with Katie as she dragged her into the kitchen. Two Bears was already there, sliding the heavy pine work table so that he could pull up the trap door that led down into the root cellar below.

"You must hide from the evil," he cried, his frail hands shaking as he pulled on the iron ring and lifted the hatch. "This man is old, but he will defend you. Do not fear."

Katie pushed Sarah into Two Bears' arms so that he could lower her onto the wooden ladder. "What evil, Two Bears?"

"The pir-rates! The pir-rates they come to Sarah's Stand!"

"Where? How many?"

"This man does not know. He only knows that Rob saw them landing on the beach from the hay loft and called out the warning." Two Bears grasped Sarah by the armpits and swung her over the dark hole. As he swung her, the medicine bag, hung around her neck, caught on the corner of the table. The seam on the tiny leather fringed bag burst open and its contents spilled onto the swept floor.

Sarah's black cat, Puddum, curled around Katie's ankle, purring, and she pushed it aside with her boot.

159

"My magic! My magic!" Sarah cried, struggling in Two Bears' arms.

"Sarah!" Katie spoke sharply. "Into the cellar! I'll get the magic!"

As Sarah allowed herself to be lowered into the root cellar, Katie immediately fell to her knees and began to pick up the contents of the torn leather bag with Josh still slung on her hip. A small feather, a red bead, a bit of fur, a miniscule seashell. Then she saw it . . . there at her fingertips. A piece of turquoise.

In an instant her father's face came to her, a handsome, angular face with skin as red as turned Virginia soil—and the necklace he had worn about his neck . . . She picked up the piece of blue turquoise with the hole in it. It had belonged to her father, the Lenni Lenape brave. She knew it as well as she knew her own name.

Katie looked up at Two Bears, and he stared at the turquoise in her palm. Then he reached out and grabbed the baby from her arms and lowered him into the dark root cellar, to his sister's waiting hands.

"My father—" Katie heard herself say.

"No time, now, granddaughter of mine. Time later to explain. Into the root hole now, so that this man can protect his granddaughter and great-grandchildren."

Tears clouded Katie's vision as she leaned over the hole, still on her knees, and handed Sarah the handful of treasures. Two Bears, her grandfather? But there was no time to think of this now. "Stay here and keep your brother quiet," she instructed Sarah. "I'll be back for you."

"What if you don't come back?"

"I'll come!" Katie insisted.

Sarah sniffed. She was young, but she had heard tales of these pirate attacks. She knew the tidewater had seen death at the hands of the pirates. "What if you don't?" she repeated forcefully. "Then what do I do?"

Katie bit down on her lower lip to stifle a sob. "Then

wait—wait a long time—and then take Joshua to Widow Hartly's, not by the road, but through the fields. Now get down so I can close the door, Sarah."

"It'll be dark," the little girl whimpered. "I want you to come down, too."

"Be brave. Be brave for your baby brother."

Sarah nodded, lifting her chin. "I will be brave."

On impulse, Katie grabbed the black cat that still curled annoyingly around her ankles and dropped it down into the root cellar with the children. "Here, Puddum will keep you safe." She blew the children a kiss and closed the trap door.

"You must go down," Two Bears told her from across the room where he grabbed a musket from beside the fireplace.

Katie shook her head fervently as she slid the table back over the hole and pushed a slop bucket under it, hoping to break up the lines of the trap door. At that moment she heard the first blast of musket fire. "Rob," she murmured, not knowing why she had said it. "I have to get to Rob."

"Inside, woman!" Two Bears ordered gruffly, pushing her toward the table. "Get into the root hole!"

Katie thrust out her chin. "This is my land now. These are my children, my husband, and I'll defend them!"

Two Bears' dark-eyed gaze met hers, and for the first time Katie realized their eyes were identical in color. He tossed the musket through the air, and her hands shot up to catch it. He threw her the powder flask and small leather bag containing musket balls and patches of cloth. "You guard the children, and I will go for your husband. If this man has need of you, he will come."

Katie nodded, trembling, as Two Bears grabbed a carving knife from the pine table and thrust it into his quilled leather belt. Then he took the scythe left in the doorway to be repaired and went out the kitchen door.

As the door swung open Katie heard the cows mooing,

the horses whinnying, hogs snorting, and chickens screeching as they scattered. She caught a glimpse of a man in a red shirt, his hair drawn back in a tarred pigtail. He ran by with a red hen under each arm. . . . more musket fire and the strangled scream of a man. The smell of smoke . . . Then the door swung shut and the sounds were muffled, her view cut off.

Katie's hands were trembling so hard that she feared she wouldn't be able to shoot if she had to. But there wasn't time for fear, not now. She had to protect the children. She had to find a place to hide. But there was nothing to get behind. The kitchen was open and airy. Then she spotted the jelly cabinet Rob was making, with its freshly planed doors and punched-tin panels. It was empty; he'd not yet put in the shelves that lay stacked on the floor.

Katie raced across the kitchen and pulled open the door to the cabinet. She backed in and sank her blunt fingernails into the tiny ledge of the tin panel to pull it shut.

The inside of the cabinet smelled of fresh pine shavings and her own fear. Pinpricks of light from the kitchen candle sconces pierced the darkness, making a swirled pattern on the embroidery of her stomacher. She knew she should pray, but no words came to mind. All she could think of was the happiness she'd found here at Sarah's Stand and how easily it could be shattered. She gripped the oak stock of the old musket, her knuckles white, waiting, listening . . .

When the kitchen latch lifted, the click of the iron hardware echoed harshly in her ears. Katie prayed against all reason that the intruder was Rob or Two Bears, but she knew better. She could feel the evil . . .

She heard a pot fall and a great hissing as her venison soup was turned over into the fire. Glass shattered and Katie knew her new oil lamp now lay smashed on the floor. She heard several metal items hit the pine table.

The silver tea service that had belonged to Rob's mother, she assumed. Then the footsteps passed the jelly cupboard, and the pirate walked into the parlor. Katie tried to get a look at him, but the holes in the punched tin were too small. All she saw was a flash of a French, white and blue, military coat with gold braid.

There was more crashing in the parlor and then footsteps up the staircase. The intruder came down a minute later and reentered the kitchen. She heard him gathering up his booty. Another minute and he would be gone . . . the children would be safe.

Then she heard the silver clatter onto the table again . . . the scrape of wood against wood. It was the table, he was moving it. He had seen the hatch in the floor!

*Dear God, not the children! Not my children!*

Katie tightened her grip on the stock and barrel of the musket. Another instant and she would jump out.

She heard the squeak of the trap door and Sarah's shrill scream.

Katie kicked open the jelly cabinet door with her boot and swung the musket to draw a bead on the black-haired pirate in the French coat. At the same instant Sarah's cat came flying up out of the root cellar. The pirate hollered out in surprise and batted at the creature with his pistol, but the cat leaped into his face, sinking its claws into his flesh before falling to the ground unharmed to race for the cover of a stool.

Katie clicked back the hammer of her musket as the pirate swung and lifted his pistol. She squeezed the trigger without hesitation. The pirate's pistol went off at the same instant, but the ball struck the jelly cabinet, missing Katie. The pirate went down on one knee, dropping his smoking weapon. He gripped his chest, staring at her with empty eyes. Blood oozed through his fingers.

Katie immediately began to reload where she stood. Her hands knew the routine, even though her mind couldn't remember. *Bite the lid off the powder flask . . .*

*dump . . . patch and ball in the barrel . . . ram . . . load*
*frizzen pan with powder . . .*

"Katie!" Sarah called hysterically from down below. "Katie, where are you?"

Baby Joshua was screaming.

The pirate pitched forward onto his face, and didn't move again.

"It's all right," Katie soothed, her musket reloaded. She sidestepped the dead pirate and leaned over the root-cellar hatch. "It's all right, sweetness."

Katie heard more musket fire in the direction of the bay and the shout of a man. Was that Rob?

Katie grabbed the ring on the root cellar door to lower it again. "Be brave," she said.

Little Sarah, holding tightly to her brother, tears running down her pale cheeks smiled up. "I'll be brave. Just like Puddum. If he can fight a pirate, I can, too!"

Katie laughed through her tears as she kicked the dead pirate's hand aside and lowered the trap door again.

"Kat-ie!" Two Bears came bursting into the kitchen as she dropped the root-cellar door. "Kat-ie must come," he said grimly.

"The pirates?"

"Your Rob-man set fire to their ship. Must come, Katie."

"Where's Rob?" She ran for the door. "Is he all right?"

"Must hurry. Time comes too quickly. Only a moment between life and the death of forever. Must save him."

"Rob's been hurt?" She ran out into the twilight, following the old Indian who spoke in riddles. "Has Rob been injured?"

The old Indian refused to answer. Instead, he grasped her sleeve and led her around the house and down toward the bay.

Katie glanced over her shoulder at the path of destruction the pirates had left behind them. Half a dozen hogs

164

ran loose, squealing; one lay half butchered near the barn door. The mule, Sugar, brayed and raced through a broken place in the fence, headed for the cover of the woods. Chickens, set free from their wire coops, scattered in every direction, feathers flying. Several piles of still-damp hay burned, sending billows of black smoke into the night air. The bodies of four pirates lay, bloody, on the path between the house and barn.

She turned away from the carnage and the sweet smell of warm human blood. It was almost dark now.

As Katie and Two Bears rounded the side of the house and started down the bank toward the beach, she saw a blaze on the edge of the shore. Acrid smoke and cinders filled the air. The pirate's sloop was engulfed in flames. The pirates had tried to set sail, but the fire had overcome them and now the small, sleek vessel listed heavily to one side.

By the orange light of the setting sun and the glow from the blaze aboard the pirate sloop, Katie caught sight of Rob's silhouette. He battled two pirates hand-to-hand, standing tall and brave in the fiery glow.

Katie stopped dead, clamping a hand over her mouth in fear that she would cry out and distract him. Two Bears caught her by the arm and dragged her behind him down the hill. "Must hurry, grandchild. There will only be seconds."

Katie ran as fast as she could, her loaded musket cradled in one arm.

Rob swung his empty musket like a war club, striking first one pirate and then the other. A man in a red coat swung an axe, the other a sword. Rob was not more than a hundred yards from her now, but it seemed a million miles. She wanted to take aim and shoot, but the sights were so bad on the old musket she carried she feared she'd miss the thieving bastards and hit Rob instead.

Rob spun around in a circle wielding his musket, buttfirst, over his head. The pirate in the red coat swung his axe, Rob ducked, and brought the musket stock across the man's head. Even from this distance, Katie heard the sickening crack of the scoundrel's skull. He fell without uttering a sound.

Without a moment's hesitation, Rob stepped up to the pirate with the sword, becoming the hunter rather than the hunted. The pirate took a swordsman's stance, laughing at the farmer with his unloaded wheel-lock.

But Rob's face was grim with determination. He side-stepped each of the pirate's parries with the swift, sure-footed grace of a dancer. His concentration was unfailing. For him, there was nothing at this moment but the man who threatened his family.

Not more than ten feet from them, Katie and Two Bears came to a halt.

Rob's gaze never strayed, though he must have known they were there. He took two steps back, one forward, he ducked and dove, still swinging the only weapon he had to defend himself and those he loved.

The pirate made a sudden start forward, but instead of stepping back, Rob swung around and caught the tip of the sword with the musket butt. The pirate gave a strangled cry as he tried to hang onto the sword and went down on his knees in the damp sand. Rob struck again with his musket, this time hitting the pirate's wrist. The man howled with pain, drawing back his hand. Rob reached down for the sword on the ground and came up with it grasped in his gloved hand.

"Surrender," he bellowed, breathing heavily. "Surrender yourself and you'll be turned in to the High Sheriff for trial and hanging, that or meet your maker now!"

Katie saw the flash of metal.

Time seemed to tilt on end and cease moving. It was as if she was there, but was not there.

The pirate had drawn a derringer from his leather boot. Katie heard a woman's scream . . . her own . . . the

166

scream she had heard on the wind in the barnyard last week.

The pirate pulled the trigger at point-blank range.

Rob had already begun to move forward to sink the sword into his chest. The pirate screamed in agony.

The night air filled with the smell of gunpowder and burned flesh.

"No!" Katie screamed. "No!"

She felt Two Bears' hand on her shoulder, pushing her forward, and she flung the musket aside and ran to Rob.

The pirate had fallen backward to stare up unseeing, the sword buried deep in his chest.

Rob had fallen into the sand.

Katie dropped to her knees beside him, sobbing. She grasped him by the shoulders and, with a heave, rolled him over. Dear God, where was Two Bears? Why wasn't he here?

"Rob?" Katie murmured. "Rob?"

He was covered with blood, a gaping hole in his stomach. He was so pale. His eyes were shut as if he were sleeping . . . so peaceful.

"Rob!" she screamed, shaking him violently. "Rob Cameron, don't do this to me. Don't die!"

But how could he not die? The hole in him was wide and deep. He was covered in blood. She felt no rise and fall of breath in his chest.

Katie sank back into the sand, cradling Rob's head in her lap. He was still warm to the touch. How could he be dead?

Then she felt Two Bears' hand on her shoulder. "Hurry grandchild of mine," he murmured. "The magic cannot wait."

Katie looked up at him, barely able to see through her tears. She was on the edge of hysteria. Rob was dead! He was dead . . .

"Hurry!" Two Bears insisted.

Katie shook her head, threading her fingers through

Rob's blond hair, pressing a fervent kiss to his forehead. "No, no. I can't."

"You can. You must," the old man whispered. "Use your powers."

She shook her head harder. "I can't," she sobbed, her tears falling on Rob's pale face. "This is not a bird! He's a man! A man!"

"It's inside you, child of my child. Look deep. Believe."

"They killed my mother for healing!" she screamed.

"Your choice," Two Bears said, his voice barely a whisper on the wind. "Believe or don't believe. Let the man you love live, or let him die."

Katie watched in disbelief as the old Indian man walked away, abandoning her. He headed back toward the farmhouse.

Through a veil of tears she looked down at Rob's strikingly handsome face. Where was his laughter now? Their laughter?

Taking in a deep breath, Katie moved out from under him, lowering his head gently to the sandy ground. Then, leaning over him, she placed both hands on the gaping mortal wound, and slowly she lowered her face to her hands.

She whispered beneath her breath . . .

A second passed.

Then another.

She waited, feeling nothing but emptiness and stark fear.

Then a strange tremor shook him.

His chest rose as he sucked in a deep breath.

Katie lifted her head, in utter disbelief to see his eyelids flutter.

"Hinny?" he whispered as if awakening from a deep sleep. "Katie girl, is that you?"

Her lower lip trembled. "It's me, my love, I'm here."

"The children?"

"Safe."

"The pirates?"

"All dead. Their boat is sinking."

He lifted his head and then let it fall back. He licked his dry lips. "I feel like I've been to hell and back. What happened?"

Katie was afraid to speak. "You . . . you were shot . . ."

He looked confused. "Shot? Shot where?"

"Here," she whispered. She was afraid to move her hands for fear of what she would see, but she knew she must.

He laid his hand on hers, looking up into her face. There was so much blood, on him, on her.

He watched as she slowly lifted her hands from his stomach.

Rob swore beneath his breath.

There was nothing there now but a large powder burn in his linen shirt.

He looked up at her, his blue-eyed gaze locking with hers. "I was dead," he said, his voice barely a whisper.

She couldn't look away from those eyes. She couldn't lie. "Yes . . ."

"Then you really are a—"

She leaned over him and pressed her lips to his to silence him. "Don't say it," she whispered. "You must never say it. Just tell me that you love me and that you'll always love me."

Rob sat up, pulling her into his arms and crushing her to him. He smoothed her long black hair with his broad hand. "I love ye, hinny," he said through his tears. "I'll always love ye, no matter who or what ye are . . ."

*Spirit of The Manor*
by
Ashland Price

# One

*Glendalough, Ireland*
*Late October, 1878*

Lysandra Mc Gill winced, as her mother flung the back of her hand to her brow and launched into the same dolorous harangue she'd been spouting for the past seven days.

"He's *dead!* God help us, he's perished, and the rest of us are certain to do the same now. You may be sure!"

"Oh, Mum," Lysandra sighed, her tone filled with the resignation she always exhibited, when her mother was beginning to wear her down.

Gertrude Mc Gill's nostrils flared, and she let her jaw drop a bit, so that her lower lip might go into the side-to-side shift that always signaled her indignation. "We're lost, I tell you, you impudent girl!"

With that, she rose from the Gypsy's reading table and began pacing about the fortuneteller's shop, her shawl clutched melodramatically about her.

"Maybe not," her hostess tendered, offering Lysandra a surreptitious wink, then fixing her eyes upon the crystal ball that sat just before her on the table.

Gertrude waved the Gypsy off and crossed to look fretfully out of the shop door's window. "Ah, what do you know of it? You've never even been wed, let alone widowed and left with three children and an ailing father-in-law to provide for!"

The Gypsy pursed her lips at this retort, and her raven eyes cast a warning look over at Lysandra.

The eighteen-year-old, in turn, found that she could only offer their hostess an apologetic smile and a shrug in her mother's defense. Madame Safina had been Lysandra's mentor, and partner of sorts, in the soothsaying business for nearly three years. So surely, by this time she must have to come to realize that Lysandra had long since given up any hope of reining in her mum's bouts of tactlessness.

The middle-aged Gypsy cleared her throat emphatically and returned her piercing gaze to Mrs. Mc Gill. "It is not my personal knowledge I draw upon in saying this, Gertrude. It is what I see in the ball. This nobleman, this heir to Sloan Fitzgerald will, indeed, come to claim the manor and take up residence within it, and you and yours will *not* be set out to beg in the streets."

"Ah, twaddle," Gertrude retorted, not bothering to take her eyes from the window. "You are simply telling me what you know I wish to hear, as the pair of you do with all of your customers." With an exasperated exhalation of breath, she struggled with the door's handle. Then, fighting its tendency to stick, she jerked it open, as though craving some fresh air.

Rather than stepping outside, however, she seemed content to simply leave the door ajar and stand before it for several seconds more.

"No, Mother," Lysandra quickly protested. "You know what danger there is for a reader if she lies about what is seen in the cards or the crystal. Madame would never, never do that."

Madame *would*, however, consider putting a hex on her mum, if she continued to be so impolite, and Lysandra knew she had to do all she could to prevent that. She and her family would have trouble enough in the months

174

ahead, with her mother's employer, the lord of Fitzgerald manor, now dead and buried. They hardly needed some Gypsy spell bringing insomnia or facial warts down upon them.

Gertrude crossed her arms over her chest and raised a blatantly skeptical brow. "Well, you won't have to look too long or hard into that ball, Madame, for I can already see, from over here, a manor with its roof torn off to keep the taxman at bay and its staff lying fallow."

"Shhh!" the Gypsy hissed, leaning in toward the crystal and cupping her hands about it. "Come, Lysandra," she said to her associate. "Come and confirm for your mother that it is not a roofless great house I see."

Anxious for any good tidings on the subject, Lysandra sprang to her feet and circled around to where the Gypsy sat.

Madame Safina slid her chair out of the way a bit, so her apprentice could bend down and get an eye-level view of the ball. "What do you perceive then, child?" she asked with a smile in her voice.

Lysandra peered into the hazy crystal, its clumps of veins like an early morning mist rising from a glen. Crystals were, by no means, her media. Her strength as a fortuneteller—a gift she and Madame had discovered quite by chance when Lysandra had come to the Gypsy for a reading three summers earlier—lay solely in the tarot cards. Nevertheless, Lysandra did her best now to make out the dark objects that were rising to the ball's surface.

"Oh, Mum, it *is* the manor," she declared with a delighted smile. "And, sure as the devil's in London, it does still have its roof upon it, just as Madame said."

"And there's something more," the Gypsy prompted. "Can you see it?"

To Lysandra's chagrin, she didn't at first. All that seemed visible to her was the great house. Still, serene, and well kept on some sunlit day in the future.

It was embarrassing, straining so and coming up with nothing. It was like floundering in a foreign language in which one was supposedly fluent.

"Umm . . . uh," she stammered.

"Ah, look, look, look, child," Madame Safina urged, her tone reflecting the precarious impatience of a frazzled piano instructor.

How Lysandra had managed to find herself saddled with two such overbearing women as her mum and the Gypsy, she wasn't sure.

Don't tense up, a voice within her counseled. The gift of foreseeing never comes to those who aren't relaxed enough to receive it. Mindful of this, she drew in a great breath, then exhaled it, ever so slowly, through her mouth . . . And yes! In that very instant, another figure did come into view for her.

"'Tis a man," she said triumphantly.

Madame clapped her hands and gave forth a soft laugh. "Oh, aye. And how does he look? Describe him."

"Well I can only see his back."

"Yes, yes. He's walking away from us, toward the manor."

"Yes. And he is tall and wears a cylindrical black hat and a long greatcoat."

"Aye. And who is he?"

Lysandra again felt her stomach sink with uncertainty. "Umm . . ."

"Come on. You know. In the depths of you, I know you know."

"He's . . ." Lysandra squeezed her eyes shut, straining for the information. "Why, he's the new lord of the manor!"

"¡Muy bien! Just so," Madame confirmed, giving her a congratulatory pat on the back. Though she was several generations removed from the Spanish Gypsies who had given rise to her, she still possessed a foreign accent of

# MORE PASSION AND ADVENTURE AWAIT... YOUR TRIP TO A BIG ADVENTUROUS WORLD BEGINS WHEN YOU ACCEPT YOUR FIRST 4 NOVELS ABSOLUTELY *FREE* (AN $18.00 VALUE)

Accept your Free gift and start to experience more of the passion and adventure you like in a historical romance novel. Each Zebra novel is filled with proud men, spirited women and tempestuous love that you'll remember long after you turn the last page.

Zebra Historical Romances are the finest novels of their kind. They are written by authors who really know how to weave tales of romance and adventure in the historical settings you love. You'll feel like you've actually gone back in time with the thrilling stories that each Zebra novel offers.

## GET YOUR FREE GIFT WITH THE START OF YOUR HOME SUBSCRIPTION

Our readers tell us that these books sell out very fast in book stores and often they miss the newest titles. So Zebra has made arrangements for you to receive the four newest novels published each month.

You'll be guaranteed that you'll never miss a title, and home delivery is so convenient. And to show you just how easy it is to get Zebra Historical Romances, we'll send you your first 4 books absolutely FREE! Our gift to you just for trying our home subscription service.

## BIG SAVINGS AND FREE HOME DELIVERY

Each month, you'll receive the four newest titles as soon as they are published. You'll probably receive them even before the bookstores do. What's more, you may preview these exciting novels free for 10 days. If you like them as much as we think you will, just pay the low preferred subscriber's price of just $3.75 each. *You'll save $3.00 each month off the publisher's price.* AND, your savings are even greater because there are never any shipping, handling or other hidden charges—FREE Home Delivery. Of course you can return any shipment within 10 days for full credit, no questions asked. There is no minimum number of books you must buy.

# 4 FREE BOOKS

## TO GET YOUR 4 FREE BOOKS WORTH $18.00 — MAIL IN THE FREE BOOK CERTIFICATE T O D A Y

Fill in the Free Book Certificate below, and we'll send your FREE BOOKS to you as soon as we receive it.

If the certificate is missing below, write to: Zebra Home Subscription Service, Inc., P.O. Box 5214, 120 Brighton Road, Clifton, New Jersey 07015-5214.

## FREE BOOK CERTIFICATE

## 4 FREE BOOKS

### ZEBRA HOME SUBSCRIPTION SERVICE, INC.

**YES!** Please start my subscription to Zebra Historical Romances and send me my first 4 books absolutely FREE. I understand that each month I may preview four new Zebra Historical Romances free for 10 days. If I'm not satisfied with them, I may return the four books within 10 days and owe nothing. Otherwise, I will pay the low preferred subscriber's price of just $3.75 each; a total of $15.00, *a savings off the publisher's price of $3.00.* I may return any shipment and I may cancel this subscription at any time. There is no obligation to buy any shipment and there are no shipping, handling or other hidden charges. Regardless of what I decide, the four free books are mine to keep.

NAME _____

ADDRESS _____ APT _____

CITY _____ STATE _____ ZIP _____

TELEPHONE
( ) _____

SIGNATURE _____
(if under 18, parent or guardian must sign)

Terms, offer and prices subject to change without notice. Subscription subject to acceptance by Zebra Books. Zebra Books reserves the right to reject any order or cancel any subscription.

ZB0793

sorts, and she slipped into speaking a word or two of her ancestors' tongue when excited over something.

This added to her air of mystery, Lysandra acknowledged, feeling at the moment far too fair-haired and green-eyed for the business of soothsaying. Yet, there was no denying Lysandra's accuracy. Her ever-growing clientele had confirmed that her predictions were correct at least seventy-five percent of the time; and, according to Madame, it appeared that she was right again now.

"Do you hear, Mum? It *is* the new lord of the manor. Master Fitzgerald's sole heir will, indeed, come to take up residence here in Glendalough and you won't lose your position as cook!"

With a disbelieving cluck, Gertrude Mc Gill strode across the room to have a look for herself. Upon reaching the table, to her daughter's horror she snatched up the crystal ball, stared into it, then began shaking it with all her might.

"Where?" she demanded. "I see neither man *nor* manor in this thing. You're mad, the pair of you!"

Both Lysandra and the Gypsy rose in that instant, their hands extended in an effort to prevent Gertrude from dropping the precious gazing ball.

It wasn't difficult to retrieve, however, for upon one more glance into it, Gertrude gasped and shoved it into Madame Safina's hands as though ridding herself of a burning coal.

"The Saints be with us, just look at the face on that creature! 'Tis enough to make my heart stop," Mrs. Mc Gill exclaimed, sinking into the closest chair and clapping a hand to her chest. "You're a vengeful woman, you are," she said to the Gypsy, withdrawing a handkerchief from the off-the-shoulder neckline of her frock and beginning to dab her forehead with it. "You could simply have asked for the ball back, you know. There was no call to go scarin' the wits out of me with your conjurin'!"

Her mother was genuinely discomposed, Lysandra acknowledged. One could always tell, because she abandoned all effort to sound like the landed English gentry and slipped back into the Irish habit of dropping her *g's*.

Madame Safina seemed not to notice, however. Instead, she elbowed Lysandra and stood studying the crystal with rapt attention.

"Oooh," Lysandra said recoiling a bit, as she gazed into the ball as well. "Whatever is that?"

"What does it look to be?" the Gypsy asked, demonstrating her usual flair for teaching with questions rather than answers.

"A ghost?"

Madame Safina placed one of her icy hands upon her apprentice's forearm. "Ah, you can do better than that, surely."

"It's a woman," Lysandra continued vaguely, unable to give a better description because of the deep fog that surrounded the apparition. "A woman in a flowing white gown. A . . . a *banshee?*" she ventured.

"Aye! Just so, you silly goose. A banshee it is! God," she went on, dropping back into her chair and emitting one of her cacklelike laughs, "I haven't spied one of those in the ball in ages! What a thrill!"

Lysandra continued to study it. "But what . . . what could it signify? I mean, we were asking about the fate of the manor, weren't we?"

" 'Signify?' Ah, rubbish," Gertrude interjected. "If 'tis indeed a banshee, it's simply the one who foretold Lord Fitzgerald's death. And what news is that to any of us now?"

"No. 'Tis a new fairy spirit entirely," the Gypsy said firmly. "One presaging the passing of a very different man."

"And what man might that be?" Gertrude snapped. "Not for any lowborn, haggling, half-bloods waileth a banshee, mind! And Fitzgerald was the only aristocrat of Gaelic roots for as far as the eye can see . . . Ah, Sweet

178

esus," she continued, leaning forward. "You don't suppose 'tis the *new* lord of the manor goin' to die as soon
as he arrives?"

The Gypsy shook her head. "No. Someone else, I
think." Still cradling the ball in both hands, she suddenly
squeezed her eyes shut and began to moan as though
slipping into one of her receptive trance states.

Then her dark eyes fell open and locked upon Gertrude
with an abruptness that took her companions aback.
"*You,* Mrs. Mc Gill," she said in a low voice, which was
very unlike her own. "You must work to see your only
daughter wed to the new lord of the manor, for it is fated
that, only because of Lysandra, will he choose to take
up residence in the great house."

Both Gertrude and her child gaped at this news.

"A lord marrying the daughter of a cook? Good heavens, woman, you *have* taken leave of your senses!"

"Please, Madame," Lysandra chimed in. "From all
we've heard of him, he's an old man. Not long behind
his uncle, the former master, in his march to the grave.
So how can you possibly wish such a fate upon me?"

The Gypsy scowled. " 'Wish?' *Wish,* Lysandra? You
know full well that the ball does not convey my wishes!"

Lysandra drew back slightly at this scolding. "Well,
aye, I know. But, as Mum just said, why would he want
one of my humble birth, in any case?"

Madame's eyes sparkled with intrigue. "Because he
will think you of royal Gaelic roots, of course. Of
course," she said again, raising one of her long crooked
fingers to her mouth, as though destiny's grand design
in all of this was finally dawning upon her. "Because
the banshee we just saw in the ball will wail at the death
of your ailing Grandfather Mc Gill and will lead the new
lord to believe you are, in your blood, highborn."

"Why on earth would a banshee do that?" Lysandra
shot back, growing angry now at the thought of being

179

handed over to some craggy old man in exchange fo
the security of the manor and its staff.

For the first time in Lysandra's memory, she saw the
sagacious Gypsy shrug as though lost for an answer. "
don't know. Perhaps she was not a banshee, in truth, bu
merely a woman dressed as such."

Lysandra gave forth an uneasy laugh. "Oh, Madame
what mortal would be foolish enough to do that, to spite
one as powerful and dangerous as a queen of the fairies?"

At this, to her apprentice's dismay, the Gypsy lifted a
taunting brow and smiled over at Gertrude. "One who
is in far more danger, if she does not. 'Tis time you took
better charge of the fate of yourself and your children
Mistress Mc Gill, instead of bemoaning it so ceaselessly
Perhaps, since it was you who first spotted the banshee
in the ball, 'twas *you* she rose to address."

Gertrude sank back into her chair and pursed her lips
once more. But this time her expression was different
It did not bespeak indignation but the calculation of one
who fully intended to take up the challenge just laid before her.

"Ah, Mother Mary preserve us!" Lysandra raised her
hands and let her face fall into them. "How dare you
put the seeds of such a preposterous plot into her head
Madame?" she snarled, as she uncovered her eyes once
more. "And, how dare you even consider such a thing
Mum?"

"Well, lest we forget, it was *you* who suggested I come
to see your Gypsy for counsel on our plight," Mrs. Mc
Gill retorted defensively. "I'm simply listening, as you
asked."

"I only suggested it because I could no longer bear
your going on and on about us ending up in the poor-
house now, with the master dead," Lysandra blared. Before she could say a thing more, however, there came a

clattering from out on the portico at the front of the fortuneteller's shop.

The three of them turned to lock eyes upon the still-
ajar door.

"Go and see who it is," Madame whispered to Lysandra. "I'm not expecting a client for another fifteen minutes, so perchance it is simply a browser."

Still fuming, Lysandra slapped her palms down on the
table and pushed herself to her feet. Then, straightening
her posture as though she'd suddenly found herself
among enemies, she strode to the door.

Lysandra swung it open to see a man bent over from
the waist, vigorously brushing what appeared to be dirt
from one of his trouser legs. He was modestly dressed
in somewhat dated apparel, and even with him bowed
so, Lysandra could see that the cuffs of his coat sleeves
were rather threadbare.

She stepped out onto the porch, shutting the shop door
behind her. "What is it?" she heard herself growl. "What
are you doing, sneaking about out here? Eavesdropping,
were you?"

He instantly straightened. He looked to be in his late
twenties, and his face—one Lysandra was certain she'd
never seen before—showed unmistakable surprise at having been addressed so rudely. "Why, no . . . no, miss."

"Well then, what do you want, pray? Have you an
appointment with Madame?"

He knit his brow, and his lips and eyes said that he
was fighting a smile at this title. " 'Madame?' " he repeated rather incredulously, in a tone that seemed far too
insinuating for Lysandra's tastes.

She, in response, cinched her colorful silken shawl
more tightly about her. "Aye, *Madame*. She's a Gypsy
fortuneteller, in case you failed to read the shingle before
*stumbling* up to our door."

He sobered and offered her a penitent nod. "Ah, 'Madame,' yes. I should, indeed, have guessed as much from your sign."

"Well, what is it you want, then, sir?" Lysandra demanded again. She was beginning to realize that she was wrong in taking her lingering anger out on this stranger, but she truly felt no will to right the situation.

He shrugged with an insouciance which only served to irritate her further. "My fortune told, I suppose," he said; but it seemed far more a question, than a reply.

"Then you'll have to make an appointment, as do the rest of our clients! You can't just come barging in for such a service any time you please."

*"Our* clients?" he echoed with the hint of a smirk tugging at one corner of his mouth. "You keep saying 'our,' young lady. Am I to understand that you are a fortune-teller as well?"

"I am. But I only read the cards. Madame does palms, tea leaves, cards, *and* the crystal ball."

"Cards alone will be fine," he quickly replied, smiling fully now; and the blatant interest he showed in Lysandra in those seconds unnerved her.

What a stupid, broad, love-stricken grin, she thought with a critical cluck. What sort of a man displayed such attraction after only a moment or two of discourse with a female?

"I think you'd be happier with Madame's work, just the same."

"No." He reached out and placed a disquietingly warm palm upon her left arm. "I want you."

Shocked, she raised a brow at him.

"You to . . . to read for me," he quickly added, apparently also seeing the need to complete the request.

"Ah, Lord, *fine,*" she said with a snort, losing all patience with finding herself manipulated by everyone she'd encountered that morning. "Come back at half past three, sir. I should have some time for you then. And

182

bring with you a pound exactly," she snapped. "We're not running a bank here, mind!"

Trevor Walsh drew his head back with a start, as she fled inside, slamming the door of the establishment behind her. Good God, she was glorious! A *treasure*. The last sort of woman he'd expected to come across in this staid little town.

She was a green-eyed, golden-haired gem of a girl in the exotic, and most provocative, garb of a bona fide Gypsy. The raven black, crimson, and yellows of her almost Oriental shawl and long skirt were terribly out of place with her soft Irish features . . . as if she were a niveous gardenia shoved into a garish cloisonné vase. Yet, somehow, she did seem to belong in such a place. Her emerald eyes had, indeed, shone with an astuteness that said she might actually be good at the business of soothsaying.

Yes. He'd definitely be back at half past three for his one-pound reading. He wouldn't miss it for the world!

On second thought, however, perhaps he'd be just a couple minutes late—thereby giving her reason to rail at him again. She was so lovely, so exciting when she was angry. Oh, that he might, one day, have the opportunity to unleash her rage upon him *in bed!*

But no! a voice within him scolded. He'd never before sunk to introducing one as young as she to his often too-worldly ways, and he knew he shouldn't start now. Glendalough was a decent, respectable town with a monastery as its founding stone; and he was, in truth, nothing more than a stranger, a transient here. Much as he might wish to, he couldn't allow himself to become involved with any of the locals. It was very likely, after all, that he'd be leaving as quickly as he'd come.

# Two

Lysandra went back inside to find her mother rising from the table, as though to take her leave.

"Who was out there?" Madame asked in a hushed voice.

"A man. I've never seen him before."

"What did he want?"

"To have his fortune told, I guess. I said he could come back at half past three and I'd read for him."

The Gypsy scowled. "Oh, but I've some free time before then."

"I know, Madame. But he insisted upon having me divine for him. I explained that yours would be a more thorough reading, but he seemed rather adamant in the matter."

"Well, to each his own, I suppose. 'Twill be good practice for you, anyway . . . reading for a total stranger. We don't get many of those."

"Off so soon, Mum?" Lysandra asked, as Gertrude gathered up her drawstring purse and began walking toward her.

"Aye. I must get back and prepare lunch. I was forced to leave that imbecile Busby in charge of the kitchen in my absence, and you know what a hash he'll make of things if I don't get back before the provisions are delivered."

She stopped to give her daughter an obligatory peck on the cheek, before leaving.

Lysandra, still vexed by their previous conversation, was not inclined to reciprocate the gesture. "Well, just don't take Madame's jest too much to heart. Only one who has spent as much time with her as I can hope to understand her curious sense of humor," she declared, turning back as her mother reached the door.

"But I was perfectly serious," the Gypsy protested.

"Of course you weren't. Please stop it now, Madame. Your joke is wearing thin."

Gertrude Mc Gill paused, as she took hold of the door's handle, and turned back to flash her daughter a parting smile. "Thank you for suggesting a visit with her, Lysandra. It has proven far more helpful than I'd dreamed possible. I feel worlds better now. See you back at the manor, and don't be late for supper."

She made her exit an instant later, and Lysandra turned about to face the Gypsy with the most ireful look she had ever dared give her. "How *could* you? Don't you realize she's just distraught enough to follow through on that hairbrained proposal? She's come absolutely unraveled since Lord Fitzgerald died! Hence, I brought her here that you might try to console her, not send her off to begin gadding about in the night in some ludicrous get-up!"

"I'm surprised at you, child," Madame returned sternly. "Three years of reading and you still have not learned that the crystal, the cards, *none* of them are for comforting. They are for telling the truth. The bare, unsettling, and ofttimes 'hairbrained' truth! I didn't reveal anything to your mother that she wouldn't, in her own measured time, have come to think of herself! Besides, your hitching up with a moneyed lord does not sound so foolheaded to me. There's no fortune to be made in divining, as you well know."

"Yes, yes," Lysandra retorted, beginning to mimic Madame's voice, " 'the only future I'll see in this business is *everyone else's.*' " It was probably very true, though, she thought, instantly regretting having mocked this admonition from her mentor. Were it not for the fact that Madame had to tend to stocking and selling the healing stones and elixirs in her shop, there wouldn't be enough demand for soothsaying to keep one reader busy in Glendalough, let alone two.

It was, nevertheless, an ideal part-time position for Lysandra. One that had always accommodated both her studies and her chores at the manor. She wanted to acknowledge this again. She knew she should thank Madame for her generosity in granting her this apprenticeship. Before she could do so, however, the Gypsy took her leave. Her ebony eyes slanted a look at Lysandra that said she wished to hear nothing more from her for a while. Then she picked up her fortunetelling ball and went into the back room to await her next client.


The rest of the day seemed interminable to Lysandra, with Madame still too miffed at her outburst to do anything more than sniff resentfully whenever they chanced to pass one another in the shop. She was, therefore, in a discomfited frame of mind when it came time for her three-thirty appointment.

The stranger was a few minutes late, and save for the fact that she'd so recently had angry words with two very important people in her life, Lysandra would have chided him for it. Being at heart mild-mannered, she'd had her fill of clashes for the day and chose to simply hold her tongue.

He seemed a gentleman, in any case. He was quick to remove his hat as he entered and wipe his feet on the mat Madame left just inside the front door for that purpose. Lysandra rose to usher him in after he knocked,

186

and he was most careful not to sit down at the reading table, until she was seated again herself.

That suggestive grin of his had abated, thank Heavens. And, all at once, he struck Lysandra as the sensitive sort—the kind of man who might actually prove caring, if ever she found the need to confide in him.

Now that the anger she'd shown earlier had subsided, she was finally calm enough to be able to take in his features; and he wasn't a bad-looking fellow. He had thick black hair and a wholly masculine face, with high, angular cheekbones and a shadowed jawline that bespoke a heavy beard were he to let one grow. A couple of short locks of wind-blown hair had fallen onto his forehead, helping to frame his dark eyes and give him the rather careless, yet appealing, look of a rogue. And though Lysandra was hardly the sort of young lady who would allow her gaze to stray too far below a man's neck, she did note that the stranger was wonderfully broad-shouldered and long of limb.

"What should I do, miss?" he asked with a slightly ruffled laugh. "I'm afraid I've never had my fortune told before."

She cocked her head and offered him a smile. "Why, nothing. Just answer my questions as they are asked, and then I shall try to do the same for you."

"Do I pay you now?" he inquired, reaching into one of his pants pockets.

Lysandra's cheeks warmed a bit at this. She wasn't sure why, but the inquiry seemed so much like something a "customer" might ask a courtesan that suddenly this otherwise upright business felt somehow improper to her.

She waved him off and gave forth a light laugh. "Oh, no, no. Let us see if, in fact, I am proficient at reading for you, before I am paid for it."

His broad black eyebrows drew together. "But how might we do that?"

She smiled again, reaching out to take her deck of

187

tarot cards from the silken scarf in which she always stored it. "Simply enough. If you judge me to be at all good at telling you about your present, I'm likely to be adept at telling you your future."

"You mean to say you're not always good at it?"

"I wouldn't know. I've never read for you."

He chuckled. "No. I meant, you don't read well for everyone who comes here?"

She shrugged, beginning to shuffle the cards. "For most, yes. However immodest, I must confess that is so. But you could be the rare exception, sir."

"Trevor," he supplied.

"What?"

"Trevor Walsh, miss. That's my name," he explained, extending a hand to her.

With some reluctance, she reached out and gave it a hurried shake. To her maidenly dismay, she found his grasp, in those seconds, very strong, warm, and just a trifle moist.

"And might I know what you're called?"

"Lysandra Mc Gill."

"Lysandra," he repeated, his voice suddenly deep, almost caressing. "Ah, that's lovely. And so fitting for a fortuneteller, isn't it? So foreign and mysterious."

"'Tis Greek is all. Hardly so foreign, when one considers how many other Greek words have found their way into our language."

He drew back in his chair a bit, clearly respectful of this subtle rebuff from her. "Aye. I suppose."

"You're from the north," she declared.

"Why, yes. That's exactly right! From Donegal. It's amazing, your knowing that without having yet turned over a card!"

She rolled her eyes. "I could tell from your *accent*, Mr. Walsh. Anyone would be able to."

His cheeks colored slightly at having committed another blunder with her. "Yes. Sorry. Of course." She wasn't going to be easy, this one, he acknowledged. Very quick. Very bright. And despite how young she appeared to be, obviously experienced enough to know when she was being charmed. He'd have to try a more direct, less manipulative approach.

He leaned toward her once more, trying to glean what he could from her eyes, her expression. He just as quickly recoiled, however; for, all of a sudden, she thrust her arms out before her like ramrods. Then, with her eyelids squeezed shut, she let her palms hover just an inch or two apart.

"Whatever are you doing?"

Her eyes fluttered open once more, as though he'd roused her from a deep sleep. "Building up a charge. It requires great concentration, so kindly remain silent until I've finished."

"But a charge for what, Miss Mc Gill? This isn't some sort of witchcraft, is it? For I've no intentions of being party to that."

Clucking with exasperation, she let her hands fall to the table. "No. Of course it's not. 'Tis just something we diviners do, so that our fates won't become entangled with those for whom we read."

"You can't be serious. Does that sort of thing actually occur?"

"Oh, yes. Indeed it does, sir. I've seen it happen more than once, in fact, and always when I'm reading for someone who also possesses some talent for prophecy."

Go ahead, then, pretty little lass. Lovely green-eyed lady, he thought with delight. Become "entangled" in my fate for heaven's sake. There is nothing I'd like better!

Intrigued, he leaned forward again, placing both of his elbows on the table and resting his chin in his upraised hands. "And what happened? Do tell!"

Lysandra drew her head back slightly, as that solicitous grin of his appeared once more. What a curiosity-seeker he was! Hadn't he anything better to be doing with his

189

time than picking some maiden's brain for what most would interpret as merely a coincidence or two?

"Well, on one occasion, I predicted that a girl friend of mine would receive a parcel from Dublin with gold in it, and within a fortnight, it was I who was sent such a package. A gold ring it was, from one of my aunts who's a Dubliner. Another time, I saw in the cards that my youngest brother would fall from a tree and break his arm. And, faith and begorra, it was I who had that very same mishap in his stead. Both times, as God is my witness, I'd forgotten to clean and seal my aura before reading for them."

He shook his head with amazement and flashed her an admiring look. "Gracious, my dear. I've never heard such stirring accounts. Then, you really must build up a charge and seal yourself with me; for I'm a vagabond of sorts, and there is no telling what might befall you in *my* place."

"You're making fun of me," she said defensively.

His large brown eyes widened with seeming sincerity. "Oh, no. Not at all. In truth, I find all of this fascinating. I can't remember when I've met anyone quite so refreshing. So, do go on with your preliminaries. 'Clean,' 'seal,' and I shall be quiet and just watch."

"All right," she replied tentatively, hesitant to shut her eyes again in so overly enthusiastic a presence.

It was all most distracting: the feel of his gaze upon her, the sound of his breathing as she again shut her eyes and began trying to build up a charge between her palms. Ordinarily she would have taken her time with this important precaution, waiting until she could feel a pronounced warmth and tingling in her fingers before she ran her hands along her torso and up over her head—first cleansing her spirit, then sealing it away from possible contamination, as though enclosing it in an imaginary bubble. But she was strangely unnerved by this man; and

190

all she really wanted to do was get his reading behind her and move on to another, *safer* client.

Her hands, therefore, sped through the procedure, finally coming to rest before her, rather tremulously, upon the table. Her eyes fell open an instant later to confirm what she already knew: he was positively perusing her, as though watching a lover sleep.

"Are you all 'sealed' now?" he inquired, with what Lysandra found to be an irksome smirk tugging at the right corner of his lips.

"I am."

He stifled a laugh against one of his fists. "Ah, good," he replied, but his tone said that he still found the safeguard rather ridiculous. "Now, Miss Mc Gill, how do I determine if you can, indeed, tell me about my 'present'?"

She pushed the deck of tarot cards over to him. "Shuffle, please, three times, and then we shall do a Keltic Cross on you."

" 'On' me?" he echoed, raising an intrigued brow.

"I can do without your lewd remarks, Mr. Walsh," she scolded in a low voice.

He didn't appear in the least bit chastened, however. Getting a rise out of her was obviously his aim, she suddenly deduced; and this made her realize she'd be best off simply ignoring such ploys. "I merely meant 'about' you, on whatever sphere of your life comes most often to mind these days."

He seemed to sober at this, as though there was, indeed, some issue that was troubling or perplexing him.

When he'd finished shuffling, he handed the deck back to her. "Oh, aye. There is one matter that has been in my thoughts of late."

Starting at the far left side of the table, she fanned the cards out, facedown. "In what area of your life is it?"

"What area?"

"Aye. Business? Romance? Family?"

191

He knit his brow as he gave this some thought. "Why, *both* business and family. They are rather inseparable for me, I'm afraid. I certainly hope this won't make it impossible for you to read for me."

"No. But just remember that 'tis you who must sort out my answers, once you have them. I will not necessarily know which I am speaking of, family or your work."

"Very well. I shall endeavor to do that on my own."

"Choose ten cards and hand them to me, please."

He proceeded to do so. To Lysandra's surprise, he didn't vacillate over any of them, as most of her customers usually did, but plucked them up from every part of the arched line with a decisiveness that only the most cocksure of men could display.

Lysandra laughed to herself as he pushed his selections into her grasp an instant later. This, in turn, seemed to make him smile slightly as well, and his commanding dark eyes locked upon hers once more.

"Now what?" he asked, as though truly beginning to enjoy having this novel service performed for him.

"Now I lay them out into a Keltic Cross, and we see what we can see, good sir."

"Mother Mary, it looks as though they're hand painted," he noted with awe, as her delicate fingers placed them all face up in a formation that did rather resemble a crucifix.

"Aye. From Northern France, I believe Madame said about this particular deck."

Her eyes dropped back to the cross she'd created, and Trevor sat admiring the long darkish lashes that shaded her emerald orbs like two tiny, Oriental blade fans. As though she were doing some complex calculation, her cherry-red lips began to work slightly, as she squinted, seeming to take in every detail of the brightly colored cards.

Of a sudden, she drew a breath in through her teeth.

"Ah, heavens, man, the Tower is before you. A card that almost always speaks of ruin. What on earth can that pertain to?"

Her green eyes were upon him once more, as though demanding an answer. He scowled with confusion and, somewhat sheepishly, leaned over to get a better look at the card to which she pointed.

There was, indeed, a tower shown on it. What was more, it was ablaze, its roof seeming to have been ripped off by a lightning bolt. Its hapless occupants had jumped from it and were plummeting to their deaths on the rocks far below.

"I don't know."

"But you must. This shouldn't be a mystery to you."

Despite the intensity of her gaze, its almost accusatory nature, he remained silent on the subject.

Yes. He had an inkling of what it meant, but that was for him alone to know. He'd be damned if he'd share it with some prying little diviner! "Let us move on to the other cards, if we might, and perhaps it will become more clear to me."

Those vernal orbs of hers pierced him a bit longer, as though she somehow knew that he was being evasive. Then, mercifully, she returned her gaze to the spread.

"Well, this is *you,* sir," she said, tapping one of the center cards, whereon there was painted what looked to be a merchant. He had his hands crossed over his chest like a genie, and there was an arched row of golden goblets situated on a table behind him.

"A man of plenty," she said pointedly; though, judging from his simple apparel, she wouldn't have guessed it. Nevertheless, the cards did not lie. "You're certainly well enough shod that you need never work again, if you don't wish to. And yet, so emotionally starved, Mr. Walsh," she observed, a soft curious smile coming to her lips, as she again raised her face to him. "How could you have

193

come to be? Is it that vagabonding you mentioned earlier?"

For the first time since she'd met him, he honestly seemed to need to pull back from her. She was *right* about his loneliness! Oh, God, the depths of it! She suddenly felt it so profoundly, that she wanted to reach out and place a consoling hand upon his arm. And were he any of her other clients, she would have. Because he was a stranger, however, she somehow managed to refrain.

Heaven help her, *this* was the biggest drawback of the soothsaying business. She'd known it from the first, so she could hardly protest too much now. More often than she cared to tell, she not only saw into people's joys, warmth, and love, but into the very wrenching depths of their despair, causing discomposure all around. It was very much like going out for a stroll and suddenly sinking into a peat bog. It seemed she was always up to at least her knees in the awful, sloppy stuff before she had the presence of mind to try to get herself out.

"Ah, sir, is it that you've been widowed of late? For I do sense some loss in you and something very recent, at that."

"No. I've never been married. So that can't be it."

"A death in the family, then?"

He nodded. "But only a relation on my mother's side, no one I knew personally."

Lysandra felt herself flush slightly at this. How could she be so off with him? How could she have been struck so deeply by his need for kith and kin and then looked up to see such a relatively untroubled face?

By the Saints, she wasn't proving much of a match for him, as readers went. But, perhaps, as he'd suggested earlier, it was best to move on to the other parts of the cross and see if a connection could still be made.

"This second card in the spread, Mr. Walsh, the King of cups, is, or has been, your obstacle in the matter you're questioning now. He, like yourself, is a man of some

194

means. Generally kind, but he has unwittingly stood in your way for quite some time now. Do you know of whom I speak, sir?"

"Aye. I think I do."

Oh, thank God, Lysandra inwardly sighed. There was nothing worse, naught more embarrassing than missing the mark on all counts with a querent. So it was with great relief that she received this affirmation from him now. "Is what I've said true of this man?" she asked charily.

"Yes. But, as you mentioned earlier, he is no longer an obstacle to me."

"This, the nine of coins," she continued more confidently, pointing to a card with a lovely maiden upon it, "is what you now have to work with in the matter."

"What does it signify?" he asked, cocking his head as he studied the card.

"She, the lady pictured here, is to become a friend or lover to you. You will meet her in a public house, perhaps. Some place where she renders a service."

"In a shop?" he inquired hopefully. "One such as this, perchance?"

Lysandra, feeling as though she'd just gotten caught in a spider's web, reflexively straightened in her chair. "Oh, no! No, sir. I wasn't referring to myself, and I am sorry if I gave you that impression."

"Oh, don't apologize, my dear," he replied, reaching out to place one of his large warming palms over hers where they still rested upon the table. "I've seen far worse presumptions made in my day."

Swallowing uneasily, Lysandra slid her hands out from under his. Dear Lord, what an onerous reading! She felt as though she were in a newly dug graveyard, falling into one deep hole after another as she struggled to make her way through it.

Despite her promptness in drawing away from him, his tone was arrantly provocative as he spoke again. It

195

was as though he was utterly undaunted now by the staving off messages she'd been sending with her body and words.

"My *friend,* Lysandra," he said softly, almost tenderly. "What possible wrong could there be in your spending a bit of time with a man who is, as you already know, so very alone, so much a stranger in your fair town? Were you on your own in my native Donegal, I certainly would not deny my friendship to you."

She must have gaped at him in those seconds. Surely he had seen how taken aback she was by this sudden and most heart-rending appeal from him.

"What say you to a walk sometime, near the cottage I am letting on the western outskirts? You may certainly bring your Gypsy friend along or anyone else you wish, if you think it improper to be seen alone with me."

"Mr. . . . Mr. Walsh, I am paid to tell fortunes, not keep company with our patrons," she stammered.

His speech became as faltering as hers. "Oh, of . . . of course. How forward of me to have made such a request. I'm sorry." He dug about in his pants pocket, then withdrew several pounds sterling. "Here. Here you go, my dear. For your trouble." With that, he rose.

"But I haven't finished your reading. And you haven't yet asked me any questions."

He tried to smile, but his eyes suddenly glistened with deep emotion. "Oh, but I have. I only just did. The most important question. The only one I came to you for, in truth. And now, I fear, I do have my answer."

He looked in that instant, despite his goodly height and build, like a little boy to her. His face was as blotchy with abashed color as one of her younger brothers' would be when caught misbehaving.

Lysandra stood up as well, never having driven a customer away and rather distressed at seeming to have done so now. "Oh, but, Mr. Walsh, you must understand. In spite of my vocation here, I'm really quite the innocent.

Though people say I look older, the truth is I've only just turned eighteen, and I'm afraid you might not have realized that."

"I should have though," he admitted. "Indeed, I should have." His hands were folded before him at the level of his loins, and he appeared both penitent and strangely worshipful of her in that instant. Then, without giving Lysandra a second longer in which to further clear the air, he strode to the coat rack and retrieved his hat.

"Oh . . . but, good sir, I feel badly about your leaving me so much money! Do come and take some of it back. Why, you're not even letting me finish the simplest of readings for you. I don't want you thinking those of us in Glendalough an ungracious lot. I mean, I know I spoke rather sharply to you this morning on the porch, but that was because my mother and Madame were hatching some dotty scheme to see me married off to the new lord of Fitzgerald manor. And it roiled me more than you can know, the very thought of them trying to serve me up to some old man, for the sake of a dower! So, you see, I am guilty of taking some of that ire out upon you, and I do most heartily apologize. I'm not usually rude to clients, you see. I'm not usually rude to *anyone,* but—"

"He's old, you say, this new lord of the local manor?" he interrupted, reaching back and letting his hand come to rest upon the door's handle.

"Aye. I'm told he is."

"Well, then, I can't blame you, lass. I would be angry, too, in your place."

Lysandra sidled out from behind the reading table and took several hurried steps toward him, holding out the extra money he'd left. "Oh, good, then. I knew you'd understand."

"Indeed I do. And should you ever wish to unburden yourself regarding your mother's plans for you, please feel free to come and chat with me at Murphy's thatch.

I should be there for the next week or so. Now you know my name, and you know where to find me. I can't promise that I'll hold the power to influence the situation with your mum, mind. But I do know a thing or two about the law in such matters, and I can, in any case, offer you a listening ear. As you have so kindly done for me today."

Lysandra wanted to differ with him on this last point, to stop him and again apologize for having been anything but sympathetic. If nothing else, she wanted to see his overpayment stuffed into one of his coat pockets, but he was gone in that instant. Tipping his hat a bit before putting it back on, he slipped outside and closed the door behind him. And by the time she reached the threshold, he had boarded a passing livery carriage and was headed off toward the west.

Shaking her head at how abruptly he'd departed—and how successful he'd been at making her feel as though she were the only one of them who had acted improperly—she stepped back inside, shut the shop door, and returned to the table.

She was about to collect the cards he'd drawn and shuffle them into the rest of the deck. But she hesitated for a second or two. Only one card remained, within the actual body of the cross, to be spoken of; and curiously, he hadn't stayed to be told about it. It was the two of coins, the card that represented his past in whatever matter it was he'd been querying about.

The two of coins, Mr. Walsh, she thought. A card that signified a lifetime of great emotional ups and downs and sudden changes of heart. Well, this was true of him. Given his precipitant exit, that much was apparent.

The card continued its silent revelations, nonetheless. His had been a past filled with too many business dealings and uncomfortable concessions. A past bereft of anything but hollow love affairs in which true feelings were never revealed. But then, Lysandra didn't need the cards to tell her that either. She'd seen it in his eyes. Those dark entreating orbs.

He was like a ship too long afloat upon very turbulent seas. He was finally looking for a place to come to port. He was considering Glendalough, yet he still wasn't sure. And, Lysandra reminded herself regretfully, as she finally gathered up her cards and returned them to their silken resting place, she certainly hadn't proven much of a welcomer.

What harm would there have been, after all, in having agreed to walk with him for a while? Simply strolling and taking in the bright colors of the autumn leaves? Why had she felt it necessary to refuse him in so biting a fashion, when he'd made it clear that she was free to bring along any chaperone she wished? What, having seen into his battered, yet gentle, soul through the cards, did she honestly think she had to fear from him?

# *Three*

Five days had passed since that fateful morning in Madame Safina's shop when Lysandra's mother and Mr. Trevor Walsh had come to call. The nights were growing longer and chillier, and the rustle of fallen leaves could be heard all about the little servants' cottage where Lysandra and her family had lived since her father's death some six years earlier.

It was late afternoon, and the local physician had again come to check on Lysandra's ailing paternal grandfather, Shane Mc Gill. Her two younger brothers were still off at school, and wishing to stay out of the doctor's way during his visit, Lysandra lay upon the saggy bed she shared with her mother and stared out of the room's only window at the great house that lay hundreds of yards away.

When her family had first moved here, just after her mother was widowed, Lysandra had fantasized about one day living in that grand old manor. During the summers when she'd worked as a chambermaid in it, carrying linens up and down the manse's backstairs, she had sometimes pictured herself taking occupancy of one of the suites and dressing in the elegant fashion of the many female guests.

Lord Fitzgerald had been ages younger back then, it seemed. A convivial bachelor, he was forever entertaining marriageable noblewomen who hailed from far and wide. The hope had always been, of course, that he'd settle upon one of them so that he could wed and beget an heir for the estate.

He hadn't, however. Finally stricken with a debilitating heart condition, he had spent his last years in a wheelchair. Save for a nephew, who had never visited the manor, there was no direct descendant to take up residence and continue employing its sizable staff, as well as the many craftsmen and merchants in Glendalough proper.

Fitzgerald had been no spring chicken, of course. It was said that he was over the age of eighty when he died, so Lysandra acknowledged with a shudder that the rumor his heir was in his late sixties certainly seemed founded.

She had hoped, as the days had passed and she'd heard no more talk of Madame Safina's crazy scheme to see her married off to Fitzgerald's heir, that her mother had forgotten about it. Yet just now, before sinking wearily upon the bed, she had spied a highly falsified lineage chart of the Mc Gill family upon her mum's night table. Proof positive that her parent still intended to try to pass her off to the new master as being half descended from a blue-blooded Gaelic clan.

Lysandra had seethed at first spotting it. But knowing that her dustups with her mother only caused the woman to become all the more mulish in her stands, her anger had quickly shifted into a tight, nervous knot in Lysandra's stomach. And now she simply lay aching and rocking a bit, her belly upon the mattress as she searched her mind for the best way to dissuade her mum from this ridiculous and devious course.

It was possible, Lysandra supposed, that Fitzgerald's successor simply wouldn't believe Gertrude's claim. Or that, though believing it, he would find Lysandra unattractive or unsuitable for him.

In any case, Lysandra knew that she could never bring herself to reveal her mother's deceitfulness to him or anyone else in Glendalough. She was, in spite of her occasional quarrels with her mum, basically obedient. And though she suspected that her father's death had been more a result of Gertrude's henpecking than anything else, she did understand how difficult life had become for her remaining parent since his untimely demise. So, no matter what the outcome, she would not add to her mother's suffering by betraying her confidences.

Gertrude meant well, after all. Though bossy and manipulative most of the time, she did seem to have her children's best interests at heart. But this . . . this *sham,* this falsification of records was simply carrying things too far!

With a troubled sigh, Lysandra rearranged herself. Tossing her long blond hair over her right shoulder, she pushed up to a sitting position. Then she reclined against the bed's headboard so she could clutch her cramping stomach.

Oooh, she thought with revulsion, the very idea of losing her maidenhood to some wrinkled codger with icy feet and hands sickened her! How heartless! How cruel of her mum not to realize that most young ladies wished to give their hearts and bodies to men of roughly their own ages.

A couple of days earlier, there had still been some hope for Lysandra. It hadn't yet been determined whether Fitzgerald's nephew would come to visit the manor with an eye to settling therein. But just that morning word had finally arrived that the new lord could be expected at any time. The estate and town were now buzzing with expectancy, in fact. Everyone was preparing for him—including, to Lysandra's deep dismay, her *mother.*

It was all unfolding just as Madame's crystal ball had shown, as inevitable as most presaged events revealed themselves to be. And, all at once, Lysandra felt as though she couldn't breathe! She was smothering in this tiny room. This confining cottage.

She had to get out and talk to someone. Had to share her misgivings with somebody she could trust to keep her mother's daft plot a secret. She sat up and slid her legs around to the side of the bed. She was not sure whom she sought, but she knew it must be an individual with no vested interest in how matters turned out with Fitzgerald's heir.

An outsider with little call or opportunity to gossip and thereby risk divulging whatever she chose to tell.

After several seconds, it came to her: Mr. Walsh. He was just the listening ear she needed, and moreover, he had actually offered to function as such when she'd mentioned the situation.

She wasn't sure what had possessed her to disclose so much to him. Perhaps she had simply been too flustered by his suggestion that she visit him to consider the ramifications of being so open. But whatever had moved her to it, she was now rather glad that she'd done so.

She got up and groped about under the bed for her shoes. Then she crossed to her mother's dressing-table mirror and began pinning her hair into the upswept style of the day.

Walsh was a stranger, admittedly. A man whose smile had, in truth, struck Lysandra once or twice as being somewhat iniquitous. Yet he'd touched and flattered her when he'd confessed that he'd only come for a reading because he wished to get to know her better.

She certainly hadn't spotted anything in the cards that indicated his was truly an evil or deviant nature. So . . . what harm would there be in paying such a lonely sojourner a call? What risk was there in confiding all to a man who was only planning to stay in Glendalough for a few more days?

Fortunately, the physician was engaging Gertrude Mc Gill in a heated discussion as Lysandra finally emerged from the bedroom. She was, therefore, able to slip out of the cottage without having to answer her mum's usual battery of questions about where she was going and when she'd be back.

With any luck, she could hitch a ride with those of the part-time staff who headed back into town at this time of day. Then the coins she carried in her tiny drawstring purse would buy her transportation to and from Murphy's thatch in plenty of time for her to return to the manor for supper.

The thatch looked strangely uninhabited, as Lysandra approached it nearly an hour later. Almost hidden by the surrounding forest, the dwelling was darkened by shade at this late hour of the day. She, therefore, expected to see some lights glowing within or smoke coming from its chimney. Yet, there was neither.

Her gait slowed, as she reached the stone walk that led to the cottage. She was beginning to wish she'd had the forethought to ask the liveryman who'd conveyed her to remain until she'd made certain the current resident was at home. But she had foolishly dismissed the driver, and now she'd have to wait alone out here for a full hour if it was revealed that Mr. Walsh had already vacated the place.

"Trevor?" she called out timidly.

How unlike you! a voice within her scolded. How totally against all good sense to let herself be abandoned in so remote a wood! No one, save the liveryman, knew where she was, and he could hardly be expected to come searching for her if she wasn't standing at the side of the road when he returned as requested.

"Mr. Walsh?" she shouted, her voice heightening with her growing apprehension.

She took a couple more steps forward, then stopped again, feeling strangely frightened of the towering oaks that stood all about her. They suddenly seemed like a lynch mob with their long limbs creaking ominously in the wind and the conspiratorial whispers of fallen leaves whirling about them.

God help her, her heart was racing as though it might pop right out of her chest! What had possessed her to come here? What had made her believe that a fifteen-minute reading on a man was vindication enough for her to call upon him unescorted so near nightfall? Lord, she *deserved* whatever fate lay ahead of her for having acted so impetuously!

Doing her best to swallow back her fear, she closed her woolen shawl more tightly against another rush of October wind and forced herself to start moving forward once more. "Mr. Walsh, 'tis I, Lysandra Mc Gill," she announced loudly. "You said I might come to you for a walk one afternoon, and I'm here."

"Are you, now?" someone whispered from very close behind her.

Feeling as though she'd just leaped several feet from the walk, she wheeled about with a thoroughly startled expression.

"Oh, sweet Jesus, you scared me half to death," she exclaimed, noting, with both annoyance and relief, that it was indeed the man she sought standing just a foot or two from her.

He smiled, clearly glad to see her. Then, after she'd had an instant or two in which to collect herself, she did the same.

"Are you alone?" he asked. "You were welcome to bring a chaperone, you know . . . Miss Mc Gill?" he prompted, when she simply stood staring mutely up at him.

She knew she should respond. Somewhere, in some anteroom of her mind, his last inquiry echoed, undeciphered. And yet, she was so enthralled with taking in his dark, princely features again—with viewing this intriguing stranger in the casual light of day rather than that of

Madame's shop—that she couldn't seem to bring herself to answer him.

"Lysandra? Are you all right?"

"Oh . . . oh, aye. I'm fine, sir. I just"—she swallowed dryly—"just was afraid that you'd already left Glendalough. I mean, with the thatch looking so unlit, I feared you'd gone away."

He shook his head and continued to smile, as though he couldn't imagine what had gotten her into such a distraught state. "No. I'm still here, I'm glad to report."

Lysandra clapped a palm to her chest. "Ah, faith, not half as glad as I!"

His dark eyes instantly filled with concern. "Why? What's the matter?"

"Oh, I . . . I just desperately need to speak with you. Might we go inside? I'm suddenly feeling cold."

"But of course," he replied, wrapping an arm about her shoulders and ushering her to the cottage with the practiced manner of one who had handled many women in his time.

Oddly though, Lysandra took great comfort in the gesture. In her wrought-up condition, it struck her as almost fatherly, in fact. "In answer to your earlier question, I've no chaperone with me. I needed to speak to you alone, you see."

He pushed the thatch's wooden door open and guided her inside. "Oh?" he returned, his tone revealing the pleasure he took in this revelation. He hung his hat up on the peg beside the door and led her over to the hearth, where he knelt and began at once to rekindle its fire.

"Yes. Well, I don't know if you recall or not, but I mentioned that my mother and Madame Safina were scheming to see me married to the new lord of the manor. Do you remember that?"

"Yes."

"Well, you said that I could talk to you about it, and, well, I surely would like to."

He looked up from his work at the fireplace and smiled softly, apparently at her faltering. "Do be my guest, then, my dear. I promise I shall hang upon your every word."

"Oh, please! Don't tease me. I don't think I can bear it today."

He rose, having finally poked the embers into a good flame, and turned to face her with a look of the utmost sincerity. "But I wasn't teasing, Lysandra. I'm delighted you've come to see me. It is what I wanted from the first. I told you that. So, of course I'll listen. To anything you might have to say. Anything at all. Please sit down," he said, guiding her to a wing chair that stood just a few feet away. "Is this near enough to the hearth? You did feel cold as I led you in."

"Oh, aye. This is fine."

"I've been walking about the grounds all day," he explained, crossing to the wing chair that stood opposite hers and sliding it over to close the distance between them. "So I let the fire die down, I'm afraid. I wasn't expecting to have company."

"Of course not. I mean, how could you have known?" she replied, watching him settle into the chair and taking a measure of comfort in being face-to-face with him once more, as they had been at Madame's reading table the day they'd met.

"*You'd* have known a visitor was coming, in my place, though, wouldn't you?" he said with a chuckle. "You'd only have to lay out those beautiful cards of yours, and you'd have seen me coming."

Her cheeks warmed slightly at this unexpected praise. "Oh, I don't know. I didn't think my reading for you particularly accurate. Was it?"

"Yes, my dear. You couldn't know it, of course, because I'm rather a private sort and, as you're well aware, a stranger to Glendalough. But I thought your divining quite good. I confess it made a believer of me. Were I planning on staying here for a while longer, in fact, I would certainly ask you to read for me again . . . Oh, but how thoughtless of me. I should already have offered to bring you something to drink. Some tea or ale, perhaps?"

"Oh, no. Thank you just the same, sir. I won't keep you long. I just wondered what you meant the other day when you said you knew a thing or two about the law in such matters as my mum trying to wed me to the new lord. Are you a barrister, perchance?"

"No. But I've engaged more than my share of them in my business. And one just sort of learns things from them, you know. Rather like a sponge soaking up water. So much of the law is just common sense, after all."

Lysandra nodded, beginning, finally, to feel somewhat at ease with him. "Well then, have I any recourse, do you think?"

"Recourse?"

"Against marrying the new master, Lord Fitzgerald's nephew? Surely you've heard about him. The town's positively atwitter with news of his imminent arrival."

His face brightened with a suddenly knowing smile. "Aye. It is, isn't it? What's his name, by the way?"

"It's Fitzgerald as well, of course. Why?"

He shrugged. "I've traveled widely, as I told you, and I simply thought perhaps I'd heard tell of him somewhere."

"Well, have you?"

He gave his head a slight shake.

"So, what do you think? Is there any way for me to get out of marrying him, should he decide he likes me?"

She could see him beginning to bite the inside of his cheek in that instant, as though fighting some amusement. "I would hope, Lysandra, that the dear man would do more than 'like' you, if he becomes intent upon taking you to wife."

"Well, you know what I mean. Can he and my mother lawfully force me into such a union?"

He leaned back in his chair, obviously pondering the question. "And where, may I inquire, does your father stand on all of this? Might you not ask him to take your side?"

"Oh, no. He's deceased. He passed away six years ago, leaving Mum in rather a bad state to support us children. Thus her interest in procuring a good marriage hold through me, you see."

"Aye. I'm afraid I do. Well, you look to be old enough to have a legal say in such matters, Lysandra. And were you to promise yourself to another man, I think you would pretty much scotch your mother's plan . . . Tell me, have you some other suitor in mind?"

She sat back as well. "Heavens, no. Between working for Madame and my chores at the manor, I've never had time for courting."

"But surely you've been pursued, my dear. A girl as lovely as you? I can't believe you haven't caught the eyes of several men in this county."

Again she blushed a bit and dropped her gaze. "A few, I suppose. But, I'm told I don't appear very approachable. And then there's the fortunetelling. You know how God-fearing Catholics feel about that!"

A smile played upon his lips at her wonderful candor. She was every bit as forthright and refreshing as he remembered her being, and he adored her for it. He wouldn't permit it to show, however. He wouldn't dream of letting his great attraction to her repel her a second time. "I certainly do."

"It's not so very sinful, though. I mean, a lot of the men in the Bible possessed the gift of prophesying. And, really, what harm is there in people being forewarned of danger? Or given the sweet hope that comes with good news?"

209

"Why, none, my dear. You're absolutely right. Since you have such a gift, why not share it with others?"

"Precisely."

"You're not dressed as a fortuneteller today, though, I see," he noted evenly, though inside, his response to this was anything but even. As enticing as he'd found her in the Gypsy apparel she'd been wearing when they'd met, he liked her even better in the bustled green frock she'd donned today. He was especially pleased by the fact that it wasn't the severe, high-collared sort of gown most women wore in public but a softer, lower-cut variety. And her lovely pale throat was adorned with a thin choker of verdant gemstones, which seemed to match the color of her eyes to a breathtaking tee.

"No. This is my day off, sir."

They locked gazes for several seconds; and though Lysandra saw the same come-hither message in his dark orbs that had shocked her so at the shop, she felt, for some reason, drawn by it now.

It was somehow mesmeric in this light, this soft fire glow that was so clearly meant to warm her against the cold reality she'd come here to escape.

She leaned toward him a bit, and he, smirking ever so subtly, toward her. Sweet Jesus, she had never felt anything quite like this: the magnetism that seemed to dance between their bodies in those seconds! It was calling, beckoning her into some sort of unspoken sin, as though this man were the devil himself!

By the Saints, how easy it would be to simply let herself go with him! To fall back limply in her chair and allow him to come and swoop down upon her, enfolding her in his arms as though they were the wings of an enormous hawk.

She let it continue for just a bit longer, let his expression grow almost wolfish in his obvious desire to cross and have his way with her. Then, knowing that she had to try to get a grip upon herself and her situation once more, she straightened and cleared her throat.

They were completely alone, after all, a voice within her reminded. She was probably miles from anyone who could hear her scream if he decided to descend upon her, and she'd been a damned fool to have allowed their silent, smoldering interplay to have gone on as long as it had.

"Now, back to this matter of my needing a suitor to fend off the new lord, Mr. Walsh. Would it have to be genuine?"

"What?"

"My relationship with another man. Would I have to actually become engaged to someone else, in order to discourage the new lord's interest?"

"No. I suppose not. As long as you and the fellow in question both kept up the facade of such a liaison. At least until Fitzgerald's heir moves on to considering some other woman, that is. But you know, Lysandra, you haven't even met the man. Don't you think you ought to wait and see what you feel about him before inviting one of the local lads to take part in such a precarious ruse? What if it turns out you find him attractive?"

"A man in his *sixties?* You can't be serious!"

Trevor pressed masking fingers to his mouth and chuckled at her adolescent revulsion at such a suggestion. "Well, perhaps you could simply come to think of him as a father of sorts. You know, someone to take care of you over the long haul."

"I do wish you wouldn't make light of this, Mr. Walsh! You know full well I'd be obligated to do a great deal more than let him 'take care of' me, were we wed. I'd have to—" Her words broke off, and she felt a mortified blush spread over her cheeks.

"To sleep with him?" her host graciously supplied.

"Yes. How hideous!"

"But of course, you're right, my dear," he agreed, finally seeming to sober at her plight. "I'm afraid I didn't

211

fully consider the situation from your young perspective. Naturally you don't want to risk falling into his hands, so I suppose you ought to scare up an alternate 'beau' as soon as possible."

At this, she rose and began pacing anxiously about the hearth rug. She was searching her mind for the name of a male she might trust in such a feigned partnership. Sadly, however, she was coming up blank. She'd been so busy with her studies and with trying to help her mother earn a living in the past several years, that the only close bonds she'd formed were with other girls of her age, and she doubted that she could rely on any of their older brothers to ally with her in this undertaking.

"What about you?" she asked finally, crossing to the fireplace and leaning up against the mantelpiece for support.

He was plainly astounded. *"Me?"*

"Yes. I mean, I know you're planning on leaving here soon, but perhaps you could stay to attend the welcoming ball for the new lord with me next week. Simply linger long enough to help me give the impression I'm spoken for."

Despite all of his tacit solicitations, he appeared genuinely uncomfortable at this suggestion. She, in turn, felt rather wounded.

"Oh, I don't know, my dear. I've never been one for even pretending at such involvement. And what will people think, when I just up and leave town a couple weeks hence? It could be construed as breach of promise."

"By whom? I'm the only one you'd have made such a promise to, and I'd be content to let everyone believe that *I* chose to break things off."

To her continued dismay, he dropped his gaze and shook his head. "Ah, God, Lysandra. I don't know. I want to help you avoid this plot of your mother's, since it seems so abhorrent to you. But I simply hadn't reckoned on your asking me to take such an active stand against it."

He looked up at her once more, his dark eyes wide with apology; and Lysandra found herself near humiliated tears at having been desperate enough to have made such a request.

"Oh, say no more, sir, please," she choked out. "Clearly I was out of line in even suggesting such a thing, and I'm terribly sorry. It's just that, if you only knew the insane lengths Mum intends to go to in this matter! I mean, it's outrageous! She's had a fake lineage chart drawn up to try to convince the new master that I'm of blue-blooded Gaelic descent on my father's side. And she's actually considering dressing herself up as a banshee, so that she can 'presage' the coming death of my ailing Grandpa Mc Gill, thereby further backing her claims! We'll be disgraced, Mr. Walsh, if the truth is ever revealed! We'll be the laughingstocks of the county and likely forced to leave town! But she . . . she just doesn't seem to realize any of that," Lysandra faltered, growing angry with herself for beginning to weep, but feeling unable to fight back her tears.

With an exasperated snort, she turned her back to him and began digging through her purse for a handkerchief with which to dry her eyes. "I mean, Mother didn't cook up this ludicrous scheme by herself, mind you. She saw it in Madame's crystal ball," she continued to lament, in spite of herself. She knew, in her heart, that this man, this stranger, was the only one she dared tell it all to, and she just couldn't seem to stop from doing so now. "'Tis not as though Mum would ever hatch such a plot on her own. And I must say, in her defense, that it's not simply our family she seeks to help with this wangling, but all of Glendalough; for Madame also foretold that 'twill be the new lord's interest in me that will cause him to choose to take up residence in the manor."

"Oh, really?" Trevor interjected, raising a brow which

seemed to indicate that, though he was just a visitor, he'd taken an interest in the town's talk about the coming aristocrat.

But then, Lysandra recalled, the cards had told her that he was considering settling in Glendalough himself. So, perhaps he too wished to benefit from Fitzgerald's legacy.

"Aye," she went on. "And there may end up being some truth to it. Who knows? 'Tis just that mother is taking it all so seriously, you see. It's as though she thinks she saw it chiseled in granite, rather than simply floating in a crystal. She believes it with all of her heart. And the worst part is"—Lysandra stopped to give her nose a loud blow with the hankie—"I do, too!"

She turned back to him, not caring now what a swollen mess her outburst was making of her face. "That is to say, I've spent the last three years of my life advising my clients to believe in the art of divining and put their trust in the workings of destiny, and then, when I don't like what's spotted in *my* future, I just want to disavow it! But one *can't*, don't you see? Your fate comes for you, whether you want all of it or not. And I can already feel mine beginning to drag me downward, like a gigantic, relentless whirlpool!"

With that, she crooked her arm over her eyes and turned away to sob into the wall of hearthstones.

"Oh, Lysandra," Trevor said softly, finally realizing that he had no choice but to rise and go over to comfort her. The poor girl was obviously anguished, and he couldn't bear to watch it any longer.

As he came up behind her an instant later, he was surprised to find how reflexive it all was. He had always found crying females rather enervating; but fortunately, he had the presence of mind now to turn this particular one about, pull her into his arms, and stand rocking and shushing her like a seasoned charmer.

"Now, now. I think we can both agree that the future

hasn't come to pass yet. So, it must be, at least somewhat malleable."

He felt her shake her head where it rested against his waistcoat, but he simply chose to go on rocking and cooing. "Yes, my dear. Trust me in this, please. If you really do not wish to marry the new lord, you'll somehow find a way to repel him."

She leaned back slightly and gazed up with a set of tear-rimmed eyes which he found positively wrenching. "No I won't. I wanted to repel you last week at the shop, and now, just look. Here I am, in your arms."

"Aye. So . . . so you are," he acknowledged, his breath catching in his throat.

If she'd only let her gaze fall in those seconds, if she had only buried her face in his chest once more, he was fairly certain he would have succeeded in resisting temptation.

She didn't, however. Her emerald eyes remained fixed upon his, searching his soul for the solution to her predicament; and before he knew it, his mouth was claiming hers. He was kissing her with the fervor he might impose upon the most experienced mistress, and she wasn't doing a thing to stop him!

"Oh, God," he whispered urgently, somehow managing to take his lips from hers and slide them over to her ear. He was certainly worldly enough to have felt such dangerous chemistry with women a couple of times before. It was the kind of alluring energy that went totally undeterred and unslowed by such obstacles as having to unbutton fly fronts and untie bustles. It was the sort of energy that could lead to seething, writhing passion upon a coarse hearth rug in just the space of a heartbeat. And the truth of the matter was that he'd already come to like this young lady far too much to allow himself to take her in so heedless and explosive a fashion. "God, Lysandra, we must get you home at once!"

"Why?"

"Stop it now," he said firmly, trying to be strong enough for them both. "You know why. A lass with eyes as wise and deep as yours knows perfectly well what will happen between us if I let you stay a moment longer. Now, I'm going out to hitch up Murphy's carriage. Where do you live?"

"The manor."

"The manor?" he echoed with an astounded rise to his voice. "I thought you just worked there part time."

"I do. But Mum was Fitzgerald's cook, so we live on the grounds, in one of the servants' cottages."

Continuing to look as though he was fighting the urge to ravish her, he pulled away and began heading for the front door. "Stay by the fire. Go on warming yourself. We've a bit of a ride ahead of us."

"But I've already arranged to have the liveryman return for me," she said weakly.

"Then we'll stop in town and you can cancel the order."

"It's because of my reading for you, you know. This inclination we both have to . . . to let things go too far between us."

He turned back to her with an uneasy expression. "Why do you say that?"

"Because I . . . I was so flustered by you that I did rather a careless job of sealing my aura, and I fear I entangled my fate in yours. I'm sorry, Mr. Walsh. I truly didn't mean to."

"It's *Trevor,* Lysandra. Sweet Jesus, I've just kissed you. With such ardour I can scarcely think straight! So, I believe we can dispense with the formalities now. Don't you?"

She bit her lip and nodded meekly at his annoyance.

"And do stop attributing everything that happens to that divining of yours," he continued to chide. "The truth is I became hopelessly enamored of you the instant our eyes first met. And that, for the record, was a full four

216

hours *before* you did any 'cleaning' and 'sealing' with me. So your infernal cards had nothing to do with it!"

With that, he plucked his hat and greatcoat from the wall pegs and took his leave, slamming the door behind him.

Lysandra wouldn't have known it from the harshness of his tone, but she could have sworn he'd just confessed to falling in love with her!

# Four

"Hit me once more with the powder, child," Mrs. Mc Gill ordered, studying herself in a hand mirror. "Square in the back of the head."

"Ah, Mum, you're white enough," Lysandra countered with a groan. She was perching on the end of their bed, taking in her mother's preposterous banshee get-up via the reflection from the vanity looking glass before which the matriarch stood.

To Lysandra's dismay, Gertrude looked every bit as ridiculous as she'd imagined she would. Clad in nothing but an ivory dressing gown, she'd covered herself from head to toe with a mixture of flour and talcum. Then she'd combed out her long wiry hair, only to smother it with powder as well.

Knowing it was no use refusing her, Lysandra rose again and, per her mother's request, gave Gertrude's head a whack with their large powder puff.

"By the Saints, girl, you didn't have to hit me that hard!"

"Sorry."

"You still don't agree with any of this, do you?" Gertrude arched a thoroughly floured brow at her.

"No."

"That's because you are, by nature, disobedient. You've no respect for your elders. Never have had."

"That's not true. I think I've been very helpful to you since father died. 'Tis just that this is so dishonest. Don't you see? Going about, pretending to be something you're not and getting a fake family tree drawn up—so that I might deceive others. Just think of the disgrace that will be brought upon us if the new lord learns of these deceptions!"

"He won't. I mean, I thought my wailing was very convincing last evening. Didn't you? I went off to practice in the woods to the north, and I do think the sounds I made came very close to those we heard from the banshee who bewailed Sloan's death."

"Aye. They were good," Lysandra conceded. "Haunting to be sure. But what if the lord didn't hear you? You're not planning on dressing up like this *every* night, are you?"

"Of course he heard. He'd have to have been deaf not to. Everyone on the grounds heard. The kitchen staff was humming with talk of it this morning. And if your grandfather would only *die,* as that doltish doctor keeps saying he will, I could retire this accursedly skimpy guise for good and all!"

"Oh, Lord, mother! How can you speak of Grandpa that way? Why, he's just in the next room!"

Gertrude waved her off. "Ah, the door's shut, isn't it. And I'm keeping my voice down. Besides, he's suffering and only wants to be put out of his pain. And 'tis time the old goat did his part to help support us! I've kept him fed and clothed, lo, these past six years, so you'd think the least he could do for us is croak on cue now. Before I catch *my* death dancing about in the cold night air this way!"

"Sweet Jesus, you're so heartless sometimes," Lysandra replied, narrowing her eyes at her mum's reflection. "It doesn't matter one wee bit to you, does it? What happens to Grandpa. What happens to me. You don't care if marrying Fitzgerald's heir would make me miserable for the rest of my days."

"Miserable, is it? Well now, how would you know that? Despite my repeated requests, you haven't stepped one foot into the great house since the new lord arrived. You haven't so much as caught a glimpse of him. So how, for the sake of heaven, can you know what you might come to feel for the man?"

"I only know that you don't care what I feel. You'll push me at him, no matter what I decide, just so you can get your pot of gold out of the arrangement!"

To Lysandra's surprise, her mother responded to this by wheeling about and slapping her across the face. It was one of Gertrude's rare shows of violence, and her daughter was accordingly stunned by it. Before she could respond, however, the matriarch launched into a caustic, if hushed, lecture.

"What are you saying, Lysandra? That I'm *greedy?* Am I greedy for wanting a guarantee of food and shelter for you children? For wanting to see you well wed? For needing a nest-egg to see me through when the three of you have grown and left me? For not wishing to spend the rest of my days standing before a hot stove and plucking chickens, until I drop from exhaustion?

"There are two kinds of women in this world, daughter. The sort who have to kick and claw all of their lives in order to carve out an existence and the kind who win a tolerable one through the men they marry. I wanted with all of my heart to be one of the latter. And for a few years I was. Until your father died, leaving me with his untold gaming debts."

Until *you* killed him with your endless nagging, Lysandra thought. But there seemed no point in fanning the flames by saying as much now.

"Take it from someone who knows," her mother continued, "the very worst fate of all, is having had a decent life, then, through no fault of your own, losing it. I *won't* let that happen to you, my dear. And if that makes me seem heartless and greedy, so be it!"

With that, she set down her hand mirror and, crossing to the casement window, pulled it open and sneaked out into the darkness. Fitzgerald manor was, for the third evening in less than a fortnight, about to be "serenaded" by a banshee.

Careful to leave the sashes unlocked for her mother's return, Lysandra went over and closed the window behind her. It was cold outside, just two days from Halloween now; and Lysandra hoped to God her mum wouldn't catch pneumonia in the freezing evening air.

On the afternoon when Trevor Walsh had brought Lysandra back to the manor, he had promised that they would see one another again before he left town. Lysandra had certainly hoped so, because apart from her wishing to enlist him in the role of fiancé, she had also come to realize that she was as fond of him as he claimed to be of her.

It was with great relief, therefore, that she had again received him at Madame's shop a few days later. He hadn't stayed long. Pretending to be looking for an elixir or two, he had simply passed Lysandra a note, which asked that she meet him near the east end of Fitzgerald manor on October twenty-ninth at nine P.M.

Hurriedly reading the missive, Lysandra had nodded her consent to the request and whispered that she'd do her best to slip away from the cottage at that hour.

That hour, as it turned out, was very nearly upon her now, and she knew that she should take advantage of her mother's brief absence and sneak up to the great house for a few minutes.

She didn't know what it was Trevor wanted. But, in truth, the enamored, sportive part of her didn't care. She simply wished to have him hold her in his arms and kiss her once more. Having had plenty of time now in which to mull over every detail of his advances—his provocative smile, his loving touch, his obvious adoration—she was more than ready to let matters progress with him. Amidst her anger at her mother, her concern for her dying grandfather, and her dread of finding herself forced upon the new lord, Trevor Walsh had become her only cause for joy. And she honestly believed that had he left town without attempting to contact her again, the very core of her would have been shattered.

Knowing there wasn't a moment to waste, she hurried to the room's wardrobe and withdrew her heaviest shawl. She considered leaving the cottage by way of the front door, but quickly decided against it. Though her grandfather was likely too stuporous from his painkillers to notice her departure, her little brothers probably would; and she naturally wanted her meeting with Trevor to be as clandestine as possible. It was *scandalous,* after all, to have a rendezvous with a stranger in the cloak of darkness.

She crossed to the window and, reopening it, slipped outside with the same furtiveness her mother had displayed. Then, once she found her footing on the ground below, she reached back up and closed the sashes as best she could behind her.

His note had said "the east end" of the manor, she reminded herself, turning about to scan the moonlit terrain that lay between her and the great house. If she traveled along the shading edge of woods to the north, she believed she could reach their rendezvous without being spotted by anyone. But as she hunched a bit and headed into the forest that marked the manor's boundaries, she soon discovered she was wrong.

Her *mother!* Dear God, her mother was just a little ways ahead of her on the winding footpath that led through the woods.

Lysandra stopped abruptly at seeing this. Her eyes hadn't yet adjusted to the darkness, and she had to squint to make out her mum's form. The matriarch was moving

222

away from her, or so Lysandra reasoned. If Gertrude was intent upon doing what she had the night before, she would head for the knoll, some distance to the north, and let her spurious wails resound for everyone in the manor to hear.

Lysandra, therefore, remained where she was, waiting for her mother to veer toward the left, toward the knoll. All at once, however, it became apparent that Gertrude was *facing* her! Perhaps she'd even caught sight of her in the eerie moonshine that was filtering down through the shedding trees of the forest.

"Oh, Sweet Jesus," Lysandra exclaimed under her breath. She had let a few minutes pass before leaving the cottage, so why hadn't her mother reached her destination by now?

Perhaps she'd forgotten something. Or maybe she had become so cold in the evening's chill that she was heading back to *powder* a matching cloak for herself.

Whatever the reason, Lysandra knew she must turn about and dash home at once. She couldn't risk getting caught out here. She wasn't at all sure she could think up a plausible excuse for it.

She turned on her heel and began running away, praying that her mother wouldn't hear her footfalls. This was probably in vain, however, for the rustle of the fallen leaves she passed through, the sporadic cracking of twigs beneath her, seemed to her panicked mind to be as loud as a torrential rain.

Blessed Mary help her, what would she say to her mum? How would she explain this odd flight into the darkness?

Her head was bowed, her body hunched, as she continued to run. She strained to hear whether or not her mother followed; but the only sounds for miles seemed to be the thundering of her own feet.

And then, of a sudden, her nemesis was no longer behind her but *before*. She heard a spooky sort of groan, just a few feet ahead of her, and she came to a halt once more.

"Lysandra Mc Gill?" someone inquired in a weird monotone.

She looked more closely and saw a luminous form in a flowing white gown.

A *banshee,* some part of Lysandra's stunned brain acknowledged. A *real* banshee! For what else could look as this being did? Vaporous. Hovering. Its tresses and robes billowing all about it, as if blown by some force quite apart from the evening's wind.

"Answer me, girl," the creature ordered. "I've no patience with those who run from me as you just did!"

Though Lysandra's throat seemed too constricted by terror for her to squeak out a sound, she somehow managed to say, "Aye. That is my name."

The spirit floated before her, its white mane and raiment making it appear to be swimming through some sort of heavy yet invisible liquid.

"You conjured me up, you and your Gypsy familiar," the banshee hissed. "You deal enough with the spirit world to know better than to do that, yet you did so! And if you don't tell your mother to stop impersonating me at once, I shall claim her, Lysandra! You two put her up to this, and you had better make her stop!"

There was a great blast of wind from the banshee's direction in those seconds; and feeling too weak to stand against it, Lysandra dropped to her knees. "Oh, yes. Oh, God. Oh, Lord! Of course I will, banshee! It won't happen again, I swear it," she cried out, never having experienced such a formidable presence.

"Good," the specter replied, suddenly lifting a comb from out of her voluminous garment and beginning to run it through her long hair with comfortingly tranquil strokes.

She was absolutely breathtaking in those seconds; her eyes huge and dark, her features as pale and delicate as those of the finest alabaster figurine. As she struggled back up to her feet, Lysandra didn't mean to gape at her, but she just couldn't seem to help herself. Having worked with Madame Safina, she knew how rare such a look into the spirit world could be, and she simply found herself spellbound by the apparition.

"Go then, and pry no more into matters not meant for mortals," the banshee exclaimed, her angelic visage turning almost demonic. "Get ye out of my sight, before I haul you to the Under World with me," she threatened. This final warning was accompanied by a stench so awful it could only have come from the portal of a grave.

Needing no further prompting, Lysandra pushed a hand up to her nostrils and turned away to begin racing toward the east side of the manor. Had the banshee not been in her way, she probably would have sprinted home and slipped back inside to hide herself, trembling and sickened, beneath her bed. But the specter was blocking the path in that direction, and after the words she'd just spoken and her dire expression, the only sane course seemed to be to get as far away as possible!

# Five

Trevor Walsh was filled with both relief and concern, as he peered around the east side of the estate and spotted what looked to be Lysandra running toward him. On the one hand, he was happy to see that she'd been able to sneak away from her family's cottage in order to meet with him. On the other, however, she was proving most careless in choosing to dash out across the back green to him, rather than taking a more covert route.

"Lysandra," he called out in a sharp whisper, as the runner finally got near enough for him to be certain it was she.

"Trevor! Oh, God, Trevor," she said breathlessly, as she reached him. "The *banshee!*"

"Aye. I know," he replied with a chuckle. "I saw her heading into those same woods a couple of minutes ago. Most impressive! Had I not known it was your mother, I would have thought for certain 'twas the real thing."

To his surprise, this formerly reserved maiden reached out and hugged him to her with all her might. "But it *was,*" she exclaimed, keeping her voice hushed. "That wasn't Mum. She set out for the knoll to the north. That was a *real* banshee, and she told me that she'd 'claim' mother if she doesn't stop this impersonation!"

Trevor took hold of her upper arms and pushed her

away just enough to look down into her eyes. "A 'real' banshee, you say? Are you certain?"

"Yes! I've never seen such a monstrous face! And that horrible odor she called up, when she threatened to take me back to the Under World with her! Oh, Trevor, I . . ." Her words broke off, and she grew even paler. "I'm afraid I'm going to faint."

She was right in fearing this, for within the instant her eyes rolled back, then her lids drifted shut and she became limp in Trevor's hold.

He wasn't sure what to do with her in those panic-filled seconds. This was absolutely the last thing he'd expected to happen during their hurried rendezvous, and he knew, given the circumstances, that he couldn't take her up to the manor for help.

He bent down and gathered her up into his arms. Then, spying what appeared to be a vacant servants' lodge off to the east, he began carrying her toward it.

The dwelling was unlocked, fortunately. With a thrust of his knee, he managed to push up on the door's handle and make his way inside. The place smelled musty, was evidently long-unoccupied, and he had to rely entirely upon the moonlight from its windows in order to spot a settle upon which to deposit Lysandra's dead weight.

"Faith, girl, how you and that silly mum of yours have complicated matters," he muttered, as he walked to the divan situated in the far right corner of the cottage's front room and laid her carefully across it.

Feeling rather shocked by it all, he lifted her head and shoulders, making room for himself to be seated. Then he lowered the upper half of her onto his lap and sat fanning her face with his hand.

"Lysandra," he said. "Do wake up, my dear. Our time together will be short enough, as it is."

She didn't respond, but lay perfectly silent and still. The only sound he heard, in fact, was the faint and eerie wailing of what he hoped to be merely her mother, to the north.

With a worried sigh, he again dropped his gaze to Mrs. Mc Gill's daughter.

Even in that dim light, he could see that she'd again changed her appearance entirely. As though with a flair for keeping him off balance, she was neither the Gypsy tonight nor the properly corseted gentlewoman. Instead, she was clad in the soft, unhampering dress of the classic Irish peasant.

Beneath her loosely knit shawl there appeared to be nothing more than a light-colored flaxen blouse and a long dark skirt of wool. And her blond hair, though upswept, was framing her face with the silky, fine wisps one most often saw on wind-blown children.

God, how easy she was making it for him to love her, he thought with an apprehensive swallow. How easy, with her body so unbridled and her face looking so angelic, to simply pretend to be trying to revive her with a *kiss*.

But *no*, he told himself sternly. No matter how irresistible she was, he would never take advantage of a woman in such a defenseless state!

He, therefore, began lightly slapping her cheeks with the back of his hand. As much as he hated striking her in any manner, he knew she must be roused before her mother became concerned about her absence and began searching the grounds. "Lysandra, darling, please come to for me," he urged.

To his great relief, she finally did so. Her eyes fluttered open after several seconds, and she lay staring blankly up at him.

"Oh," she groaned. "Where am I?"

"In a cottage near the manor, love. You fainted, and I didn't know what else to do with you."

"Trevor?" she inquired, still blinking.

He gave forth a soft laugh. "Aye. Please don't tell me

you were expecting some other man or I shall be quite jealous, I'm afraid."

She tried to smile, but she still felt terribly dizzy. "No. Of course I wasn't."

"Ah, good." He reciprocated her smile, glad to see that she seemed to be feeling better. Of a sudden, however, she again appeared horrified.

"The *banshee,*" she exclaimed, obviously recalling the awful encounter.

He held her tightly, fighting her impulse to sit up. "Shh," he directed, brushing some hair from her eyes. "Let's not speak of her again in what little time we have left together."

"But she was *real,*" Lysandra protested weakly, allowing herself to sink back into his lap.

"I've no doubt. And I'll walk you back home in a few minutes, so you're protected from her. But for now, love, let us talk only of you and me?"

Lysandra didn't need to be told, of course, that their rendezvous had definitely gone awry. Standing before Murphy's hearth last week and kissing a virtual stranger had been risky enough. But now she somehow found herself sharing a sofa with him. Lying in his *lap,* for heaven's sake! And even by the moon's dim light, she could see that he was as drawn to her as he'd seemed the last time they'd been together.

He tried to go on smiling down at her in those seconds. His lips curved upward, as though in a herculean effort to make her believe that she was utterly safe in his arms.

She knew she wasn't, however. An instant or two later, the corners of his mouth quivered with the weakness that overcame them both whenever they were alone; and before Lysandra knew it, his face was covering hers and he was kissing her with abandon.

"Oh, God, I *ache* for want of you," he confessed in a feverish murmur between kisses. "I think of you constantly. Can't get you out of my mind."

"I know," she replied, keeping her voice equally hushed. "I've been feeling the same way about you."

His words were again a hot stream at her ear. "No, but 'tis worse for me, my angel, because I'm not an innocent such as yourself. I know all too well what ecstasy men and women can bring one another, and it is all I can do to keep from ravishing you."

Lysandra felt an unspeakable surge beneath her skirts at this admission. "But why must you keep from it? I wouldn't stop you, you know," she replied, his candor giving her the courage to exhibit some as well.

Drawing a pained breath in through his teeth, he let one of his palms travel down the side of her, tracing her profile, from the swell of her bosom to the sharp indentation of her tiny waist and back out again at the level of her hips. He groaned, his hand closing, almost angrily, over the gathers of her skirt. "Ah, but you *should*," he growled. "Were there any justice in this world, you'd yet have a father to look after you. One who would horsewhip me for wanting what I want right now!"

"Can it be as bad as all that?"

He issued a dry laugh against her cheek. "Oh, no. That's just the trouble, my sweet. It isn't bad at all. It's as good as anything gets in this life," he added, and the telling waver in his voice again caused the depths of Lysandra to well up with both fear and anticipation.

In the moon's bluish glow, her eyes were like a siren's to Trevor. Almost against his will, he felt himself being sucked down into them, down and down—until his mouth was upon hers once more and he was able to feel her stirring receptiveness to the sudden introduction of his tongue.

She shouldn't have been permitting this, a voice within him raged. She shouldn't have fainted, and he should have been able to go on simply conversing with her beside the manor.

There were things about him, about his past, that she

230

was entitled to know. Things he'd summoned her tonight expressly to tell her. Yet, just as at Murphy's thatch, they weren't talking anymore. They were both so overwhelmed with animal longing that neither of them seemed capable of speech.

Continuing to kiss her, he slipped his hand down into the drawstring neckline of her blouse. Then his fingers closed about the soft peak of her right breast with a roughness he hoped would bring her to her senses and cause her to pull away.

To his dismay, she didn't, however. Issuing only a tiny gasp from beneath his plundering mouth, she allowed this fondling to go on until her nipple grew hard from his relentless attentions and his hand progressed to do the same to its twin.

"Stop me," she heard him command in a heated yet vexed tone, as though he was unable to do so on his own. "Bring this to a halt, like the virtuous lass I know you truly are."

"No," she whispered back, moaning blissfully at his touch. "I'd much rather lose myself to you than that revolting old man in the great house. And if that makes me a loose woman in your eyes, so be it."

"Damn it, Lysandra!" he snarled, withdrawing his hand from her blouse and reaching down to pull up her skirt with a brusqueness that made her breath catch in her throat.

He was genuinely cross with her for letting nature take its course between them; and lying in his lap this way, she suddenly felt as she had when her father took her over his knee in her childhood. Trevor's vehemence was the same. He was even pinning her waist with one arm, holding her down for the infliction of his wrath as her father always had. But instead of feeling pain in the seconds that followed, she knew only the most ineffable pleasure.

With continued abruptness, he pulled her pantalets

down to the level of her knees. Then he parted her secret sheath and began stroking the tiny swell within her, his fingers inching upward all the while as though goading her to pull away while she yet could.

Though she still felt his gaze upon her, she couldn't bring herself to reciprocate it in those mortifyingly intimate seconds. She clearly wasn't the seasoned lover he was, and she couldn't pretend to be. It was all just too new to her. Being touched in such a way, in so private a place—by one of the opposite gender—she had to let her eyes close and her face turn to the side.

"Lysandra, look at me," he murmured.

She shook her head. He was simply trying to ruffle her, to make her realize how serious a realm they were entering now.

"Yes. Look at me," he ordered again, his tone more insistent as his fingers continued their skillful manipulation within her.

She suddenly felt compelled to obey, and as she locked gazes with him, she saw, to her surprise, that his eyes were almost teary for some reason.

"Now, having had a taste, are you sure this is what you want?"

She nodded.

"Knowing so little about me and that no other man may want you when 'tis done, are you *certain?*"

"Aye," came her enraptured whisper, and all at once she sensed that she was no longer a child, a novice to him. His expression became so attentive, so concordant that she knew he at last viewed her as an equal, a consort

"God help me, I love you. I've never felt this for a woman before," he declared, finally taking his hand from her and sliding out from beneath her torso to stand up beside the divan.

She was aware, through her peripheral vision, that he threw off his coat and began unbuttoning his fly in those seconds, that his fingers were working to bare him to

232

her, much as she'd been bared to him; but she couldn't bring herself to look.

She only wanted to gaze into his eyes, those dark orbs that bespoke the soul she now trusted to guide her through this passage, this bittersweet rite she'd heard such mixed and fragmented accounts of through the years.

As he returned to the divan and knelt between her legs a moment later, as she felt him spread her thighs more fully and replace his fingers with the masterful length and breadth of himself, she was amazed at what an extraordinary blend of pain and pleasure it caused.

Something tore and burned within her. Her body actually began to cramp at this invasion, as though echoing his warning about the gravity of the act.

She whimpered a bit and clutched his torso, her nails digging, talonlike, into his shoulders. Yet, even now, when her distress was at its zenith, the pleasure of their joining prevailed.

His intimate flesh soothed and caressed hers with the gliding motion of his body. Again and again and *again*— until all that remained was sheer bliss.

Trevor fought to last for her in those passionate moments. Against her virginal tightness, against the warmth and wetness that seemed to draw him deeper and deeper still, he struggled to keep breaking free of the consuming vortex within her.

And for a while he succeeded. For several long minutes, he clenched his teeth at the irresistible tug of her hidden folds as he moved in and out of her.

But she claimed him in the end, of course. Just as her emerald eyes and full cherry lips had the day they'd met.

In a final frenzy of motion, his hard thighs slapped heedlessly against hers. His hands brought her hips down to meet his thrusts, and he felt himself empty into her, giving her all of the warmth and ardor such a young beauty deserved.

They lay limp and winded for several seconds, their

hearts seeming to race in satiated unison. Then she spoke again.

"Please save me from the master, love. Come and be my partner at his welcoming ball on All Hallows," she beseeched.

"Oh, just don't attend it," he suggested, feeling too dreamy and drained by their coupling to converse.

"But I must. I've been avoiding Fitzgerald's heir since his arrival, and I know Mother will force me to go, if she has to take me there at gunpoint."

"All right then. I'll come," he agreed, unable to refuse her. Though he knew what she asked was nearly impossible for him, that he was entirely the wrong man for such a role, he said yes.

In light of what he'd just claimed, of what she'd just so sweetly *given,* he knew it was the very least he could do.

# Six

"Well, thank God you're getting ready," Gertrude Mc Gill said absently to Lysandra, as she entered their bedroom with a pile of remnants from the Halloween costumes she'd been hurriedly preparing for her sons. "May I assume, then, that you don't intend to give me call to drag you up to the ball by your hair?"

Lysandra laughed under her breath, her mother's knack for exaggeration amusing her. "No. I'll go willingly. You've got to take the boys out to gather treats, and I did agree to tell fortunes in Madame's place this year."

"Mercenary beast, that Safina woman! She's always agreed to read for just five pounds at the ball before."

"I know. But can you honestly blame her? She was offered fifteen to read at McGee's pub tonight. That's practically a small fortune, and the shop does have its expenses."

Gertrude clucked her continued disapproval and tossed her armload onto the bed. "Just the same, I thought it rather ungracious of her to refuse us, what with this being our welcome to the new lord . . . Oh, Lysandra," she snarled, finally catching full sight of her daughter in the dressing-table mirror. "What on earth have you done to your face? It looks green!"

"But witches *are* green, Mother. Well, green*ish*. You

don't like my costume?" she asked, turning about to afford her mum a better look.

"Mercy, no! It's dreadful! You look as though you've been dead for centuries. I don't want you meeting Fitzgerald's heir that way!"

*But it's perfect,* Lysandra inwardly gloated, biting her lip to keep from smiling at what an ideal opportunity All Hallows was giving her to repulse the new master.

Mrs. Mc Gill crossed to the wardrobe, flung its doors open and began rummaging through it. "No, no. Where's that sweet little shepherdess guise you wore last year? You looked so lovely in it."

"Teddy spilt punch down the front of it. Don't you remember?" Lysandra replied, grateful in this instance for her youngest brother's clumsiness. "The stain wouldn't come out, so we tore it up for rags."

"Oh, that's right." Her mother stepped back from the wardrobe with a discouraged sigh. "Well . . . at least try to smile at the lord as much as possible, child. And do take that pointy hat off from time to time, so he can see there's some pretty blond hair beneath it."

"Aye, I will," Lysandra agreed, wanting to rush through making up so that she could get up to the manor as soon as possible. With any luck, she could complete her card readings within a couple of hours, then sneak off with Trevor for another tryst in the empty servants' cottage before her mum arrived at the festivities.

She hadn't told Gertrude about her intimate encounter with Walsh, of course. Much as she wanted to celebrate her passage from maiden- to womanhood, she knew there was probably no one she could tell of it and not sully her reputation. But how blissful she'd felt as he'd seen her home two nights before! How warm and tremulous she'd still been as she'd climbed into bed and tried to brand every melting detail of his ravishment into her memory.

Her mother had scolded her for having gone out after

dark, naturally. But luckily the tongue-lashing hadn't spoiled the heavenly mood in which Lysandra's clandestine lover had left her. And once she'd explained to her mum, however falsely, that her outing had simply been caused by her spotting the *real* banshee from their bedroom window and then going out in search of Gertrude in order to pass on the apparition's warning, the matriarch had fallen silent and let her daughter go to sleep.

It was difficult to tell whether or not Gertrude had taken the secondhand admonition to heart, however. As convincing as Lysandra knew she'd been in recounting her nightmarish conversation with the banshee, the fact remained that Grandpa Mc Gill still hadn't died. So it was very likely her mother would see cause to don her white guise once more.

"Well, I'm off," Lysandra announced seconds later, having finally put the finishing touches upon her warty nose and chin.

Mrs. Mc Gill winced again at her costume. "Sweet Jesus, just promise me you'll try to look your prettiest for the lord the *next* time he sees you," she pleaded, sinking down on the bed and staring into the wardrobe, as though in search of something to wear to the ball herself.

"Aye, and *you* promise me you won't be seen in that banshee get-up again," Lysandra returned sternly, gathering up her tarot deck and the hem of her black witch's gown before taking her leave.

The matriarch merely shrugged at this.

"I mean it, Mum! All Hallows is absolutely the *last* night one ought to be out taunting those in the spirit world. 'Tis a threshold to the afterlife, and you know it as well as I."

Gertrude waved her off. "All right, all right, you pest. I'll bear that in mind. I promise. Just get yourself up there, and give the lord a proper curtsy when the pair of you meet."

Lysandra did precisely that, as it turned out. Within

ten minutes of her arrival at the manor, she was led up to Fitzgerald's successor by the estate's steward; and after being introduced as the cook's daughter, she genuflected and told the lord she sincerely hoped he'd choose to stay in Glendalough.

The geezer didn't say much in return, fortunately. Costumed from head to toe as some sort of Roman deity, he simply clasped one of Lysandra's hands between his gloved fingers and drew it up to his masked face to grace it with a mock kiss.

It was difficult for Lysandra to judge his age in those seconds, for he issued little more than a hello, and his features and hair were almost completely obscured by his golden headdress.

His posture was good, however. He didn't appear at all hunched, as she would have expected for a man of his years. But this proved to be of little consolation to her.

After a moment, obviously aware that the lord had no interest in engaging her in further conversation, the steward mercifully led him off to make the acquaintance of some newly arrived guests. Lysandra was, therefore, freed to proceed to the reading table, which one of her mother's kitchen staff had set up for her near the door that led to the terrace.

The *terrace*. That was where Trevor had agreed to enter, when he finally arrived. Though he had no formal invitation to the ball, Lysandra had felt certain that he could sneak into the gathering via this route, if suitably costumed. Once the drinking began, even the servants were sure to lose track of who had been admitted through the front door and who hadn't. So as long as Lysandra kept an eye out for him, she felt fairly sure that he could reach her and make his presence known without incident.

He hadn't been able to tell her two nights before just what guise he would be wearing. Though she had made it a point to offer such enticing suggestions as vampire and white knight, he had remained annoyingly uncommitted, and they had simply settled upon his coming and finding her in her witch's get-up. She hadn't known then that she'd be taking Madame Safina's place as the evening's fortuneteller, but that, too, would serve to help her lover find her tonight.

After a couple of hours passed with no sign of him, however, she couldn't help becoming concerned. She was kept busy, of course. Most everyone in Glendalough made an appearance at Fitzgerald's prestigious Halloween ball each year, so there was no shortage of people wanting readings from her.

But this wasn't distraction enough. Beyond wanting Trevor to save her from the new lord, she was beginning to realize how much she cared for him, how much she craved his company. And the thought of being let down by him now was heartbreaking.

When another half hour passed without any sign of him, she finally took a much-needed respite from her divining and went outside to have a look about.

He was nowhere in sight, not amidst the clusters of guests, who stood laughing and talking along the terrace's balustrade. And when her eyes finally lit upon a couple who were billing and cooing in a shadowed corner of the promenade, her chest began to ache all the more with the fear that Trevor had chosen to leave town and simply hadn't found the nerve to tell her so.

Of a sudden, she realized what an unforgivable fool she'd been. What could have possessed her to give her virginity and, far worse, her *heart* to such a stranger? Such a confessed vagabond, who very likely had a paramour in every town he visited? She'd probably been nothing more to him than another conquest.

Fighting the urge to become tearful, she went back inside, fleeing the evening's chill and anxious to help herself to one of the glasses of white wine which servants were carrying about on trays.

"Lysandra?" she heard a man say from behind her. Though it didn't sound a bit like Trevor's voice, she turned about in the vain hope that it was.

To her disappointment, it was the steward once more. "Lysandra, the lord says he wants you to read for him. Would you please return to your table?"

She blushed at the question, at having been caught away from her agreed-upon post and in search of spirited drink, no less. She could feel her cheeks color, but gratefully realized that her pale, witchy makeup was probably concealing it. "Aye. Of course," she replied, letting him take her arm.

She'd get through it, somehow, she told herself with a brave swallow. The shrewdest thing to do, clearly, was to make a botch of the master's reading, so he'd come to think of her not only as witchlike, but as a charlatan to boot. So, all things considered, a voice within her observed this request was probably more a blessing than a curse.

"I'm told you wish a reading, your lordship," she acknowledged in a quavery voice, as she took her seat across the table from the old man seconds later.

He nodded his gilded head.

"Very well," she agreed, beginning to shuffle her deck. To her dismay, her fingers trembled quite noticeably, as she did so. "I'm nervous," she explained with a wavering smile. "I've never read for a nobleman before, you see."

"Oh, but you have," he replied, his low, gravelly voice continuing to sound very muffled by his mask.

Her eyes flew up in an effort to meet his. Unfortunately, however, his headdress revealed very little of the orbs that lay beneath it. "What?"

"You already have, my dear. Just last week in the Gypsy's shop you read for a Mr. Trevor Walsh, did you not?"

"Well, y-yes," she stammered, nonplussed. "But how would you know that?"

"I'm the new lord, child. And if I'm to take up residence here, I feel I must learn as much about Glendalough and its people as possible. I even know," he added with a roguish laugh, "that the pair of you took refuge in one of my servants' cottages just the other night. And you were inside it for rather an unseemly length of time, don't you think?"

Lysandra's hands froze about her cards, and she bristled with both indignation and dread at this disclosure.

"Oh, don't worry, lass. Your secret is safe with me. I'll not tell your mother. Walsh is kin to me, after all."

Gaping, Lysandra locked her gaze upon him now, wanting to bore larger holes in his infernal mask so that she might study his elusive eyes. "He's a relative of yours?" she asked incredulously. "But why wouldn't he have said so? Oh, no," she gasped, remembering with horror how she'd told Trevor every detail of her mother's plot to wed her to the lord and, worse still, how abhorrent she herself would find such a marriage.

Why, for the sake of heaven, hadn't Trevor told her this? a voice within her demanded to know. How could he have simply let her go on and on about the situation? Blazes, what a shameless spalpeen he'd been!

She suddenly heard prankish laughter from under the mask, and she once again felt bedeviled by the new master. "This . . . this isn't in the least bit funny, Lord Fitzgerald," she sputtered, almost crazed with hurt and betrayal, as she rose from her chair. "I demand to know what relation Mr. Walsh is to you!"

*"Lysandra."* It was a mere whisper. An utterance so tender and familiar, that a lump formed in her throat. It was unmistakably Trevor's voice she'd just heard, and she instantly looked about her in search of him. In those befuddling seconds, she even sneaked a peek beneath the cloth-draped reading table.

"Lysandra. 'Tis I. *I'm* Trevor, don't you understand?" the lord asked with a chuckle.

And suddenly, yes! His voice and Trevor's did seem one and the same!

"Trevor *Fitzgerald* Walsh," he continued. "That relative you told me had died when you read for me, that was my mother's brother, Lord Sloan Fitzgerald. So it appears I'm the master of the manor now, whether I want the title or not. But, of course, having met you and learned of your family's plight, I do."

"Are you all right?" he inquired, when, after several seconds, she failed to respond. "God, you're not going to faint again, are you?"

"Trevor?" she asked in amazement, sinking numbly back into her chair.

"Yes, love."

Her mind raced to piece it all together. The tarot cards did not lie, so the truth must have been spread out before her from the day they'd met. And all at once the reading did, indeed, begin to make sense.

The Tower card. Aye! Roofless with its occupants in peril. *That* was precisely the fate that would have befallen Fitzgerald Manor had Trevor decided not to stay. And the King of cups, his "obstacle." That had symbolized old Sloan himself. Inadvertently standing in the way of his nephew's inheritance, until, of course, he'd died.

"But *why?*" Lysandra choked. "Why would you keep your identity from me? Why would you lie to me that way?"

He reached out and placed a consoling hand upon one of hers. "I didn't lie exactly. I just refrained from letting you know the whole truth, my dear. And I had my reasons, rest assured. Once we're married and you become lady of the manor, you'll soon learn how it is to have everyone for as far as the eye can see dependent upon you for a livelihood. I had never been to Glendalough, you see. I didn't know Uncle Sloan had named me his heir. So, having never met the man, I'd felt no call to visit here. Then, when he died and word reached me that

I'd been named in his will, I realized the locals would, understandably, pressure me to take up residence in the manor. That is, were I to arrive in Glendalough in the usual, straightforward way." He shook his head. "All those hopeful faces, all those lives I'd adversely affect if I decided I didn't like the place and simply wished to let the manor go."

"So you came to town well before you were expected," Lysandra interjected, starting to understand. "Dressed as a commoner, letting a thatch as a true transient might, you came to have a secret look about."

He nodded, then gave forth a dry laugh. "How was I to know that the very first person I'd meet here would be a heart-stealing lass such as yourself? How could I have known that just a few minutes with you would bring me bang on with one of the very tales of woe I'd come so furtively to avoid?"

Lysandra's eyes narrowed discerningly. "So your plan was simply to catch the next coach out of town, if your backdoor stay in Glendalough proved disappointing?"

"Oh yes, my dear. We moneyed lords have feelings, too, you know. And 'tis far easier to express one's regrets from across the country, than to have to refuse an entire town of people in the flesh."

Lysandra settled back in her chair, pondering all of this. Then, probably out of sheer shock, she shook her head and began to laugh.

"What? What is it?" Trevor asked, sounding as though he wished to join in her amusement.

"If you're Fitzgerald's nephew, why aren't you old, as everyone was told you'd be?"

He shrugged. "I don't know. I can't imagine where that rumor started, so you can believe me when I tell you I had nothing to do with it. My mother was the last-born of her family," he continued. "There were many years between her and her brother Sloan, so that accounts for my relative youth, I suppose."

"Hmmm. So, Madame Safina's prediction that you'd become taken with me was right, and you didn't bother to tell me?"

"Well," he drawled sheepishly, "a man would like to believe he possesses at least some measure of say in his fate, you understand. It galled me at first, finding myself so helplessly smitten with you, just as some Gypsy's *crystal* had foretold. I wanted to fight it, naturally. Then, when I realized it was inevitable and I'd be miserable without you, I knew you had to be told the truth. Your mother kept assuring me that she'd bring you up to the manor so we might meet and talk, but you never came. So I arranged a meeting on my own. But once you fainted, once I saw what a shock the banshee had given you, I realized you probably couldn't bear any more for a while. And then matters just seemed to get out of hand. You know how we are together, Lysandra," he added, lacing his fingers into hers in a most suggestive manner.

"I'm afraid I do."

"You will marry me, though, won't you? I do so want a bride who loved me *before* she knew of my wealth and title. I mean, I would go through proper channels and ask your mother for your hand first. But under the circumstances it does seem a moot point."

Lysandra bit her lip and hung her face abashedly. "Ah, faith, I can't believe you let me go on and on that way at Murphy's thatch! All that rambling about Mum's silly scheme and such. You must think us terrible connivers."

"Heavens, no. No more so than I was in coming to Glendalough so covertly. People do desperate things at times, my dear."

Lysandra looked up and rolled her eyes. "That they do."

"But you haven't answered my question," he noted, lowering his voice to a vulnerable murmur. "Would it be presumptuous of me to conclude that you may have finally changed your mind about being 'married off' to the new master of the manor?"

A smile pulled at one corner of her lips, and a warm surge of arousal moved through her, as she recalled how adeptly he'd made love to her two nights before. "No, Trevor. Not at all," she returned in a tone as enamored as his.

They stared at each other for several long seconds, seeing beyond one another's guises as only two such soul mates could.

"You don't suppose the new lord would mind, if we sneaked off to his empty servants' cottage again tonight, do you?" she asked, arching a gamesome brow.

Beneath his mask, Trevor's expression was equally sportive. "Not in the least, I assure you."

Lysandra gave his hand a squeeze, and she was about to tell him how happy this response made her, how much she looked forward to being alone with him again, when an awful wailing was heard in the distance. "Oh, God, Trevor, I think that's Mum! I told her about the banshee's warning, but I fear she's decided to ignore it!"

"Sweet Jesus! Well, what can we do?"

"You'll have to come with me. Out to the knoll past the woods. Once she sees you, once she learns that we intend to be wed, she'll stop, of course."

Needing no more prompting than this, Trevor sprang from his chair. Then, grabbing his beloved's hand, he brought her racing along after him. It seemed Lysandra's feet scarcely touched the ground as they hurried out across the terrace, down its three steps, and over the manor's back lawn toward the woods.

It was too late when they finally reached the knoll, however. Before Trevor could do a thing to stop her, the *real* banshee—now several times the size she'd been when she'd stopped Lysandra—swooped down upon Gertrude and, with the rapacious screech of an eagle, carried her off toward the starry sky.

Lysandra watched for several seconds, as her mum, dangling from the huge apparition's enfolding arm like a rag doll, was borne up over the treetops. "Oh, dear Mother Mary, she's lost," she cried in horror, turning to bury her face in Trevor's chest.

"No, love. Take courage, please. She's still in sight, and the banshee's certainly floating slowly enough for us to keep up with her on horseback. We'll go fetch some mounts. I'm sure the good spirit only intends to scare her."

Lysandra, having known the banshee's wrath firsthand, was anything but sure. Seeing no other course of action, though, she ran after her fiancé as he turned and dashed back toward the manor's stable.

# Seven

Lord Trevor Fitzgerald Walsh was right about Gertrude's fate, as it turned out. While he and Lysandra traveled on horseback with a couple of his stablemen, across the rolling land to the east minutes later, it became apparent that the banshee did not intend to carry the woman off into oblivion. Rather, the specter kept her flight low in the Halloween-night sky. Just above the skeletal fingers of the molting trees, she and her pendulous captive passed, well below the glowing full moon.

It was a spectacular display! Had Trevor not known the circumstances behind it, he would have found it exceedingly entertaining. Many bands of trick-or-treaters were seen to stop dead and watch the luminous apparition quite raptly, in fact.

She swept down toward several of the bonfires, which always dotted the Irish countryside on this hallowed eve. Each time she'd near one, she'd seem to threaten to let Gertrude fall into it. Shifting her hold upon the matriarch, until only their hands were joined, the banshee dipped down to the flames, letting them nip at the hem of the mortal's white garment. Then, laughing demoniacally at Gertrude's resultant screams, she'd jerk her back up again, into her huge, enfolding arms.

And on and on this went, until, seeming to tire of the game, the spirit saw fit to drop Mrs. Mc Gill in the middle of a lough. Then, issuing another booming warning to her, the banshee jetted straight upward, vanishing into a clump of clouds which suddenly appeared in the indigo sky.

"Dear God, can she swim?" Trevor shouted over to Lysandra, as their party rode on toward her mum.

"I think so."

Gertrude evidently could, for by the time her would-be rescuers reached the lake, she was emerging from it, drenched and mortified.


She didn't speak much in the days that followed. Though she was clearly delighted at the news of her daughter's betrothal to the new lord, the terror of her ordeal seemed to quell her accustomed imperiousness.

A couple of things seemed certain, however. She would never again take the spirit world lightly. Nor would she, by henpecking or wailing, hasten a man to die before his time.

# The Seventh Bride

## by
## Becky Lee Weyrich

# One

Captain Jerusalem Caine crafted words as smoothly, intricately, and beautifully as any Down East sailor ever scrimshawed a piece of whale ivory. The letter that someone had slipped under Aurora Holloway's door earlier this morning—before the nightmare woke her—was positive proof of this, if she needed any further proof.

For over three years he had been at sea, and the neat stack of letters on Aurora's marble-topped vanity attested to the captain's elegant penmanship, his dedication to wooing her, and his single-minded intent to return to Maine and make her his wife—*someday*.

"But how much longer must I wait?" Aurora sighed, thinking back over all the springs, summers, autumns, and winters she had been forced to endure without the man she loved.

Opening the silver locket she always wore, a gift of farewell from her captain, Aurora gazed down into Salem's handsome face, done in miniature on an oval of porcelain. A warm feeling crept through her whenever she looked at his likeness.

She smiled, remembering the laughter in Salem's deep voice when he'd told her about the Boston artist's frustration with his subject. "He said to me, my love, before he would begin with his brushes and paints, I should comb down my rampant locks. Aye, he did! But I told him this head of hair had been so long before the mast, it knew naught but to curl wild as the tradewinds had fashioned it."

"Ah, and how those wondrous locks do curl," Aurora said with a sigh, "all tossed and gleaming as if he were caught forever in the turbulent breath of a nor'easter."

Salem's dark halo framed a long, serious face. But there was a merry twinkle in his storm-gray eyes, and a half-dimple at one corner of his mouth signaled a laugh in the offing. His brows were straight and dark and bold, his nose fine and sturdy like all the rest of him. Although the tiny portrait showed only his face, Aurora knew her man by heart—broad shoulders, trim waist, long arms and legs, and hands so large he could span her round the middle with ease. His voice, too, she recalled. Deep and rumbling, it was. So loud most times that when he was in company, he almost seemed forced to whisper. He was not a boisterous man, but neither was he the thoughtful, silent type like her professor father.

Salem Caine simply loved life, and his very great joy in living made him yearn to do everything in an exaggerated fashion. His manner of loving Aurora proved no exception. He had wooed her lavishly before taking to sea and had kept her heart throbbing, her head spinning with his passionate words, all the while he'd been away.

Aurora glanced down at the unopened letter in her hands. Her heart pounded with anticipation. How she longed to tear into it and read her beloved's words. But she stayed her urge a moment longer, hoping against all hope that this would be *the* letter—the one announcing that after all this time the good ship *Sankaty,* her crew, and captain were at long last homeward bound.

Pressing the letter to her heart, Aurora rose from her green-velvet slipper chair and paced across her bedroom. Tears misted her eyes as she stared out of the second-story window of the tall white house on Washington Street, away toward the river. In the stout breeze, gold

252

and crimson maple leaves danced against the bubbled glass of the panes. It was fall, that glorious carnival of sunshine and color before the cold, dismal gray of winter gripped Maine's coast in its tight, hard fist for six long months or more.

She closed her eyes. Her lips moved, but only the barest whisper issued forth. "Please! Dear God, let him be safe, let him be well." She dared not utter aloud the prayer that was always uppermost in her mind—the selfish prayer of a lonely woman: *Let him come home to me soon!*

Aurora had to admit to herself that she was more than lonely, she was afraid. The same ominous dream had troubled her sleep since the night Salem went away. First, she would envision a ship's carved figurehead—the likeness of a woman with flowing hair like flame and wide, blue eyes staring fixedly out over a storm-tossed sea. Then, suddenly, Aurora herself took the place of the wooden lady, lashed to the prow of the foundering ship, unable to move, knowing there was no way to save herself. The angry black waves, cold and stinging, tore at her until she could no longer catch her breath. She strained against her bonds, screaming Salem's name, only to have the fierce, icy wind dash the sound back into her face. Each time she experienced the dream, the agony was prolonged. In last night's dream, she knew she had nearly drowned.

"What will happen when the nightmare comes again?" She hugged her arms, shivering, wondering what it could mean.

Forcing her mind away from such dire thoughts, Aurora settled on the candlewick bedspread in a pool of sunshine as yellow as warm butter, trying to chase away the chill of last night's terror. She stared down at Salem's unopened letter, then eased off the initialed wax seal and unfolded the single sheet of vellum slowly, carefully—as if she were handling some object rare and fragile to the touch.

The very sight of his boldly shaped letters made her heart beat faster. Brushing angrily at the tears that blurred her vision, she finally permitted herself to read her beloved's sweet words.

> At Sea
> July 3, 1879

My dearest Aurora,

I have thought of you and this moment since we weighed anchor, outward bound, on that dreary, sad day thirty-nine months ago. I thought of you and this moment all along the way, down and across the great Atlantic, rounding the Cape of Good Hope, passing Madagascar, putting in at Bombay, Calcutta, and Hong Kong. And now, at last, dear heart, we are homeward bound!

Aurora gave a cry of mingled disbelief and joy. Tears flooded her eyes so that she had to stop reading for a few moments until she had her emotions in check. Finally, she was able to continue.

I do hope this letter reaches you before my return. Perhaps we shall speak another, faster ship at sea. If so, I shall charge the captain with the delivery of this missive into your own dear hands. Even if this reaches you by the fastest route possible, I shall follow on its heels very shortly. So you have little time to prepare for our wedding, my love. Something simple will suffice. I am a plain man, as you well remember.

Even as I write this, I know that on reading it you will be battling mixed emotions. Do not mistake my words. I believe in your love for me as much as I believe that I could not go on living without you by my side. However, I do remember well that our engagement sent your poor mother into a fit that caused her to take to her bed. I could never knowingly cause you or your family unhappiness. Therefore, I have made a decision. This is to be my final voyage. The profits from this last venture, coupled with the inheritance I will receive upon my return to my family's estate will stand us in good stead financially. I may have mentioned to you, on some earlier occasion, my ancestral home up the coast. I never considered returning there until now. If you are willing, my dearest, we shall leave Bath immediately following our wedding and travel to The Ledges, where we will honeymoon in glorious seclusion, then make the old place our home.

Spend your days from here out on the widow's walk with your spyglass in hand. Watch for the *Sankaty*'s red sails, for, even as I write this, those very sails are singing with wind, driving me ever nearer to the one who owns my heart.

> With all love and yearning,
> Captain Jerusalem Caine
> (Your Salem)

Aurora kissed the letter, then, still clutching it in her hand, she ran to her wardrobe and flung the doors wide.

"It's real!" she sang out. "It *is* going to happen! I'm going to marry Salem Caine!"

Of course, she had supposed all along that they would wed, but her mother's disapproval of the match, simply because he was a seafaring man, had cast a gloomy shadow over Aurora's happiness. Now her joy was total. She felt she might burst with it, flying about the room in bright, glittering particles of sheer joy.

Suddenly, she paused and caught a sharp breath. She shuddered as if someone had just walked across her grave, and for an instant the image of the ship's doomed figurehead flashed through her mind. She mistrusted such total joy. Enough Irish blood ran in Aurora's veins from her mother's side to make her wary.

"What if something should happen?" she warned aloud.

Just then, one short, curt knock sounded at her bedroom door. "Aurora? Have you read your letter yet? I want to hear what your captain had to say."

Casting off all grim thoughts, Aurora grinned and ran to welcome her Aunt Persia, her mother's younger sister.

Persia Hazzard, a tall, handsome woman in her fifties, bustled in, a twinkle in her knowing blue eyes. "Well, my girl, was this the letter you've been waiting for? I hurried right over the moment it fell into my possession and slipped it under your door. Your mother might have led it astray. Europa is a dear woman, but, as we both know, she is somewhat overprotective. And she's certainly made her feelings about your marriage to Salem plain enough."

Aurora stared at her pretty, red-haired aunt, the rebel in the family, the one who had traveled the world with a seafaring husband.

"So that's how the letter got here. I couldn't imagine. I woke early—another of those terrible dreams—and there was Salem's letter, lying on the floor. I nearly fainted with joy, but then I couldn't bring myself to read it right away."

"Why on earth not?"

Aurora shrugged, embarrassed suddenly. "I suppose I was afraid of bad news." She brightened and said, "It was so good of you to bring it to me, Aunt Persia, but how did you come by it?"

"Oh, well, easily enough. Captain Winslow of the *Delhi* gave it to your Uncle Zack earlier this morning down at the Bath wharf. It seems the *Sankaty* spoke the *Delhi* somewhere in the middle of the Indian Ocean. Salem went over in a whale boat and entrusted the letter to Captain Winslow, begging him to see that it was delivered into your hands. But that's neither here nor there," Persia said, waving a slender hand impatiently. "What did Salem have to say for himself?"

"He's coming home, Aunt Persia!" Aurora cried. "And, best of all, he's giving up the sea. So Mother won't have any further objections."

Persia sat up very straight and gave a quick nod. "Well, there you are, my girl! Didn't I tell you that all this fretting was pure idiocy? I knew things would work out. They always do where love is concerned. They did for me and your Uncle Zack, didn't they? Even if he was betrothed to Europa. So now you've stopped worrying, you can begin to enjoy preparing for your wedding."

A frown creased Aurora's smooth brow. "I don't dare stop worrying until Salem is here with me and we are man and wife."

"Poppycock! What do you have to worry about now?"

"There are still those awful dreams." She glanced at the other woman. "Aunt Persia, what am I to do?"

Persia shook her head in disbelief. "Silly child, you must simply ignore your persistent nightmares, marry Salem at the first possible instant after he sets foot on land, and then live happily ever after. One night with your husband will chase away all unpleasant dreams. You've been a virgin far too long. That's your only problem."

After stating that blunt fact, Persia rose, gave her blushing niece a swift peck on the cheek, and left.

Quickly, Aurora dressed in a soft, indigo cashmere skirt—the same shade as her eyes—and a crisp, white bodice. She brushed vigorously at her dark red curls, then tied them with a black velvet ribbon. Snatching her shawl from a chair, she flung it around her shoulders and hurried into the hall and toward the stairs to the attic, headed for the widow's walk, high atop the house. She meant to spend every waking hour there until she spied the *Sankaty*'s red sails on the Kennebec River.

The instant before Aurora would have disappeared into the safe gloom of the attic, she heard someone call her name and her mother came bustling toward her, her dark bombazine skirt rustling ominously.

"Aurora?" Europa Holloway's voice was shrill and accusing. "What business did Persia have here so early this morning? She was bent on mischief, I could tell. She barely spoke to me when she flew in. And she had that gleam in her eyes. I don't trust her—you know that. Ever since she stole Zachariah Hazzard away from me, I've held my breath, waiting for her next trick."

"Mother, that was over thirty years ago," Aurora reasoned. "And you've admitted that you never really loved Uncle Zack, that Aunt Persia did. You love Father, so everything worked out for the best. Aunt Persia says that's usually the case where love is concerned."

Petite, plump Europa smoothed a hand over her salt-and-pepper hair, vain to this very day, though her legendary beauty had long since paled. "Well, everyone knows I could have had Zack had I truly wanted him," she commented. Then her ice-blue eyes snapped with accusation. "You're purposely leading me off the subject, Aurora. What was my sister doing here?"

Aurora's face positively glowed as she answered breathlessly, "Aunt Persia brought me good news, Mother. The *best* sort of news."

"Oh, really! Is she moving away?"

In spite of her mother's caustic tone, Aurora trilled a laugh. "No, Mother, but *I am!* Captain Caine is returning any day now and we'll be married."

Europa's eyes narrowed and she opened her mouth to protest, but Aurora cut her off. "He's giving up the sea, Mother. He has made a fortune on this voyage, and he says we can live in fine style in his home up the coast. The Ledges he calls the place, and I'm sure it's grand, indeed. So we must begin plans for the wedding immediately. Salem could arrive any day."

Aurora's tension eased as she watched her mother's face undergo a startling transformation. An instant before, Europa had been puffed up for battle. Now her whole countenance glowed with an excitement that nearly matched her daughter's. She caught Aurora in her arms and hugged her soundly.

"Let's tell your father at once, my dear. How exciting! A fall wedding! You'll wear your grandmother's gown, of course."

Mother and daughter hurried downstairs to the study, where they found Dr. Seton Holloway, as usual his balding head buried behind stacks of books.

"Seton!" Europa shrilled. "Do listen to what I have to say!"

"Of course, my dear," he answered automatically, not looking up.

"Well, it is simply the best news we could have," she ran on. "Do tell him yourself, Aurora. Maybe he'll listen more keenly to you."

Her pretty face beaming, Aurora approached her father's cluttered desk. "Captain Caine is coming home, Father, and we'll be married. Mother no longer objects. Isn't that wonderful?"

He glanced up at the child who was his pride and joy, his only daughter after six sons. "Oh, my dear, that is good news. I am mightily impressed with your captain. A fine man, Salem Caine!" Then he turned his warm, brown gaze on his wife. "I knew you'd come around, Europa. You're not as stubborn as you used to be."

Europa stamped her tiny foot, infuriated. "I most certainly am!" she cried. "It's not *I* who came around but Captain Caine. He's agreed to leave the sea for our Aurora. He plans to take her to his ancestral home, The Ledges."

But Europa had lost her husband's attention once

more. It was enough that he knew his daughter would be wed and happy. He did, however, note mention of The Ledges a moment before he dismissed the women mentally. After they'd left him, a certain worm of doubt began to wriggle through his mind. An hour later, after some intensive research, he discovered in an old book on the tales of early Maine what he had sought.

"Shocking!" he muttered. "Shocking! I'll have to tell them of course. But later."

Dr. Holloway sank back into his books on medieval history, dismissing all thoughts of The Ledges and Captain Gideon Caine for hours to come.

Not until he was seated at the supper table that night, partaking of boiled cabbage and beef and trying to ignore the hum of wedding plans going on around him, did his research return to plague him. Lifting his spectacles from his nose to his forehead, he glanced down the long table toward his wife.

"Excuse me," he cut in. Shocked silence followed. Seton Holloway hadn't spoken during supper since the spring of '69.

"Yes, dear?" Europa asked with unexpected solicitude in her voice. She really thought he might be ill.

"About this marriage," he said, avoiding his daughter's glowing eyes. "I'm afraid I must withdraw my permission. There'll be no wedding, Europa. Now, if you'll excuse me, I'm going to my study." He rose and left the table without another word.

Seton Holloway's calm, quiet voice had far more impact than all of Europa's shrill harping. Aurora sat stunned, unable to believe what she had heard but knowing full well that her father never spoke without a reason for his words.

"Mother?" Aurora, fighting tears, turned to Europa, pleading for some explanation, some ray of hope.

But for once Mrs. Holloway sat paralyzed with shock, unable to utter a sound.

The silence was as deafening as a banshee's scream. It hung over the two women like thick, gray, smothering sea-smoke—the kind that causes ships to wreck, sailors to die, and widows to weep.

# Two

Aurora fretted herself nearly ill for the next two days. But she did her fretting, spyglass in hand, atop the widow's walk, scanning the length of the Kennebec for any sight of Salem's *Sankaty*. It was there that her uncle, Zachariah Hazzard, found her on a gray and blustery October afternoon.

"Ahoy there!" he called up from the ladder. "Retired captain coming aboard. With your permission, of course."

"Uncle Zack!" Aurora cried, always delighted to see her Aunt Persia's handsome rascal of a husband. "Do come up. The wind is fresh and the view is fine."

His sea-boots echoed hollowly on the boards as he climbed the last few stairs. Aurora ran to him, giving him an enthusiastic hug. He smelled of salt air and tar and exotic winds from far-off lands.

"Oh, Uncle Zack, I'm so glad to see you."

Untwining her stranglehold on his midsection, Zack said, "There, there, 'Rora. Take it a bit easy on an old man, won't you?"

She stood back, hands on hips, matching the twinkle in his dark eyes with her own. "Old man, indeed! You'd better not let Aunt Persia hear you talk that way. She always says a body's as young as he feels."

Zack shook his mane of snow-white hair. "I'm feeling

every one of my sixty-odd years since I heard of the ruckus over here. Damned if I'm pleased about it, 'Rora!"

She stood her ground against the brisk winds and against the tears that were threatening at the mere mention of her father's edict. "Do be pleased for me and Salem, Uncle Zack. We'll wed as planned, with or without my father's permission."

"You're that much in love with him, eh, child?" Zack's rough voice softened with some deep emotion when he spoke. "Aye, I can see it in the set of your jaw and the glint of your storm-blue eyes. You're the image of my own Persia when she was your age. Ha! And look where her stubbornness landed her, married to an old sea dog who's had to go into dry dock before his time."

Aurora shook her head until her bright curls slipped their ribbon to dance about her shoulders. "You're wrong about that, Uncle Zack. Aunt Persia's stubbornness got her the man she loved, the man she still loves. I mean to have my chance at the same."

When one rebellious tear escaped Aurora's eye to streak down her wind-flushed cheek, Zack muttered an embarrassed oath and closed his big arms around her somewhat clumsily. "There now, don't you cry. I've come to tell you that I talked to your father. Seton only wants what's best for you, Aurora. He told me that not an hour ago."

Aurora drew back and stared her uncle full in the eye. "Then he's given his permission for me to marry Salem?"

"Now, I didn't say that, did I, girl?" Zack's defensive tone sent a chill through Aurora.

Turning back toward the river, she put the glass to her eye once more. "So nothing's changed," she said in a tone as icy as the hand clutching at her heart.

"Aurora, hear me out," Zack begged. "It's not the man your father objects to. It's his taking you away. You're

263

Seton's only daughter, after all. He loves you something desperate, child."

Aurora whirled to face her uncle, her blue eyes flashing fire. "He loves me, does he? Enough to ruin my life? Enough to deprive me of the only man I'll ever care for? If that is love, then I'd sooner he hate me."

"Aurora Holloway, belay that talk!" Captain Hazzard bellowed the order as if his niece were a lowly sailor caught in some serious shipboard transgression.

She lowered her gaze, ashamed of her outburst. "I'm sorry," she whispered. "You know I didn't mean that, Uncle Zack. But having Father against me is ever so much worse than having Mother barring the way. What can I do? Salem could arrive at any moment. It's not as if he meant to whisk me off to another country or sail me across the oceans as you did Aunt Persia. We're only moving up the coast."

"Your father knows that—knows it well, he does," Zack muttered. "And therein lies the problem." He cocked his head and looked curiously at his niece. "Have you never heard the tales of The Ledges, child?"

Aurora moved closer, all attention suddenly. "No, Uncle Zack. I'd never even heard the name of the Salem's home until Aunt Persia brought me his letter two days ago. What sort of place is it?"

"A castle," he said with an odd tremor in his deep voice. "A castle moved stone by stone from a country in Europe that no longer exists. The place is old—old and tainted, so the stories say, with centuries of madness and evil. Some say witches—"

"Poppycock!" Aurora cried, echoing one of Aunt Persia's favorite expletives.

"Not to your father, whose specialty, if you'll recall, is medieval history *and* the witchery of those times."

Aurora laughed, a dry, humorless sound. "Are you telling me, Uncle Zack, that my own father, a renowned scholar and teacher, is forbidding me to marry the man

I love because he's afraid of some ancient witch tales from Europe's Dark Ages? I refuse to believe it!"

She turned away quickly to scan the river once more. The moment her eye adjusted to the lens, she cried out. "The *Sankaty!* Uncle Zack, he's home—home at last!"

Before Zachariah Hazzard could say another word, Aurora flew past him and down the stairs to the attic. "Tell Mother I'm going to meet the ship," she called over her shoulder as an afterthought.

Zack stood atop the widow's walk, staring after his niece. He smiled. What a curious wonder that she and his Persia were so alike!

A short while later, Aurora stood on the wharf with the others awaiting the arrival and docking of the *Sankaty.* A brisk, cold wind whipped her hair about her face and tossed her wool skirt with such force that the lace of her petticoats peeked out from time to time. But Aurora noticed none of this. Shading her eyes against the dull glare of the leaden sky, she focused all her attention on the tall, dark figure standing on the quarter deck as if his boots were rooted to the spot.

"Salem," she breathed, hardly able to believe her eyes. She had imagined him so often that actually seeing him after so long was almost more than her limited grasp of reality would permit.

Gulls circled overhead, riding the low-scudding drifts of clouds. "Looks like snow, ayuh!" someone in the crowd muttered. Aurora didn't care. She would stand fast in a blizzard until she could touch the man she loved, feel his arms around her, see his steely, love-filled eyes gazing into her own.

Time crawled and the skies grew darker as she waited for cargo to be off-loaded, sails to be lowered, gear to be stowed. She found herself suddenly in the midst of dozens of happy reunions of sailors and wives, children, or sweethearts. Still the captain manned his ship. Still Aurora waited.

She was cold, shivering by the time she heard his call. "Miss Holloway, can that be you?"

A strangled sob escaped her. Suddenly, he stood there before her—tall, handsome, alive, home, *hers!*

He gripped her cold hand in his. "Steady as you go, my love," he warned in a whisper. "If I took the action I most long for at this moment, your reputation would be besmirched forevermore."

Aurora's cheeks flamed and any trace of a chill deserted her body.

Then in a louder voice, Captain Caine said for all to hear, "How good of you to come out on such a cold evening to meet the ship. Your father wishes to speak with me, you say? Then let us away at once."

Salem hailed a carriage to drive them up the hill. Once inside the closed conveyance, the captain cast off all inhibitions and drew Aurora close for a long, soul-rending kiss.

She truly thought she would swoon in his arms. Before he'd left, their courting had been of the most proper sort. She had been a shy girl, while he was a grown man. Her parents had seen to it that the two of them were never left alone. Only once before had he kissed her lips. The night he boarded his ship to sail with the tide next dawn he had braved the wrath of her parents by stealing one quick parting embrace in the dark, front hallway of the house on Washington Street. Aurora had cherished that kiss all these months, going over many times every detail of her own feelings at that moment. The quiver of her heart, the sweet weakness that had flooded her limbs, the delicious taste of Salem's wine-flavored lips pressing hers.

But *this!* This kiss was something altogether different. His hands eased inside her cloak and around her, kneading her back and shoulders, pressing her breasts tight to his hard chest. His mouth parted over hers and she could feel his breath, warm and teasing. After a moment, his tongue flicked out, urging, pleading, enticing. When her own lips opened to him, it was as if they did so with no conscious effort on her part. And a moment later, she was drowning in his taste and feel and urgency.

He made her feel like a scone, hot from the oven, drenched in warm honey and melting butter—all soft and warm and crumbly, waiting to be devoured.

The coachman pulled up in front of the Holloway residence and only then did their kiss come to an end. They sat for a moment, staring at each other, breathing hard, and wondering how they could face Aurora's parents without the sweet wildness of their secret kiss being discovered.

"They'll see it on my face, in my eyes," Aurora whispered, as if she could read Salem's own thoughts.

"Thank God I'm wearing a long coat," he replied, making Aurora wonder why on earth he was thinking of clothes at a time like this.

He took her hand, then opened the door of the carriage. "Come, love, we might as well face the music. Soon enough we'll be married. Then we won't have to give a good damn what anyone else thinks."

Salem paid the driver while Aurora stood close to him, shivering, wondering how to tell him that her father was no longer on their side. As they started up the front walk, Aurora caught his arm.

"Salem, wait! There's something I must tell you before we go in."

He turned to her, his brow furrowed and his dark eyes gleaming with suspicion and something akin to fear at the strange tone in her voice. "Your feelings for me haven't changed?"

Aurora leaned her head against the warmth of his sleeve and uttered a quivery sigh. "Oh, no, my dearest! Never! How can you even ask? I loved you more each day we were apart. And at this moment, I love you so much that I think it must be sinful."

Salem quelled the urge to take her in his arms again. Glancing up toward the lights in the front parlor, he could almost feel Dr. and Mrs. Holloway hovering near, watching his every move.

"It's Father," she blurted out. "For some reason unknown to me, he rejects your idea of taking me to live at The Ledges. Uncle Zack told me Father's feelings have to do with some nonsense about witches."

Salem hugged Aurora's shoulders with one arm, threw back his head and laughed. "Glory! What a fright you gave me, 'Rora. The witches, is it? Those old wives' tales never seem to die. Sometimes I think my great-grandfather, Gideon, invented those stories to keep people at a distance. He was something of a recluse and liked it that way. But surely Dr. Holloway can't believe such meaningless clack."

"I'm afraid he does, Salem. He's withdrawn his permission for our marriage." Aurora's voice trembled as tears threatened.

"Don't worry, darling. I'll explain everything to your father. He'll understand." He hugged her again and dropped a soft kiss on her brow. "And if he doesn't, then I'll climb into your window some midnight and steal you away as if I were a Gypsy, mad with love."

Aurora smiled up at him, feeling a weight lift from her heart. He did look like a wild Gypsy, there in the shadows cast by the waxing moon. And Gypsies, so she'd heard, could cast spells and work miracles. Her Salem could do that. He could do anything. She was certain of it.

"Do you love me?" he asked. "I want to hear the words once more, to be sure."

"I love you, Captain Jerusalem Caine. I do!"

"And I love you, Aurora Holloway." He brushed her temple with his lips and she burned. "Now that that's settled, my darling, shall we go declare our intentions to your parents?"

She made no objection. She had none. With Salem at her side, Aurora could and would go anywhere, do anything. He was a giant of a man, and beside him petite Aurora grew into an Amazon of a woman.

Europa Holloway met them at the front door, her smile of greeting for Salem warm but brief before worry showed in her face. "Your father's in his study, Aurora. I think the three of us should go in and confront him. Surely, he can't stand his ground so stubbornly if we present ourselves united."

"Mother Holloway, how good of you to support us." Salem leaned down and planted a kiss on his future mother-in-law's plump cheek. When he'd left so long ago, Europa had been staunchly against their engagement. In a towering, foot-stamping rage, she'd called down all manner of curses on his head. But now, under the onslaught of his charms, she became as flustered as a shy young girl.

"Oh, my!" She giggled, beaming up at the tall, handsome captain her daughter meant to marry. "Well, how sweet of you, my boy. Come along now, both of you. It's high time we put an end to Seton's foolishness."

A snapping fire of birch logs glowed warmly in the study. For once, Dr. Holloway was not hidden behind his stacks of books. He stood at the mantelpiece, a brandy in one hand, frowning down into the leaping flames.

"Sir?" Salem said hesitantly.

"Captain Caine," Seton answered, leaning forward and offering his hand. "So good that you're back. A safe and profitable voyage, I hope?"

"Indeed, sir." Salem nodded and smiled. "And I needn't tell you how happy I am to be home." He looked

269

down at Aurora and winked. "Especially now that I have someone to come home to."

Dr. Holloway glanced about as if he'd only just noticed the two women in the room. He straightened, and his long, lean face fell into serious lines. "I hadn't planned on discussion on this point," he said brusquely. "I never said this topic was open for discussion, ladies."

"Please, Father," Aurora begged, "listen to what Salem has to say. For me?"

Never one to stand firm against his daughter when she used that sweet, besieging tone, Dr. Holloway nodded. "Oh, very well. Speak your piece, Captain, but I make no promises."

Salem cleared his throat almost nervously. "I know you never were a man of the sea, Dr. Holloway, so it's difficult to explain how much your daughter's affection has meant to me these past forty-three months. We fell in love before I went away. She was only a girl then, so I agreed to wait until my return to make her my wife. But look at her now." Salem paused and spread his hands toward Aurora, who blushed as all eyes in the room turned her way. "Your daughter is a woman, sir. A woman grown, ripe for marriage. I promise you that she will never know an unhappy moment as long as she is my wife. I will do anything and everything to assure that. Already I've notified the owners of the *Sankaty* to find a new master for their ship. I love the sea, sir, but I love your daughter far more."

"I have no quarrel with that," Seton Holloway said abruptly. "But what about The Ledges? Can you possibly mean to put my own dear daughter—the very woman you profess to love—in such danger? Think of it, man!"

"What danger, Father?" Aurora asked. "You can't truly mean that you believe in witches."

Her father turned a dark frown on her. "The witches of Coven Cove are real enough."

Salem shook his head. "Sir, I beg to differ. I was born

270

and reared at Coven Cove, at The Ledges. Granted, the old castle can be a frightening place of a dark and wintry night. But fear, like beauty, is only in the eye of the beholder. Gideon Caine, though he was my own flesh and blood, was an odd character, right enough. To transport such a place across the Atlantic, then rebuild it on that isolated spit of land had to be the work of a madman. But I assure you, sir, whatever evil lurked there died and was buried in my ancestor's grave."

Dr. Holloway still looked unconvinced. "And Gideon's bride? Have you an explanation for her disappearance?"

Salem forced a laugh. "I never believed those sordid tales for a moment. My great-grandmother didn't *disappear*. She simply ran away from her loveless marriage."

"She left her child," Dr. Holloway challenged.

Salem nodded. "That she did," he admitted.

"And 'twas one of the witches that raised that child."

"Not so!" Salem said. "Gideon himself spread tales that the nursemaid was a witch. My own father told me that. Don't you see, sir? Old Gideon wanted rumors of evil linked with The Ledges. But as a lad I hunted every inch of the place, explored every cave along the shore, searched the castle from turrets to dungeon. There is nothing there to fear. Would I take my bride into danger?"

"There you are, Seton," Europa interjected. "A fine man like Salem wouldn't think of putting his wife at risk."

"Oh, please, Father," Aurora begged. "We won't be that far away. We'll visit often, and you and Mother will always be welcome at The Ledges."

Maybe it was the tears brimming in his daughter's blue eyes or maybe he was just worn down by all the persuasion. Whatever the cause, Seton Holloway finally reluctantly nodded his agreement. Hugs all around followed; then the women left the men alone to their brandy, cigars, and the obligatory father-in-law and son-in-law talk.

271

From her bedroom late that night, Aurora watched her future husband leave, headed for the hired rooms he kept near the wharves. How sad that they must spend this first night apart! She glanced from Salem's tall figure on the walk below toward her own wide bed. There would be plenty of room for him—plenty of love.

As if sensing Aurora's thoughts, Salem paused and looked up at her window. He blew her a kiss. She blew one back. Then he disappeared into the night, whistling a lonely, sailor's tune.

Aurora fell asleep immediately that night, exhausted by the emotional upheaval she had undergone over the past few days. She smiled in her sleep, reliving in dreams Salem's marvelous kiss. But soon, stranger, darker dreams invaded her mind. Red-eyed hags flew at her, cackling unfathomable threats. Salem remained in these nightmares, but it seemed the witches kept them apart. He was far, far away. She kept calling to him, crying out his name, but he couldn't hear for the evil laughter of the coven. Finally, it seemed that same ugly sound erupted from Aurora's own mouth.

She woke with a start, shivering and sweating.

Dawn was breaking. With relief she realized that this was one of the few dawns left when she would awake alone.

# Three

Aurora and Salem's wedding day—October 24, 1879—dawned cold but brilliant. A sparkling sapphire of an autumn day. The front parlor of the tall, white house on Washington Street mirrored the flaming riot of fall colors outside. Branches of scarlet maple and golden elm leaves shimmered, glowing, in vases around the room, while evergreen boughs graced the marble mantelpiece.

Family and friends, armed with lavish gifts, had streamed in from all points of New England for the festive occasion. Now the guests were assembled in the parlor, still and silent, smiling at the nervous groom who stood beside the minister while they awaited the bridal procession down the long, mahogany staircase. The wife of one of Aurora's brothers perched, sparrowlike, at the antique harpsicord, her fingers poised to begin the wedding march.

Upstairs in her bedroom, Aurora anxiously awaited her cue. A final glance in the mirror assured her that her grandmother's ivory satin wedding gown was still every bit as lovely as it had been over half a century ago when young Victoria Forsyth had married Captain Asa Whiddington. Aurora, a surprise child of her parents' later years, had never known her grandparents, but she had heard so much about them all her life from her mother and Aunt Persia that she felt almost as if they were both here today, smiling and blessing her marriage to Salem Caine.

Aurora's Aunt Persia, her only attendant, came to stand beside her. "My goodness," she said, "except for your coloring, you are the image of your grandmother. She was so dainty and delicate looking, but a pillar of strength to our family. And, I will tell you a secret; both you and I share some of her other characteristics."

"Like what?" Aurora asked, always fascinated by tales of her legendary grandmother.

Persia hesitated, as if considering what to say. A slight frown passed over her face as if she had changed her mind concerning her answer. Finally, she said, "We both inherited her fiery temper, I'm afraid."

"Is that where we got it? I'd like to think that I also possess Grandmother Victoria's strength. But, oh, Aunt Persia, I'm so afraid suddenly!"

Persia patted Aurora's hand. "You've every right to be, my dear. You'd hardly be a proper bride if you weren't a bit jittery."

Aurora smiled at her aunt, so beautiful in her emerald-velvet gown with her flaming hair swept up. More than beautiful, Aurora thought, serene and wise and strong.

Suddenly, Persia frowned again at her niece. "Do you have questions, Aurora? I mean, your mother has talked to you, hasn't she?"

Aurora laughed softly. "Mother has told me very little, blushing all the while as she imparted her few bits of insight. But I'm not worried about that, Aunt Persia. My husband is a man of the world. I'm sure he'll show me the way."

Persia sighed with relief. She had miscarried during the early months of her one and only pregnancy, so she had no experience with tutoring virgin brides on the facts of life.

"What's bothering me most," Aurora went on, "is our going to The Ledges so soon."

"Why on earth would that frighten you, dear?"

Aurora blushed, embarrassed by her own foolish fears. "All this talk of witches and such. Do you believe it, Aunt Persia?"

"Do I believe there are witches at The Ledges? Of course not!" Persia scoffed. "No more than I believe all those poor women who were persecuted down in Massachussetts back in 1692 were practicing the black arts. Do you know that women used to be burned at the stake simply because they were left handed? That alone was thought to be the sure sign of a witch."

Aurora laughed nervously. "Then it's certainly a good thing I was born into such modern times." She reached up and adjusted her veil with her left hand. "I would have been a prime candidate for the witch-hunters' pyres."

"Goodness, child! Don't even think such a thing!"

Just then, the first tinkling music from the harpsicord floated up to the second floor.

"It's time, dear," Persia said, giving her niece a final hug.

A sharp knock sounded at the door. "That will be Father to escort me down."

All heads turned moments later as Persia Hazzard, a bouquet of autumn leaves clutched in her slender hands, entered the parlor. Then, a soft sigh rose from the company when the bride herself appeared on her father's arm. Aurora was a vision in the old-fashioned gown with its sweetheart neckline, high waist, and flowing lace sleeves and overskirt. Even through the misty white of her veil, Aurora's tremulous smile as she gazed at her groom was evident to all.

For once Seton Holloway did not look distracted. Instead, he wore a serious expression. To some, it seemed

275

he almost glared at Captain Jerusalem Caine, the man who was about to steal his daughter away.

From the moment Aurora took her place before the black-clad minister, she had eyes only for Salem. His handsome face was flushed with happiness. His storm-gray eyes gleamed with the soft light of love. In his dark, formal suit, he looked taller, broader of shoulder, altogether more imposing than Aurora had ever seen him. She quivered inside, trying to think how she was going to feel once she was truly the wife of such a man. Her thoughts hurried ahead to their first night together. She only hoped he would be gentle and patient with her. But then, of course, he would. He was the love of her life, after all.

Oblivious to the minister's words, lost in her own loving thoughts and the depth of Salem's eyes, Aurora did not realize her father had given her to her groom until she felt Salem's hand grip hers. He was closer now, standing so near that their bodies touched. She could feel his heat, smell his warm scents of bay rum, salt air, and something else, indefinable but peculiarly masculine.

By the time the minister reached the "I do's," Aurora could only manage a whispered response. But that was enough. "Now you may kiss the bride," the clergyman intoned.

An instant later, Aurora was in her husband's arms. His lips came down to meet hers—gently, sweetly, lovingly. Aurora felt the kiss a thousand times over. The delicious heat of it sizzled through her blood and made her heart race, her mind spin. It was as if she had been waiting for this particular kiss since the beginning of time.

When they parted, Aurora and Salem stood staring into each other's eyes for a long, moving moment. So much love swelled her heart that tears squeezed from the corners of her eyes. In fact, there was not a dry eye in the house. Even the groom grew misty.

"Well, you've done it, lad. You've stolen my only girl-child." Dr. Holloway was the first to break the fragile silence. "She's the apple of my eye, you know. The love of my heart. Treat her well, or by all that's holy, man, I'll—"

Europa bustled up in time to quell her husband's threat. "Seton, have you never heard of *congratulating* the groom? I think a handshake is in order. As for me, dear boy," she said, beaming up at Salem, "I'll have another of those kisses on my cheek. I found that quite nice, actually."

The guests all laughed as the groom paid proper homage to his new mother-in-law. Then best wishes were extended all around. Music followed, then dancing and food as the afternoon wore on. Near the end of the celebration, Europa insisted that the couple open their gifts. The merriment continued while Salem helped his bride unwrap the bright packages to discover comforters, bedwarmers, crockery, crystal, and cookery books. Finally the heaped table was cleared, save for one thin package.

"Why, there's no card with this one," Europa said. She held the slender gift on high, but none of the guests claimed it. Personally, she wasn't surprised since it was done up in ugly brown paper and twine.

"Never mind, Mother," Aurora said. "The card must be tucked inside."

Salem helped Aurora untie the thick twine. A moment later, she had the paper off. A murmur went through the crowd when they heard the bride's cry of alarm, then watched her face go ghostly white.

"What is it, darling?" Salem asked. He took the gift, a sheet of what looked like old parchment, from Aurora's trembling hands. "My God!" he gasped as he gazed down at the thing. Quickly, he folded the brown paper around the parchment. "It's only a joke," he told the guests, who were whispering and craning their necks to

277

see. "And one in rather poor taste. Shall we all have some champagne now?"

Once the guests dispersed, Salem turned to Aurora. She was still pale, a stunned look in her eyes. "Never mind, darling. It's nothing."

"How can you say that, Salem?" she whispered. "It's signed by your own ancestor, Gideon Caine, in what looks to be blood."

Dr. Holloway had caught a glance at the old piece of parchment, enough to let him know that it was some sort of document. "Salem, I'd like a word with you in my study. And bring that!"

Aurora clung to her husband's arm, refusing to be left out when her husband begged her to let him handle her father. "I want to hear what you have to say, too. I'm a part of this now. The *main* part, it would seem, if I'm the 'seventh bride.' "

Seton Holloway was waiting when they entered the study. "Spread it out here, on my desk," he ordered, "where I can get a proper look at it."

Reluctantly, Salem did as his father-in-law instructed, then stood back, holding Aurora's cold hand.

Taking a magnifying glass, Dr. Holloway leaned down over the parchment. For several moments, he studied the document silently. When he straightened, his face was grim. "It appears to be authentic. Have you ever seen this before, Salem?"

"Never!" he said. "Of course, I'd heard of it in old tales my nurse used to tell me when I was a boy. But I never for a moment believed her."

Aurora could stand the suspense no longer. "Please, will someone explain to me what this means? Am I the seventh bride mentioned there?"

"My God, no!" Salem exclaimed. "That can't be!"

Holding the parchment to the light, Dr. Holloway cleared his throat then read the document aloud. "This is dated All Hallows' Eve, seventeen hundred and thirteen. It states: 'I, Gideon Caine, do hereby grant the Coven of this place—Witches' Head at Coven Cove—the Seventh Bride to marry into Clan Caine in return for peaceful cohabitation of these premises and my castle, The Ledges, for the duration of my earthly existence. This oath, duly sworn and signed, is not to be canceled by any power on Earth, in Heaven, or in Hell.' Below is Gideon's signature, probably fashioned in his own blood."

Ominous silence followed Seton's reading of the document. "Well?" he said at length. "What about this, Captain Caine?"

Salem sank into a chair, covering his face with his hands. "I don't know," he muttered. "I simply don't know what to say."

"I do!" Dr. Holloway answered. "I say that it would be dangerous folly to remove my daughter to The Ledges. You've vowed to me that there are no witches at Coven Cove and never have been. I say that this document disproves your words. Someone at The Ledges has sent this as a warning or, more probably, a threat. I refuse to allow Aurora to go there."

Salem reached for Aurora's hand. Staring up at her, he said, "Of course I'd never take her there under these circumstances. I had no idea. This is as much a shock to me as it is to you, sir."

"What?" Aurora cried, the temper she had inherited from her grandmother erupting. "Deny me my home and my rightful place as your wife because of this spiteful jest? I see why there was no card from the sender—probably some disgruntled soul we forgot to invite to our wedding."

"Aurora, please!" Salem begged. "You can wait for me here while I go up to The Ledges and investigate the situation."

"Wait for you? I've been waiting all my life! I won't hear of it. Do you both believe me so faint of heart that

I would let some bizarre document mar my happiness? You show me witches, and I'll show you a grown, level-headed woman who will stand up to them and banish them as quickly as I would send any trickster on his merry way."

Ignoring his daughter's outburst, Dr. Holloway turned once more to Salem. "Is Aurora truly the seventh bride in the family?"

Salem uttered a pained sigh and shook his head. "I don't know. I suppose it would be easy enough to figure out."

For the next few moments, the two men worked over the problem. Dr. Holloway listed names while Salem combed his memory reconstructing his family's history.

"Gideon's bride was the first," he began. "Their son was my grandfather, Timothy. He married Lydia, who bore him five sons, one of which was my father."

"Did all the sons marry?" Seton asked.

"I know four of them did. The youngest son ran off to sea when he was in his teens. The family never heard from him again."

"That makes five brides, possibly six," Seton reasoned, "if your other uncle married. In that case, Aurora would be the seventh bride."

"Father, you're simply forcing this to work out the way you want it," Aurora accused. "What of all the brides of all the other sons, Salem's cousins? Surely the women they married count in this foolish scheme as much as I do."

"You have a point, my dear." Dr. Holloway brightened and looked to Salem for an answer. "I hadn't thought of that."

Sadly, Salem shook his head once more. "I am the only descendant of Gideon Caine left, except perhaps for offspring of my uncle who ran away to sea. Of my father's other brothers, one couple remained childless, another couple had only one daughter, who never married,

280

and the children of the third couple perished along with their parents in a fire. I alone survive to inherit The Ledges." He gazed at his lovely bride, his face mournful. "And old Gideon's curse."

"Curse, indeed!" Aurora fumed. "How do you know that document isn't a forgery? It could simply be a cruel joke perpetrated by some disgruntled sailor from you ship. I refuse to allow you to take this seriously, Salem. I certainly do not!"

At his daughter's words, Dr. Holloway once more examined the parchment with his magnifying glass. "Hm-m-m-m. This is odd," he muttered.

"What, sir?" Salem asked, a ray of hope dawning. "Could it be a forgery?"

The professor shook his bald head. "No. There's no question that it's quite old. The odd thing is the parchment itself. I've examined hundreds of antique documents, but I've never seen a sheet quite like this. The skin of a sheep or goat is normally used and can be quickly identified by the follicle marks left after the hair of the animal had been scoured away. But such marks are absent from this parchment. Still, it is undeniably some sort of skin."

Salem felt his blood curdle. Suddenly, a voice from his childhood penetrated his consciousness. His old nurse, Zenda, was speaking to him across the years. "You see this book, lad? Read whatever else you will from old Gideon's library, but touch not this wicked tome. 'Tis called *Malleus Maleficarum,* the medieval witch-hunter's guide. And the curious leather binding, you ask, my boy? 'Tis fine parchment made from the actual skin of witch. See how smooth and pale it is."

"Curious, indeed," Dr. Holloway muttered, interrupting Salem's gloomy thoughts.

"Well, I'll have you both know," Aurora announced, "that I resent having my wedding day disrupted in this manner. And I refuse to listen to another word. Salem,

281

I'm going up to my room to change now. When I come downstairs, I'll be ready to leave on our honeymoon journey. *To the Ledges!"*

In a swirl of antique satin and lace, Aurora turned and left father and husband staring after her. She was acting far braver than she felt. But she kept reminding herself firmly that Aunt Persia would not be frightened by all this *poppycock!*

# Four

Salem didn't want to spoil their wedding day for his bride. Reluctantly, he agreed to take her to The Ledges as planned. Perhaps this was all some fiendish joke as she insisted. And even if the parchment and the pact were real, any witches who had known old Gideon would be long since dead. Wouldn't they? Or were witches, like vampires, immortal?

"Get a grip," Salem muttered to himself as he waited for Aurora to come down from her bedroom. Vampires did not exist outside of horror stories. Nor did witches!

A stir among the guests brought Salem out of his gloomy reverie. He looked up. Aurora—his wife, he reminded himself with a rush of wonder—stood at the head of the stairs, dressed in a peacock velvet traveling suit trimmed in silver fox fur. The sight of her caused a pleasant tightening in his groin. He had never seen her look lovelier. There was a glow about her that seemed to radiate from within. He met her halfway up the stairs and took her hand. His eyes locked to the sapphire glimmer of hers. Slowly, Salem brought her fingertips to his lips.

"You're of another world," he whispered. "A vision!"

She leaned down close and murmured in response, "No, my darling. I am no vision, but flesh and blood . . . and *yours!* All yours, to have, to hold, and to love."

Salem felt his blood rush at her words. Slipping his

arm around her waist, he leaned close to her ear and said, "Keep talking that way and we won't make it to The Ledges tonight. I'm likely to stop our sleigh and have my way with my bride in the very midst of this blizzard. Cold work, that!"

Aurora gave an excited cry. "It's snowing? How could I not have noticed?"

"The first true snowfall of the season," Dr. Holloway confirmed. "If you two had your wits about you, you'd stay here overnight until this storm lets up."

"Oh, shush, Seton!" Europa told her husband. "Where's your sense of adventure? I think it's terribly romantic that they'll be driving up the coast in a sleigh with snow swirling all about them and love keeping them warm and safe."

Hugs and kisses all around, and then the newlyweds hurried out the front door. Salem lifted Aurora into his arms and placed her gently on the soft leather seat of the sleigh. Then he climbed in beside her and spread a black bear robe over them both, taking care to tuck it in firmly about his bride.

"Oh, this is cozy!" Aurora said with a shy smile.

He leaned down and kissed her, warming her chilled lips while one hand stole under the lap robe to press her thigh.

"Yes, quite cozy," she murmured, resting her head on his shoulder.

A moment later, Salem touched up the horses and they were on their way, speeding through the drifts of new snow while the bells on the harnesses jingled cheerily. The cries of farewell slowly faded into the distance, and at last they were alone in an enchanted world of sparkling snow, icy stars, and love.

Soon they escaped from the town and were in the country with its bleak and rocky landscape. Snow whirled and danced in the air, dusting the green-black firs and cedars that sped past on either side like shapeless spirits. The silence was total, save for the cheery song of the bells and the sleigh's runners whispering smoothly over the blanket of white.

"Tell me about The Ledges, Salem," Aurora pleaded, snuggling closer.

"What would you like to know, darling?"

"Well . . . why is the place called that?"

"Because old Gideon had it reconstructed on a high, rocky cliff, a ledge that juts out over the sea. You almost get the sense of being on board a ship when you're there. During storms, waves crash into the promontory with such force that water is dashed up into windows of the upper stories. Only on the ebb of the tide, you can see the narrow peninsula extending below. I'll take you out to the point. The view of the castle is grand from there."

Beneath their lap robe, Aurora slipped both of her hands inside Salem's coat to make the best use of his body heat. He smiled down at her, his dark eyes flashing.

"There's an inn up ahead, 'Rora. Would you like to stop for the night?" His voice was low and husky, caressing her with its warmth and promising untold wonders. "It's likely to get colder and stormier before we reach The Ledges."

The thought was tempting, Aurora had to admit. She had waited so long for his return—for their marriage—that waiting several hours more before she actually became his wife seemed cruel punishment. But, at the same time, this ride through the night, with his arm holding her to his side and her hands intimate with his chest made her dizzy with pleasure. Now that they were here, together, married, she saw no reason to rush through their happiness. As it lingered, so did it grow.

In answer to Salem's question, Aurora said, "I'll always remember this night, my darling. Riding through the cold, snowy night so close to you, feeling you with me at last, realizing that we'll always be together from now on, that I don't have to fear the pain of another

285

parting." She gazed up at her husband, happy tears starring her long eyelashes. "I don't want this to end, Salem, not just yet."

She turned slightly, to rest her head against his chest, hearing his heart thunder in response to her words and her nearness.

"I'll keep you warm," he whispered, kissing her forehead. "I'll keep you close—always. Nothing and no one can part us again, my love."

The arm he'd had around her shoulder slid down and around, cupping her breast. Aurora stiffened for an instant. No man had ever touched her there before. But the gentle kneading of his fingers through the heavy cloak she wore soon had her tingling through and through. She sighed and relaxed, revelling in her husband's fondling touch. It seemed as if a roaring fire had been kindled beneath their shared robe of fur, a fire hot enough to warm her very soul.

"Tell me more about your family, Salem," Aurora said at length. "About Gideon."

"You'll see him when we reach The Ledges, darling."

"What?" Aurora half-rose from her relaxed position.

Salem laughed. "Oh, not in the flesh. You'll see Gideon's portrait, I mean. Along with those of the other members of my family. But Gideon's portrait is different from the rest."

"How do you mean?"

Salem thought for a while before he answered. "It's hard to explain, darling. The others all look like stalwart New England settlers—salt of the earth and all that. But Gideon seems otherworldly by comparison. Very dark and European, with perhaps a touch of evil lurking in his gaze and a sneer on his lips for the whole world."

"Oh, Salem, stop! He sounds dreadful! But I know you're only teasing me because of all that witch business."

"You'll see," he answered cryptically.

286

"You told Father there had never been any witches there," she reminded him, "so I don't believe any of that foolishness for a minute."

"Good!" he answered, giving her breast a firm squeeze for emphasis. "Because I don't want our lives complicated by a lot of superstitious nonsense. You may be the seventh bride of Clan Caine, but you're *my* bride. And I mean to have you—every sweet inch of you—darling."

Fire sizzled through Aurora's blood at his tone and his words. Maybe they should stop at the inn after all. Salem had been at sea without a woman for a long time, and Aurora had been without a man even longer—her entire life. Suddenly, she was beginning to sense what she'd been missing all those loveless years.

Shortly after that, Aurora must have fallen asleep. The swaying motion of the sleigh, the caress of Salem's hand, the darkness holding them in its silent grasp all worked to soothe her like a sweet-sad lullaby. She was next conscious of Salem kissing her awake, his mouth warm and insistent over her icy lips. She snuggled into his arms, purring with sensual pleasure.

"We're here, darling," he said, drawing slightly away. "We're home at last."

Aurora opened her eyes to find the stormy breath of the sea whipping the snowflakes to a fury. Using one hand to shield her eyes against the gale-driven snow, Aurora stared up at the colossal structure before them. The Ledges was a monstrous pile of blood-red stone, rising high above them with its turrets, gargoyles, and towers. Sputtering torches lent uneven beams of light at either side of the massive entrance. And the moat, sea water surrounding the castle—how were they to bridge that gap?

As if sensing his bride's dismay, Salem clanged a huge metal gong suspended near the moat. Within seconds the clank of chains and the groan of old wood sounded eerily through the night. Aurora watched as the drawbridge slowly descended.

"Is someone here, Salem?" she asked, wondering why it hadn't occurred to her before that the place must be staffed.

"The housekeeper, Mrs. Romney, and her little daughter Krystine. Then, too, there's the stableman, Bodwell."

"Oh!" Aurora sighed her disappointment. "I had thought we would be alone—just the two of us, darling."

Salem laughed. "You'd planned then to cook and tend castle yourself, my love, while I saw to the stock, chopped the wood, and repaired the old homeplace according to its daily needs? Well, I *might* have managed all that single-handed, but I doubt I'd have had much strength left at the end of the day to see to my husbandly duties. Believe me, darling," he added, still chuckling, "there are enough rooms here for us to be alone as often as we like. Besides, Mrs. Romney and Bodwell have their own quarters below the main floor."

"Of course," Aurora answered. "How silly of me! I'm glad I won't have the worry of hiring servants. Thank you, darling."

Just as Aurora pressed herself against her husband to offer him an appropriate kiss of gratitude, a dark shape caught her eye, looming near the edge of the woods. Aurora gave a startled cry.

Salem turned toward the tall, gaunt figure and raised his hand in greeting. "Bodwell! Good to see you again. Come meet my bride."

As the stableman came nearer, into the circle of light cast by the torches, Aurora saw that he was not the twisted ogre he had appeared to be in the shadows, but a large, sturdy man, perhaps in his sixties. His head was entirely bald, while his eyebrows formed a dark hedgerow over his sunken eyes. A long mustache drooped past his chin, framing the straight line of his mouth.

Bodwell glared at Aurora from beneath his shaggy brows and muttered, "How do, Mrs. Caine?"

As Salem and Bodwell turned away for a moment to deal with the horses, Aurora thought she heard the man say to her husband, "Why did you bring her here?" The words made her slightly uncomfortable. She could not hear Salem's reply, which only caused her further uneasiness.

Salem rejoined her a moment later to lead her across the drawbridge, now firmly in place over the wide moat.

"Did I hear Bodwell ask you why you brought me here, Salem?"

Refusing to meet her steady gaze, her husband answered lightly, "Of course not, darling. Why would he have said such a thing?"

"I haven't a notion," Aurora replied. Perhaps she was letting her imagination run away with her. All this talk of witches and such.

Once they had crossed the drawbridge, a great oaken door studded with metal spikes barred their way. Aurora thought she caught sight of someone peering through a narrow window slit at them. A moment later, the door swung inward.

Salem swept her up into his arms and kissed her soundly, all but taking her breath away. "And now, Mrs. Jerusalem Caine, your husband is going to carry you over the threshold in the time-honored tradition."

"Ah, isn't it more superstition?" Aurora quizzed, hugging his neck happily. "I thought we were not going to pay attention to such foolishness, darling."

"You're right, of course, about superstitions being foolish. But this is one tradition I mean to honor. It goes far back into the shadows of European history, I believe, back to the days when barbarians stole their brides and carried them off. Most of those poor young women were still struggling to escape when they reached their new homes. Their grooms were forced to carry them in or

289

lose them." He clutched her close and kissed her again. "I think those barbarians had the right idea."

Aurora purred in his arms. "If you expect me to resist you, darling, you'll be sorely disappointed, I'm afraid. That last kiss just took all the fight right out of me."

Someone cleared her throat in the shadows of the entranceway. Aurora flushed, knowing that words meant for her husband's ears alone had been overheard by a stranger.

"Mrs. Romney!" Salem's deep voice boomed in the stone cavern of the entranceway. He hurried into the dimly lit hall, still carrying Aurora in his strong arms.

A tiny, withered woman in a shapeless black dress presented herself, candle in hand. "Captain Caine," she said warmly, "welcome home to ye."

"This is your new mistress, Mrs. Romney," Salem announced, holding Aurora forth in his arms so that she felt most undignified.

"Put me down, please," she whispered, but Salem continued to hold her to him as if he hadn't heard.

"Lame, is she?" Mrs. Romney said, peering over her round spectacles at the slip of a girl in his grasp, but speaking only to Salem. "More's the pity. But mayhap old Zenda can fix . . ."

Aurora struggled out of Salem's arms and to her feet, extending a hand toward the housekeeper and cutting her off in mid-sentence. "Mrs. Romney, I'm happy to meet you. As you can see, I'm neither lame nor deaf."

Once more directing her words to the master of the house, Mrs. Romney said, "Speaks her mind, right enough, sir." Then, dismissing Aurora totally, the woman said, "You'll be wanting to greet Krystine, I'm sure. I'll rouse her, Captain."

"No need for that, Mums." A sultry, rich voice flowed into the dim hall like warm, sticky honey.

"Krystine?" Salem said, wonder in his voice.

Aurora's eyes went wide as "Mrs. Romney's little

daughter" moved into the light. She looked to be just shy of Aurora's own age of twenty-one. And by her figure, plainly visible through her thin, linen shift even though she clutched a long shawl about her shoulders, she was every inch a woman. Her blue-black hair was long and straight, tangled from sleep. A lock snaked sexily down over one gleaming dark eye, giving her the look of some wild animal peering out at them from the deepest gloom of the forest.

"Salem," she sighed in a husky whisper. "I dreamed you were coming back."

He laughed nervously. "You knew, of course. I sent word ahead last week that we would be here tonight."

"Krystine knew before that. She always knows," Mrs. Romney told them. "Well, what do you think, Captain? She's grown a mite, eh?"

Salem cleared his throat, trying not to stare at the girl who had been his shadow when they were both much younger. "It's been over ten years, Mrs. Romney. I should hope she'd have grown."

Krystine's dark gaze locked on Aurora, who squirmed with discomfort under her pouting scrutiny. She touched Salem's arm. "Dear, if you don't mind, I'm quite tired. Could we go up now?"

"Of course, darling," he answered quickly. "Mrs. Romney . . . ?"

"Your supper'll be right up, sir, and Bodwell's got a fire going in the master suite like you instructed. He'll bring your bags directly."

"Thank you." He nodded to Mrs. Romney, then Aurora noticed that his gaze went back to Krystine, lingering on her voluptuous form for a moment longer than it pleased Aurora. She tugged at his sleeve. He turned back to his wife quickly, smiling down at her.

"Shall we?" He offered his arm.

Although torches sputtered along the tapestry-hung stone walls, Aurora saw little of the place as they hurried up the wide staircase to the floor above. An uneasy feeling was at work inside her. She hadn't bargained on another woman her own age living under the roof at The Ledges—especially a woman who looked at Salem in exactly that way.

"Brr-r-r! It's cold as a tomb in here," Salem said, rushing Aurora toward the closed door to their warm suite.

"Really?" Aurora commented. "I thought it rather *too* warm down below."

Ignoring her remark, Salem opened the first door to the left of the stairs. It glowed like a polished jewel. A fire roared in the wide fireplace, making the whole room seem to shimmer in light and welcoming warmth.

Forgetting all else, Aurora gave a delighted cry and rushed in. "Oh, Salem! This is perfectly marvelous! I've never seen such a place."

He smiled at her obvious pleasure. "When this old castle still rested atop its mountain in Europe, this was known as the King's Chamber. Legend says that every crowned head on the continent slept here at one time or another."

Aurora moved about caressing her surroundings: the green and gold silk-draped walls, the billowing curtains that opened onto a balcony that overhung the sea, the great bed with its high, gilt coronet.

When Salem could wait no longer to hold her, he came to Aurora, drawing her into his arms, his mouth hovering over hers. "I'm so glad you like it, darling. Tomorrow we'll explore the castle. Right now, I thought we might indulge in a more intimate sort of exploration."

His kiss was just gaining momentum when a knock interrupted. Before they could break their embrace to answer it, the door opened. Aurora gave a startled cry.

"Oh, I do beg your pardon, Salem," the deep, honeyed voice said, but without a trace of true apology. "I brought your supper."

"Krystine!" Salem said in an exasperated tone. "Please wait from now on until I answer your knock."

She strode into the room and threw Aurora a spiteful glance as she set the tray down on a table near the window. "I'll *try* to remember."

"See that you do." Salem hurriedly escorted her back to the door and slammed it behind her. "That girl!"

"She's hardly a girl, darling," Aurora said, pointing out what she felt was disturbingly obvious.

"Where were we?" Salem said, changing the subject abruptly. "Ah, yes, I remember now."

Drawing his bride back into his arms, he applied his lips with even more dedication. This was yet a new feeling for Aurora. For the first time in her life, she was alone with her husband in their own room with the bed waiting and the whole world locked out. As he held her with one arm about her waist, he quickly divested her of her cloak, then began unfastening the jacket of her traveling suit. Beneath that, he found only a thin blouse over her camisole. Still holding her captive with his deep kiss, Salem let his hands stray to her breasts. Aurora shuddered with pleasure as his strong fingers played over her taut, aching nipples.

"Why don't you change, darling?" he whispered against her mouth. "We'll have our supper and then . . ."

"If that's what you wish, Salem," she answered softly, feeling suddenly shy with her husband.

He hugged her tightly for a moment, pressing her head to his chest. "Yes, my darling," he moaned. "Oh, yes, that's what I wish!"

# Five

Supper passed quickly and without much conversation. Seated next to his bride on a loveseat by the French door to the balcony, Salem spent most of his dinner hour alternating between feeding Aurora slivers of cold lobster and nibbling at her succulent lips.

"Aren't you hungry, darling?" Aurora asked between kisses.

"Starved," he admitted. "But I can't seem to keep my mind on eating."

Aurora knew exactly what he meant. She was having the same problem concentrating on food, yet she was nervous over what would come next. She knew so little about love—about men. What if she didn't please Salem? What if she did it all wrong?

Trying to delay things as her husband became more amorous, she stood and walked to the French doors, staring out over the sea. The snow had stopped and the moon was now peeking out of the clouds, forming a silvery trail over the water.

"What's that?" she asked, her eyes focusing on some distant dark shape in the moonlight.

Salem rose and came to her side. "That's the peninsula I told you about. The tide is out now so it's above water. There used to be a tunnel that ran from the dungeon of The Ledges out to an opening in one of the caves in the cliff. I assume a good deal of smuggling was carried on here at some time in the past."

"How intriguing!" Aurora said. "Is the tunnel still open? Can we use it to get out to the point?"

"No." Salem shook his head and grinned down at his bride, who sounded as excited as a child. "My father closed it off when I was a lad. You see, the tunnel floods at high tide. Father was afraid I might get caught down there and drown if he left it open. He was probably right. I was quite the explorer when I was young."

Aurora leaned closer to the glass, squinting to get a better view. She could hardly believe what she saw next—a figure moving about in the dim moonlight.

"Salem? Someone's out there on the point. Look!"

He laughed softly. "At night it does look like a person, doesn't it? Actually, it's a large, upright stone. I've always believed it was a Viking rune-stone. There are strange markings all over it."

"No! I don't mean the stone. I saw a figure moving about."

Salem frowned at the nervous edge to Aurora's voice. He took her hand. "Come away, darling. We've better things to do than watch moon shadows."

His next kiss told Aurora that she could stall no longer, nor did she wish to. He led her about the room, blowing out candles, until only the dim glow of the embers gleamed in the shadowy darkness.

Leading her toward the bed, he motioned for her to sit down.

"Do you know what I thought about while I was at sea?" he asked.

Befuddled by his question, Aurora said, "I can't imagine."

He placed one hand on either side of her on the bed and leaned down over her, staring into her eyes. "I thought of this very moment," he whispered. "I thought of coming home, marrying you, of our raising a family

295

together, growing old side-by-side. But most often, I thought of our wedding night—of how it would feel to hold you and kiss you and make you mine forever, Aurora darling."

Leaning closer, he pressed his lips to hers in a light, sweet, devastating kiss. With his mouth still on hers, Salem slipped the dressing gown from her shoulders and caressed her warm flesh until she sighed and trembled.

"I hope I won't disappoint you," she murmured. "I've thought of this night, too, and wondered . . ."

"You've nothing to fear, darling. You couldn't disappoint me if you tried."

So saying, he proceeded to undress before her, letting her see for herself what lay in store for her. If Salem Caine had been handsome clothed, naked he was magnificent. Aurora trembled at the sight of his gleaming flesh—wanting him, fearing him, needing him.

After giving her a few moments' contemplation, Salem gently raised her to a standing position once more. Slowly and carefully he stole his bride's dressing gown completely away, and after that her nightshift, until she too, had the light from the fire dancing over her bare pearl-like skin. Soon now, Aurora knew, her loving thief would also steal her innocence.

"You're so beautiful," he whispered. "I knew you would be, darling. But I could never have imagined . . ."

In answer, she said, "Once Aunt Persia showed me a painting of a Greek god . . ." She could bring herself to say no more, but her meaning was clear enough.

Aurora shivered in Salem's arms, her tingling flesh pressed to his. She could feel his hardness, his heat. His hands moved over her, leaving a trail of fire and ice in their wake. When he dipped his head to her breast and suckled gently, Aurora moaned aloud and sagged against him.

Salem lifted her in his arms and carried her to their waiting bed. The moon sailed lower, the embers died down, a clock somewhere in the castle struck once and then again, and all the while Salem kissed her and stroked her and gentled her toward madness with his lover's touch.

"Please, darling," she moaned when she felt she might die from wanting him. "Oh, please, make me yours!"

Only then did he cover her, kissing her deeply as he gave his first thrust. Aurora stiffened beneath him and uttered a sharp cry. He tried to pull out, but she gripped him, gasping a wordless plea. A moment later, the motion of her hips picked up his steady rhythm. Aurora could feel his heartbeat against her breasts—faster and faster, stronger and stronger. And so the pleasure built as well, spiraling up and up into the night heavens, carrying her over the clouds, beyond the sea and the moon.

And then it came!

Aurora clutched Salem's damp shoulders, feeling his muscles ripple under her own sweating palms. She held on for dear life. Nothing had ever prepared her for this. She felt as if every pleasure in life were combined to bring this moment of pure, perfect ecstasy.

For a long while afterward, Salem held her and kissed her murmuring words of love and amazement. When he rolled away to lie beside her, Aurora lay as still as the stone pillar on the point. She had to concentrate all her efforts just to keep breathing.

"Darling, are you all right?" Salem whispered. "I tried to be gentle, but—oh, God, Aurora!"

She reached out to touch his face, her first move since she'd reached the pinnacle. "I love you," she said, amazement in her trembling voice. "Salem, I never . . . I mean, how could I have guessed. . . ? It was so beautiful."

He leaned over and kissed her breast, then slipped his arms around her, drawing her close again. *"You* are so beautiful, Aurora. And to think that you are mine!"

Soon, they slept, still clinging to each other, waiting

for the dawn and renewed strength so that they could make this new-found miracle happen again.

But sometime before dawn, Aurora woke. She lay tense beside Salem, listening. Listening for what? She didn't know.

Suddenly, out of the corner of her eye, she thought she saw a slight movement in the shadows. She lay very still, feigning sleep, but shifting her gaze in that direction. Her whole body ached with tension. She reached out, meaning to wake Salem, but her hand never touched him.

Everything happened so quickly that she never quite knew what transpired. Even as she saw the shadow move again—perhaps a curtain rustling in the wind, she thought at the time—something covered her face and she breathed in a sickly sweet smell. Her gasps carried the odor deep into her lungs and straight to her head, dulling her senses, making her mind spin in a dark vortex. She tried to cry out for Salem, but words refused to come. She tried to reach for him, but her arms seemed as lifeless as her mind.

Soon any sort of struggle became a thing of the past. Aurora drifted off, a vile-smelling curtain of black closing over her.


The morning sun shone in, slanting across the rumpled bed. Salem covered his closed eyes with one hand and reached for his bride with the other. How many mornings at sea had he dreamed of *this* morning?

"Darling?" he whispered, groping farther along the sheets, assuring himself that he would touch her warm, soft flesh at any moment. "Aurora?"

He started to leap out of bed, sure that she was gone or that he had only dreamed their wonderful love-making last night. "The best damn dream *you'll* ever have!" he told himself with a happy laugh. Then he lay back, closing his eyes again, and waited. Aurora would be in the little water closet off the dressing room, of course. There were certainly delicate things that needed taking care of this morning.

He waited . . . and waited.

Finally, he could wait no longer. Something wasn't right. A dull buzz in his brain signaled a warning.

Salem hauled himself out of bed and quickly pulled on his trousers. He dashed for the water closet and jerked the door open. Nothing in the little room had been touched since the night before. Back in the bedroom, he glanced about. Aurora's blue velvet robe and white gown lay on the floor where he had discarded them before they made love. His own clothes, too, were scattered about. Opening the door, which was bolted from the inside, he stared out into the hallway. Their bags sat untouched where Bodwell had deposited them hours ago.

Shaking his head, trying to sort out the million or so dire thoughts that were crowding his brain, Salem went back inside. He glanced through the French doors to the balcony. The slightest breeze moved the drapes. The doors had been opened!

He ran across the room and flung them wide, stepping out onto the tiny balcony to face a brisk, cold wind.

"My God!" he gasped, staring down at the sea dashing against the jagged rocks far below. "Aurora?"

Salem stumbled back inside, slamming the door shut with such force that the glass rattled. He couldn't think. Black bile was rising in his throat.

"The seventh bride," he moaned softly. "Oh, my God, what have they done to you? Why did I bring you here?"

Snapping himself out of it, Salem quickly dressed, then dashed downstairs, shouting Aurora's name as he went. She had to be here somewhere. Maybe she'd gotten up earlier to investigate her new surroundings.

He all but ran over Mrs. Romney in the hallway. They both started to speak at the same moment, Salem's "Have you seen my wife?" overlaid by the housekeeper's "Have you seen Krystine?"

"Krystine's missing, too?" Salem asked, suspicion beginning to paint an ugly picture in his mind.

"Well, sir, I wouldn't exactly say Krystine's missing, but she didn't sleep in her bed last night. And I've seen neither hide nor hair of her this morning."

"Aurora's gone!" Salem exclaimed, looking wild-eyed to Mrs. Romney.

"I'll summon Bodwell from the grounds, and we'll give the place a thorough search—top to bottom. Could be Krystine's only showing Mrs. Caine around."

"I don't think that's likely," Salem muttered. Then a thought struck him. "Aurora questioned me last night about the tunnel out to the point. She might have gone down there, hoping to find an opening."

Mrs. Romney was already headed for the door. "You search down there, then, Captain," she called over her shoulder. "I'll get Bodwell. We'll find them, sir. Don't you worry!"


Aurora could still smell the sickly sweet odor. It seemed to cling to her body and fill the blank space in her brain. A wave of dizziness swept over her, followed by a twin wave of nausea.

"I have to open my eyes," she moaned. "I have to see where I am, what's happened."

But when she raised her hands to her eyes, she found that they were open. Yet she could see nothing. Lying very still, she listened. Off in the distance, she could hear the thunder of the sea. Yes, the air about her, she realized, felt thick and damp. In fact, she was lying on wet ground.

She strained to remember what had happened. Was this simply her nightmare in some new and hideous form? Was she really lying in bed next to her husband and only dreaming this awful, black place?

300

"No," she moaned as memory came creeping back. Someone had come in the night and done something to her. She vaguely remembered that terrible, suffocating smell and then being dragged from her bed. She'd been naked when she was forced outside. She could remember the cold wind slashing at her body like icy knives, shocking her back to consciousness for a moment.

Was she still naked? Yes! But she was wrapped in some sort of thick, rough cloak.

She reached out, trying to feel her surroundings. Her hand touched cold rock. Trickles of water oozed from cracks. She remembered that Salem had mentioned caves by the sea.

"A cave," she murmured. "Yes, this smells like a cave—feels like a cave. But how did I get here?"

She forced herself to lie still, gathering her strength to call for help. Whoever had brought her here could still be lurking nearby. But surely Salem must be searching for her by now. Her only chance was to make him hear her and come to her aid. Although she wasn't tied, she dared not try to move in the total blackness. If she was in a cave, for all she knew, she could be lying on the very edge of some bottomless pit. An incautious step and she could plummet to her death.

Then another, even more frightening thought came to mind. "I must be the seventh bride," she whispered. "And last night the witches came to claim their own. What did they do to me while I was unconscious?"

She heard pounding in the silence, then realized it was her own heart. Terror closed in, thicker than any blackness, more evil-smelling than any drug.

"Help," she whimpered, then she called out, "Help!" Then loud enough to bring the cave down, she cried, "Help me, Salem! Salem, please!"

# Six

With cold sweat stinging his eyes and fear lashing his heart, Salem clattered down the rough stone steps to the dungeon. Grabbing a flaming torch from its steel bracket in the wall, he hurried into the wine cellar to reach one of the underground tunnels that led toward the old, closed-off passage to the sea. For all he knew, the boards his father had placed over the entrance to that one dangerous tunnel had long since rotted through, giving Aurora easy access, but proving a deathtrap once she was inside and the tide started to rise.

In his haste, Salem tripped over a wine barrel and cursed. A moment later, he heard a soft moan. Raising his torch higher, he scanned the dusky shadows of the chamber. Racks, cobwebs, dusty bottles, a rat scurrying for cover, but nothing else.

"Aurora?" he called. "Can you hear me?"

He stood stock-still, listening with his very soul. He heard a muffled sob, then another moan.

"That way!" he cried. "The sound's coming from the torture chamber."

Stooping to make his way through a low, connecting tunnel, Salem entered the room that had both fascinated and horrified him as a lad. Among Gideon Caine's other perversities had been a fascination with instruments of torture. This dank, low-ceilinged chamber had been fully furnished by his black-hearted ancestor with ancient tools once used by witch-hunters to extract confessions from their hapless victims. Stocks, whips, chains, a dunking stool, an iron maiden, a torture rack. On first glimpse, Salem saw no one. The figure on the rack appeared to be no more than a bundle of dirty, mildewed rags. Then the rags moved and uttered a soft moan.

Flinging his torch aside, Salem cried, "Aurora!" as he ran to the torture rack.

"Salem," came a ragged sob.

He fell over her, fumbling at the rusty shackles that bound her to the monstrous contraption. Then he drew back, stunned.

"Krystine?" he said, half-choked with disbelief.

"Oh, God, it hurts, Salem! Get me off this thing," she begged.

Quickly, in a bewildered daze, Salem unlatched the iron cuffs from her wrists and ankles. A moment later, Krystine, sobbing her loudest, threw herself into his arms.

"Are you all right? What the hell happened here?" Salem demanded.

Krystine gave another choked sob. "You wouldn't believe me if I told you," she said.

"Who did this to you?"

She clung to him, seeming faint. "Salem, please! Just get me out of here. Then I'll answer all your questions."

Retrieving his torch, Salem slipped one arm around the limping girl and helped her back through the low tunnel, then up the stone stairs. Mrs. Romney came running to meet them.

"Mother of God!" the woman cried, her hands fluttering to her face in shock and fear.

"She's had a bad fright, but she seems all right," Salem assured his housekeeper, turning Krystine's care over to her. "Has anyone seen Aurora yet?"

303

"Not a trace," Mrs. Romney answered, staring at her daughter with a strange look in her eyes.

"I'm going back down, then," Salem said. "The tide's coming in. I have to check the tunnel before it's flooded."

"Wait, Salem," Krystine called after him. But he was already gone.

Retracing his steps, Salem dashed through the torture chamber into the tunnel opening. Sure enough, he found his father's carefully constructed barrier lying in a rotted heap. Kicking the bits of old wood aside, he plunged into the icy darkness.

"Aurora!" he yelled. But only the sound of the incoming tide roared an answer to his frantic call. Glancing down, he saw that water was already inching up his boots. He pushed on, brandishing his torch, shouting her name.

Aurora roused herself. Had she heard someone call or had she only imagined the sound? She couldn't seem to keep herself awake. Try as she might, she kept drifting in and out of consciousness. What did it matter anyway? She was going to die. Already, she was so cold that her limbs had gone numb. Cold and *wet,* she realized suddenly. She was lying in water now, not the trickle that came through cracks in the cave wall but icy, rushing water that kept creeping higher and higher.

"Aurora, answer me!"

She shook her head, trying to clear it. That was Salem's voice. Her heart gave a joyous leap of hope. He was coming. He would save her. Then she glanced about. How would he ever find her in the blackness?

She tried to call out to him, but his name only whispered brokenly from her mouth. Aurora bit her lip and closed her eyes, summoning all her strength and all her courage. She concentrated only on calling Salem's name. She held the sound inside for long moments, not allowing it to escape, forcing it to gain momentum. Finally, as the water crept up toward her neck, she screamed, "Salem, I'm here!"

A moment later, she saw a wavering light coming toward her. She recognized the grotesque mask of anguish as her husband's face. Tears of love and relief welled up.

"Aurora!" he gasped. "Oh, my darling!"

Carefully holding the torch high above the water, Salem bent down and scooped her up in his arms. He kissed her cold lips and murmured low curses along with mumbled prayers of thanks.

Aurora clung to him. Allowing the effort of her scream and the relief at her rescue to have their way with her, she drifted off, losing consciousness in her husband's strong, protective arms.

Salem felt her go limp against him. He tried to quicken his step, but the fierce current of the incoming tide—boot-top high by now—slowed his progress. He slogged on, keeping a tight grip on Aurora and on the torch. Without light to show him the way out of the winding maze of tunnels, he might take a wrong turn. Then they would both be lost.

By the time he reached the main floor of the castle, he was already shouting orders to Mrs. Romney. "Get blankets, hot water, brandy!"

As he dashed for the stairs, headed for their bedroom, Salem caught a glimpse of Krystine. She lounged against a far wall, her nightshift in tatters on her voluptuous body, her long, black hair damply matted, her wrists and ankles marked with angry bruises from the torture rack. He noticed something else about her, too. Her face wore the same pout he'd often seen when she was a child—a pout that presaged a temper tantrum or some scheming misdeed. But most of all it was her eyes that held him, glittering black eyes that radiated some pure, icy emotion. He turned away and hurried on, anxious to see to

Aurora's needs, to get her dry and warm, to find out what had happened.

Once he brought her into the room, Salem realized that she was naked, wrapped in a grimy boat tarp. He stripped the filthy thing away and stared at the gray-blue tint of her skin.

"Damn!" he muttered. "A few more minutes down there and she would have died from exposure."

He managed to slip her limp arms into her warm, velvet robe, then he placed her on the bed, piling the covers high, chafing her icy hands with his.

Mrs. Romney appeared at the door. "I brought the brandy, sir."

"Good! Bring it here."

Slipping one arm around Aurora's shoulders, he raised her enough to give her a sip.

"Slowly, darling," he warned. "Take only a bit at first."

Aurora felt herself hovering just this side of unconsciousness. Parting her lips, she accepted whatever Salem was offering, only to cough and choke when the fiery liquid flowed over her tongue. But the coughing itself seemed to revive her somewhat.

As eager as Salem was to question her, he dared not press her just yet. She looked so weak and pale. Clearly, her ordeal had sapped all the strength from her.

"It's a wonder they aren't *both* dead," Mrs. Romney said pointedly.

Salem, having forgotten that the other woman was in the room, glanced over his shoulder. "How's Krystine?" he asked.

"A mite shaken, as you might suspect," the housekeeper answered, "but she'll survive."

"Did she tell you what happened?" Salem asked.

"A bit of it—as much as she can remember. Seems she was sleeping and someone slipped into her room. The next she knew, her abductor was holding a foul-smelling rag over her face; then she blacked out. When she came around, she was down below, lashed to the torture rack with no way to get loose and the tide coming in." Mrs. Romney glanced at Aurora, her gaze narrowing in suspicion. "What about her?"

Salem felt a twinge of anger at Mrs. Romney's tone. *"My wife,"* he said pointedly, "almost lost her life. If she hadn't asked me about the tunnel last night . . . if I hadn't guessed that she might be there, she'd have drowned by now."

"What do you suppose she was doing down there?" The woman's words sounded more like an accusation than a question.

"She saw something on the point last night. She said it was a figure moving around the rune-stone. Do you have any idea who that might have been, Mrs. Romney?"

The woman didn't seem surprised in the least by this revelation. "Probably old Zenda."

"Zenda?" Salem made no attempt to hide his shock. "You mean my old nurse?"

"Ayuh!" Mrs. Romney said with an abrupt nod.

"But I thought she was long dead by now."

"Not that one. She's stayed about the place ever since you left home. She always said you'd come back in spite of everything, and that you owed her and she meant to collect. Mayhap she's been waiting all these years for the seventh bride to come."

Boyhood tales of servants at The Ledges practicing the black arts swarmed back into Salem's mind. Krystine had always sworn it was so. And maybe it was. But surely not his dear old Zenda!

"I need to talk to her," he said. "Tell her to come up here."

Mrs. Romney shrugged. "I can't do that, sir."

"Why not?"

"There's no telling where she is."

307

"You mean she's not in the castle? But you said she lives here."

"Begging your pardon, sir, I said she's still around. She lives sometimes in the old gamekeeper's cottage way back in the woods. Other times, she just vanishes for long spells."

A moan from Aurora diverted Salem's attention. He leaned over her, relieved to see that some of her color was returning.

"Darling?" he whispered. "Can you hear me?"

In answer, Aurora reached up and slid her arms around his neck, clinging to him as if to life itself. Suddenly, she was sobbing, trembling, begging him not to let them take her again. Her words confirmed Salem's suspicions. Aurora hadn't simply wandered down to the tunnel. Someone had forced her to go, then had left her there to die.

"Easy darling," he soothed. "Everything is going to be all right. No one's going to harm you. I'm here. You're safe."

Salem smoothed back her damp, tangled hair and stared into her eyes. The pain and fear in them he had never seen before. He hated himself for letting this happen to Aurora.

Turning back to Mrs. Romney for a moment, he said, "Please bring up some hot broth and tea. Have Bodwell heat water for a bath."

"Yes, Captain," she answered crisply, then left.

Holding Aurora close, Salem continued whispering reassurances to her until her trembling ceased. Then he pressed her back on the pillows and tugged the covers up to her chin.

"Can you tell me what happened, Aurora?"

Her eyes went wide with fear as she thought back over the past hours. "Not really," she confessed. "Shortly after you fell asleep, I thought I heard someone in the room."

"But the door was bolted," Salem reasoned.

308

"Then there must be another way in. Someone was here, Salem. Whoever it was put a drug-soaked cloth over my face. I fought, but it was no use. I lost consciousness. When I came around, I was lying down there in that cold, black, awful place where you found me." She threw her arms around him again, trembling with fright at the memory. "Oh, Salem, I was sure I was going to die."

"Easy, darling, easy," he murmured, holding her, his own heart racing in response to the frightful flutter of hers. "You're safe now. Now and always."

Suddenly, Aurora pulled out of his arms, her face going pale, her eyes glittering feverishly. "It was the witches!" she cried. "They came for me, didn't they? They really do exist and they know I'm the seventh bride!"

It seemed to Salem that Aurora's words brought a dark cloud over the dawning sun. He felt a coldness grip his heart. "Of course not, Aurora. I told you—there are *no* witches here. Would I have brought you here if I thought. . . ?"

"But don't you see?" she interrupted. "The pact with old Gideon was made so that the witches would leave him and his descendants at peace. All of them except for the seventh bride. I'm to be sacrificed in the name of Clan Caine. We can't fight them, Salem. The pact was made generations ago—signed in *blood!*"

"Don't, Aurora!" Salem begged, clutching her close as her voice rose to a hysterical pitch. "It's not true. It's not!"

"I wouldn't be so sure of that if I were you."

Salem shot a glance toward the voice at the bedroom door, anger rising as he spied Krystine. Once more she had entered their bedroom with neither a knock nor permission to come. But considering what she'd been through, he couldn't bring himself to chastise her for her continued impertinence.

309

"Mums said I should bring up this broth and tea."

"You're feeling better, then?" Salem asked as he rose and took the tray from her hands, noting as he did so the bruises and scrapes on her slender wrists.

"I'm tough, as you well know, Salem. You and I, we've been through a lot together, like the time you dared me to scale the cliffs and I almost killed myself trying to please you."

Salem frowned. He remembered the incident all right. He'd been a brash and fearless teenager while Krystine had been a sassy, fearless girl of around ten. But as he remembered it, Krystine had dared *him* to make the dangerous, foolhardy climb. He'd made it all right, but Krystine had become stranded when some rocks gave way beneath her. He'd had to scale the heights a second time to save her from a plunge into the sea. For his efforts, he'd received a caning from his irate father, while Krystine had been pampered, petted, and excused from all work for the following week so that she might recover from the ordeal Salem had supposedly put her through.

At the moment, Salem was in no mood to argue the past with Krystine. He had much weightier business on his mind.

"Your mother said someone drugged you and kidnapped you from your room last night, Krystine."

"That they did," she answered, gazing levelly at Salem, ignoring Aurora.

"The same happened to my wife. I mean to find out who did it."

Krystine tossed her mane of black hair over her shoulder and smiled—an icy, emotionless smile. "I can tell you that, and I'll tell you, too, that it's all *her* fault." She pointed an accusing finger at Aurora.

"What are you saying?" Aurora asked. She didn't like this mean-tempered, black-eyed woman at all!

"It was old Zenda and her coven who took us both. The bumbling idiots! They mistook me for your wife."

310

She tossed her head and laughed without humor. "Fat chance, eh, Salem? But I might have died for their mistake. When they saw they had the wrong woman, they left me on the rack and came back for her."

"This is insane!" Salem roared, jumping up from the side of the bed to confront Krystine. "I've never heard such witless babble. Zenda is not a witch, and she would never hurt anyone. She's the kindest woman I've ever known. Why, she was like a mother to me."

"Believe what you will, Salem, but I know I'm right." A feline smile curved Krystine's full lips. "They may have bungled the attempt this time, but they'll be back. It's barely a week until All Hallows' Eve. You mark my words, Zenda and her crew will have their seventh bride for the blood sacrifice on that night of nights."

Whirling away without another word, Krystine vanished through the door, leaving her prediction hanging ominously in the heavy silence.

Salem turned back to Aurora. She looked stunned and horrified. In that awful moment, Salem knew that his bride believed every dreadful word that Krystine had uttered. He gripped her trembling hands tightly.

"Darling, don't think about what she said. The girl is half-daft. She's always been just this side of mad. She's only trying to frighten you."

Aurora bent her head to rest on Salem's shoulder and heaved a weary sigh. "She's done a fine job of it. After last night, the very thought of them coming for me again is enough to chill my soul." She looked into Salem's eyes. "Hold me, darling, love me. That's the only thing that will make me brave enough to stay here."

Remembering Krystine's habit of popping in when the spirit moved her, Salem went to the door and bolted it. Then, slipping quickly out of his clothes, he slid into bed with Aurora. He cuddled her close, kissing her eyelids, her cool cheeks, and finally her lips, while his hands smoothed over her peaked breasts. Aurora sighed and snuggled closer, her body warming to his.

Salem let his hands trail over her arms, down her back, and across her narrow hips. Soon his desire reached such a fever pitch that he could wait no longer. But as he kissed her, he realized that Aurora was no longer with him. Feeling safe and warm at last, she had slipped into a deep, dreamless sleep.

With a sigh of regret, Salem let her rest. But he stayed beside her, filling his eyes with her delicate beauty, touching her lightly, kissing her softly.

As his hands and lips roamed, so did his thoughts. Could Krystine be right? Could Aurora really be in danger? Looking at her sleeping here beside him, her dark red-gold lashes soft against her pale cheeks, he couldn't imagine anything terrible ever befalling her. But then the grim sight of her huddled in the cave came back to haunt him. If anything happened to this woman he loved with his very heart and soul, how could he ever live with himself?

"I couldn't!" he said.

He leaned down and kissed her soft lips. "Sleep well, my darling. When you wake, I'm taking you away from this place. You may be the seventh bride, but you're *my* bride, the love of my life. We're leaving The Ledges!"

# Seven

Aurora slept through the rest of the day and into the night. Salem stayed with her, pacing their bedroom, trying to piece things together.

Shortly before noon the following day, Mrs. Romney knocked and called to him softly. Salem slipped back the bolt and opened the door.

"Pardon me, sir, but could I have a word with you?" The woman looked strained, frightened.

Salem stepped out into the hallway, wondering what could have happened now.

"Yes, Mrs. Romney? What is it?"

"It's Krystine," she whispered, glancing about as if to make sure no one was listening. "She's talking out of her head."

Salem thought that was nothing new, but he managed to curb his tongue, asking simply, "What's she saying?"

"A lot of nonsense, I'm sure, but I thought I should tell you just the same." The woman paused for so long that Salem thought she'd changed her mind. He was about to press her when she finally continued. "Krystine claims now that she remembers clearly what happened to her."

"Yes?" Salem said eagerly. "Has she identified her assailant?"

Mrs. Romney shied away, unable to meet his direct gaze. "Well, sir, she claims your wife attacked her."

*"My wife? Why, that's absurd!"*

"I agree, sir. But I thought I should tell you anyway. Krystine says the witches came for Mrs. Caine as she knew they would."

"Because of Gideon's pact with them?" Salem couldn't believe he was even asking such an outlandish question.

Mrs. Romney nodded. "Krystine believes that the coven put your wife under a spell. Then they ordered her to take Krystine down to the torture chamber. Krystine believes that if you hadn't interrupted things, your wife would have tortured her and then killed her. She says Mrs. Caine dashed into the tunnel to hide when she heard you coming. She said they both heard you trip over something and curse loudly, then your wife fled."

"Well, yes, that's so," Salem recalled. "One of the small wine kegs had fallen. I did trip over it. I did curse. But this doesn't make any sense, Mrs. Romney. Why would my wife try to harm Krystine? How could Aurora even manage it? Your daughter is much larger, much stronger."

The woman shook her tidy, gray head wearily. "I'm only reporting to you what Krystine told me. I knew you'd want to know. Especially if it's true that Mrs. Caine has been put under a spell."

"Yes, of course, Mrs. Romney." Salem touched her arm appreciatively. "Try not to worry about any of this. I'll handle everything."

"Oh, thank you, sir. I hope I did the right thing. Krystine begged me not to tell anyone."

"You were right to come to me, Mrs. Romney."

Dismissing the woman, if not her wild accusation, Salem went back into the room. Aurora was still sleeping, but now she seemed restless. She tossed on the bed and muttered unintelligible words.

"Darling?" Salem sat down beside her and shook her gently. "Can you hear me?"

Aurora curled her lips and made a low, hissing sound in response, like an angry cat. Salem drew back, his brow beading with perspiration. He shook her none too gently this time, but still she slept, frowning and grimacing and making threatening, spitting sounds when he touched her. She was clearly not herself. This was more than a nightmare. Try as he would, Salem couldn't wake her.

Finally, he had to admit that he half-believed Krystine's words. He rubbed a hand over his eyes and sighed. "Oh, my darling. What have they done to you? What have I done to you?"

All day Salem sat with his wife, trying to wake her, trying to soothe her. But, as if she were still drugged, she slept on and would not be soothed. Whatever had happened to her during those dark hours when she was away from his side, it must have been horrible indeed.

Mrs. Romney brought his supper to the room and reported that Krystine was sleeping soundly.

"Any nightmares?" Salem asked.

Mrs. Romney shook her head and smiled. "No, thank the Lord! She's sleeping like an angel."

Salem glanced back toward the bed as he shut the door. He wished he could say the same for Aurora. There seemed nothing he could do for her. Leaving his supper untouched, he stripped off his clothes and slid into bed beside her.

"At least I can hold you," he whispered, trying to kiss her snarling lips. For his tender efforts, he received a vicious bite. But he would not give up, he could not!

Talking quietly, soothingly, he said, "Aurora, I want you to listen to me. I'm going to take you away from The Ledges. As soon as you're able, we're going back to Bath. Back to your mother and father, to your Aunt Persia and Uncle Zack. I'll never bring you here again. I promise."

"Sal-em?" Aurora's voice in the darkness was thin and high pitched, the sound of an old, old woman. But her grip on his arm was like iron. "No, Salem!" she spat. "I won't go. I can't!"

"Oh, my darling!" he cried, crushing her in his arms, deliriously happy that she was finally awake, that she was finally herself again, or so he assumed. But he was unprepared for the woman who awoke beside him.

After declaring her demand to remain at The Ledges, Aurora shoved him down on the bed. "I want to make love," she declared fiercely, unashamedly.

"So, do I, darling. That is if you feel up to it. You've been through so much."

If Aurora had been through a lot, she put her husband through his share as well. She made love to him—not gently and sweetly as she had their first night together, but with a fierceness and passion that was unlike anything he had ever experienced before. She took total command, torturing him with tenderness, taunting him unmercifully until he begged, nearly weeping, for her to give him the sweet release he craved.

With another of her feline snarls, she mounted him, grinding her body down over his, riding him at a dizzying pace. She would bring him almost to the point of release, then dismount to torture him further toward madness.

Hours later, when she finally finished with him, Salem lay limply prostrate on the bed, drained and exhausted, his body an empty, used-up vessel of her pleasure.

He could only stare at the woman who sat beside him in a pool of moonlight, smiling her catlike grin as her hands played over his spent body, trying to arouse him anew.

"We'll stay then, darling," she whispered in an oddly triumphant voice. "It's all settled."

He meant to argue. He meant to leap from the bed, pack their things, and go. Now, in the dead of night.

He meant to do a lot of things, but what she was doing

316

to him drained the last of his will away. The thought suddenly struck him that perhaps the witches had taken Aurora last night and replaced her with this woman who only looked like his sweet wife.

"I'm as mad as Krystine," he said with a hoarse laugh.

"Krystine is not mad," Aurora said, matter-of-factly. "Krystine knows things—all things. You and I have until All Hallows' Eve, my darling. Shall we make the most of it?"

Salem groaned with a new tide of desire and surrender as Aurora continued her wonderfully arousing and innovative torture. It was almost dawn before she let him sleep.

When she woke hours later, Aurora groaned and squinted into the bright autumn sun. She felt drugged, disoriented, and her whole body ached as if she had been beaten or worse.

Bits and snatches of the past thirty-six hours flitted through her dulled mind. She tried to fit the pieces together, but it was impossible to make any sense of the jumbled puzzle. As she lay on the bed, trying to keep her eyes closed against the sun, she heard footsteps in the room.

"Salem?" she whispered.

"Yes, Aurora. I'm here." His voice sounded tired, dull.

With some effort, she propped herself up on one elbow and squinted at him. The sight of his face brought a cry of alarm from her. Claw marks down his cheeks had left it streaked. His lips looked swollen as if he'd been in a fight. There was the perfect imprint of teeth in his bare shoulders, and his chest, too, looked as if it had been raked raw by the claws of some vicious beast.

"Darling, what happened?" she gasped.

"Don't you know?" he replied, still in the same dull

317

tone. But this time Aurora caught a hint of accusation in his voice.

"How should I?" she asked. "I've been sleeping. I just woke up."

"Yes, I imagine you were quite exhausted."

"After being in that cold, black cave, you mean."

"Not exactly," he answered cryptically. He moved to the side of the bed and stared down at her, unsmiling. "Tell me about the witches, Aurora. What did they do to you?"

"Witches?" she stared at him blankly.

"You know—Zenda and the coven. You slipped out the other night and joined them, didn't you? Or maybe they truly took you away." Salem knew his words sounded harsh, but what else could he think after last night. No normal wife would leave her new husband so scarred and bloody in the name of love. "Did you participate in any sort of ceremony? Did they make you drink something? The thorn apple causes hallucinations, Zenda used to say. Nightshade? Monkshood? They must have given you something."

Aurora looked at him solemnly. "I don't remember any witches, Salem. I don't remember any ceremony or being forced to drink anything. Honestly, I don't!"

"Then they must have given you mandrake. Did you eat any little green berries that looked like apples? The witches call them 'love apples' because they work"—he paused, clearing his throat self-consciously, and glanced at the teeth marks on his right shoulder—"they cause a strange longing of sorts."

Aurora shook her head gently. Gently because it ached. "I don't remember eating anything in quite some time. Not since the lobster right after we arrived. Salem, can't you tell me what's wrong? You seem so different."

Losing control for a moment, he flung his hands up. "*I* seem different? Good God, Aurora! Look what you did to me last night!" He leaned over her, bringing his

318

clawed face close to hers, angling his bitten shoulder toward her. "And you say I seem different? The night we came here, you were my shy and blushing virgin bride. A sweeter, tenderer woman no man ever held in his arms. Then, last night—my God!—last night you were an insatiable, lusting witc—" He caught himself just in time, or so he thought.

*"Witch?"* Aurora finished for him. "Is that what you were going to say? You think *I'm* a witch?"

Salem sagged down on the bed and blindly reached for her hand. "Oh, Aurora," he sighed, "what would you have me think? What were you thinking when you did this to me?" He raised his head and searched her face for some clue. She looked the same; she looked beautiful.

Slowly, she brought his hand to her lips. For a moment, he thought she meant to sink her teeth into him again. Instead, she kissed his knuckles, then his fingertips.

"Darling, I'm sorry," she whispered. Then a tear slipped down her flushed cheek. "I don't even remember last night."

"You don't *remember?*" he gasped. "How could you forget such a night? You don't believe that you made love to me right in this bed as if you meant to destroy me with your passion?"

Aurora's cheeks flushed crimson and she shied away from his gaze. "I believe I did something strenuous," she admitted softly. "I ache as if I'd been the one on the torture rack." She met his eyes once more, her own pleading through a mist of tears. "I'm sorry, Salem. I don't know what more I can say. I don't remember what I did and I can't account for my actions. Was I so dreadful, my darling?"

At the little-girl tone in her voice, Salem almost laughed aloud. How could his blushing, nearly innocent bride have given such pain and, yes, pleasure last night without remembering a shred of her wantonness?

"Let's forget it, darling." He leaned over and kissed

319

her very softly with his bruised lips. "Obviously, whatever came over you, it has passed. You seem yourself again this morning. We'll pack our things and leave. Right away!"

Aurora shook her head. "No, Salem! I'm not going," she said firmly. "This is your home—*our* home. I refuse to let anyone drive us away."

"Damnit, Aurora!" he growled. "What am I going to do with you?"

She smiled up at him, her blue eyes shining. "Love me," she whispered. "Just love me, my darling."

He was half-tempted, but far too fatigued for such sport.

Dressing hurriedly, Salem said, "I have to talk to Krystine this morning. Do you want to come with me? It might help to have both of us confront her." He paused, wondering how much he should tell Aurora. He decided to be as vague as possible. "Krystine claims that everything that's happened here is somehow your fault."

*"My* fault?" Aurora cried. "But how can that be?"

Before Salem could answer, Aurora murmured, "Of course, the curse of the seventh bride."

Salem was quick to reassure her. "Krystine's lying, Aurora. I know the things she's said are pure fabrication. But I can't figure out what the truth really is. I mean to get to the bottom of this, though. One way or another. If we're going to live here, we're going to live in peace."

"I'll stay here," she answered. "I don't think I feel up to any confrontations this morning."

"As you wish, darling." He gave her a kiss on the forehead. "I won't be gone long."

Aurora looked up with a worried frown. "You're going out, Salem? Like *that?"*

"Like what?" He glanced in a mirror and touched his scratched face and frowned at his image. "I'll tell anyone who has nerve enough to ask that I tangled with one of the castle's cats." He grinned at her suddenly. "Not far from the truth, actually."

Leaning down, he embraced his wife tenderly. "You rest, darling. I'll have Mrs. Romney bring you something to eat."

Aurora swung her legs over the side of the bed. "No, I'm going to dress, too. It seems I've spent half my married life so far naked. I haven't even seen the castle yet— other than the bedroom and the torture chamber."

Salem chuckled. If last night was any example, those two rooms were very nearly one and the same.

"Do as you please, my love. After I've had a chat with Krystine, I'll take you on the grand tour, if you like."

She smiled brightly at her handsome but scarred husband. "I'll be downstairs shortly. Please tell Mrs. Romney that I'll take my breakfast below."

Even as her husband left, the fog was clearing from Aurora's brain. She intended to get more than breakfast from Mrs. Romney. She needed answers—answers that Salem didn't have or wouldn't give her. First, she would talk to the housekeeper; then she intended to get to the bottom of all this weirdness. She meant to search out old Zenda and find out the truth about the witches once and for all.

"I waited for Salem to come back to me for over three years," she said aloud. "I do not intend to allow anything so outrageous as a coven of witches to spoil our happiness."

Once she was dressed, Aurora set out, determined, denying to herself that she was the least bit afraid of what she might learn on her quest.

# Eight

Aurora was neither mad nor witch-tainted. She knew exactly what she was doing and she guessed who he enemy was. But Salem would never believe her—not yet at least. She had to prove her beliefs for herself.

When she entered the kitchen, Mrs. Romney eyed he suspiciously.

"The dining room's through there," the woman said "Captain Caine said I should have your breakfast wait ing. I hope you like porridge with gallberry honey. It' what we have here of a cold morning. The captain's fa vorite."

"Thank you, Mrs. Romney." Aurora smiled, trying t reassure the woman, who looked as if she thought th new mistress of The Ledges might cast a spell over he at any moment. "I'm sure that will be delicious. Bu might I eat here in the kitchen so we can talk? I enjo conversation with my meals."

Looking decidedly uncomfortable, Mrs. Romne mumbled, "Suit yourself, mum," then hastily began put tering about the large kitchen as if to indicate that sh was far too busy for idle chitchat.

Aurora sat at the large pine table in the center of th room and tried a taste of the hot, spiced dish. "Hm-m-m This really is delicious, Mrs. Romney. You must teac me how to prepare it."

The ploy worked. Mrs. Romney's ramrod stiffness gave way just a bit. "I'd be pleased to, Mrs. Caine," she replied.

Aurora eased into conversation, asking the housekeeper how long she had been at The Ledges, what she knew of its history, what Salem had been like as a boy. Finally she got to the question she'd been tiptoeing around for the past moments. "Where can I find my husband's old nurse?"

Mrs. Romney dropped a pan, which clattered noisily to the stone floor. Whirling around, she stared Aurora straight in the eye for the first time. "Whatever would you be wanting with old Zenda, Mrs. Caine?"

Aurora shrugged, took another taste of her porridge, and smiled. "Since I'm the new mistress and plan to live here for a long, long time, I think I should meet everyone at The Ledges, don't you?"

"I don't know that Zenda's up to company, mum." Mrs. Romney turned away, back to the dishes she'd been drying, as if to put an end to the subject.

"Is she ill?" Aurora persisted. "If so, then I really must see her. She might need medicine or a doctor."

Mrs. Romney gave a muffled, humorless laugh. "Not that one!"

"I'm going to find Zenda and talk to her, Mrs. Romney. If you won't help me, I'll ask someone else. You'll soon learn I'm a very determined—some say stubborn—woman. Once I set my mind to something, there's no stopping me."

The housekeeper turned back around, a look of surrender on her wrinkled face. "I'd figured that about you already, Mrs. Caine. If I knew where you could find Zenda, I'd tell you. Truthfully, I don't know, but I caution you. There's evil hereabouts. Powerful evil! You've witnessed it yourself. You've got a fine, loving husband. Why don't you do as he says and leave this place while there's still time? Captain Caine vowed once he'd never

323

come back here. He should have stuck to that vow—fo his own good and for yours."

"This is Salem's home," Aurora reasoned. "Wh should he not live here?"

Mrs. Romney shook her head. "That's not for me t say. If you want the answer—mark my words you won' like it—go to Zenda. Bodwell will take you to her."

Aurora should have felt only triumph at the though of receiving answers, but that triumph was mingled with dread.


Meanwhile, Salem was trying to wring some answer to his questions from Krystine. He'd found her stil abed—a tousle-haired, gleaming-eyed hoyden more than willing to invite him into her cluttered bedchamber.

Clad only in a thin nightshift, she ushered Salem into her small, untidy room, smiling at him all the while. Immediately, she poured him a cup of tea from the kettle on the hearth. He tasted it and grimaced. Krystine would never be the cook her mother was.

"So, you've come to me at last," she purred. "Wha took you so long, Salem? Has your little wife been *tha* demanding? I see she's left her marks on you." She trailed one long-nailed finger along the scratches on his cheek. "Spirited for so frail a woman, isn't she?"

Ignoring her questions, Salem scowled at her. "You mother told me what you said about Aurora. You're lying Krystine. Why?"

She put on a pretty pout. "Salem, would I lie to *you*? It's not my fault that you brought her back here, and he the seventh bride. Poor girl! Does she know that her marriage will last less than a week? How sad a fate! I know it will be hard on you, Salem, but I'll be here to comfor you—afterward."

Salem's eyes narrowed. "You sent that old parchment didn't you?"

She shrugged, causing one sleeve of her shift to slip down off her shoulder as she lounged seductively on the bed. "I thought I did right to warn you. But then, too, I guessed you wouldn't heed the warning, that you might even take it as a challenge." She sighed and smiled at him. "I was right. You always were such a strong-willed, hard-headed, lusty man. There was never anyone else like you, Salem. Not in my eyes, at least."

Quickly changing the subject, Salem accused, "You claim old Zenda's a witch. Why would you say such a thing?"

Krystine yawned and stretched, her actions feline. "Because she is. I know that for a fact."

"How do you know?"

"I've spied on their gatherings for years. Remember the strange circles of stones we used to find in the woods, the blood and feathers all about on the ground, the burnt offerings?"

Salem remembered well enough, but he'd always thought Krystine created those scenes to amaze him. She was always telling witch stories and making up legends and tales. Once she had dared him to eat some green love apples from the mandrake plant, claiming that they had the power to make one fly, that the witches used them for just that purpose. Salem had soon discovered that love apples had power, all right. He had been overcome with such desire that he had engaged in his first sexual experience, with Krystine as his more than willing partner. Afterward, he had been sorely ashamed, but Krystine had been pleased, telling him, "We are now mated for life."

"What are you thinking about, Salem?"

There was a strange hum in his ears. His mouth suddenly felt as if it were filled with cotton. He cleared his throat, trying to make his words come out plainly. But he slurred them in spite of his efforts. "Something I haven't thought about in years. Something I don't want to think about." He looked up and narrowed his eyes at her. "Tell me why you lied about my wife."

She trilled a laugh and purred her next words. "*I am* your wife, Salem. The witches say that those who make love after partaking of the mandrake fruit are mated for life. Remember?"

Salem rose with a growl of disgust. He stumbled slightly, dizzy as he rose. "That was no more than an adolescent prank, Krystine. Forget it!"

"You haven't. Why should I? I've spent years waiting for you to come back to me, and now you have. We'll soon be together. You might as well be happy about it Salem. You see, there's nothing you can do to change things. It would take another witch to undo what the witch of The Ledges has already done."

He was on his feet, ready to bolt from the room. " can leave!" he shouted at her. "That's exactly what I intend to do. This very day!"

His agitation had no effect on Krystine. She merely smiled and stretched again. "She won't go. The witches won't let her."

Salem had heard enough. He tried to stalk out of the room, but stumbled to the door instead. What on earth was happening to him? He felt so odd.

Once he had slammed the door behind him, he felt the full weight of his desperation. He had to get Aurora away from here—now! Away from this place and away from Krystine. She was surely as evil as any witch!

But when he went in search of his wife, Aurora was nowhere to be found.


After finishing her breakfast and her chat with Mrs Romney, Aurora headed straight for the stables, hoping that Bodwell would be there. Sure enough, she heard him talking to the horses as he gave them their morning feed.

326

"Mr. Bodwell?" she said, entering the sturdy, stone structure.

He turned toward the sound of her voice, squinting his eyes at her.

"Oh, it's you, Mrs. Caine," he said, obviously caught off guard. "I figured after all the strange goings-on you'd stay abed for a few more days."

"I'm not quite that fragile, Bodwell," Aurora answered. "Nor that easily frightened."

"'Scuse me, ma'am, but I'd be more than a bit wary were them witches after me."

Aurora cocked her head quizzically. "You believe in the witches, then?"

"Considering all that's happened around here of late, I'm inclined to believe. Yes, ma'am."

"Do you know the woman named Zenda?"

Bodwell scratched his bald head. "I do. I've known her some thirty-odd years."

"And do you believe she's a witch?"

"I never did before," he admitted. "She raised young Jerusalem, you know, and did a fine job of it. She was a good woman back in those days, tough as a ship's master but kind and fair. Jerusalem's pa was a great one for not sparing the rod, but Zenda never raised a hand to the lad, though he got in his fair share of scrapes, I can tell you. Especially when that little hussy Krystine was in tow."

"Yes, Krystine," Aurora murmured.

"Pardon, ma'am?"

Aurora dismissed her comment with a wave of her hand. "Oh, nothing. I was just thinking aloud."

"Is there something I can do for you, Mrs. Caine?" Bodwell suddenly looked puzzled again. Ladies didn't usually pop into his stable unannounced. Or even announced, for that matter.

"Perhaps," Aurora answered. "I'd like to meet Zenda. Can you tell me where to find her?"

He grinned, the first time Aurora had seen anythin[g] close to a pleasant look on his face. "As a matter of fac[t] I can take you there myself. I was about to hitch up [the] wagon and fetch her some firewood. She don't ge[t] around as good as she used to, and I try to see she's go[t] plenty of supplies up to the shack. She'd be might[y] pleased at a visit from Jerusalem's bride."

A short time later, Aurora perched on the board sea[t] of the wagon while, next to her, Bodwell guided the team through the flaming, autumn grandeur of the woods.

Aurora clutched the front of her green wool cape closely about her chin. The air was as clear as fine crysta[l] and as cold and crisp as new snow. She breathed deeply feeling exhilarated as they rode deeper and deeper int[o] the very heart of the woods. The sun shone down throug[h] the thick canopy overhead, dappling the trail in warm spots and dark shadows. A bright cardinal darted pas[t] like a tongue of flame on the wing.

"She'll be to home, then," Bodwell commented, rousing himself from a long silent contemplation of the road ahead.

"I beg your pardon?" Aurora said.

"That redbird yonder," he answered, pointing throug[h] the trees. "That's old Zenda's. He's no doubt telling he[r] this very minute that company's on the way."

"Her bird can talk?" Aurora asked, puzzled.

Bodwell shook his bald head. "No, ma'am, but Zend[a] can listen."

Sure enough, when they pulled into the small clearing ringed by tall fir trees, an old woman with white hai[r] nearly to her heels stood waiting for them on the stoo[p] of the gamekeeper's stone cottage.

"Mornin', Zenda!" Bodwell called, waving casually.

"Mornin', yourself, Jock!"

Aurora smiled. She'd wondered if Bodwell had a firs[t] name. Now she knew, thanks to Zenda. She was hopin[g]

Salem's former nurse could clear up a lot of other questions as easily.

"You brought company, I see." Zenda looked frail, but took the stairs down to the dooryard with the agility of a young girl. "High time you were bringing Salem's bride around to say how do."

This comment took Aurora by surprise. How did Zenda know who she was? How did she even know that Salem had married?

"I reckon her bird told her," Bodwell said with a chuckle, as if he'd just read Aurora's thoughts.

Aurora glanced back to find Zenda standing beside the wagon, staring appraisingly. "Well, well, well!" Her silvery eyes, as young as her light step, twinkled with pleasure and a touch of mischief, Aurora thought. "It's about time that boy of mine settled down and took him a wife. Been years since I heard the laughter of wee ones echoing through these ancient woods." She leaned close and peered right into Aurora's face. "You in a family way yet?"

Aurora blushed and tried to think of an appropriate reply. But before she could say a word, Zenda clucked her tongue and said, "Never you mind, child, I have something that will do the trick quick as you please. Come on inside now."

The two women were on the steps, about to go in, before Zenda remembered Bodwell. "Jock, come have some cider with us after you stack my wood."

"Thank you, Zenda, but not this morning. I got things to do back to the stable. I'll come back for you in an hour or so, Mrs. Caine."

Zenda leaned close to Aurora and said, "He's got nothing special to do this morning, but—bless his soul—he knows you and I need time to talk alone. Jock's a good man. He can be trusted," she added pointedly. Then guiding Aurora by the elbow, she ushered her toward the blue

329

door. "Well, come along, now, and let's get at it, shall we?"

Zenda's cottage was a place of wonders. A fireplace took up almost one entire wall. On the mantelpiece lay what Aurora took to be a stuffed gray cat until the fat, lazy thing switched its tail.

Zenda laughed at the expression of surprise on Aurora's face when she saw the cat move. "I call him Rigor Mortis because it seems like it's been setting in ever since the day that old tom was born."

The cat opened one golden eye, stared at them, then went back to sleep. Aurora let her gaze drift on past the animal. Seashells, barnacle-encrusted bottles, colorful fishing floats, and a branch of autumn leaves festooned the mantel. Beside it on hooks in the stone wall hung copper pots of all sizes. A sleigh-bed rested in one corner, covered in a bright, patchwork crazy quilt. Two pine chairs and a small table sat before the fire on a mellow-hued, hooked rug. From the smoky rafters above hung bunches of dried flowers and herbs that mingled their spicy scents with the mulled cider on the hearth. The atmosphere in the cabin was sweet and pungent.

The other things Aurora noticed, lying all around in nooks and corners, were toys—tin soldiers, a sled, worn alphabet blocks, tiny carved animals, and a softy, shaggy creature that looked like it might have once been a rabbit, but its ears had long since departed.

Observing her guest's interest, Zenda volunteered, "They were his—our Salem's. When he was a boy, they were his friends. The only friends he had until Krystine came along. You can't fault him, you know."

Aurora stared at the bright-eyed woman, who seemed to be one jump ahead of her in the conversation.

"Fault Salem? I don't understand, Zenda."

"For her—and what they were to each other once."

"Oh!" Aurora gasped softly. "I didn't know . . ."

Zenda, her long hair falling over her shoulders like a

330

fine, silk cloak, poured cider into two cups on the table, but kept one eye on Aurora. "Yes, child, I think you did know, whether you allowed yourself to admit it or not. It was a long, long time ago, and Salem left here to be done with her."

Aurora felt the sick fangs of jealousy sink into her heart. Her Salem and Krystine? Why, he was with that woman at this very minute! She rose as if she meant to leave, but Zenda put a strong hand on her shoulder.

"Stay!" the old woman ordered. "You came here today to ask me about the witches of Coven Cove, and before you leave I mean to tell you *everything.*"

"The witches, yes," Aurora murmured, but her mind was no longer on the questions she'd come here to ask. Her mind and her heart were with Salem.

# Nine

"Let's get one thing straight right up front, then we can go from there," Zenda said. "You *are* the seventh bride."

The words went through Aurora's heart like a knife. "Then I'm doomed," she murmured hopelessly.

"Indeed, not!" Zenda voice boomed in the still cottage. "Whoever filled your pretty head with such poppy cock?"

At the sound of her Aunt Persia's favorite word—so much a part of her home, her family, her innocence— Aurora smiled. She truly liked old Zenda. She felt as if she'd known her forever.

"There's something else I must know. Are you a witch?" Aurora asked, point-blank.

Zenda spread her arms, making her black robe flair about her tall, thin form. "Do I look like a witch?"

Aurora gazed at her lined but still lovely face, her star silver eyes, her flowing white hair. "Yes," she said at last. "I think you do."

"Ah! You *think!* But how many witches have you seen in your short lifetime, child?"

"None that I know of," Aurora admitted.

"Then bear this in mind. Things are not always what they appear."

Aurora nodded, puzzled at the way Zenda had so easily sidestepped her question. "Yes, I'll remember."

"Why don't I begin at the beginning? It will all be clearer to you then. We have to go back many centuries, to a dark, dismal mountaintop kingdom in the European country of Luxitrynnia."

At Aurora's thoughtful frown, Zenda waved a slender hand in the air. "Never mind trying to recall the name, child. Chances are, you've never heard it before, nor ever will again. It was smaller than tiny, not much larger than the mountain itself. It seemed to come out of the mists one day, hover atop its lofty perch for a brief, dark span of time, and then it faded into the past. The country and its evil would have vanished for all time had not Gideon Caine bought the crumbling castle and brought it here to the coast of Maine. In so doing, he transported its mysteries as well."

"Then you're saying that the witches somehow came with the castle?"

Zenda shook her head, making her long hair move like a cloud. "No, child. The so-called witches of Coven Cove were a poor, ragtag band of women who barely escaped with their lives during the hysteria in Massachusetts back in 1692. They took refuge in this isolated place and lived in peace until Gideon Caine bought the land and reconstructed his sinister castle. The women tried to scare him away. They never managed, but they did extract a promise from him."

"The parchment document, promising the seventh bride to the coven." Aurora stared down into her cup as if she might find answers to all her questions there. Then she looked up at Zenda again. "But I don't understand. If the women weren't witches, why have there always been stories of witchcraft here at The Ledges?"

"I never said there were *no* witches at all," Zenda reminded her guest. "One among that original group had been practicing the black arts, unbeknownst to the others.

333

As the story goes, old Gideon delighted in her evil magic and fathered her child—a daughter. His wife found out and that's why she left him."

Aurora remembered the discussion of this she'd heard earlier in her father's study. "Why didn't she take her son when she left?"

"Because Gideon demanded that she leave the child and had the witch-woman threaten to put a curse on the boy unless his mother did so. Poor woman! What choice did she have?"

Aurora was seeing a pattern begin to form. "And was Gideon's daughter a witch?"

"Ayah!" Zenda nodded. "And her daughter after her, who was worse than her grandmother ever thought to be."

Aurora was beginning to realize where Zenda was going with this. "You are that witch's daughter, aren't you? And you've spent your whole life trying to right their wrongs."

Zenda laughed until her whole, frail body shook. "Nothing quite so romantic, I'm afraid. I'm not from this place. I came shortly before Jerusalem was born to act as his nursemaid. I will admit to being a healer, and at times I dream dreams and see visions, but I'm not a black witch. Far from it! I come of quite a normal and religious family. My father ran a lobster boat out of Quoddy Cove. You know the place, I believe?"

Aurora's blue eyes lit up as she remembered tales her mother and aunt had told her. "Why, yes! My mother and all her family were born there. I wonder if my grandparents knew your people."

"Ayah! As a matter of fact, your grandmother Victoria and I were girls together. But that's another story, child. Let me tell you the rest of the history of The Ledges."

"You mean there's more?"

Zenda leaned close and whispered, "The best—or the worst—is yet to come. It was good that your Salem's

334

mother hired me to watch over her son. She was a sickly woman, who never quite recovered after his birth. She died before he was a year old. Jerusalem's father became a bitter man and took his grief out on the boy. Most times, I could, and did, protect him from his father's wrath. On one occasion, however, I failed. Jerusalem's father found him with Mrs. Romney's girl, Krystine. It seemed only a bit of youthful foolishness to me, nothing to become alarmed over, but Mr. Caine flew into a towering rage. He gave the boy a brutal whipping."

Aurora winced at the thought of anyone harming her husband. Her left hand trembling, she raised her cup to her lips. Old Zenda's eyes followed the movement, and her head nodded imperceptibly.

"That's when Jerusalem decided to leave home and take to the sea. I never quite knew what to make of Mr. Caine's rage that day. I suspect that he might also have been Krystine's father. Mrs. Romney was quite a pretty woman back then—and without a man of her own. She came here as a young widow, then had her baby, claiming it was her dead husband's. But if that was the case, I calculated that she must have carried Krystine for at least thirteen months."

Aurora sighed with relief. "I was sure you were about to tell me that Krystine was a witch."

Zenda's eyes narrowed as she thought through her next words carefully. Finally she decided Aurora was ready for the full truth. "That well may be."

Aurora gasped. She had been trying to make a joke. But obviously this was no laughing matter.

"I don't believe she was born a witch," Zenda added. "But as she was growing up, she often visited the old caves by the sea where the first witch had lived and where the last witch still resided in seclusion. I believe the old woman passed along everything she knew to Krystine. Whether the girl possesses any real power re-

335

mains to be seen. But she could be dangerous, of that I have no doubt."

A new kind of fear crept through Aurora. "Then it must have been Krystine who drugged me the other night and took me to the dungeon."

"Ayah." Zenda only nodded, allowing Aurora to figure out the rest for herself.

"But Salem found Krystine on the torture rack. If she kidnapped me, she must have had an accomplice who bound her so no one would suspect."

"Not necessarily," Zenda answered. "Krystine has been fascinated by that torture chamber since she was a child. When Salem left home, she spent days down there lying on that rack, crying her eyes out, when another girl might have taken to her bed. She knows tricks no one else would think of. I believe she fastened herself there, knowing that Jerusalem would come to her rescue and believe whatever she wished to tell him."

"And he did," Aurora admitted. "Why, this very morning he told me that Krystine said *I* kidnapped *her*. I almost felt I had to defend myself. But how could she have gotten into our room? Salem bolted the door."

Zenda chuckled. "Hasn't your husband ever told you about how he and Krystine climbed that very cliff? Jerusalem tried it only once, but Krystine has climbed it so often over the years that she's worn a path up to that balcony. Then, too, there's the secret passage behind the water closet."

Aurora jumped up so suddenly that she almost overturned the table.

"Here now!" Zenda cried. "Where are you going, child?"

"Salem's with Krystine right now. I have to get back to the castle. I have to warn him."

Zenda caught Aurora's left hand and held it. "Sit," she ordered. "He'll come to no harm because Krystine still believes that he belongs to her. You see, you've yet to

336

do the one thing that will both bind you fast to your husband and put him safely away from that self-styled witch-woman."

"What's that?" Aurora had sat down again, but on the very edge of her chair. She had heard more than enough to make her realize what danger The Ledges posed for both her and Salem.

As if in answer, Zenda reached into a deep pocket of her robe and drew out three lengths of soft leather. She placed them on the table.

"You and Jerusalem have yet to participate in the ceremony called 'handfasting.' You must take these leather ribbons with you back to The Ledges. When Jerusalem would make love to you, have him help you plait a strong bond instead. Then, on All Hallows' Eve, the two of you will meet me at the rune-stone on the point at midnight."

At mention of the dreaded spot, Aurora glanced up, staring into Zenda's gleaming eyes.

"Have no fear, child. The tide will be at its ebb."

"But why, Zenda? What is this *handfasting?*"

"It is something you *must* do—the witches' ceremony of marriage."

"I still don't understand. What have the rites of witchcraft to do with me?"

Zenda motioned toward Aurora's cup, clasped tightly in her left hand. "You truly don't know, do you?"

"Know what?"

"That *you* are a witch, my child!"

Aurora's cup slipped from her hand and clattered to her saucer. She gasped aloud and tears filled her eyes. "No!" she whispered.

"You never knew your grandmother Victoria, did you, Aurora?"

Finding no voice when she opened her mouth, Aurora simply shook her head.

"I knew her—probably better than most anyone else. You see, I knew her secret. Although she tried all her

337

life to live normally, she could not deny her birthright. When another witch in the village sought to destroy your Aunt Persia with her wagging tongue and evil spells, Victoria even then could not bring herself to evoke her own magic to defeat her enemy. She took her secret to an early grave, when she might have used her talents for good. You see, Victoria was the best kind of witch—a seer, a healer—as are you, Aurora."

Aurora's mind was reeling. "And my mother?" she asked. "Is she, too, a witch?"

Zenda smiled and shook her head. "No, child. Your powers come by way of your Aunt Persia, passed on to you since she had no child of her own."

"I never knew," Aurora whispered.

"Neither did Persia until after she'd been in India. She learned a great deal in that far-off land—about love and hate and power."

Suddenly, remembering how much closer she'd always felt to her aunt than to her mother, Aurora believed. Then her thoughts turned to Salem. "Does anyone else know about us? About me?"

"Krystine senses your powers even though she, like you, may not yet fully understand them." She gripped Aurora's hand. "Trust me when I tell you that you can fight her black evil with your white magic. Be cautious! Be alert! Only then will you be able to defeat her."

Aurora's head was spinning as she tried to take all this in. "What if I choose not to fight her?"

"Are you willing to give her your husband?"

Tears welled up in Aurora's eyes. "I would fight the devil himself to keep Salem!" she exclaimed.

"Very well, then." Zenda rose to signal an end to their interview. "I'll send Bodwell with a message for your family. There is strength in numbers. I think it wise that they all be in attendance at the handfasting. And Persia may be especially important in the dark scheme of things.

338

Go now, child, and begin plaiting your bond for the hand-fasting on All Hallows' Eve."

Bodwell was waiting in the wagon when Aurora—dazed—stepped outside. Their ride home was silent as Aurora's emotions did battle within her.

*A witch!* How strange it all seemed. Still, there were things she remembered from her earlier years that gave credence to Zenda's pronouncement. Precognitive dreams, her strange restlessness at the full of the moon, the cures she concocted to heal ailing animals, and always the sense that she was not one but two people—her normal self and a vague entity shaped in mysterious darkness.

When the wagon rolled to a halt in front of The Ledges, Aurora looked up. Krystine, wrapped in a long black-and-silver cloak, stood by the drawbridge.

"I've been waiting for you," the black-eyed woman said, smiling. "Salem asked me to tell you that he's decided to send you away—back to your family. We've talked it over, and he's realized it's far too dangerous having you here. Too dangerous for everyone!"

Aurora's first impulse was to burst into tears and dash into the castle to plead with Salem. Instead, she climbed down from the wagon with great dignity and walked directly to Krystine, her bright sapphire eyes challenging glittering onyx.

"I won't be leaving. This is my home. You'll excuse me now. It's time I begin preparing for the handfasting." Then she swept across the bridge into the castle, calling Salem's name.

What she found sent a new stab of fear through her heart.

# Ten

Aurora found Salem in the great hall with its high, beamed ceiling and twin fireplaces—each large enough to roast an ox—and battle lances, shields, and armor all about on the walls. From the wall over the fireplace, old Gideon glowered down at them from inside his gilded frame. Salem slouched in a heavy oak chair, his long legs stretched before him.

"Salem?" Aurora called softly.

He seemed not to hear her, but remained in his weary pose, head down, forehead resting against palm.

"Salem dear, I've just come from visiting Zenda. She hopes you'll pay her a call soon."

He roused and turned, staring at his wife, but seemingly through her. "Zenda? Is she well?"

"Indeed!" She gazed at the pallor of his face and the glazed look in his eyes and felt immediate alarm. "But are *you* well, Salem?"

He sighed deeply and tried to rise to his feet, but staggered and clutched at the back of the chair for support. Aurora ran to him.

"What's wrong, darling?"

"I don't know," he answered, shaking his head to clear it. "It seems I've lost my memory. I don't remember coming back to The Ledges or even getting up this morn-

340

ing." He stared oddly at Aurora. "Excuse me, ma'am, but I don't seem to recall your name."

A sharp jolt of fear raced through Aurora. Forcing herself to remain calm, she gripped her husband's arms and helped him back into the chair.

"Sit down, Salem, and listen to me. Look at me and try to concentrate on what I'm saying."

He stared into her eyes, his own dull and glazed like tarnished silver. Something was very wrong with him, there was no doubting it.

"Salem, I'm your wife Aurora." She said each word slowly, distinctly. "We were married at my parents' home in Bath only a few days ago, shortly after you returned from sea."

The deepening of his frown told her that he remembered none of this.

"Do you know where you've been this morning?"

He nodded. "With Krystine."

"Did you eat or drink anything while you were with her?"

He bit his bottom lip and glanced about thoughtfully, obviously trying to recall. Then he nodded. "I hadn't had breakfast. She brewed us some tea." He grimaced. "Bitter stuff, but I drank mine rather than offend her. She's no cook like her mother."

"Oh, God!" Aurora murmured softly. She remained silent for a time, trying to think what to do. Maybe she should take him to Zenda.

No! she told herself, silently, but firmly. Salem is my husband. I will see to his welfare. I must show Krystine that my power is greater than hers.

Drawing out the three leather ribbons Zenda had given her, she said, "Help me plait these, won't you, darling?"

As his large fingers worked at the tricky task, he glanced at Aurora.

"You're my wife?"

"Yes, I am, Salem. And I love you with all my heart—more than life itself."

He offered her a faint smile. "I think I must love you, too. You're very beautiful and kind."

While they worked at plaiting their bond for the handfasting, Aurora casually told Salem about their life together. She went back over their first meeting at the clam bake, his wooing of her before he sailed away, his wonderful letters—each one like a kiss from afar. Finally, she told him of his return, their wedding, and their wonderful first night together. She failed to remind him of any of the unpleasantness that had occurred at The Ledges, either past or present.

Finally, she said, "Salem, look at me." Once she had his undivided attention, she asked, "Will you marry me again on All Hallows' Eve in the old way, the handfasting?"

He seemed to hesitate. Frowning deeply, he asked, "Who is Krystine?"

The simple question spoke volumes about what had happened here while Aurora was with Zenda. Obviously, Krystine had given Salem something in her bitter tea—something that would take away his memory of the present, of anything having to do with his wife, so that Krystine could steal him away.

Aurora thought over her answer carefully, finally deciding to tell him the truth. As calmly as if she were saying that the sun was shining, she replied, "Krystine is a witch, darling. An evil, black witch, who is trying to kill the love we share."

Salem remained silent, obviously wrestling with her unexpected answer. After a moment, Aurora leaned forward and kissed him tenderly on the lips, then smiled.

"But you see, darling, I'm a witch, too, a good witch. And I don't intend to allow Krystine to work her black magic on you."

* * *

The next days were harrowing for Aurora. Salem remained dazed and confused. All she could do was stay by his side, keep reminding him of their love for each other, and make sure that he was never alone with Krystine. Aurora got little sleep, dreading to close her eyes at night for fear Krystine might slip into their room and do unspeakable evil.

Finally, the morning of All Hallows' Eve arrived and with it Aurora's family. Even though Aurora was thrilled to see her parents again, along with Aunt Persia and Uncle Zack, the day proved an agony for her. Salem was still not himself, prompting many questions from her family. Only Aunt Persia asked for no explanations. She seemed to know exactly what was going on.

Late in the afternoon, Persia managed to get Aurora alone in the library for a time.

"Aurora, who's done this to him?" she asked immediately, putting no name to what exactly "this" was. Persia knew; she needed no explanations.

"That terrible girl, Krystine," Aurora told her with a deep sense of relief. "Oh, Aunt Persia, she's a witch!"

"Tell me something I didn't already know," Persia replied. "She's tried to charm Salem for a long time, hasn't she?"

Aurora nodded. "Since they were children."

Persia paced the room, muttering angrily to herself. Finally, turning to her worried niece, she said, "This is all my fault. I'm sorry, Aurora. I should have told you years ago that you and I are gifted, too. I almost told you the day of your wedding. When I was asking you how much your mother had confided in you, you thought I meant about men and love. I let that pass, too nervous to tell you of your powers or to explain how to use them. There's much you must learn, and there's not much time. You go to Salem now and stay with him until the ceremony tonight. Don't let him out of your sight."

"But what about Krystine?" Aurora was verging on panic.

Persia smiled and her blue eyes twinkled with mysterious lights. "You leave that one to me. I promise you she'll rue the day she mixed her first concoction of powdered bat wing and henbane."

Aurora hugged her aunt gratefully, then hurried away to find Salem. For the first time, she felt hopeful that tonight's ceremony might actually take place—that she and Salem might be allowed to live the normal, loving life together that they had craved. She meant to take Salem to their room and keep him there until time to leave for the point where they would be bound together under the midnight moon in the shadow of the ancient rune-stone.

Amazingly, the afternoon slipped past without an incident. Salem slept peacefully on their large bed while Aurora paced, watching the clock. She had dressed already in the flowing white robe Zenda had sent her to wear at the ceremony. Salem's similar robe hung on the door of the armoire, awaiting his attention once he woke.

Darkness had long covered the restless sea, and the clock had just struck eleven when Aurora answered a knock at the door. Zenda herself stood in the drafty hallway.

"Come in," Aurora invited, noting that Zenda, too, had changed to a robe of white for the handfasting.

The old woman glanced at the bed. "It's time you roused him," she said. But as Aurora started toward her husband, Zenda interposed, "No, let me."

"Jerusalem!" the woman called loudly. "Wake up, you lazy boy!"

The moment Salem came awake, Aurora realized why Zenda had insisted on waking him. Salem was a little boy again, at least in his mind. He kicked at the covers

344

and shook his head, throwing a childish tantrum at being disturbed.

"Aw, Zenda, what do you want? It's still dark outside. Go away and let me be!"

"Time to get up, you sleepyhead." She leaned closer and whispered. "We're going on an adventure—out to the rune-stone to see if the witches will dance this All Hallows' Eve."

His eyes shot open and a grin spread over his face. "Hey, Zenda, why didn't you say so in the first place?" He leaped out of bed.

For a moment, his gaze stopped on Aurora. She thought she saw a gleam of recognition, but then he looked confused.

"What's *she* doing here?" he demanded of Zenda. "And why are you two wearing those funny clothes?"

Zenda moved to the armoire and whisked his robe down. "We have a costume for you, too, lad. If the witches should spot us, they'll think we're ghosts and leave us be."

He laughed and pulled the flowing fabric over his head. "You think of everything, Zenda." Then he stopped and glanced around. "But what about Krystine? She'll be mad if she doesn't get to come. Besides, she promised to bring love apples next time we slipped out."

Aurora tensed.

"She'll meet us there, lad. Now, do hurry!" Zenda glanced over her shoulder at Aurora. "Do you have the bond that you and Salem plaited?"

Aurora reached into her jewel box and handed the woven strip of leather to Zenda, who quickly pocketed it somewhere in the folds of her sweeping robe.

"I believe we should use the secret passage tonight so no one will hinder our progress."

Hurrying into the narrow water closet, Zenda pressed a certain stone and the wall turned, revealing a dark flight of narrow stairs. "I'll go first," she said. "Jerusalem, you follow me, and the girl can come along behind."

The climb down was torturous and almost lightless. Zenda carried a small lantern, but it guttered and smoked, threatening to go out at any moment. Holding to the back of Salem's robe, Aurora stepped carefully, praying that they would soon reach open spaces.

When they did break out of the confines of the tunnel, they were in the torture chamber. Aurora tried not to look at the awful implements collected there as she hurried with the others into the damp, slime-walled passage that led, eventually, to the point. Aurora shuddered and tried not to think of her previous experience in the dank place.

As they came out into the fresh, cold, salt air, Aurora saw that torches blazed on the point, and her family, along with Bodwell and Mrs. Romney, were all there waiting. She uttered a prayer of thanks that Krystine was nowhere to be seen. But her relief came too soon. Even as they gathered around the rune-stone to begin the hand-fasting, Krystine's black-robed form appeared at the edge of their circle. Breaking in between Europa Holloway and Bodwell, she clasped her hands to theirs.

Aurora stood with her back to the rune-stone, facing out to sea. For a moment, she recalled the nightmare that had plagued her for so long. This seemed the very setting of that terrible dream. But tonight was far different. She was no longer alone with the wind and the sea. Salem was with her, his hand holding tightly to hers.

The others, all except Zenda, formed a circle around the stone. Aurora watched tensely as Zenda, holding the leather bond in both hands, raised her arms and face to the moon, whispering a haunting chant in some foreign tongue. Tears threatening, heart thundering, Aurora saw the plaited bond glow silver in the moonlight.

Krystine, too, saw the silver thread and instantly understood its meaning. Once the handfasting was done, Salem would be lost to her forever.

While everyone else watched Zenda, Aurora's Aunt Persia kept her eyes on Krystine's every move. Persia kicked a pebble across the clearing to strike the witch's leg. Instantly, Krystine's ominous, black eyes, the moon reflecting in them like twin disks of death, turned on Persia.

Persia had not felt such a wilting power of evil since her long-ago days in India. But she had learned there, how to combat such a threat. She concentrated all her senses on the woman across the circle until she saw Krystine give a visible shudder.

Zenda was still chanting, lost in her own world. At the moment that she approached Aurora and Salem to twine the bond round their joined hands, an ear-splitting scream tore through the night. The other members of the circle gasped and dropped their hands.

With all the sorcery she possessed, Persia glared at Krystine, battling her evil will and praying to all the powers of light to give her strength. She was beginning to feel drained and faint from her effort. Krystine was stronger than she had bargained for. Suddenly, Persia knew that she had failed.

At that very instant, Krystine broke free from the circle, her black robe swirling in the wind. Another flash of silver matched the glow of the bond. It was the deadly, dull gleam of a knife.

"If I can't have you, no woman can!" Krystine cried as she lunged toward Salem, her wicked blade raised for the death blow.

Aurora stood stunned and seemingly helpless as she watched Krystine fly across the circle toward them, bent on murder. Suddenly, something powerful and unfamiliar stirred within Aurora's breast. She saw not Krystine in her black robe but a huge carrion bird swooping down on them. Clinging to Salem's hand Aurora willed the great, black bird begone.

Wind whipped the waves, and dry leaves flew in fu-

347

rious spirals. Screams and moans issued forth from the ancient rune-stone. Everyone seemed frozen in an eerie tableau.

Suddenly, there was the sound of wings beating the air and a great, angry squawking. The knife clattered to the ground at Salem's feet. The enraged raven swooped once and then again toward the shining blade, trying to clutch the weapon in its talons. Aurora kicked the knife away. At last, the fierce bird flew off into the night, out over the sea, its grating cry dying in the sound of the waves.

Aurora suddenly became aware of a band tightening around her wrist. She gazed down to see Zenda slowly binding her hand to her husband's. Looking up, she saw that Salem was staring into her eyes, his own clear and glowing with emotion. He knew her again. He loved her.

"Now, darling," he whispered, "we are truly one. No one can ever come between us. I love you more at this moment than I ever thought I could love in my life."

"I love you, too, my darling," Aurora said through happy tears.

Cups of wine were passed and congratulations offered, but Aurora and Salem did not tarry long at the scene of their handfasting. Once more the master of The Ledges carried his bride over the threshold of the old castle, then through the doorway to their chamber.

Long after the silver moon had sunk into the distant waves, they lay in each other's arms, making sweet, passionate love as if for the first time.

As Salem held his twice-wed bride in his arms, kissing her deeply, cherishing her with his very soul, he whispered, "I used to think this place was evil. But you, Aurora, have banished all witchery from The Ledges for all time, and I do love you even more for that."

He kissed her breast, and Aurora smiled. Even now, the hopeless cries of the raven were fading into the distance out over the dark, placid sea.

348

Aurora touched her husband's face and smiled, feeling her heart brim with love for this man she had almost lost. She might be the seventh bride of Clan Caine, but she was also the last witch of The Ledges and, most certainly, the best loved.

## ABOUT THE AUTHOR

Caroline Bourne lives in Pineville, Louisiana. Her previous Zebra historicals include *LOVE'S PERFECT DREAM* and *RIVERBOAT SEDUCTION*. Her newest Zebra historical, *EMERALD DREAMS*, will be on sale in December 1993.

Colleen Faulkner lives with husband, three sons and daughter in Seaford, Delaware. Her previous Zebra historicals include *FLAMES OF LOVE, SWEET DECEPTION, SAVAGE SURRENDER* and *PATRIOT'S PASSION*. Her newest Zebra historical, *FOREVER HIS*, will be on sale in November 1993.

Ashland Price lives in Eden Prairie, Minnesota. Her previous Zebra historicals include *VIKING ROSE, WILD IRISH HEATHER, CAJUN CARESS, AUTUMN ANGEL* and *CAPTIVE CONQUEST*. Her newest Zebra historical, *VIKING FLAME*, is on sale now.

Becky Lee Weyrich lives on St. Simons Island, Georgia. Her previous novels for Zebra's Pinnacle imprint include *WHISPERS IN TIME* and *SWEET FOREVER*. Her newest Pinnacle release, *ONCE UPON FOREVER*, will be on sale in March 1994.

# SURRENDER TO THE SPLENDOR OF THE ROMANCES OF F. ROSANNE BITTNER!

| | |
|---|---|
| CARESS | (3791, $5.99/$6.99) |
| COMANCHE SUNSET | (3568, $4.99/$5.99) |
| ECSTASY'S CHAINS | (2617, $3.95/$4.95) |
| HEARTS SURRENDER | (2945, $4.50/$5.50) |
| LAWLESS LOVE | (3877, $4.50/$5.50) |
| PRAIRIE EMBRACE | (3160, $4.50/$5.50) |
| RAPTURE'S GOLD | (3879, $4.50/$5.50) |
| SHAMELESS | (4056, $5.99/$6.99) |
| SIOUX SPLENDOR | (3231, $4.50/$5.50) |
| SWEET MOUNTAIN MAGIC | (2914, $4.50/$5.50) |